Dear Betsy,

Thanks for all
your support - I
hope you enjoy
after the kiss).

With love,
Patti 3/5/06

After *the* Lies

by
Patricia A. Graves

authorHOUSE™

1663 LIBERTY DRIVE, SUITE 200
BLOOMINGTON, INDIANA 47403
(800) 839-8640
WWW.AUTHORHOUSE.COM

First published by AuthorHouse 01/26/06

ISBN: 1-4208-9609-1 (sc)

Printed in the United States of America
Bloomington, Indiana

This book is printed on acid-free paper.

PROLOGUE

Nick slipped quietly out of bed, hoping to make a quick getaway. He glanced over at the nightstand and noticed that the dial on the clock read 4:30 A.M. He figured that with luck, he could make his way silently down the hall, take a quick five-minute shower, dress, say a thirty-second goodbye to the woman still asleep in bed, and be on the road in fifteen minutes flat.

Even though every cell in Nick's body was screaming out for a cup of strong, black coffee, he knew he would have to make do with only a shower to clear his head. All he had to do now was gather his clothes without making a sound, which he was pretty damned good at. Not making a sound was second nature to Nicholas Fallen, and a skill he had perfected over the years.

As Nick scooped up his discarded clothes, he felt an unwanted but noticeable twinge of guilt. He hated to skip out on Susan this way, but he hated even more that he might have to face a long, uncomfortable goodbye. And he told himself, as he took one carefully placed step toward the bedroom door, that the reason he was in such a hurry was because he really, really needed to get to L.A.

"Nick?"

He heard the soft, sleepy voice just as his hand reached out for the doorknob.

"Shit," he muttered under his breath, as he turned halfway around toward the rumpled bed. "Go back to sleep, Susan."

"But where are you going? It's not even light yet." This time he noticed that there was a note of concern in her softly spoken words. And suddenly and not surprisingly, he heard a voice in his head telling him that Susan deserved better than this. She certainly deserved more than a thirty-second good-bye, and the same voice was telling him that he really didn't want to leave her with the impression that he was a total bastard. Even if he could be a bastard at times, deep down he really wanted her to think better of him. So he dropped his hand from the doorknob, and made himself walk back over and sit down on the side of the bed.

"I need to take a quick shower and then hit the road, Susan. It'll probably take me six hours to get to Los Angeles, and you know how bad traffic is, even this early in the morning." He knew that his explanation for his disappearing act sounded lame, but he couldn't seem to help it. Without a cup of coffee, his brain was just not working.

"Not the way you drive, Nick."

He could detect a hint of teasing in Susan's voice, and he smiled in spite of himself. "Yeah. Well, I plan to take it nice-n-easy. No point in getting a ticket on my way out of town."

There was just enough light from the streetlamp coming in through the bedroom window to outline Susan's shape, and to allow Nick a glimpse of her soft, rounded breasts. And against his will, he felt an unwelcome pull of desire. A pull he fought hard to control. So instead of reaching out as he wanted to do and running the back of his fingers along the swell of her breasts, he just watched as Susan sat up, tucking the tangled sheet around her, almost as if she were embarrassed by the flash of sexual awareness in his deep, green eyes. Almost embarrassed, but not quite.

"Why don't you come back to bed, Nick?" As she whispered the words, she let the sheet slip down just a notch. "I'm not finished with you yet."

Nick was tempted for only a second, because he knew it would be a really bad idea for him to get back into that bed. Forcing his eyes away from the blatant invitation now evident in her smile, he also knew that precious minutes were ticking away.

"I'm sorry, Susan, but I really can't stay. I'm going to help myself to your shower if you don't mind, and then I need to get going."

Both her smile and her sexual invitation disappeared at his words, and he could tell that she was trying not to let her disappointment show. "Then I'll make some coffee while you shower." And Nick watched as she slid gracefully out of bed.

"Please don't get up. I'll get some on the road."

"Don't be ridiculous, Nicholas. I've worked with you long enough to know that you barely function without a hit of caffeine in the morning. And besides," she added before he could protest further, "my coffee is probably the best you're going to get for a while. It never ceases to amaze me how homicide detectives survive on the world's worst coffee. And I expect the coffee in L.A. will be no better than here." With that, she slipped into her robe, sent him a sweet, understanding look, and walked out of the room.

Nick looked over at the clock and realized that ten minutes had ticked by. So without further hesitation, he made his way into the shower and turned the water on full blast. Bracing both hands on the tile in front of him, Nick leaned forward, hung his head, and let the hot water beat down on his shoulders. He counted away two minutes before finally lifting his face, trying desperately to clear his muddled mind and to shake off the fringes of a hangover. As the hot water started to work its magic on his body, he felt a knot form in the pit of his stomach.

"How in the hell did I let this happen?" he muttered out loud. And as his mind started to clear, so did his memory of last night.

Spending the last eight years as a detective with the San Francisco Police Department, Nick warranted a going-away party in his honor. The party last night had started out with a large crowd down at a local bar. Somewhere around ten o'clock, a smaller group had moved the party over to Susan Bradley's house — and that's when the drinking got serious. There seemed to be one crazy toast after another, and once the beer ran out, tequila became the drink of choice. And that's when Nick broke two of his long-standing rules.

First, he got completely shit-faced, which he figured he hadn't done in almost seven years, when he was twenty-eight years old, and newly divorced. Second, he had slept with someone that he works with — and *that* he never, ever did before, until last night. Nick knew that technically he and Susan no longer worked together, but that really didn't help the immediate situation. Because here he was, at almost five in the morning, cursing himself for letting things get so out of hand.

And to make matters even worse, he liked Susan Bradley. He really did. He just didn't want to have a committed, romantic relationship with her. And he certainly didn't want to have a long-distance, romantic relationship with her. He liked and respected Susan as a fellow cop, as a woman, and as someone he could call a friend. And now, because of his total lack of control, he had probably fucked everything up.

It really didn't help to remind himself that Susan was the one who had come on to him last night. He shouldn't have had so many shots of tequila, and he shouldn't have let her get so close. He knew that Susan was interested in him, because she had made no secret of the fact that she would go out with him in a second, if asked. But he hadn't asked. And now he was madder than hell at himself, because he had managed to keep her at bay for over two years, and then poof — in one reckless night, all his good intentions were gone, and he had ended up smack dab in her bed. And if he could drum up the courage to admit it, they had quite simply screwed each other's brains out.

But that was last night, and this was a new day for Nicholas Fallen, and a new beginning. And if he didn't get moving, he would never get to L.A. in time for his noon meeting with his new boss. Because one thing he knew for sure, he didn't want to keep Lieutenant Alexander Kendall, Homicide Division, LAPD, waiting.

Still desperate for a cup of coffee, but anxious to get the inevitable over with, Nick made his way into the living room with his duffel bag slung over his shoulder. He was wearing a pair of comfortable blue jeans, an old SFPD T-shirt, and well-worn loafers without socks. His dark brown hair was a little too long, and it looked as if he'd combed it with his fingers. Nick Fallen was what most women would call too sexy for his own good. He had a perfectly sculptured six-foot frame, long legs, wicked green eyes, and a smile to die for. And to add to the package, he could be as charming as hell. Or, he could be cold and distant, depending on his mood or the situation at hand.

But even Nick was smart enough to know that the current situation at hand was going to call for a great deal of charm — and then some. So with his eyes fixed steadily on Susan, standing with a cup of coffee in her hand, he gave her one of his most endearing smiles.

"I'll give you a hundred bucks if that's for me."

Susan said nothing as she handed Nick the coffee.

"God, that's good." He took another long sip. "I had no idea you were so talented in the kitchen."

He was trying to keep things light between them until he could make a hasty retreat.

"Talented in the kitchen and talented in the bedroom," was her unexpected response, and Nick knew that he'd just run out of time.

He took one more taste of the delicious coffee, handed her back the cup, and started making his way toward the front door. "It's way past five and I'd better get going. I want to reach Fresno before I stop for a quick breakfast."

Nick reached out to pull the door open, but something stopped him dead in his tracks. Even though now he could make a clean getaway, he couldn't quite bring himself to just flat out walk out on her like this. He just couldn't walk out this way after two years of working together and two years of friendship. And for the second time in less than an hour, he realized that he really didn't want to play the part of an unfeeling bastard. So with a sigh, and a twinge of regret for the way they had ended up, Nick turned back toward Susan and let his duffel drop to the floor. In two long strides, he was standing before her, taking her gently into his arms.

"I haven't a clue what to say," he whispered into her ear. "I really didn't expect last night to happen, and I don't want to just dismiss it away. But..." he added as he lifted her face up to his with the tip of his finger, "I ..."

Before he could continue, Susan surprised him by gently placing her lips against his. The kiss was sweet and simple. "I have absolutely no regrets about last night, Nick, and I don't want you to either. I also have no expectations about us. You're an incredible lover and I enjoyed every second being with you. I only hope that when you come back to visit, you'll give me a call. Because," she continued as she ran her hand slowly along his unshaven cheek, "you have a great imagination in bed Detective Fallen, and I wouldn't mind trying out some of the things you suggested that we didn't get around to doing."

Nick's laughter rang out in the room, and he felt the guilt and the unease drain instantly away. He knew that Susan was trying her hardest to make the best of this awkward morning after, and he was deeply grateful. So, wrapping his arms more tightly around her, he brought her up against the length of his body, lowered his head, and gave her a goodbye kiss worthy of the woman he was holding in his arms.

"You're one helluva woman, Susan."

"And you're running late, Detective."

Nick saw in her eyes a silent goodbye, so he didn't waste

another second. And truth be told, he couldn't really think of anything else to say. With more effort than he would have believed was necessary, he drew his eyes away from her lovely face, reached down and lifted his duffel bag onto his shoulder, sent her one of his sexy smiles, and walked out the door.

As he reached his car, parked outside of Susan's apartment, Nick threw his bag carelessly onto the passenger seat. He got in behind the wheel, flipped on a Rolling Stones CD, and without even a glance in his rearview mirror, he headed south. South to Los Angeles, where he would be starting a new phase of his career, and unknown to him at the time, a new and dramatic phase in his life.

CHAPTER ONE

Two Years Later

"All right. If everyone will quiet down, we can get started."

Lieutenant Kendall's voice rang out over the noise of the six detectives getting settled in their chairs.

"Now that we're all here, I'd like to bring Detectives Fallen and Morris up to date."

All eyes glanced briefly toward Nick and his partner of two years, Ben Morris, before returning to their boss.

"You two were on another case when this one first went down three months ago, but now I need to bring you both on board."

Nick said nothing, and Ben shifted his bulky weight into a more comfortable position. Everyone in the room knew that Lieutenant Kendall was a detail-minded person, so they expected to be here for a while.

"Okay. Here's the lowdown. Three months ago, a woman named Cynthia Jackson contacted Detective Jensen by phone, to report her suspicions that her husband was running an illegal operation out of the small travel agency they owned. All she would tell Lou was that the illegal goings-on had something to do with false immigration papers for possible drug lords and members of the Mexican Mafia wanting to enter the country under the radar. She was nervous, scared, and didn't want to go into details with Lou over the phone."

"So we made arrangements to meet later that night," Lou Jensen interjected, "at a dive of a coffee shop, well off the beaten path in a shithole part of town. Only she didn't show. I waited for her from eight until eleven that night, and nothing. No phone call, nothing. So I called in the false alarm, thinking that the woman was nothing more than a nut case. But then, guess whose body was found at three in the morning in an alley about five miles from the designated meeting place?"

Lieutenant Kendall picked up the conversation when Lou took a sip of his Diet Coke. "Believe it or not, a homeless guy stumbled across the body. He was looking for some food in one of the dumpsters and found a dead woman instead. As far as we could tell, he was pretty shaken up, and we were just thankful at the time that he had enough sense to find a phone and give us a call. Of course, when we got there he was nowhere to be found."

"What was the cause of death?" Nick asked, wishing like hell that he could have a cigarette. But he'd finally given up smoking a little over a month ago, so he sat back and chewed on the end of the straw that he'd extracted from his soft drink.

"Bullet hole to the back of the head. Shot at point blank range." When no one in the room said anything further, Lieutenant Kendall went on. "As you might guess, we immediately suspected the husband, especially after the wife's earlier phone call to Lou. But he has an unshakeable alibi. And after weeks of questioning him, and after questioning other family members and friends, we couldn't come up with a damn thing to prove he's involved in any way. We didn't even know for sure what his wife was talking about when she first contacted Lou. But one thing we do know for sure — the late Mrs. Jackson was scared out of her wits the day she made the phone call to us, and by three o'clock the next morning, she was found murdered. Killed in cold blood."

"So what about their business? You said Mrs. Jackson suspected her husband of wrongdoings connected with their travel agency?"

"We looked at everything we could, Ben. And the business came up clean as a whistle. There was absolutely nothing we could pin on the husband. The books were in perfect order, they paid their business taxes, and after interviewing their friends, from all accounts, they seemed to be a happily married couple. The husband even cried real tears when we informed him of his wife's untimely death."

Nick and the others noticed the look of frustration on Alex Kendall's face, but wisely, no one made a comment about it.

"Anyway, we've been keeping a low profile and a watchful eye on things, but can find nothing out of the ordinary with their travel business."

"So what's changed?" This question came from Nick.

Lieutenant Kendall let his gaze wander slowly over the men crammed into his office before directing his answer to Nick.

"About a month ago, a new face came on the scene. And the new face just happens to be the sister of our deceased. Now that in itself wouldn't send up any red flags, but something about the sister just doesn't add up."

Nick sat up a little straighter in his chair, draped an ankle over his knee, and leaned forward with interest. "And that would be?"

"Let's see if you can tell me, Nick. Here's what we have. We have an older sister, age thirty-two. She's single, appears to be unattached, and she's an English lit professor at USC. She's well-educated, fairly well-off financially, and suddenly she takes a sabbatical from her teaching profession to take on a low-paying job with her brother-in-law."

Nick started to ask another question, but Alex brought up his hand to stop him. "First let me tell you what part of this finally caught our attention, and helped us to put some of the pieces in place. Last month, luck was on our side and we were able to get one of our special agents hired on part-time in the travel agency. And our agent was finally able to figure out that this low-paying job actually involves traveling around to places outside of the country, delivering packages to would-be international travelers. Packages that we now suspect include illegal documents such as fake passports, fake green cards, fake social security cards, etc., etc. Our agent has never actually seen what's inside those packages, but she knows that they exist because she's seen them handed off to Ms. Bennett. So now you tell me, Nick, how does this all add up to you?"

"One more question, Alex. I take it you feel pretty certain that these false documents are being hand-delivered to persons who may already be on the Most Wanted list?"

Nick noticed the slight hesitation before Alex answered his question. "Well, now that's the tricky part. You see what we have is only speculation. But what we can say for certain is that the sister, Ms. Rachel Bennett, has traveled to South America and Mexico three times in the last month. She leaves with a so-called travel package and returns empty-handed. And she has visited places where there are known drug rings and terrorist cells. This part of the puzzle may be a long shot, but because of the late Mrs. Jackson's phone call to us, we need to play it out and see what we can uncover."

Everyone in the room was getting a little restless. It was apparent that all but Nick and Ben were already privy to this information, but Lieutenant Kendall obviously wanted everyone to hear all of the facts of the case again. So even though there was a feeling of restlessness in the air, all attention stayed focused on their leader.

"So you think the sister knows what's in those packages?" Ben asked the question that had already crossed Nick's mind.

"Your guess is as good as mine on that one. And that's what we're going to try to find out. Like I said before, it just doesn't sit right with me that a college professor would leave a good job to take on the role of messenger girl. Unless, of course, the good professor is in on the operation and is getting a piece of the action."

Nick couldn't sit any longer. He was dying for a cigarette and he needed to move around. So he stood up and walked over to the window and looked out over the city. He really loved working in Los Angeles, but sometimes he really missed the beauty of San Francisco. And in the back of his mind, he realized that he probably needed to plan a trip back there in the near future. He needed to pay a long overdue visit to his parents, and there were friends he wanted to catch up with. But something told him that whatever Alex was getting at would involve him and Ben, and that any trip back to San Francisco would just have to wait. Nick absentmindedly rubbed the back of his neck, and then he turned his attention away from the L.A. skyline to the detectives in the room.

"So, in a nutshell," he said as he slipped both hands into the front pockets of his jeans, "we think the victim found out about her hubby's little business on the dark side, called to turn him in, and got eliminated before she could give Lou any incriminating information. And," he continued as he walked back to his chair and sat down, "you think perhaps Professor Bennett is either in on the game, or an innocent bystander. The latter of which is a bit puzzling, given that her background should make her less inclined to take a job as a delivery girl. Especially given the fact that she's a professor at such a renowned university."

"Very good, Detective Fallen. Now, would you care to guess how we're going to proceed to get to the bottom of this?"

Nick knew that this was the way Alex Kendall worked. He liked to bait the hook, keep the line dangling, and then slowly reel in the catch. Nick also knew without a shadow of a doubt that he was the fish on the end of the line. Because, as planned, Nick had taken the bait — hook, line, and sinker.

"I guess it would be way too simple to just drag the professor down here and ask her to fill in the blanks for us?"

"You're right. That would be too simple. And frankly, I don't believe for a minute it would get us anywhere other than to show our hand too soon. Especially if she's involved."

Again Nick felt like the fish on the end of the line. And because he had a strong feeling he wasn't going to like the plan Alex obviously had already mapped out, he took a stab at another option entirely.

"If your speculation seems even remotely possible, we could always turn things over to the feds. They'd love to get their hands on a case like this. And God knows we have no jurisdiction outside of L.A. So, if you really think there's a connection to drug lords, the Mafia, and maybe even terrorists, is there a reason not to call our esteemed colleagues at the Bureau?"

Nick knew he hit a nerve when he saw a muscle twitch along his boss's jaw. Most cops, including himself, rarely wanted to turn any of their cases over to the feds. And Nick didn't really want to turn this one over either. But he did want to move this chess game along and see if he could get Alex to cough up his plan. Because he and every detective in the room knew that Lieutenant Alexander Kendall always had a plan.

"First, we have a homicide on our hands and that's ours to solve, not the suits down at the Bureau," was Alex's clipped response. "Second, if we are successful in determining what the hell is going on, and if we can prove that Mr. Jackson and his sister-in-law are in fact providing undesirable individuals with fake U.S. documents, I'll be the first one to contact the FBI. But before I do that, I want to be damn sure what I'm turning over. Damn sure. And so, Detective Fallen, needless to say, this is where you come in."

Checkmate was Nick's thought as he focused his green eyes on Alex Kendall. "Why do I have a feeling that I'm not going to like this?"

"Depends," was Alex's one-word response, and Nick suddenly noticed that every man in the room was trying his best not to grin. And the knot in his stomach took a nose dive.

"Wouldn't you like to take a little vacation, Detective?"

"Not particularly."

"How about a cruise to Mexico, Nick, paid for by your friendly LAPD?"

"Not interested."

This time, Alex didn't even try to hide his smirk. It seemed to Nick that his boss was enjoying every minute of this exchange, which shouldn't be a big surprise, since it was a foregone conclusion who was going to win, hands down. And the winner wasn't going to be Nick.

"Okay, Nick. All kidding aside. It's time we get down to business and deal with why I pulled you in on this case. Right now we need to flush out fact from fiction, and we need to do it sooner rather than later."

Nick had a feeling that he knew exactly what was coming and he didn't like it one bit. And he didn't like the fact that there was an audience, including his partner, watching the exchange with amusement. So refusing to dangle from the fishhook any longer, he sat back in his chair, stretched out his long legs, crossed one ankle over the other, and tried to look completely unaffected.

"So, what do you have in mind, Alex?"

In a flash, Lieutenant Kendall took on a serious note, and all teasing was gone from his eyes. "Now before you overreact, Nick, I want you to hear me out."

This was not a request, but a demand from his superior, so Nick sat perfectly still and waited for Alex to lay out his plan.

"Our inside agent has told us that the lovely Professor Bennett is scheduled to leave tomorrow on a short four-day cruise out of San Pedro. Ports of call are San Diego, Catalina Island, and finally Ensenada, Mexico. Our agent also tells us that a package was handed to Ms. Bennett today, ready to be delivered to an unknown party in Mexico. So, here's the plan. You, Detective Fallen, are going to be on that cruise ship tomorrow. We've already made arrangements with the captain to have you seated at the same dinner table with Ms. Bennett. You need to get her attention and you need to get her to notice you — pronto. And then I want you to use all of your … um … your powers of persuasion to get close to this woman. Do whatever it takes, Nick, to get to know her. Do whatever it takes to stick to her like glue. You need to keep her a little off balance, and keep her interested enough in you so that you can get invited into her room and get a look inside that damn package."

Without being able to stop himself, Nick sat up straighter in his chair and his tone of voice was like steel, even though he was addressing his boss. "And what exactly are you suggesting, Lieutenant?"

"I think you know exactly what I'm suggesting. But in case you missed my message, let me spell it out for you. I don't care if you have to charm her, flirt with her, romance her, or lead her on. Short of going to bed with Ms. Bennett, I expect you to do what you do best with women — and that is to seduce her into wanting to spend all of her time with you. She needs to invite you into her cabin for a nice long stay, and how you go about getting her to do that is entirely up to you. But you can't get a look in the package she's carrying without getting inside her room. Now, Detective, is that clear enough for you?"

The last quietly spoken question finally got a reaction out of Nick. "No fucking way, Alex! Find someone else. I have absolutely no intention of romancing information out of any woman."

"I don't remember asking you whether or not you want this assignment, Nick. And unless I'm mistaken, I'm still the one making the decisions around here."

Both men seemed madder than hell, while everyone else in the room was enjoying the scene immensely. Everyone knew that it was only a matter of minutes before Nick was forced to concede defeat, but it sure was fun to sit back and watch this predictable battle of wills.

"Just give me one good reason why it has to be me. There are five other men on the team." Nick realized he was pushing his luck, but at the moment, he didn't care.

"How about I give you three good reasons?" The tone of Alex Kendall's voice would have put the fear of God into most men, but Nick just sat looking at him with cold, challenging eyes.

"One, you and Ben are the only two detectives on this team that the husband and the sister-in-law didn't meet during the initial investigation. Two, you have a rather well-known and indisputable reputation with the ladies. God only knows why, but they seem to fall at your feet with little or no effort on your part. Three — and this is the only reason that really matters. Reason number three is because I said so. I want you aboard that cruise ship tomorrow, and as far as I'm concerned, that's exactly where you'll be."

Even though Nick was still pissed off, he couldn't help but admire the man standing before him. He may not have liked the message, but he had nothing against the messenger. In fact, he had nothing but the utmost respect for Alex Kendall, and it was time for him to acknowledge Alex's authority and to show him the respect he deserved. Especially since he suspected that everyone in the room expected him to continue with the argument. So Nick took a deep, steadying breath and spoke as calmly as he could.

"Okay, Alex, you've made your point. Now let me make mine. Have you even considered the fact that if I'm successful at … as you put it, seducing my way into Ms. Bennett's room, and if I do find incriminating evidence, this entire case could go down the drain if the professor starts screaming illegal search and seizure?"

And for the first time since the discussion turned serious, Nick detected a hint of doubt flash across Alex's face.

"It's been considered, Nick. But I'm willing to take the risk."

Nick absolutely hated this assignment, but he knew when to throw in the towel. All he wanted to do now was to get the hell out of this room, and head somewhere so he could grab a beer. But he knew that Alex wasn't quite finished with him yet.

"One other thing, Nick. This assignment is somewhat unofficial, so I can't send anyone else with you. And you were absolutely right when you said we have no jurisdiction outside of L.A., so you're on your own. All I want for now is information, nothing else. If and when we have something, we'll decide what to do with it. Understand?"

Instead of answering Alex's question, Nick turned toward his partner. "Give me a cigarette, will ya, Ben?"

"Oh, no way, buddy. You quit. Remember?"

There was dead silence in the room and the look in Nick's eyes was lethal. He simply reached out his hand and waited for his partner to comply with his request. With a shake of his head, Ben reached into his shirt pocket, took out a pack of Marlboros, and handed Nick a cigarette.

"Thanks." But he didn't light up. He just held the cigarette between his fingers, contemplating what to do next. And everyone waited, quietly, including Lieutenant Kendall.

"You wouldn't by any chance have a picture of Ms. Bennett, so I at least know who I am expected to wine and dine? God knows I wouldn't want to put the make on the wrong woman."

The sarcasm was ignored as Alex reached into his top desk drawer and pulled out a photograph. While Nick was busy tapping the end of his unlit cigarette on the arm of his chair, Alex tossed him the picture. And for one brief second, Nick saw the bright side of this assignment. Professor Rachel Bennett was absolutely gorgeous. The picture was taken as she was leaving the campus at USC, and was obviously taken without her knowledge. She was waving at someone off-camera, and the smile on her face was enough to turn a man's head. Her face was exquisite, and her eyes looked large enough to drown in. She had long black hair, which was blowing slightly in the breeze, and Nick guessed it was long enough to hang halfway down her back. She was wearing a short skirt, which showed off her incredible legs, and complemented the rest of her figure. Which was simply outstanding.

She was a knockout, and someone Nick would have enjoyed getting to know under other circumstances. He knew that he had a reputation as a ladies' man. But the truth was that Nick enjoyed not only beautiful women, but interesting, educated, smart women as well. And when all of that came together in one nice package, all the better.

But these circumstances sucked. And Nick just wanted to get it over with. So he passed the picture over to Ben and waited for the reaction he knew was to come.

"Holy shit. This is one great-looking woman. Tell you what, Nick, if the lieutenant doesn't mind, I'll volunteer to take your place. How about it, Lieutenant?"

Alex smiled and even Nick felt his lips turn up into a grin. Everyone knew that Ben was one of the happiest married men on earth. He adored his wife Betty, and would be scared to death if he'd been given this assignment. He also couldn't charm his way out of a paper bag. He was easily thirty pounds overweight, slightly balding, and always looked like he'd slept in his clothes. But he was one of the best cops Nick had ever worked with, and Nick would put his life in Ben's hands any day of the week.

"It would serve you right to get this assignment and leave me here all alone to watch over Betty while you're gone."

Ben just laughed and handed Nick back the photograph. Without thinking, Nick slipped the cigarette into his shirt pocket and stared again at the woman he was assigned to seduce.

"Okay. So we're all set." Alex's voice brought Nick's attention back to the matter at hand. "The ship leaves San Pedro tomorrow at noon. You have early seating, so be in the dining room at 6:00 sharp. You want to be sure you sit next to Ms. Bennett. There is one formal night on this cruise, so be sure to pack your tux. You do have a tux, don't you?"

Nick suspected that Alex already knew that he owned a tux. His family background was no secret. Everyone knew that Nick's father was the successful San Francisco attorney, Benedict Fallen, and senior partner in Fallen, Hooper and Sullivan. Everyone also knew that Nick had earned his law degree before tossing that career away to become a cop. So naturally, he would own a tux. The fact that he hadn't put the thing on in more years than he could count really didn't matter. It was still hanging in his closet — cleaned, ready, and waiting.

"Yes, I have a tux, and I also have a question."

"Ask away." Nick was a little irritated that Alex managed to sound so cheerful all of a sudden, but he didn't let the irritation show in his voice.

"Just what is my cover on this assignment? If asked, what the hell do I do for a living, and why am I on this cruise? Which, by the way," he added before Alex could answer his question, "I would never, ever take a cruise if given a choice."

"Don't knock it till you try it, Nick." This comment came from one of the detectives who had been completely quiet up till now. "My girlfriend and I took a cruise last year and it was pretty cool. There's tons of free food, lots to drink if you want, and lots to do on and off the ship. I wouldn't mind this assignment myself."

Before Nick could offer up the assignment to Marc, Alex answered his question. "Your cover is pretty simple. You're an attorney working in your father's firm in San Francisco. You've been working round the clock for the past year, and decided to get away for a few days. If, for any reason, Ms. Bennett becomes suspicious and has someone check you out, this will fly. You really do have a law degree, so you should be able to pull this off without a hitch. All you need to do is call your father and fill him in. If contacted, he needs to verify who you are, that you work there, and that you're currently on vacation. Nothing more."

Nick hated to involve his father in any of this, but the cover was too logical to argue against. It fit nicely, sounded authentic, and had just enough truth to make it an easy sell.

"I'll call him this evening, Alex. He won't like it, but he'll agree."

"Good. Then why don't we call it a night. Nick, we'll have your tickets delivered to your apartment early tomorrow morning. Be at the dock early. The ship leaves at noon and everyone needs to be on board at least one hour before sailing."

Finally, the meeting was over. And not soon enough, to Nick's way of thinking. Keeping hold of the photo of Rachel Bennett, he stood and started to make his way out with the others.

"Oh, Nick?" And when he turned, he found Alex's hand extended. As the two men shook hands, Alex wished him luck. With nothing left to be said, Nick and Ben were the last to leave the lieutenant's office.

"How about a beer?"

"Sure," was Nick's half-hearted reply, because his mind was already on his assignment. Even though he'd fought it, once he gave in, nothing would stop him from doing his job.

"Want to go over to Eddy's?"

Eddy's was a local cop hangout. The bar served pretty decent booze and cheap food. Nick wasn't really in the mood, but he didn't want to go home this early, so he agreed to have one quick beer. Then he would go home, call his father, and pack for this unexpected vacation. He would also have to call Jeannette. He had a date with Jeannette tomorrow night, but of course, that was now off, which didn't bother him all that much. Jeannette was a pretty little thing he had met at Starbuck's of all places. He had gone in there early the other morning to read his paper and have a cup of coffee. The place was jam-packed, and Jeannette had asked if she could share his table. Then one thing led to another and he had asked her out. Now he had to cancel, and he was surprised that he didn't really care.

"Earth to Nick. Come in, Nick."

Ben's deep voice penetrated though Nick's thoughts about Jeannette. "Hey, buddy, want me to drive or should we take both cars?"

"Either I drive both of us, or we take separate cars. Your car is nothing but a deathtrap."

This was a discussion they had every day for the past two years. Ben always offered to drive and Nick always refused to let him. Besides, Nick loved driving, and his one and only extravagance was his fully restored 1956 Chevrolet Corvette.

"Then why don't we each take our own car? That way you won't have to bring me back here."

"Okay, I'll meet you at Eddy's in fifteen minutes. I need to make one phone call first."

Fifteen minutes actually turned into thirty, but Ben was still waiting at the bar when Nick finally arrived. So Nick sat down on a bar stool next to his partner, loosened his tie, and ordered a draft beer.

"I decided to call my father and not put it off until later."

The bartender placed a cold one in front of Nick, and he took a long, deep swallow of the refreshing brew.

"Any problems?"

"Nah. Not really. He wasn't very happy that I wouldn't tell him why I wanted him to lie. But he finally accepted it as part of my job."

Ben was the only cop on the force who knew that Nick's parents absolutely hated the fact that Nick was a cop. His father was sorely disappointed that he'd left the law firm after just two years of practicing corporate law. He couldn't understand what made his son tick, and he would never accept his career choice. But when the chips were down, his father had agreed with his request. Even if he didn't like it. And in that way at least, father and son were very much alike.

"Look, Nick. I know you're not happy about this assignment. But you also have to know that you're the best man for the job."

"That's bullshit, Ben, and you know it. No one's suited for this type of thing. No one on the force should be expected to set someone up just to intentionally seduce information out of them. Not even me."

Nick took another long drink of beer and suddenly it left a bad taste in his mouth.

"Listen to me, buddy. The fact remains that you're a friggin' chick magnet, and that alone makes you perfect for this job. You only have four nights to get invited into Ms. Bennett's cabin, and believe you me, if anyone can pull this off, it's you. No disrespect intended."

Nick started to protest, but stopped cold when he felt a feminine hand slide lightly up his back, along his neck, stopping only to caress his shoulder.

"Nick, darling, where ever have you been hiding? I've been waiting for you to call me for weeks."

With a feeling of dread, Nick closed his eyes and tugged once more on his tie. Then, after taking a deep breath, he turned slowly in his seat, only to come face to face with a woman he could barely place. He had a vague recollection of meeting her a couple of weeks ago, but for the life of him, he couldn't remember her name. And to make matters even worse, Ben was sitting next to him with a big, fat smile on his face.

"So, Nicholas, what happened, did you lose my phone number?"

The woman standing before him was quite a looker. But even that wasn't enough to jog his memory. And like earlier, when he thought about canceling his date with Jeannette, he really didn't care. But because he didn't want to appear rude in front of his partner, he played along, hoping to politely get rid of whoever this woman was.

"I'd never lose the phone number of such a pretty lady." His smile didn't quite reach his eyes, but the woman didn't seem to notice.

"Then why haven't you called?"

Nick was just way too tired to get into this. He didn't want to hurt her feelings, but he didn't want to string her along either. So he decided to be honest. Because if he could at least come up with her name, he could then introduce her to Ben, tell her it was nice to see her again, and get the hell away.

"I'm really sorry, sweetheart. But I'm afraid I can't quite remember your name. Although," he added quickly when he saw a pout forming on her full lips, "I do recall clearly that you have a very pretty name. I just can't seem to come up with it at the moment."

Ben nearly choked on his beer, but the woman with the very pretty, but unknown name was buying into Nick's line. She stopped pouting and turned her lips into a smile that said she would forgive him anything. Even forgetting her name.

"My name's Anita," she whispered, moving in a little closer to Nick.

Without missing a beat, Nick reached out and placed a hand on her waist. He could tell that she thought it was because he wanted to touch her, when the real reason was that he wanted to keep her at a safe distance.

"See, what did I tell you? Anita is a very pretty name."

When the woman responded just as Nick had hoped she would, Ben had to stifle another laugh. His partner was just too cool.

"So Anita, let me introduce you to my partner, Ben Morris. Ben, this is Anita." And with a flick of his wrist, Nick turned her in Ben's direction, and let go of his hold on her waist.

"Nice to meet you, Anita."

Nick had finally been able to distract her long enough to make a smooth exit. He slipped off the bar stool just as she placed her hand in Ben's. It took just a second for them to shake hands, but that was all the time he needed. He made his way around the pretty blond, placed himself behind Ben, and slapped his partner on the shoulder.

"We had better get going, partner. We don't want to be late."

Ben took less than two seconds to respond. He let go of Anita's hand, drank down one last swallow of beer, and stood up to join Nick. It all happened so fast that the young woman didn't even have time to recover.

"It was really great to see you again, Anita." And this time, the smile that Nick sent her was genuine, sexy, and reached into the depths of his devilish green eyes. "I'll see ya around."

And before Anita could put together that Nick had never even answered her question about why he hadn't called, Nick and Ben were out the door.

Ben draped his arm over his partner's shoulder, laughing out loud as they practically ran for their cars.

"Now you see what I mean, Detective Fallen. Like I was tellin' you just a few minutes ago, you, my man, are a chick magnet. A friggin' chick magnet."

And with nothing left to say, both men turned in the opposite direction. One turned right and headed for his old, reliable Buick, and the other headed left, straight for his bright red, classic Corvette convertible. And Nick chuckled to himself as he slipped into his car, because he couldn't quite dismiss the irony that once upon a time he actually thought of his hot, red sports car as a possible chick magnet. *But never again,* he promised himself, never again would he think in those terms. And as he pulled out of Eddy's parking lot, he pushed a button on the portable CD player. As the music started, Nick couldn't stop himself from singing along with the Eagles, as their song "Hotel California" came on, blasting out into the silence of the night.

CHAPTER TWO

Nick made his way into the dining room at precisely six o'clock. He had spent the entire afternoon familiarizing himself with the layout of this larger-than-life cruise ship. He had walked each floor, memorizing where everything was located, hoping to kill a few long hours. Because as expected, he was already bored out of his mind. And he hated the feeling of being cooped up. He knew that his thinking wasn't entirely rational, but he couldn't help it. Because he couldn't get off the ship, he felt just a little claustrophobic.

The first night's attire aboard ship was casual, so Nick wore a pair of tan Dockers and a black shirt that made the green of his eyes stand out like emeralds. His shirt collar was open, which gave him a sexy, laid-back look, that wasn't missed by many of the single women in the room. But Nick Fallen was completely oblivious to the women trying to catch his eye, because his attention was suddenly drawn to the stunning brunette who was making her way to his table.

Professor Rachel Bennett was even better looking in person, which was saying quite a lot. She was easily five feet six inches tall, and she moved with grace, confidence, and a hint of sexuality. For this evening, she had selected a simple, white sundress. The sundress tied around the neck, leaving her shoulders completely bare. The dress had very tiny buttons down the front, was cinched in at the waist, and ended almost two inches above her knees. Her hair was loose and hung, as Nick had suspected, nearly halfway down her back. She had tiny pearls in her ears, and wore no jewelry other than the tiny earrings and a slim, gold wristwatch.

Watching her approach the table, Nick realized that he would've been able to pick her out of a crowd of thousands, even if she wasn't his assignment and even if he hadn't already committed her photograph to memory. Because her looks took his breath away.

But she *was* his assignment, he reminded himself. And even though she was a beautiful woman, all she was to him was a means to an end, and nothing more. The simple fact was that she might be very involved in a very nasty business, so Nick couldn't afford to forget that for one instant — no matter how beautiful she was. So he stood as she reached the empty chair beside his, acting every bit the gentleman, keeping in mind that the stage was now set and the play was about to begin. Without saying a word, Nick pulled her chair out for her, before he sat down again.

"Thank you." She spoke very softly and followed her words with a sweet, but somewhat tentative smile.

Nick didn't speak, but turned his gaze in her direction and returned her smile with one of his own. And he had absolutely no way of knowing this, but Rachel's heart skipped a little beat when she got a good look at the man sitting next to her.

Rachel had noticed Nick the minute she had walked into the dining room and spotted her assigned table. But from such a distance, she couldn't get a really good view of him. All she could tell as she had moved through the crowded room was that there was something about the man in the black shirt that made her want to take a closer look. So she had purposely slowed down her pace and noted a couple of things at once. His hair was a glorious deep brown, and it looked rich and silky. He was also smiling at something someone at the table was saying, and his smile was both friendly and sexy at the same time.

Intrigued and not exactly knowing why, Rachel continued to study Nick. She liked his looks, and the closer she got, the more she found herself unable to look away. So she kept right on looking until suddenly, without warning, Nick looked up, caught her approaching, and then with his eyes focused on her and only her, he followed her every move until she made her way to the table. And now here she was, gazing into penetrating green eyes and trying to catch her breath.

Rachel forced herself to draw her eyes away from Nick's and greeted the other diners at the table. There were six people in all. Nick, Rachel, a couple who appeared to be in their forties, and two young women, both somewhere in their midtwenties. It was a mixed group, but not a shy group, as Nick was soon to discover.

"Well now, since we're all finally seated, how about we introduce ourselves?" This came from the only other man at the table. And before anyone could say a word, the two young women jumped right in. "My name's Dixie and this is my sister, Rhonda. We're from Dallas, Texas and this is our very first cruise."

Suddenly introductions were made all the way around, and everyone seemed to talk at the same time. Because Nick was seated next to Rachel, he took advantage of the opportunity to try to make a more personal introduction.

"My name's Nick. Nick Fallen."

He extended his hand and was pleased when Rachel didn't hesitate to place her hand in his.

"It's nice to meet you Mr. Fallen. I'm Rachel Bennett."

Nick's fingers tightened just slightly around hers, before he released her slender hand.

"Please call me Nick."

"I will if you'll call me Rachel."

And that set the tone for the rest of the meal. Everyone around the table was on a first-name basis, and there was never a lapse in conversation. The topics of conversation were the usual — what everyone did for a living, where they were from, what brought them on this cruise. Questions that Nick had already rehearsed answers to, so the lies came out of his mouth without even thinking.

One thing that bothered Nick was that there was so much noise in the dining room and so much going on around them, that it was impossible for him to do much more than listen. He never had a chance to engage Rachel in a quiet, personal conversation, so after a while, he didn't even try. He knew he'd just have to find a way to accidentally bump into her later in the evening, and so he reminded himself that patience was a virtue. A virtue that, unfortunately for him, was usually in short supply.

Even though it was impossible to have a one-on-one conversation, Nick could sense that Rachel was aware of him. As he was of her. He caught her peeking over at him a couple of times throughout the meal, which was a good thing. If she was even remotely interested, he knew his job would be that much easier. So deciding to keep her attention on him in as subtle a way as possible, Nick reached out, picked up the bottle of Merlot on the table, and poured some into Rachel's glass.

"Thank you," she whispered with a smile.

"You're welcome," he whispered back, and then he emptied the rest of the wine into his own glass.

Dinner ended in a flurry of activity as everyone hurried out of the dining room to catch the eight o'clock show. Nick didn't want to appear too obvious, so he said goodnight to everyone at the table, including Rachel. And it wasn't until an hour later, when he wandered into a quiet little bar, tucked away at the back of the ship, that he spotted her. She was sitting all alone, perched on a bar stool, sipping a glass of wine.

Rachel looked up just as Nick started making his way over

to her. And like earlier in the evening, her heart skipped a beat. The man was the best-looking man she had ever laid eyes on. He was the epitome of tall, dark, and handsome, and she just knew that there wasn't a woman alive who wouldn't be affected by his incredible green eyes. And now those green eyes were focused on her as Nick walked around a couple of tables, past a group of men arguing about sports, and headed in her direction.

"Hi," was all Nick said as he stood before her, trying to keep his eyes off her long, exposed legs.

"Hi yourself. Care to join me?" Rachel was absolutely stunned at the words that spilled out of her mouth. She had never been so forward with a man in her life, and she was momentarily shocked at her own behavior.

"Sure. I'd love to." Nick's response was very casual, with just enough sincerity to put Rachel a little at ease.

Still trying to gather her wits about her, she took a sip of wine and watched as he sat down on the bar stool next to her, turned his body in her direction, and laid one arm along the bar.

"Actually, I was going to ask you earlier if I could buy you a drink, but I never quite got the chance. Dinner was a little hectic, and I didn't want to embarrass you by asking in front of everyone."

Rachel was so pleased and so surprised by his comment that she nearly spilled her wine down the front of her dress.

"So I'm really glad I decided to drop in here for a little peace and quiet. The only problem I have now is that you already have a drink, so I guess you'll just have to let me buy you another."

Before she could respond, the bartender stepped up to take Nick's order. "Whiskey on the rocks, and another glass of wine for the lady."

God, the man is smooth, Rachel thought. In less than two minutes, he had her inviting him to join her, had another drink on the way, and all he did was walk in and say hi. For a split second, Rachel debated whether or not to decline his offer of another drink. She had already gone way beyond her limit, and something told her that she should try to keep her head as clear as possible when she was around this man. But then again, something else was telling her that one more little glass of wine couldn't possibly hurt. So she dismissed the little warning bells going off in her head.

Nick watched Rachel closely, trying to figure out just how fast he should move things along. He sensed that if he came on too strong, she might pull away. He was surprised when she'd asked him to join her, and he didn't want to blow things by moving too fast. But on the other hand, he knew that he didn't have much time to get her interested in him enough to invite him inside her cabin. They would be docking in Mexico in just three days, which meant that he had tonight and only two more nights to get a look into that envelope that was supposed to be somewhere in her cabin. With no other choice, he decided that he needed to turn on the charm, make his moves, and make them fast. So when the bartender brought their drinks, Nick lifted his glass and tipped it against the rim of the wine glass she still held in her hand.

"To new friends," he said with a smile that lingered in his eyes.

"To new friends," she echoed, and he watched her mouth as she took the last sip of her drink.

"So, you didn't want to see the show?" Rachel had to break the silence that seemed to settle between them, so she said the first thing that came to her mind.

"Not really," he responded, taking a sip of his own drink. "I'm not big on crowded places. And I'd rather have a quiet drink with a beautiful woman any day."

Rachel felt herself blushing, and for the life of her, she couldn't figure out why. She wasn't a stranger to compliments, but for some reason, this man seemed to be able to get a reaction out of her with simple words. Words she had heard a hundred times before. Words she usually had no trouble dealing with. But there was just something about this man and the way he spoke to her. Or maybe it was the way he was looking at her.

"How about you, Rachel? Why are you here all alone, and not enjoying the show?"

She set her empty glass down on the bar and picked up the drink he had ordered for her before answering. "I guess I'm a little like you, Nick. I tend to gravitate to someplace quiet. Big, noisy crowds don't excite me either."

"And what does excite you?"

Again, simple words and a simple question. But one loaded with lots of meaning. And the look on Nick Fallen's face was anything but simple. He leaned just a little closer to her, just a little, and looked right into her brown eyes. And again she felt a blush coming on. God, he was flirting with her and she was suddenly at a loss. She knew his question could be taken in about a thousand different ways, and she suspected that he did it on purpose. So she decided that since flirting was something she was pretty good at herself, she tried to give as good as she got.

Rachel tossed her hair back over one shoulder, and secretly smiled when she saw how that sexy little gesture caught his attention. Then she tipped her glass to her lips, and took a sip — a nice, long, slow sip. And again she smiled inside when his eyes traveled slowly from her hair to her mouth. Taking the glass away from her mouth, she ran her tongue over her bottom lip, noticing that Nick's eyes watched her every move. He seemed incapable of lifting his gaze from her lips. Deciding that she had probably been outrageous enough for the moment, she set her glass back down on the bar, causing him to lift his eyes from her mouth.

"Well, let me see." And she almost laughed aloud when Nick blinked his eyes, obviously to clear his head. "The ocean, right before the sun goes down excites me. Music, especially opera, excites me. Lobster dripping with butter excites my taste. A roaring fire on a cold winter's day excites me. Watching children playing in the park excites me. Learning and teaching will always excite me. And dancing excites me, because I really love to dance."

Nick was so taken aback by her words that he was actually speechless - which was a new experience for him. He always had some sort of a comeback, but listening and watching her made him forget for a second why he was with her, and what his job was. He was a little mesmerized by her softly spoken words, and not quite prepared when she turned his own question right back at him.

"Now it's your turn, Nick. What excites you?

Without thinking about the consequences, he looked her straight in the eye, and decided not to lie. He knew he was going to tell her enough lies over the course of the next four days, so for right now, the truth would serve him better. And besides, he wanted to see if he could make her blush again.

"Women excite me, Rachel. Kissing, touching, and sex excite me. Good food, friends, and fast cars excite me." Nick started to tack on that his job excited him, but he remembered at the last minute that he was supposed to be a lawyer, and that would not have been the job he was referring to. So he said nothing further.

Rachel's breath caught in her throat. Everything he said seemed so right for the man sitting beside her. He just looked like the type who would love women, sex, and fast cars. And she was a little amazed he threw in friends and food. She started to tell him so, thought better of it, and decided that it was time to change the subject. They were both treading on thin ice and it was time to get back on solid ground. Flirting was one thing, but his flirting was moving just a little too fast. But before she could speak, Nick changed the topic of conversation himself.

"Tell me a little about yourself, Rachel. I was able to pick up over dinner that you teach and travel, and I got the impression that both are work-related."

Some of the sexual tension eased with the sudden change of topic, and Nick leaned away from Rachel, still resting his arm along the bar. His hand was just inches away from touching her arm, but he made no attempt to do so. So with a little sigh of disappointment, Rachel looked over at him, noticing that the corners of his mouth were turned up into a grin. A sweet, all-knowing grin.

"What exactly would you like to know?" she asked, hoping to buy herself some time to recover from his closeness.

"Do you teach and travel as a profession? Or do you teach as a profession and travel for fun? Or do you travel as a profession and teach for fun?"

His eyes were laughing and she couldn't help it as a giggle escaped her lips. "Let's see if I can make this simple. I teach and travel as a profession, and I travel for fun. But truth be told, I love teaching so much, I guess some would say that I teach for fun as well."

"What?"

"I teach and travel for a profession," she repeated, "and I travel for fun. But," and as soon as he realized that she planned to repeat the whole thing again, he reached out and touched a finger to her lips.

"I didn't get it the first time, so saying it again sure won't help." He was laughing as he was talking and Rachel felt a deep longing to run her tongue teasingly along his finger, which was still lying gently against her lips. But she resisted that temptation and instead laughed out loud along with him.

Nick reluctantly took his finger away from her soft and inviting lips. And in the back of his mind, he wondered, not for the first time, what it was going to be like when he kissed her. But before her could even begin to entertain those fantasies, he had to try to get to know more about the woman. Then the kissing and the seduction of Rachel Bennett could begin.

"Let me try again, Nick," she said trying to be more serious. "I'm a full-time professor at USC, but I took a brief sabbatical to help my brother-in-law out for a few months with his travel business. I'm also one of those few lucky individuals who love to teach so much that it's not like a job at all. It's really a lot of fun. So see, that wasn't complicated, was it?"

"What do you teach?" He asked the question, even though he already knew the answer, because it would be expected.

"I teach English literature. I teach both graduate students and undergraduate students."

Before Nick responded, he lifted his empty glass toward the bartender, indicating that he was ready for another drink. "And what about your travel job? How does that fit in?"

"Oh no you don't. Now it's your turn. I heard you say over dinner that you're an attorney, but I didn't get any details."

It didn't get past Nick that she completely avoided answering his question about her job with her brother-in-law. And that worried him. She was pretty clever at switching the subject, and that worried him too, because he wondered if she had something to hide. But deciding that it was more important at this moment to gain her trust and not push too much for the answers he wanted, he responded to her question.

"I'm afraid I don't love my job as much as you do," he started out, slipping easily into his old and now make-believe profession. "I practice corporate law in my father's firm in San Francisco. Sometimes it's challenging, most times it's not. But it's a job and I do it well."

"Now that's a shame, Nick."

"What? That I do my job well?" Her statement caught him off guard.

"No. What I meant to say is that's it's a shame you don't love your job. We spend so much of our time at work, and I like to think that most people love what they do."

God, if she only knew, Nick thought. If she knew what he really did for a living, and how much he loved being a cop, and how he might bring her down, would she still be smiling up at him? Somehow, he doubted it.

"Okay, so now you know about my job. It's your turn again. What do you do when you're working for your brother-in-law?"

"Oh Nick, let's not talk about work anymore. Let's talk about something more fun."

Warning signals went off again inside Nick's head, but he knew better than to seem too curious about her other job. His suspicions were beginning to grow about Rachel's involvement in this whole illegal operation, and he didn't like that one bit. As much as he wanted to push, he knew that for the time being, he would be better to let things pass. There would be plenty of time to push later, if he didn't or couldn't get the answers he wanted.

"Okay, Professor, you choose. What shall we talk about?"

Rachel couldn't deny that she was getting a little tipsy, but she was having such a good time with Nick, she decided she didn't care. She may care later, but right now she just wanted to enjoy the moment. And it was because she was a little tipsy that she didn't want to talk about work. She wanted to talk about Nick Fallen.

"You said that fast cars excite you."

"Among other things," he reminded her with a slow grin, and with words that were spoken in a husky voice.

"Yes …. Well …. Do you actually drive a fast car?"

Both Nick and Rachel just sat and stared at each other for a heartbeat, before Nick finally answered her question.

"I sure do." And she watched as his grin turned into an all-out smile. "I drive the sweetest little sports car ever made. About four years ago, I got my hands on a newly restored 1956 Corvette. She's cherry red, runs like a dream, and goes from zero to sixty in less than ten seconds. That sweetheart of a car is the love of my life."

"Then you'd probably die on the spot if you saw the car I drive."

Rachel's eyes were laughing and Nick had the sudden urge to lean in and kiss her. Just a little taste is all he wanted. Just a touch of her full lips against his. But now was not the time, and sitting in a bar with other people around was certainly not the place. Because, Nick thought, when he kissed Rachel Bennett, he didn't want an audience. He wanted to have her all to himself.

"I drive a nice, reliable, and slow, 2005 Honda Accord."

"Ouch," he responded with an exaggerated frown. "A woman as gorgeous as you should never drive a Honda. A woman with your looks should be in a …. let's see … How about a Mercedes 300 SL? Now that's a honey of a sports car and one I could see you in. Especially with the top down and your hair blowing in the wind."

Completely unable to stop himself, Nick reached out and took a strand of her hair between his fingers. "My God, but you have beautiful hair, Rachel. I just knew it would be soft and silky."

Rachel sat perfectly still, unable to move even an inch as Nick took his time and toyed playfully with her hair. She actually held her breath as she watched his fingers caressing what he referred to as her silky strands. And she noticed that he had really beautiful hands. His fingers were long and sensual, and his nails were neatly trimmed. And in her mind, she could imagine all kinds of things he could do with his wonderful hands. But her thoughts about his hands were short-lived as Nick let go of her hair, then reached out to grab his glass and drained the last of his drink in one long swallow.

"Tell you what, Professor. You ever decide to buy another car, you look me up and I'll help you pick one out. How does that sound?"

Rachel laughed, more out of nervousness than anything else, but also because he was trying hard to put her at ease. She suspected that he could tell how much he'd affected her, and she was thankful he'd backed off — even if just a little.

"I usually keep a car for about five years, Nick. And since I just bought this one, I guess I'll need to know where you plan to be in five years."

"You can never tell." As Nick leaned in closer, the look in his eyes dared her to glance away. His eyes held hers, and she felt a nervousness begin all over again. And she wondered briefly if he was more than she could handle. Wanting to get control of her emotions, and the situation, she spoke without caring what she said. She just wanted to break the silence that enveloped them.

"What … what are you doing tomorrow when we dock in San Diego?" Rachel had to swallow past the lump in her throat.

"Spending it with you, if you'll let me."

So here it was — finally — the pick-up. Nick had been flirting with her ever since he sat down, and Rachel had easily succumbed to his charming ways. And now she had a choice to make. She could politely say no or she could give in and accept his invitation that they spend the day together. It was not in Rachel's nature to give in so easily, because she was usually pretty cautious around men. But all she wanted to do with this man was to throw all caution to the wind. And why not, she asked herself. Why not enjoy being with a devastatingly handsome man? And why not allow herself to have a shipboard romance? *After all,* said a little voice in the far recess of her mind, *you don't need to go to bed with him.* And just like that, she made up her mind.

"I promised my brother-in-law that I'd see a couple of clients for him first thing in the morning. But we could meet for lunch if you'd like."

"I'd like that very much."

"I should be back here by one o'clock at the latest." Rachel was having trouble keeping her voice light and casual. She just couldn't seem to stop looking into his eyes. His deep, green eyes that reminded her at the moment of a turbulent ocean.

"Then how about I meet you at Sea Port Village at one o'clock? Do you know where the Charter House restaurant is?"

She nodded, now mesmerized by his low, sexy voice.

"Good. Then I'll get us a table and wait for you there."

"Okay," was all she could manage, and briefly she wondered what was wrong with her.

Nick noticed a somewhat dreamy look in her soft brown eyes, and he wasn't sure if it was because of him or because of the amount of alcohol she had consumed. He also noticed her empty glass next to his empty glass on the bar. He wasn't sure he even wanted another drink, but it crossed his mind that with another glass of wine, he might finally be able to get Rachel to talk about her job at the travel agency.

"Would you like another glass of wine?"

Rachel blinked twice. "Oh. No, thank you. I've actually had more than usual."

"Then would you like to take a walk outside?"

Rachel was tempted. Sorely tempted. But she felt a sudden need to get away from Nicholas Fallen so that she could clear her head. Because Lord knows she would never be able to clear her head with him sitting this close.

"Thank you, Nick, but I should probably call it a night. I need to get a pretty early start in the morning, and it's later than I realized."

Nick guessed that it wouldn't take all that much to get her to change her mind, but he decided that it was probably best to call it a night himself. He had some things he needed to sort out, and he was having trouble thinking clearly at the moment. He kept forgetting that she was his assignment. He kept forgetting that she might be guilty as hell and that he might be the one forced to put her away. He kept forgetting that if he kissed her, it was all part of his job, and not because he might want to. So, all in all, calling it a night was a really good idea.

"Okay, Rachel. "I'll walk you to your cabin."

Rachel started to protest, then changed her mind. There was no reason not to accept his offer as an escort. After all, it was the gentlemanly thing for him to do. But if Rachel had been completely honest with herself, she would have admitted that her real reason was that she wanted to give Nick a chance to kiss her goodnight.

Nick watched as Rachel slid off the barstool. The act caused her dress to shift up a little further and his eyes were drawn to her legs. And with a great deal of effort, he forced himself to draw his eyes away. Hoping she hadn't noticed his sexual appraisal of her long, beautiful legs, Nick smiled up at her, took her by the arm, and led her out of the bar.

"Which way?"

"My cabin is on the Diamond Deck. Room 303. Three flights up and to your right."

Nick put his hand on the small of her back and directed her into the empty elevator. They stepped inside, both backing up to stand against the wall. As the doors slid closed, Rachel couldn't help but wonder if this was where Nick would make his move. Like most women, she had always fantasized about being kissed in an elevator. But as the ride slowly went up and up, her hopes were dashed when he didn't even try to make a pass. Instead, Nick thoroughly surprised her by reaching out and taking her hand. That's all he did. He just took hold of her hand. But that one, sweet gesture was enough.

They walked in silence to her cabin, Nick still holding her hand in his. When they reached cabin 303, Rachel felt a stab of disappointment because the evening was coming to an end. Pulling her hand out of his warm grasp, she reached into her purse to take out the coded room card. Rachel slipped the card into the slot, but didn't open her door. Instead she turned toward Nick and sent him a dazzling smile.

"Thank you for the drink."

"My pleasure," was Nick's quietly spoken response, right before he finally made his move.

Not wanting to startle her, Nice advanced very slowly. He took one step closer to Rachel, causing her to lean back against her cabin door. He said nothing as he placed one of his hands on her tiny waist, and then lifted the other to rest above her head, with the palm of his hand flat against the door. His eyes looked into hers before resting on her lips. Still he said nothing.

Nick let his gaze wander leisurely over her face, only putting off the kiss because of the heightened anticipation. But after finding her eyes again, and reading the spark of pure, female interest, he didn't waste another second.

"I've wanted to kiss you all evening." His words were low, seductive, and full of promise. And in the next instant, the promise was fulfilled, as Nick bent his head and brought his mouth down to her waiting lips.

It started out like most first kisses. Sweet and tentative. Nick didn't want to rush this kiss. He wanted to take his time and savor the feel of her mouth against his. The fullness of her lips was so intoxicating that he had to fight against the urge to explore her mouth with complete abandon. And almost without being able to stop himself, Nick took the kiss to another level, and Rachel right along with him. Because she just felt so good. Her lips were soft, her breath was warm, and she tasted like wine. And she was so responsive. So wonderfully responsive. And that is when Nick felt a deep stab of desire. A desire so powerful that he had to force himself to remember — for the hundredth time that night — that this was a job and she was a possible suspect. A beautiful, desirable, possible suspect. But before he could pull himself together and break away, Rachel surprised him by reaching up and wrapping one hand softly around his neck. And that touch alone kicked the kiss up another notch.

Rachel had not known what to expect when Nick kissed her, but nothing could have prepared her for this. Nick's mouth on hers was almost more than she could handle. The pleasure was just so overwhelming. His lips were hot and persuasive. He was a man who knew exactly how to kiss a woman, and how to make a woman respond to him without giving any thought to the consequences. And she didn't even think about stopping him when he parted her lips and slipped his tongue inside her mouth. She knew she had invited more when she had placed her hand around his neck. But she couldn't help it. She just had to touch him, and she had wanted more of him. She had wanted a whole lot more, because she couldn't remember ever experiencing a first kiss like this before in her life. So with her head filled with wine and her senses filled with Nick, she kissed him back, touching her tongue to his. And if possible, Nick deepened the kiss even more. And then he lifted his head, changed the angle of his mouth, and captured her lips again.

Taking her mouth again was almost Nick's undoing. As his fingers tightened his hold on her waist, he stepped closer, backing her flat against the door. And when he leaned into her, he could feel every inch of Rachel against his hard, throbbing body. And still the kiss didn't end. Again, Nick slipped his tongue into her mouth, and he would have sworn he heard a small murmur deep in her throat. But he would never know for sure, because suddenly his mind registered that they were no longer alone in the hallway. And he knew the instant that Rachel realized it too.

Hearing footsteps coming toward them, Nick pulled slightly away from Rachel, keeping one hand tightly around her waist. He stepped back quickly, dropping his other hand away from the door.

Nick was an expert at recovery, so in a flash, he appeared to have himself completely under control. But Rachel wasn't quite so lucky. She was having a tough time pulling herself out of the sexual daze she was in. She was taking deep breaths, trying to steady her nerves and clear her head. And Nick felt a little sorry for her, because as a cop, he had years of practice at covering up his emotions. So, wanting to help her out, he put on a gentle smile, touched her cheek with his fingers, and said nothing as the other couple walked hurriedly by them, obviously aware that they had interrupted something intimate.

Even after they were alone again in the hallway, Nick remained silent long enough to give Rachel time to compose herself. And within minutes, he felt her starting to relax.

"You okay?" he finally whispered, as he tilted her eyes up to meet his.

"I'm just a little embarrassed," she responded honestly, and tried to look away, but he wouldn't let her.

"Don't feel embarrassed, Rachel. We enjoyed a kiss. That's nothing to be embarrassed about."

Probably easy for him to say, thought Rachel. He was just way too cool and calm, and she hated it that she was the one who appeared all shook up. So she made herself stop shaking inside and tried to be just as cool and very sophisticated about the whole thing. But when she couldn't think of anything cool and sophisticated to say, she decided to give it up.

"I need to go in now, Nick." He barely heard her because her words were spoken so softly.

For a second, Nick didn't respond. He just leaned over and gave Rachel a light kiss against the side of her lips. "I'll see you at one o'clock tomorrow."

Nick sensed that Rachel wanted to say something, but she hesitated and he stayed quiet. And he waited some more. And finally she spoke. "Yes, Nick, I'll see you then. Tomorrow at one o'clock."

And before either one could say anything more, Nick reached around Rachel, pushed the door open and stepped aside, so that she could make her way into her cabin.

"Goodnight, Rachel."

"Goodnight, Nick."

As the door closed softly behind her, Nick felt an all-too-familiar knot in his stomach. But this was not a knot of desire, this was a knot of regret. Regret that he was on the job, regret that he had to play this part all the way to the end, and regret that he was beginning to like Rachael Bennett.

He had enjoyed himself way too much tonight, and that alone was eating away at him. He cursed under his breath, and sent up a little prayer that Rachel was just an innocent bystander in her brother-in-law's life of crime. But then there was the nagging reminder that each time he tried to bring up the travel business, she would change the subject. And as a cop, he knew that was pretty suspicious behavior. Behavior he couldn't ignore. Behavior he was going to have to get her to explain — as soon as the time was right.

"Son of a bitch," he muttered as he made his way outside for a breath of fresh air. He walked over to the rail and looked out over the ocean. It was pitch black out on the horizon, the only spot of color coming from the wake of water caused by the movement of the ship.

Nick stared out into the night, and as the minutes ticked away, he realized that he could not afford to have any regrets where Rachel Bennett was concerned. He was a cop on assignment. And no matter how great she looked, and no matter how great she kissed, at the end of the day, if he had to slap handcuffs on her, he would, no questions asked.

Without realizing what he was doing, Nick reached into his shirt pocket and took out the cigarette he had bummed from Ben just yesterday. He tossed it from one hand to the other, thinking about Rachel and wondering if she was having any trouble falling asleep. Deciding almost subconsciously that he had better save his one and only cigarette for another time, he dropped it back into his pocket right before he started off for his own cabin. And somewhere in the back of his mind, he knew that with or without a cigarette, he was going to have a long, lonely, and sleepless night ahead of him.

CHAPTER THREE

Nick sat outside at a small table set for two, nursing a beer. He didn't really want a beer, but somehow it went hand-in-hand with this brooding mood. He hadn't slept worth shit last night, and when he finally did fall asleep, he had mixed-up dreams about a pretty mermaid with long black hair, big brown eyes, and an innocent smile. But sometime before dawn, Nick had jerked wide awake, just as his sweet mermaid had turned into a convicted felon. His mermaid was suddenly dressed in an ugly orange prison jumpsuit, with handcuffs around her lovely wrists and shackles around her flipper. Big, splashy tears were falling from her eyes, and she kept whispering, *"Why, Nick? Why, Nick? How could you do this to me?"*

Nick took a long swallow of beer, trying to forget his disturbing dream. He also tried to push aside his disturbing thoughts that Rachel might be involved up to her pretty little neck in her brother-in-law's nasty business. His gut told him she was probably an innocent bystander, but his head kept reminding him that she was smart, clever, and perfectly capable of dodging his questions. As she had proven to him last night. He never did get her to tell him anything about her travel job, and that disturbed him more than he wanted to admit.

Nick knew that he didn't have a whole lot of time to determine Rachel's guilt or innocence, so he needed to turn up the heat and try to sweep her off her feet. He didn't plan to take her to bed, because there was no way he would go that far. But now that he was certain there was a mutual attraction, he did plan to romance her just enough. Just enough so that between kisses, he might be able to draw her out and get her to invite him into her cabin.

Nick wasn't stupid and he quickly figured out that getting inside her cabin was only one hurdle he was facing. Once inside, distracting her long enough for him to get a peek into the mysterious package was another hurdle he would have to handle. But he couldn't dwell on that right now. Because first he had to get invited inside, and then he would find a way to look around. "One step at a time," he muttered under his breath, "one step at a time."

Just as Nick started to reach again for his bottle of beer, his attention was drawn to the waiter, who was escorting Rachel over to his table. And like last night, the sight of her took his breath away.

Rachel was dressed in a short, flowing, wrap-around skirt that made her legs look miles long. She had tucked into the skirt a matching blouse that fit snugly, and which Nick thought accentuated her lovely breasts. She had done her hair in a long, single braid that was slung over her shoulder and tied at the end with a bright pink ribbon. On her feet were sexy sandals, and Nick immediately noticed that her toenails were painted the same shade of pink as the ribbon around her braid. She looked rested, happy, and pretty as a picture.

"I'm so sorry I'm late, Nick," she said a little breathlessly, as the waiter pulled out her chair for her to be seated. "I just couldn't get away from Mr. and Mrs. Cates. They're planning an extensive trip to Europe next year, and they must have asked me a million and one questions. I didn't want to be rude, but I swear I must have said my goodbyes to them at least three times. I'm really sorry I kept you waiting."

Again she sounded a little out of breath, and that caused an unexpected smile to cross Nick's face. He liked seeing her a little flustered because it brought such a pretty flush to her cheeks.

"No problem, Rachel. I wasn't going anywhere. And anyway, you're certainly worth the wait."

Nick smiled and Rachel opened her mouth to respond, just as the waiter cleared his throat. For a minute, they'd both completely forgotten that the waiter was still there.

"May I bring you something to drink, Miss?"

"Oh, yes please. I would love an iced tea."

"Would you like to order lunch now, sir, or would you prefer to wait awhile?"

"Are we in a hurry?" Nick asked Rachel, and when she shook her head no, he responded, "I think we'll wait awhile before we order."

"Very good, sir. I'll bring the lady's tea and leave the menus. Just let me know when you are ready to order."

Nick nodded to the waiter and then turned his undivided attention to Rachel.

"So. How was your morning?"

Rachel jumped a little at the sound of his voice, because she had been momentarily distracted. She had been staring at Nick, totally lost in her private thoughts. Early this morning, she had tried desperately to convince herself that Nicholas Fallen was not as handsome as she remembered from last night. But looking at him now in the light of day, she realized that he was simply gorgeous. And she was completely distracted by his looks, his smile, and the fact that she felt light-headed just being with him now. But she was not some young, foolish schoolgirl, and she had to remind herself to pull herself together and try to act like the mature grown-up that she was.

"My morning was actually quite successful. I met with two lovely couples and I think both will use us to book their trips. Especially since we offer the added bonus of hand-delivering all of their necessary travel papers. That extra little touch seems to be a real selling point in Steven's business."

Nick was instantly alert. He knew he had a golden opportunity to pursue some answers to his questions, but he also knew that he needed to be very, very careful. So he purposely didn't jump right in and ask her to explain about the papers. He took a long, slow sip of beer, sat his bottle down, and then tossed out his question as casually as possible.

"What extra touch is that, Rachel?"

The waiter came by and silently placed a glass of tea beside Rachel. Instead of answering his question, she reached out and took a long, slow drink of her own. And right at that moment, Nick could have easily strangled the waiter. He just hoped that he wouldn't have to repeat his question and that Rachel would pick up the conversation by providing him with some of the information he desperately needed. And luck was on his side today, because she responded as soon as she set her glass back down.

"The travel business in very competitive, Nick. And ever since September 11th, more and more travel agencies have gone out of business. Steven thinks he needs an edge to keep ahead of the game, so about a year ago, he came up with the idea of specializing in preparing and personally delivering travel documents. And you'd be surprised by the number of people who take advantage of this service."

"So is that one of your jobs for Steven? Do you prepare and deliver these travel documents?"

Again Nick was careful to act casual, and almost uninterested in her answer. He forced himself to glance briefly around at the other tables before bringing his eyes back to Rachel.

"Actually, Steven prepares the documents for me to deliver. This is my fourth trip for him this month, and all I do is hand over the package that contains all of the travel documents. It's really not much of a job, and to be truthful, it's only temporary. Steven came to me a little over a month ago and said he really needed my help and I just couldn't say no. I always teach summer school, but because Steven needed me, I took a three-month sabbatical from USC and here I am — on board this lovely ship, ready to deliver my package as soon as we dock in Mexico."

Nick was stunned that she offered up even this much information. His years of experience as a cop analyzing what people said and more importantly, what people didn't say, told him that she was probably telling the truth. Her story was just too smooth to be a lie. And it made perfect sense. But his years of experience as a cop also told him not to take things at face value.

"You know, my father and mother do a lot of traveling, and they're always grumbling about the paperwork. Especially when they travel somewhere that requires a visa. Does Steven take care of all that stuff?"

"I'm a little embarrassed because I'm really not sure what's in the packet I deliver. Steven stresses privacy and confidentiality, so I've never bothered to look inside. The envelope is usually sealed when he gives it to me. But I would guess that visa applications would be part of the service."

Again, Nick thought that she was telling the truth. But just because she sounded like she wasn't lying, he knew better than anyone that she could be spinning the best tale ever.

"How about I give you my dad's name and phone number and you or Steven can get in touch with him?"

"Are your parents planning a trip?"

Nick had to think fast, and the only country he could think of off the top of his head that he knew for sure required a visa was Tanzania. "Yeah. They're thinking about an African safari sometime in February."

Rachel took another long sip of tea before she responded. "Well, I'll be going back to teaching when this summer is over, so I'll pass the information on to Steven. I'm sure he'd be happy to help them, Nick."

The direction the conversation was going was really not giving Nick much more to go on for the case. He just wanted to be sure he didn't appear too curious about the documents, and so far, he didn't think he'd sent up any warning signals. What he really wanted to ask Rachel was who had this job before her, because the one thing that bothered him was that she still hadn't volunteered that her sister had also worked at this job, and that she was found murdered three months ago. And Nick found that to be rather strange. So with that, Nick had to remind himself to keep a clear mind and to stay focused. He still needed to get into her room and get a look inside that package for himself. So even though he was dying to pursue this line of conversation, what he really needed to do was get on the ball and turn up the charm.

"Well, even if you don't think this is much of a job, and even if it's just temporary, I for one am glad you're here, Rachel. So here's to Steven and his great ideas." And with that, he raised his bottle of beer and tapped it lightly against her glass. "Why don't we order lunch and then take a walk through the village?" The smile he gave her was meant to kill, and Rachel felt her insides turn to mush.

Lunch passed in somewhat of a blur. Nick kept the conversation light and fun, and Rachel couldn't remember when she had laughed so much. After lunch, as promised, they walked hand-in-hand through the charming seaport village. They went in and out of shops, laughing and kidding around like kids. They tried on silly hats in the Mad Hatter Shop, and almost got themselves kicked out by the manager.

The entire afternoon couldn't have gone better, and Nick felt just a small twinge of guilt. Not that he was having any problem having a good time himself. That was not the case at all. In fact, his guilt came from that fact that he was having such a good time. He was a cop on the job, and he was having trouble keeping that in the forefront of his mind, because this just didn't seem like a job to him. And when he looked over at Rachel, he knew that this was something he was just not trained to do.

"Oh look, Nick, ice cream. Let's have a cone." And before he could respond, Rachel took hold of his hand and dragged him over to the small ice cream parlor.

"Do you want one of your own, or do you want to share?"

"Let's share," was his response and he couldn't quite suppress his smile as he watched her trying to decide on which flavor to choose.

"I can't decide," she finally said after they stood there for what seemed like forever. "You pick."

"Vanilla." He wasn't much of an ice cream eater, so vanilla seemed like a logical choice.

"Vanilla? Oh, come on, you can do better than that."

"Okay. How about strawberry?" He said the second flavor that came to mind.

"Try again, Nicholas."

He thought about suggesting chocolate, but finally figured out that she was interested in something a little more exotic. "Okay, Rachel, how's this? How about we share a scoop of piña colada sherbet delight?"

Her smile told him all he needed to know, as they carried their scoop of ice cream over to a small outdoor table. Since they were sharing the cone, they sat side-by-side, close enough so that their legs were touching. Nick offered Rachel the first lick, and in the blink of an eye, he completely lost his appetite for the piña colada sherbet delight. Because as he watched her delicate, pink tongue swirl around the cone he was holding in his hand, he felt a knot of desire hit him squarely in the groin. The desire he felt was so overwhelming that all he could think about was how he wished that her tongue was swirling around in his mouth. Or, he was ashamed to admit, what he really wanted was for her tongue to swirl around another more intimate part of his body.

Rachel, on the other hand, seemed totally oblivious to Nick's sudden discomfort, because she was so engrossed in the pleasure of her ice cream cone. She took a couple of more licks of the smooth-tasting cream, before offering it up to Nick.

"Your turn," she said as she ran the tip of her tongue over her bottom lip. And that was enough to send Nick over the edge.

The last thing Nick wanted at the moment was a stupid ice cream cone, but he took a big bite anyway. The tangy taste exploded in his mouth and for the next second, he thought about how much better the piña colada ice cream would taste if he could lick it off of the lady sitting next to him. With that vision planted firmly in his brain, Nick closed his eyes, shook his head, and tried to clear his brain cells. He needed to stop thinking about sex and start thinking about how he was going to solve this damn case. And conjuring up visions of a naked Rachel and ice cream wasn't going to help.

With a frown on his face, he handed the rest of the cone over to Rachel. "Here, you finish this." His voice was rougher than he'd intended, but he really didn't care. He was getting pissed that he couldn't seem to get sex out of his head.

"Sure you don't want any more?" Rachel seemed unconcerned with his tone of voice, and she didn't seem to notice the sudden scowl on his face.

"It's all yours." And for the next five minutes, Nick sat silently and watched her tongue lick away at the melting ice cream.

"That was wonderful," she whispered as she licked the stickiness from her fingers.

"Glad you enjoyed it."

"How come you didn't want any?"

"Because this is what I want."

And before he could stop himself, Nick reached over and placed one hand behind her neck. Without thinking about the fact that they were in public, and sitting out in broad daylight,

Nick pulled her slowly toward him. Right at the moment, he didn't care if the entire world was looking on, because all he knew was that he had to kiss Rachel and he had to kiss her now. In a slow, unhurried manner, Nick brought his lips to rest against Rachel's mouth. He breathed in her scent, took a small nip out of her bottom lip, and then he pulled her fully into the kiss.

The kiss was shorter than either one of them would have liked, because the reality was that they were, in fact, smack dab in the middle of a crowd. Nick just needed to get a small taste of her before he lost his mind. He just needed to feel her mouth, satisfy his need to see if she tasted as good as he remembered, and then he could let her go. And reluctantly, that is just what he did. He drew out the kiss for less than a minute, felt Rachel lean into him, and then he lifted his head.

"God, you taste better than any ice cream in the world," he breathed against her wet lips.

"And you take my breath away," she responded in a whisper, as she lowered her lashes to try to cover the desire that was evident in her all-too-expressive eyes.

Nick was the one to finally pull away. "I guess we'd better head back to the ship. We sail in less than an hour." And with that, he stood up, took hold of Rachel's hand, and pulled her to her feet. He stood quietly for a second and watched as a slight blush started to creep into Rachel's cheeks, and he suddenly wanted to pull her back into his arms and kiss her silly. But before he could do something so reckless, he latched more tightly onto her hand, and started leading the way back to the ship.

They walked in silence back to the waiting vessel, both lost in their own thoughts. Nick forced the kiss out of his mind, and made himself think about how he might go about getting into her room tonight. And Rachel was thinking about only one thing. And that one thing was the kiss they had just shared.

Rachel could still taste Nick's kiss and she could still feel the sensation down to the tips of her toes. His lips had been soft and warm, and so coaxing that she thought she might die from the need to have him kiss her again. She knew that he had purposely held back because of where they were, and she was deeply disappointed, because she had wanted all of him — his mouth and his tongue. And she wasn't sure if she could wait for tonight to see if she could get more. Because sometime during the day, she had made a decision that she was going to have an affair with this man. She had decided that she was going to have that once-in-a-lifetime shipboard romance, because she was not going to have regrets for the rest of her life. She needed to do this for herself, and she was pretty sure that she knew exactly what she was getting into. She just hoped that she could pull it off, without getting her heart involved and broken in the process. But right now, none of that mattered as much as her decision to take these next few days, and to have the time of her life — in bed and out of bed with Nicholas Fallen.

Nick escorted Rachel up the gangplank and back to her cabin. He needed to find some time alone so that he could make contact with Lieutenant Kendall before the ship sailed. Once out to sea, the ship-to-shore connection tended to be iffy at best. And he wanted to fill his lieutenant in on his conversation with Rachel this afternoon. He also needed to make this phone call so that he could feel a little more grounded and focus on the real reason he was aboard this ship. So as they headed toward her cabin, he told his over-sexed brain that kissing Rachel Bennett was nothing more than a fringe benefit and part of his job. His job as a cop, and nothing more. Absolutely nothing more.

Unfortunately, no matter how hard Nick tried not to, once they reached Rachel's cabin, he felt conflicted. One part of his brain told him to hightail it back to his own cabin and get on the phone with Lieutenant Kendall. The other part of his brain was screaming at him to skip the call, wrap his arms around Rachel, pull her into his embrace, and finish the kiss he had started fifteen minutes ago.

Thankfully for Nick, logic actually won out over lust. But it wasn't his logical mind that stepped in and took over. It was Rachel who actually put a stop to the thoughts he was having that had absolutely nothing to do with his job.

"Thanks for such a fun day, Nick. I really had a good time."

Nick couldn't help but notice that as she spoke she was pushing the door open to her cabin - which, given his current state of mind, was probably a good thing.

"Yeah, I had a good time too."

Rachel stepped into her room, turned, and sent Nick a tentative smile.

"So, will I see you at dinner?"

Nick could see the uncertainty in her eyes, and that surprised him. They had just spent an almost-perfect day together, and it never crossed his mind that they wouldn't see each other at dinner. But obviously, Rachel wasn't so sure, and needed a little reassurance.

"I'll see you right at six, Professor," he responded with a smile that sent shivers down her spine. And before he could change his mind, he leaned over, gave her a quick peck on the cheek, and headed back to his cabin to make a call.

Dinner turned out to be nothing more than a dismal repeat of the night before. Everyone at the table wanted to talk at once, each person anxious to tell about their day at port. If anyone noticed that both Nick and Rachel were rather quiet, it was not brought up.

Nick was unusually quiet during dinner because he was bored to death. He wasn't the least bit interested in the conversation going on around him, and he found it nearly impossible to pretend otherwise. He was also quiet because he kept replaying and rehashing pieces of his earlier phone call with Alex Kendall.

Nick had secretly hoped that when he reported in that Alex would simply accept Rachel's story about her lack of knowledge surrounding the content of the travel documents, and call him off the assignment. But he should have known better. Because Alex had still insisted that he get a look inside the damn package himself, which brought Nick right back to square one. He still needed to get inside Rachel's room, and the only way he could see doing that was to pursue the romantic angle - which was really starting to piss him off. Not because he minded getting close and personal with the lovely professor, but because he hated using Rachel in this way. He was beginning to really like and respect Rachel, and he detested the lies and the deceit. But because Alex gave him absolutely no choice in the matter, he forced himself to fall back into the role of seducer.

Nick looked over, caught Rachel's eye, and sent her one of his most engaging smiles.

"Would you like some more wine?"

Because there was a look on Nick's face that Rachel couldn't quite read, her response was to tilt her wine glass in his direction. His smile was sweet and almost gentle, but his eyes seemed so intense that the contradiction caught her off guard.

"By the way," he added in a quiet, deep voice, "you look beautiful tonight. So beautiful that I can hardly wait to get you alone."

Rachel set her glass down and glanced quickly around to see if anyone at the table had heard his compliment.

"No one's paying us the least bit of attention, Rachel."

Nick hadn't missed her glance around the table. But because she wanted to be sure, Rachel took one more look around. Everyone was so engrossed in their own conversations that they were pretty much leaving Nick and Rachel to themselves. Which suited her just fine, because she wasn't in the mood to make polite small talk. She was in the mood to play, and she knew exactly who she wanted to play with.

Rachel took one more sip of wine to bolster her courage and then she shifted just an inch in her chair. That subtle, small movement brought her a little closer to Nick, who had still not taken his eyes off of her. Determined to live out one of her lifelong fantasies, Rachel slipped off one of her shoes, crossed her legs under the table and found Nick's ankle with the tip of her toe. And before he realized what she was up to, she started to play.

Had anyone been watching, Rachel appeared to be listening to the conversation going on around her. In reality, she couldn't have repeated one word of what was being said, even if her life depended on it - because she was so focused on her own plan of seduction, and on the reaction of the man she planned to seduce.

Rachel sent an innocent smile Nick's way right before she moved her toes lightly and fleetingly along his ankle. She waited until she noticed the flicker of awareness in his eyes and then she started again. First she caressed him with her toes, and then once she knew she had his full attention, she began a slow and sensual move up his leg. Her stocking-clad foot rubbed, stopped, slid slowly up and down, stopped again, and then worked its way back down to his ankle — where she started the game all over again.

"How about we get out of here and take a walk out on deck? I can't wait any longer to kiss you in the moonlight," he whispered for Rachel's ears only.

Unbeknownst to Nick, Rachel was pleased and relieved by his whispered words. She was not oblivious to the fact that he'd been a little distant since the moment they arrived back aboard ship. He had withdrawn from her right after he'd kissed her so sweetly, and she thought that maybe he was starting to regret where this thing between them was heading. Sure, they were moving things along pretty fast, but the trip was going to be over in three more nights, so they didn't have a whole lot of time. If she wanted a brief, romantic interlude — and she did — she needed to act now and not let him entertain any second thoughts.

"That's the best offer I've had all evening," she whispered back, as she leaned toward him to speak softly into his ear.

Before he could talk himself out of it, Nick scooted his chair back, stood up, reached out for Rachel's hand, and pulled her to her feet.

"If everyone will excuse us, we thought we'd skip dessert and call it a night."

Instantly, everyone at the table stopped talking at once and just sat and stared at Nick and Rachel as though they had both just sprouted two heads. Nick didn't give a damn what these people thought of their abrupt departure, but he noticed that Rachel seemed a little flustered. And suddenly he couldn't get away fast enough.

"Have a nice evening, everyone," was his parting comment as he slipped his arm around Rachel's waist and led her out of the dining room, through a set of double doors, and into the cool, quiet night.

"My God, Nick. We left so unexpectedly. I can only imagine what everyone must be thinking."

"Who cares?"

"I …. I think I do."

"Well I don't. And you shouldn't either."

"But did you see the look on their faces?"

Nick led Rachel over to the railing and leaned against it, bracing his weight on one elbow.

"I'm sorry if I embarrassed you, Rachel, but I just couldn't take one more second in that dining room. And," he continued as he drew her along with him and made his way to a hidden and secluded part of the ship, "I was really getting tired of sharing you with everyone."

Nick's softly spoken words had just the right effect, so he kept on talking. But this time, as he spoke, he brought her even closer to him, so that their bodies were almost touching.

"I want to touch you, Rachel. And I want to feel my mouth on yours. I've thought about our kiss this afternoon all evening, and all I can think about is finishing what we started. You are just so sweet." And this time, he lowered his head so that his mouth was an inch away from her waiting lips. "So incredibly sweet," he said barely above a whisper, and without waiting for permission, he claimed her mouth with his.

And that is when Rachel's world started to spin out of control. In the same instant that Nick took possession of her lips, he brought her even closer and molded her body up against his. He clasped both of his hands around her waist, keeping her captured within his arms. After a few seconds, his thumbs began skimming lightly over her lower back, and his kiss became a little more demanding. He made sure that his touch was gentle, but very, very persuasive. And even though Rachel was drowning in his kiss, she felt branded by his hands as they now stroked up and down her back. She felt each sensation as the backs of his fingers trailed slowly up her sides to rest right below the fullness of her breasts. And she caught her breath as he easily parted her lips and slipped his tongue inside. Like the night before, she was completely unprepared for such a kiss. And like the night before, she responded to him without giving any thought to the consequences.

Nick felt her soft, warm response and he reacted without thinking. He responded to her like a man, completely forgetting who she was and why he was there. It never even crossed his mind that he was a cop, on the job. Instead, he brought one hand up and tangled it in the silkiness of her hair. Slowly, he lifted his mouth from hers, tilting her head back just enough to give him full access to her long, inviting neck. With a hot, open mouth, he placed his lips against her soft skin and drew in her wonderful, womanly scent. And when Rachel let out a tiny sigh and stepped even closer into his body, his mouth started a slow, wet journey down her throat. With a destination clearly in mind, Nick took his time as his mouth made its way down to the swell of her breasts.

Rachel clung to Nick, hanging onto him for dear life. She was reeling from his touch and his mouth was driving her crazy. She knew that she had initiated this kind of response from him with her playfulness under the table, and she didn't regret his ardor for an instant. In fact, she wanted him so badly that all she could think about was how she couldn't bear to let him go. So she leaned up against Nick, tangled her legs with his, and issued a silent but clear invitation. And Nick responded to her in an instant. Nipping, sucking, and kissing, his lips stalled for just a moment while his hands found their way to the buttons on Rachel's silk blouse. One by one, Nick's fingers worked at her buttons, until he could see the lacy contours of her bra. And causing her to grasp tightly onto the front of his shirt, he dipped his head and placed a series of kisses right at the top of her breast. Nick took his sweet time as he allowed himself to savor, feel, and taste the soft skin that was peeking out above her bra. With a soft wind blowing through her hair, and the scent and feel of Nick taking over her senses, Rachel couldn't fight the overwhelming desire that crashed through her.

Rachel simply melted against Nick, allowing him complete access to her to body as well as her mind. Somewhere in the far recess of her brain, it registered that he had hidden them away in a dark, cozy alcove, giving them at least an illusion of privacy. But somewhere it also registered that they needed to find their way to her cabin or to his, so that they could make love totally and completely assured that they would not be interrupted.

With a great deal of difficulty, Rachel took a small step away from Nick's hard and responsive body. As he was forced to raise his head she noticed how his eyes had taken on a sensual, almost drugged look. His green eyes had turned dark as the night, and the look he was now giving her was full of questions.

With shaking hands, Rachel tried to straighten her clothes, and started to button up her blouse. The only problem she was having was that her fingers were shaking so badly that she kept on missing the buttonholes. Without saying a word, Nick gently brushed aside her hands and began the task of refastening her blouse. As he put each button in place, his head began to clear, and he knew that he had taken things way too far.

Nick had made himself a promise that he was not going to go to bed with Rachel during this rotten assignment. He would not use her that way. He had decided over dinner that he might need to continue the seduction of Ms. Rachel Bennett in order to gain her trust — but for no other reason. Seduction took many forms, he well knew, and ending up in the sack was just not going to happen. How he was going to get a look into the package was beyond him, but he was not going to get her into bed for that reason. He would not do that to her or to himself. Alex could threaten to feed him to the wolves, but he had made up his mind. And he had to put a stop to this madness now. But before he had a chance to say a word, Rachel caught him completely by surprise.

"We can go to your cabin or mine, Nick."

His fingers froze on the front of her blouse and his eyes narrowed as he studied her face in the shadows.

"I'm not sure you know what you're saying, Rachel." As he spoke, he calmly finished with the buttons on her blouse.

"I know exactly what I'm saying, Nick. And I think you do too."

Nick had to call on all his willpower to keep to his promise not to take Rachel straight to bed. And because he didn't trust himself enough not to give in to temptation, he figured his best bet was to put her off the idea himself. So he purposely chose words that were meant to discourage her. Words that were blunt, somewhat insensitive, but very much to the point.

"I don't think it's much of a secret that I want to make love to you, Rachel. God knows that I can barely keep my hands and mouth away from you. And each time I touch you, I can hardly think about anything else. But you need to understand something. You need to understand that if we go back to your cabin or to mine, for me it will only be about sex. I'm not in any position to have a relationship right now, and as much as I like you and as great as sex with you would be, it will all come to an end in just three days. At the conclusion of this cruise, I'll go my way and you'll go yours. Now, knowing this about me, and knowing that in three days it will all be over, do you honestly think you can handle this?"

"I am not a child, Nicholas. And believe it or not I've already given this a great deal of thought over the last twenty-four hours. I admit that I'm not the most experienced woman in the world when it comes to these things, but I'm experienced enough to know what I want. And I want to be with you, Nick. I want to be with you for the next three nights, and I promise you that I won't expect anything from you after this trip is over. As you said, I fully expect you to go on with your life, and I'll do the same. So you see, I really have thought about this."

"Please think it over some more, Rachel." Nick was trying desperately to buy himself some more time. "I don't want you to jump into something that you may regret later on."

"Oh, my God. You're not married, are you?"

"No, I'm not married. I was once, but that was a long time ago."

"Do you have a girlfriend? Is that what you're trying to tell me?"

"No."

"Then why are you asking me to think over my decision?"

God, she was making him crazy, but the last thing he could do now was to back down.

"Listen to me for just a minute. I'm asking you to think this over some more because something tells me that deep down inside, casual sex is not really your thing. I want you, Rachel, more than you can imagine. But not enough to take advantage of you, and not enough to hurt you in the process of getting what I want."

"So you're turning me down?" she asked. And only a fool would have missed the slight quiver in her voice.

"God no!" And as soon as he realized what he said, he tried again. "Only for tonight, Rachel," was his amended reply, as he reached out to run the back of his hand lightly down her cheek. "Please understand that I just need to be sure you're ready to accept something that cannot last between us. I need to be honest with you about this and all I ask is that you're honest with yourself. So do us both a favor and give yourself another night to think this over."

Nick stepped closer to Rachel and leaned down to run his lips over hers. "Just one more night to think it through."

Rachel closed her eyes and drew in a deep, sobering breath. She was embarrassed and disappointed by Nick's response to her open invitation to have sex with her, and she wasn't sure what to do next. She really was way, way out of her element. As sophisticated as she was trying to be, she really was in over her head. And in her heart of hearts, she knew that everything Nick had just said made perfect sense. But because his words and his lack of enthusiasm had hurt her more than she cared to admit, she decided to get back at him and to give him a little something to think about.

Rachel reached up and wrapped her arms around Nick's neck. Then she brought her lips to his ear. "All right, Nick, I'll do as you ask and I'll think about everything you've said. But in return there's a little something I want you to think about." Nick didn't say a word, because with her warm breath in his ear he couldn't quite find his voice.

"I had a dream about you last night. In my dream we made love to each other and it was wonderful. We both made love with our hands, our mouths, and finally with our bodies. And my dream was so clear and so erotic that I swear I could actually feel every inch of you as you slipped deep inside me. So, even though I promise to think about everything you've said tonight, I want you to know that if I get the chance, Nick, I want to know what you will feel like for real."

Even though Nick knew exactly what she was up to, he still couldn't prevent a groan from escaping. His mind latched onto the description of the two of them in her dream and wouldn't let go. He became instantly hard, and he silently cursed himself, Alex Kendall, this assignment, and the entire LAPD.

Rachel knew she had made her point and decided not to push her luck any further tonight. So she unwrapped her arms from around Nick's neck and took a tiny step backwards.

"So, will I see you tomorrow?"

How the hell she could now sound so damn cool and collected was beyond him.

"How about a picnic on Catalina Island?" he choked out, still trying to get her all-too-vivid dream out of his head.

"I'd love that."

Nick just nodded and started to pull away from the railing so that he could walk her back to her cabin. But Rachel stopped him by putting up her hand.

"It's probably best if I make it back on my own, Nick. If you walk me back to my room, you will probably kiss me goodnight at my door, and I will kiss you back. And before you know it, our kisses will get out of hand and you'll be trying to undress me right there in the hallway. And then I'll never be able to keep my promise and think things through clearly. So stay where you are, Nicholas Fallen, and I'll see you in the morning."

Rachel was obviously teasing him now and having a great deal of fun in the process. So deciding that he could afford to lose a round or two, and deciding that he liked the idea that she was trying to lighten things up between them, he leaned back against the rail, and blew her a kiss.

"I'll pick you up at ten."

"I'll be ready," was her only reply as she swept through the nearest door and disappeared back inside the confines of the ship. And for the first time all evening, Nick finally took a long, deep breath.

A smile tugged at the corners of his mouth as he made his way back to the same spot where he had stood last night. Staring down into the depths of the ocean, he thought that Professor Rachel Bennett had actually gotten the best of him. In the end, she had managed to turn things around and get the upper hand. And her teasing had helped tremendously. At least Nick thought so. Because she had been able to walk away from an awkward situation as the winner, leaving Nick to deal with images of her erotic dream and a world-class hard-on.

But as Nick struggled to get his body under control, which wasn't easy, his brain finally allowed him to think a little less about sex, and to concentrate on this God-awful case. As he continued to look out into the night, he had to admit to himself that the more time he spent with Rachel, the more he became convinced of two things. First, he was pretty sure that she didn't have a criminal bone in her body. Second, he was convinced that he was not going to cross over the line and have sex with her. Never mind that she was willing to the point of being the aggressor. Never mind that he couldn't remember the last time he'd wanted a woman this badly. And never mind that they were both single, consenting adults, whose sexual attraction to one another was way off the charts.

The other thing that Nick was absolutely certain of was the importance of this case. And until he could prove otherwise, Rachel was still considered a possible suspect. And he could not, would not, sleep with her to get the answers that he needed — because sleeping with Professor Rachel Bennett was simply out of the question.

*   *   *

Rachel crawled into bed with only one thought on her mind — how she was going to get Nick Fallen into bed. And the more she thought about it, the more she was absolutely determined to have this fling. She had never done anything like this in her life, and she strongly suspected that she never would again. But she wasn't about to let this opportunity pass her by. Rachel wanted to make love with Nick, even though she had to work on convincing herself that she wasn't in the market for anything long-term. He was so clear about not being able to give her anything more, and she needed to accept it. It was just that simple. And even though she was pretty sure she might have a hard time walking away from him in just three days, she was still willing to take the risk because she had finally met a man who could bring her to her knees with just a look — never mind what he could do to her with his hands and his mouth. "Oh … yes," she muttered to herself as she snuggled even deeper into her pillow. "This is going to be the best sex of my life." And as Rachel drifted off to sleep, her last thought was that *not* sleeping with Nicholas Fallen was simply out of the question.

CHAPTER FOUR

"No, Alex, I haven't gotten inside her room yet."

"So what's the problem, Nick? When you checked in last night, you said you were pretty certain you'd manage to get invited in."

"Things changed."

"What things?"

Nick had no intention of explaining to Alex what had happened between him and Rachel last night. It was none of his business.

"It just didn't happen, Alex." Nick snapped out the words and refused to offer up an apology.

"Okay, so it didn't happen last night. I don't need to remind you that you only have tonight, and tomorrow morning you dock in Mexico and she will hand off her package."

Nick ran his hand down his face, already weary and fed up. But Alex was his boss, and he needed to know that Nick hadn't completely fucked up this assignment. At least not yet.

"I've come up with an idea that should get me inside her room this morning."

"It's about time. So what's your idea?"

Nick hesitated for just one second. "Before I go into that, there's one other thing, Alex."

"And that would be?"

Nick dreaded this part of the conversation, but he wasn't going to back down now. He had too much at stake.

"If everything goes down according to plan, I want to make a deal with you."

The silence on the other end of the line stretched from one second, to two seconds, to three seconds before Alex spoke. "I'm listening." And Nick could tell that he wasn't happy. Nick also knew his plan was full of holes, but it was the best he could come up with as he had tossed and turned all night long.

"We're spending the day together and I'm supposed to pick her up at 10 o'clock. You and I both know that there isn't a woman in the world who's ever ready on time, and never, ever ready early. So I plan to knock on her door at 9:30. And when she invites me in to wait until she finishes getting dressed, I'll see if I can locate the package. And if I do, there should be enough time for me to get a quick look inside."

"Not the best plan you've ever come up with, Detective, but I guess it'll have to do since we're running out of time."

"Now I want to make a deal with you, Alex."

There was a long pause on the other end of the line, and Nick knew that Alex wasn't going to give in easily. In fact, he wasn't even sure that Alex would agree to hear him out. Making deals with his detectives was not usually done.

"Okay, Nick. Even though it goes against my better judgment, I'll hear you out. But no promises."

"Fair enough." And before he continued, Nick reached out and took a sip of strong, black coffee, waiting for the jolt of caffeine to kick in.

"So let's hear it."

"If my plan works, Alex, and I find out there's nothing in that package of Rachel's but regular, everyday travel documents, I want this investigation called off until I get back to Los Angeles. I want to officially be off the job for the next two days. We can always figure out what to do next when I get back in town."

"Anything else?" It didn't get past Nick that Alex had not agreed to a thing.

"Yeah, there is. If I get a look inside that package and find that it's full of illegal documents, I still want to be called off this assignment. I want off this ship today and I'll come up with some trumped-up emergency to explain my sudden departure. We can wait for Ms. Bennett to disembark in Los Angeles and pick her up for questioning then. But I've got to tell you, Alex, that even if I find a shitload of illegal documents, my gut tells me that she's not involved."

"Is it your gut telling you this, Nick, or another part of your anatomy?" This time the long silence was on Nick's end of the line. "Don't answer that. I'm out of line for even asking you such a question."

"Listen, Alex…"

"No, you listen, Nick. I'm not sure this plan of yours will even work. But if it does, I'll agree to the first part of your deal. If there's nothing suspicious in the package Ms. Bennett is delivering tomorrow, then you are officially on vacation for the next two days. Do whatever you want, with whomever you want to do it with. But when you return to L.A., you're back on point, because we still have a murder we're trying like hell to solve. But what I won't agree to is the second part of your deal. My God, Nick, if you find evidence of illegal documents, then the last thing I need is for you to disappear. If you find anything in that package that you don't like, you need to stick even closer to our Professor Bennett. Understood?"

Nick had the urge to tell his boss to take this assignment and shove it. But he knew that losing his temper would get them absolutely nowhere. And in the end, he was still a cop. A damn good cop. And a cop who could see the logic in what Alex was saying.

"I know you're right, Lieutenant, but I gotta tell you that I really hate this assignment."

Nick could hear Alex's sigh of relief coming across the phone line. "Yeah, me too. But we both have a job to do, and I need you to see this thing through."

Nick drained his cup of coffee and wished he had ordered a full pot. "I'll let you know what I find out as soon as I have a chance. Don't worry if you don't hear from me right away. As soon as I have something solid to report, I'll call in."

"Don't hang up, Nick. There's someone here who wants to say hello."

Nick knew who it was even before he heard his partner's voice. "Hey buddy, how's it going?"

"Don't ask."

Ben laughed and Nick could hear him take a long drag off a cigarette. Nick wanted one so badly, he felt his stomach tighten.

"Oh come on, buddy. It can't be that bad."

"I wouldn't bet on that if I were you. I hate this damn ship, this assignment sucks like hell, and tell Marc that cruising is way overrated."

Ben laughed again. "How about you tell him yourself when you get back. Which, by the way, couldn't be soon enough."

"What? You miss me already?"

"Hell no. But I'm sure gettin' sick and tired of being your friggin' secretary. I've got three messages for you here somewhere."

Nick could hear Ben rustling around, obviously searching through all the crap in his pockets. "Okay, partner, here they are. Now the first message came in the day before yesterday, and was from a very nice lady by the name of Jeannette. She asked me to remind you to call her as soon as you get back into town so that you two can reschedule your date. The second message was from some gal named Betsy. And let's see, oh yeah, she wanted you to know that she'd be in town this weekend in case you're free and wanted to get together. And the third message — which, in case you're interested, is the one I liked the best

— was from a sweet-sounding thing named Darla. Seems that Darla scored a couple of tickets to some highbrow concert this weekend and she'd just love to take Nicky darling along. Jesus, Nick, with all these women calling you all day, it's a wonder you have any time to work a case."

This time it was Nick's turn to laugh.

"And since we're on the subject of women, how's it going with the beautiful professor?"

No way did Nick want to talk about Rachel right now. "We'll talk about it when I get back. Because I gotta go."

Ben knew his partner well enough to know that this subject was closed. At least for now.

"Okay, Romeo. But hurry and get your ass back here. My head's spinning just trying to keep all your female admirers straight."

Nick didn't even bother to say goodbye. He just muttered a good-natured "Screw you," and hung up.

*   *   *

Nick waited patiently for the door to cabin 303 to open, and when it did, his smile died on his face. Because there stood Rachel, dressed and ready to go, a full thirty minutes early. *Shit,* was his only thought as she stood in the doorway and sent him a smile of her own, before she whirled back around.

"Come on in, Nick. I'll be ready in a second. I just need to put on some lipstick."

Nick walked into the room, closed the door, and grabbed onto her arm before she cold slip away. "And good morning to you too, Professor," he said right before he pulled her gently to him and kissed her on the tip of her nose.

Rachel laughed at his sweet gesture, and as she drew away, she noticed the picnic basket he held in his other hand.

"What's in the basket?"

"Got me. I just called and asked the kitchen to put together a picnic lunch for two. I haven't a clue what's inside."

"Oh good. I love surprises," she threw over her shoulder before she disappeared into the bathroom. "Make yourself at home. I'll only be a minute."

Now was finally Nick's chance to look around. He was inside her cabin, and pretty much alone for a few minutes. So, not wasting a second, he wandered around the small cabin, his eyes quickly scanning all the tabletops. And bingo, right there, sitting on top of a cluttered vanity, was a ten-by-twelve envelope. Nick walked over, read the name typed in bold letters, and committed it to memory. *Miguel Ernesto Bautista,* Ensenada, Mexico. He was debating whether or not to turn it over to see how hard it would be to get it open, and decided to leave well enough alone. Now that he knew where it was, he knew he would just have to find time tonight to get back in here and take a look inside.

"Okay. I'm ready to go."

Nick was smooth as silk. He turned toward Rachel without giving any indication that he'd even noticed the package.

"I though we'd rent one of those small electric carts, explore the island, and then search out the perfect spot for our picnic."

"I think that's a wonderful idea, Nick."

If Rachel had even a hint of suspicion that Nick was snooping around, she didn't show it. But then again, he was an expert at disguising what he was really up to.

The day on Catalina Island was picture perfect. The island was filled with cute, one-of-a-kind shops, lots of restaurants, and just enough attractions to keep the tourists entertained. But Nick and Rachel avoided all of those things as they spent their morning as far away from the crowds as possible. As promised, Nick rented a golf cart and he took them all over the little island. They took their time and skirted around the island, exploring everything at their leisure. Nick never let on, but he'd been to Catalina enough times that he was familiar enough with the island to know right where to find a secluded, out-of-the-way place for their picnic.

"This looks like a pretty good spot."

Rachel nodded with delight as he led the way over to an area shaded by a wonderful old tree. The grass was deep and springy and made a perfect cushion for the blanket they spread out. Nick sat and took off his shoes, encouraging Rachel to do the same. And as they got comfortable, Nick fished into the basket and took out cold chicken, fresh fruit, and a piece of chocolate cake for each of them. Nick was both pleased and a bit surprised that a bottle of red wine had been included in their basket.

Both Nick and Rachel enjoyed their lunch, each telling the other stories about their past. The more Rachel drank, the more she talked, whereas Nick became that much quieter. He preferred to just sit back and listen. And when she started talking about her sister, he became very alert and didn't want to distract her by saying a word.

"My sister and I were very close growing up. I was two years older and she used to follow me around like a little puppy. In my teens, I resented that a little, but as we both grew older, she became my best friend. We did as much together as we could over the past five years, especially after both of our parents died four years ago. Cynthia got married three years ago, so her priority was her husband of course, but we still saw as much of each other as possible. She died this year, and I miss her so much."

This was the opportunity Nick had been waiting for. "What happened?"

Rachel's eyes took on a faraway, haunted look, and Nick thought for a moment that she wasn't going to answer his question. So he reached out and took her small hand in his. "What happened, Rachel?"

She closed her eyes and took in a deep breath. "My sister was murdered three months ago, Nick."

He felt her fingers squeeze tightly around his hand. "She was found in an alley, shot in the back of the head." Her hand was now clutching even more tightly onto his, but he ignored it as he waited for her to continue. And when she didn't, he tried to gently urge her on.

"I'm so sorry, Rachel."

"I am too." He couldn't tell if she was speaking to him or to herself. So again he prompted her with another question.

"What did the police say? Have they solved the case?"

Rachel opened her eyes and looked at Nick with such sadness that he felt his heart turn over a little in his chest.

"The police are still working on it."

He could tell that this was hard for Rachel, and he sensed that he should stop, but the cop in him had taken over and he needed to push her a little more.

"Do they have any theories as to why she was killed?"

"I'm not sure. They don't talk to me. If they have anything to report, they speak to her husband. You know, Steven, my brother-in-law."

"The one you're working for."

"Yes," was her only response.

"Doesn't Steven talk to you about the case?" Nick watched her very, very closely. He wanted to see her reaction to this particular question.

"It upsets Steven too much to talk about my sister, so I stopped asking. He's promised to tell me if the police come up with anything. And since he hasn't said a word, I guess they aren't any closer to finding her killer than they were three months ago."

"You could go to the police and talk to them yourself, Rachel. I'm sure they'd see you." Again, he watched her closely, wanting to gauge her response to his suggestion that she talk to the police on her own.

"Actually, I wanted to do that right from the beginning, Nick. You see, after the detectives on the case interviewed me,

I was hoping they'd keep me in the loop. Which, of course, didn't happen. So after a couple of weeks went by and I didn't hear another word from anyone, I thought about stopping by the station to see if I could meet with one of the detectives. But when I mentioned it to Steven, he got very agitated and begged me not to interfere."

As she spoke, Nick felt agitated himself. He felt agitated as hell at Steven Jackson and how easily he had managed to manipulate Rachel. But he didn't allow any of his agitation to show in his voice.

"So now what are you going to do?"

"I don't know," was her softly spoken response, and Nick sensed that this conversation was over. And because he couldn't stand to see the sadness in her eyes, he decided to let things go for the time being. So they sat in silence, both lost in their own thoughts, as Nick finished pouring the last of the wine into their glasses.

Rachel sent Nick a small smile of thanks, and drank from her glass, watching him over the rim. She felt very relieved that for a few minutes, she had someone other than Steven to talk to about her sister. Lately, Steven had not wanted to talk about Cynthia at all, and Rachel thought she could understand why. Because it was hard for her too, and even now she was grateful that Nick seemed to have a sixth sense that she couldn't pursue this conversation any further. It was just too sad.

Rachel set her empty glass aside and that is when Nick noticed that she was trying hard to stifle a yawn.

"Why don't you lie back and close your eyes for a while?" Before Rachel could protest, he placed his hands on her shoulders and laid her down gently on the blanket. "We still have a couple of hours before we need to be back aboard ship."

Rachel just couldn't resist. She felt so incredibly sleepy with the sun warming her face, the feel of a very slight and soft breeze, and Nick's low voice coaxing her to take a little nap.

"I just need ten minutes." Her eyes were closed and her words were already slurred as she drifted off to sleep.

Nick stretched out beside her on the blanket, and placed both hands behind his head. But he didn't even try to sleep. His mind was focused on the fact that she had finally told him about her sister. And now more than ever, he thought that she was innocent. There was just no way she would become involved in anything that may have contributed to her sister's murder. No way at all. And then Nick thought back to the name on the package in Rachel's room. Miguel Ernesto Bautista sounded vaguely familiar to him. But no matter how hard he tried, he couldn't remember when or where he'd heard the name before. Nor could he remember in what context. But he wasn't too worried. As soon as he got back aboard ship, he would call the name in to Alex. And even if the man had nothing more than a jaywalking ticket, Alex would be able to pull up his record and he would know his entire life story in no time.

Nick tried to relax not only his body but his mind. He hadn't slept much the night before, so he allowed himself the luxury of closing his eyes. But he knew he wouldn't doze off. So he lay back and let almost an hour tick by before he turned onto his side and reached over to wake Rachel.

"Open your eyes, Professor." His words were spoken so softly, he thought she hadn't even heard him. So he leaned in even closer and stroked his thumb ever so lightly over her cheek. "Come on, Rachel. Time to wake up."

"Mmmm …"

He chuckled at her sleepy sigh, and tried again. "Come on, sleepyhead," and before he could continue to coax her awake, she reached out, wrapped both arms around his neck, and drew him down for a kiss. Rachel had caught him so off guard that Nick completely lost his balance, fell forward, and somehow found his body sprawled right on top of hers. It took all of one instant for him to become hard, and he knew he was lost as soon as her lips made contact with his.

Rachel was a little sleepy, so the kiss was slow and easy, which ended up being a real turn-on. And the man in Nick responded without hesitation. He brought both of his hands up and ran his fingers through her hair, holding her face still so that he could explore her at his leisure, and take his time drawing Rachel into his kiss. He wanted to linger, taste and seduce her with his mouth. As his kiss washed over her like a drug, he could feel Rachel's body yielding to nothing more than his lips against hers.

Nick lifted his head just enough to allow his tongue to tease the corners of her mouth, right before he expertly parted her lips and slipped inside. And when he felt Rachel tighten her hold and lift her hips to rub up against him, he made love to her with his kiss.

Rachel was completely swept away by her sexual response. Nick's mouth was wet and scorching hot. His tongue was slipping sensually in and out of her mouth, imitating the act of having sex. And because she feared he might pull away, she reached up and ran her hands through his hair, keeping him captive just as he did her. Rachel felt so gloriously alive and so sexually aroused, that she forgot all about having any inhibitions as her own tongue touched and teased.

Nick was tempted to go even further and run his hands slowly down the length of her, but he knew that he had to put a stop to things. His conscience was telling him to slow down, but his body seemed incapable of listening. Luckily, they both needed to catch their breath, so they were forced to break apart. And as Nick raised his head, his lust-filled eyes gazed down into Rachel's flushed and lovely face.

Nick would never know what it was that finally brought him to his senses. Maybe it was nothing more than echoes of his own promise not to take advantage of Rachel. Whatever it was, as he continued to look down at her, he felt some tiny element of self-control take over.

"We can't make love here, Rachel." But even as he spoke the words, he couldn't help but sink a little more deeply into her parted legs. And she responded by closing her eyes and whispering his name. "It's just too risky, sweetheart." *God, had he really called her sweetheart?* "Someone could come by any minute."

Nick didn't believe a word of what he was saying. He knew they were in a spot well off the beaten path, and even his muddled brain knew how easily they could make love right where they were and get away with it. But he didn't voice any of this to Rachel, because there was one other very, very good reason they couldn't make love. Besides his promise to himself, Nick didn't have any protection with him, and he absolutely refused to even consider having sex without a condom.

"Open up your eyes and look at me, Rachel." Very slowly, she did as he asked, and suddenly Nick felt as though he had been punched in the stomach. Her eyes were dreamy, unfocused, and conveyed to him a desire to be kissed one more time. Unable and unwilling to stop himself, he bent his head and kissed her lightly at the corners of her eyes. First one and then the other.

"We need to pack things up and head back before they sail without us." It was the only thing he could think of to say.

"I know," she sighed. And Nick felt a different kind of punch in the stomach as she trailed her fingers along his neck, up his chin, and then lightly over his lips.

"Please don't. We'll never get out of here if you keep touching me that way."

Rachel just gazed into Nick's penetrating green eyes for several heartbeats, before responding to his plea. "Would that be so bad?" she asked as again she ran the tip of her finger against his lips.

"You are a dangerous woman, Professor Bennett. A very dangerous woman."

Reminding himself that one of them had to be the voice of reason, Nick drew in a ragged breath. He knew he couldn't entertain the idea of kissing her again, because if he did, he might actually try to see just how easy it would be for them to make love. So before he broke down and gave in to his own throbbing need, Nick dropped his head into the crook of her neck, and then moved his lips to the sensitive spot just behind her ear. He didn't move for one or two minutes. He just allowed himself to rest against her and to draw in her sweet scent.

Still hard as a rock, Nick forced himself not to think any more about how her soft and welcoming body felt beneath his. So with all the self-control he could muster, he pushed his body up and lifted himself off of Rachel. And in one fluid movement, he came to his feet, reached down for Rachel's hand, and pulled her up with him.

She fell easily into his arms, wrapping hers around his waist. Rachel clung to Nick, trying to steady her rapidly beating heart and trying to pull herself together. "How much time before we sail?"

"A little more than an hour," he replied as he kissed the top of her head. "But if we hurry, we'll make it back in time to rest a little before dinner." Nick wasn't really thinking about resting, but he needed time before dinner to get in touch with Alex.

"I feel pretty rested now, Nick. But a nice, long shower would be nice."

"Then we'd better get going."

Reluctantly, Rachel pulled out of his arms. She was still so affected by him, and she suspected that he was having trouble calming his wildly beating heart as well. But she knew that Nick was right and that they couldn't possibly make love in such a public place, even if they hadn't seen another soul since they arrived for their picnic. With a small sigh, Rachel sent up a small prayer of thanks that at least Nick had the common sense to put a stop to things before they had gotten completely out of hand. Because God knew, if left up to her, she would probably have taken the risk and made love to him right out in the open — which would have been a really stupid thing to do. So again, Rachel sent up a silent *thank you,* and together they packed up the remains of their picnic before climbing back into their little electric cart.

"Did you remember that it's formal night tonight?" Rachel asked as Nick started up the golf cart and headed back in the direction from which they came.

"Yeah. I brought my tux, but I'm really not in the mood. I'd rather stay in my jeans and order a hamburger."

"We can do that tomorrow night if you want, Nick. But tonight is the Captain's Dinner and since it is an evening for grown-ups, I doubt they'll serve hamburgers anywhere on the ship. Except, of course, for the children on board."

Nick looked over at her with a grin. "Are you making fun of me, Professor?"

"Of course not!"

Nick stopped the cart, looked at her with narrowed eyes, and lifted a dark brow.

"Well ... maybe I am making fun of you. But just a little."

He put his foot back on the pedal and laughed right along with Rachel. "I guess I do sound a little like a ten-year-old. But truth be told, nothing beats comfortable old jeans, a nice worn T-shirt, and a hamburger and fries for dinner."

Rachel loved thinking about Nick as a ten-year-old kid. She could easily picture him at that age, and thought that even at ten, he had probably managed to break a dozen little-girl hearts. She was absolutely certain that he'd have been cute, mischievous, and probably smart as a whip.

"Do you have any brothers or sisters?" She realized that even though he had talked earlier about his past, he'd never mentioned any siblings.

"No, I'm an only child."

When Nick didn't elaborate, Rachel didn't pursue the subject. Instead, she sat quietly and watched him, thinking again about what he must have been like as a little boy, a teenager, and a young adult. She could certainly testify firsthand as to what a wonderful man he had turned out to be, and she suspected that he'd had a good childhood, even without a brother or sister to share it with. He just seemed so self-assured and so confident in himself. And not for the first time, Rachel realized that she liked everything, absolutely everything about Nicholas Fallen.

It seemed to Rachel that it had taken a lot less time to get back to the ship, but then again Rachel had been lost in her thoughts about the man beside her. Like yesterday, they walked quietly up the gangplank, except this time, Nick was holding onto Rachel's hand. They flashed their boarding passes to get back on the ship, and Nick was leading her in the direction of the elevator when Rachel suddenly stopped.

"You go ahead, Nick. I need to run to the gift shop. If you want, you can pick me up at my cabin before dinner."

Nick was relieved. He still needed to get in touch with Alex or Ben, so that he could have one of them see what information they could find on Bautista. And then he needed to shower, shave, and change into his tux.

"How about a drink before dinner? I could pick you up … say, in about ninety minutes."

Rachel quickly glanced at her watch, noting that it was just 4:00. "I'll be ready." Before he could reach for her himself, she stood up on her tiptoes, placed her hands on his shoulders, leaned forward, and kissed him on the cheek. And then she disappeared.

Nick grinned as he watched her hurrying away, a little intrigued by what could be so important in the gift shop. But he didn't have time to think about that, because he needed to get back to his own room and make a call. He figured that by now, Alex was going to be good and mad because Nick had waited this long to call. Nick knew that Alex would expect him to have found a way to break free from Rachel long enough to at least check in. But that didn't happen. And he would just have to explain that to his boss, or if his luck held out, he would get the chance to explain everything to Ben instead. So, dismissing Rachel's little gift shop expedition from his mind, he headed to his own room, ready to face the music.

CHAPTER FIVE

Nick glanced in the mirror to straighten his tie, slipped on his tuxedo jacket, and then headed out his door. He hated getting dressed up and he had meant it when he told Rachel earlier that he preferred well-worn jeans and hamburgers and fries. Plus he had no interest whatsoever in attending this Captain's Dinner. He had already made up his mind that he couldn't tolerate another dinner in the noisy, crowded dining room, especially in the mood he was in.

Needless to say, his conversation with Alex had gone pretty much as expected. Alex was madder than hell that he had waited all day to hear from Nick, and he had gotten even madder when Nick gave him the name of Miguel Ernesto Bautista.

They had hung up the phone, both of them a little pissed, with Nick not even bothering to hide his own frustration. Alex had told him to sit tight, and not leave his room until he called him back. Nick nearly lost his temper because he hated being told what to do — but the truth was, he wasn't going anywhere anyway, until he picked Rachel up at 5:30.

Twenty minutes after hanging up with Alex, his phone rang and it was Alex again, this time with a full dossier on Bautista. In a deadly calm voice, Alex explained that Bautista was a fairly new, but rather well-known drug dealer, wanted in the U.S. not only for transporting drugs across the border, but he was also wanted for questioning in an attempted murder case. Alex found his name on the U.S. watch list, which meant there was no way he could get into the U.S. without very good and very false papers. He was always armed, considered dangerous, and up until now, difficult to find.

Alex and Nick spent a quick ten minutes working out a plan. They both agreed that now it was even more important for Nick to get a look inside the package in Rachel's room. If it was full of illegal documents, which they were now 99 percent sure was the case, Nick's priority was to convince Rachel to take him along on her delivery in the morning. If he could pinpoint Bautista's location, Alex could call in the FBI, and they could work with the Mexican authorities to apprehend this scum of the earth.

Since time was running out, and everything hinged on tonight, Nick tried to force his bad mood into the back of his mind. As he reached Rachel's room, he ran his fingers impatiently though his hair, then he lifted one hand and knocked on her door. And the very instant she opened her door, he knew that he was a dead man.

Because standing before him was without a doubt, the loveliest woman he had ever seen. With one sweep of his eyes, he took her in. Rachel was dressed in a long, black, strapless dress that clung to every curve of her body. The bodice of the dress outlined her breasts to perfection. The gown was gathered tightly at the waist and then fell to her feet in wisps of black lace. She had on very high, strappy sandals, and she had changed her toenail polish from pink to bright red. His eyes made their way very slowly down her body and then just as slowly back up again. And that is when he noticed her hair. She had pulled her lovely hair up into a style that just begged to be let down. With her thick, black hair piled somewhat loosely on top of her head, her neck and bared shoulders were showcased. The only jewelry she wore were earrings that dangled from her ears and seemed to sparkle just a little as she moved her head. Just looking at her, Nick was absolutely breathless. She was quite simply way too sexy for his peace of mind.

Trying hard not to let his thoughts show, Nick had no idea that at the sight of him standing in her doorway, Rachel had been having very similar feelings. As soon as she had opened her door, she had to catch her breath. She had always thought that most men looked great in a tuxedo, but she couldn't even find the right word to describe Nicholas Fallen. Great just didn't do him credit. Incredible came to her mind, along with breathtaking, drop-dead gorgeous, and sexy beyond words. She did notice that he looked a little uncomfortable in the tux, but that just seemed to add to his sex appeal.

Both Nick and Rachel stood staring at each other, until Rachel finally found her voice.

"Come in, Nick. I thought we could have our drink here before we head down to dinner. I hope you don't mind, but I went ahead and ordered a bottle of wine."

Rachel turned around to head back into the room, and that's when Nick nearly lost it. Her dress was cut low in the back, and was form-fitting just enough so that it showed off every inch of her sweet, sweet butt — so much so that Nick had to fight the urge to reach out and run his hand over her bottom. It was just so tempting that he came very close to doing so. But even as he fought back his desire to grab onto her, he made himself walk into the room and calmly close the door.

"Would you please open the wine?"

Some small voice in the far recess of Nick's mind told him that this was a really bad idea. Rachel looked way too inviting, and the small cabin suddenly seemed to shrink in size. Feeling a little hot under the collar, Nick reached up and tugged on his bow tie.

"I ordered a nice burgundy. I've had it before, and I think you'll like it."

Nick hadn't moved even an inch, nor had he said a word. All he seemed able to do was to stand silently and watch as Rachel turned back around toward him.

"Would you rather have a beer? We can call and have one sent up to the room."

After one more slight tug on his tie, Nick did two things. He forced his eyes away from Rachel's clinging dress and he forced himself to speak.

"How about we save the wine for later, Rachel? Why don't we go down to the bar now for a drink and then come back up here after dinner." He wasn't sure why, but he thought he needed to get out of this room. And he needed to get out now.

"All right. We can do that." Nick noticed a little disappointment in Rachel's voice, but decided to ignore it. And before he had a chance to give in to the look in her eyes and change his mind, he turned back around and headed for the door.

Because there didn't seem to be any other choice, Rachel picked up her beaded evening bag, and slipped the tiny handle over her arm. She walked up behind Nick, and laid her hand lightly on his back, just as he reached for the door knob.

"Do you like my dress, Nick?"

"Of course," he responded as he looked at her over his shoulder. "You look incredible."

Rachel smiled at his compliment and Nick couldn't quite stop himself from turning around to face her. "You really are beautiful, Rachel."

And again she offered him one of her sweetest smiles. "Do you think my dress is too inappropriate for tonight?"

"Are you kidding?" The look on his face and the intensity of his eyes told her just the opposite. He really did like the dress.

"I just want to make sure it isn't too revealing. You know … I don't want to show too much skin."

Nick swallowed hard before his eyes swept slowly down her body for the second time in less than ten minutes. "I think it's perfect."

"I'm glad," she replied a little shyly and then she took a small step a little closer to him.

"Can I ask you another question before we go?"

Nick just knew he was going to be in big trouble. Something about the way she was looking at him made him wonder what she was up to. But she smelled and looked so damn good that he went against his better judgment and said, "Sure, go ahead."

Rachel brought her lips up to Nick's ear and whispered, "Do you think it's inappropriate that I'm not wearing anything under this dress? I wouldn't want anyone to be able to tell. Except you, that is."

And that was it. That was all Nick could take. In one instant, he didn't give a damn that he was a cop, he didn't give a damn that he was on a case, and he didn't give a damn about his promise not to sleep with Rachel.

With more force than he intended, he reached out to take hold of her arms, and then he pulled her up against his body. "You win," was all Nick said as his mouth came crashing down on hers. And that was the last coherent thing he said to her as his lips and tongue began their assault on her mouth. And what an assault. Nick didn't even try to coax Rachel into the kiss. His kiss was demanding, not persuasive, and not the sweet, tender kiss of a new lover. His kiss was taking control and setting the pace — not allowing for any hesitation. He took her lips, opened her mouth, and let his tongue seduce her mind. And as Nick kept Rachel locked tightly in his arms, he just kept on kissing her and kissing her. He didn't want to think about anything but how she felt, and how he was going to feel once he was finally inside of her. It vaguely registered to Nick that when she had first opened her door, he had thought that *he was a dead man*. And now, as she started to return his kiss for kiss, his only thought was *what a way to die*.

Rachel felt herself melt against Nick, her heart beating a mile a minute. She had hoped her seductive words would work on him, but she could never have imagined such a reaction. He was kissing her senseless and she thought she might faint from the waves and waves of pleasure flowing through her body. She knew firsthand that Nicholas Fallen could kiss, but this was different. This kiss was already taking her to bed. And she could hardly stand the anticipation of what was to come.

In a haze of desire, Rachel could feel Nick's hand slide up her back, while his other hand kept her plastered up against his body. His fingers trailed lightly over the back of her neck right before he reached up and pulled the pins from her hair, causing most of it to fall in disarray down her back. And his hand stayed tangled in her hair as he continued to tease her with his tongue.

Rachel tried to draw in a little breath, and he lifted his mouth barely an inch from hers. She sighed his name, and before she knew what was happening, he pulled her back just enough so that his emerald green eyes locked onto hers. And without saying a word, he continued to stare into her eyes as his hand began to lower the zipper on her dress.

"You need to say no now, Rachel." His voice was low and raspy. "Because in another second it will be too late."

Rachel couldn't look away from his eyes if her life depended on it. She knew he was giving her one last chance to call an end to this. She also knew that this was going to be nothing more to him than sex. Down and dirty sex. And she knew that he hadn't changed his mind about not wanting a real relationship right now. But none of that mattered. All she cared about was how she felt in his arms, and how she felt when he kissed her. So she refused to look away from the warning in his eyes. And she refused to call a halt to what she had been waiting for all her life.

Nick waited several long seconds. And when Rachel just continued to meet his eyes with a knowing look of her own, his hand continued to move down her back, taking the zipper with it. It one quick movement, Nick pushed her dress down past her hips, watching as it pooled around her feet. Slowly he lifted his eyes, catching his breath, as he gazed at her perfect, naked flesh. And suddenly he was hit with a knot of desire so strong, he didn't even stop to think about what he was doing.

Somehow he managed to struggle out of his tuxedo jacket, right before he reached out to grab Rachel around the waist. Without giving her a moment to protest, he lifted her up, swung her around, and pushed her back up against the door. He could feel Rachel's legs wrap tightly around his waist, just as he lowered his mouth to take one firm, extended nipple between his lips. A moan escaped from Rachel as Nick began to suck on her nipple. His mouth was hot and wet against her breast, and Rachel thought she might actually die from the overwhelming sensations.

Rachel started to cry out for him when he lifted his head, but her cry was caught in her throat as his mouth found its way to her neck. As he kissed her neck with his lips and his tongue, Rachel reached out to pull his shirt from his pants. She wanted — no she needed to be able to feel his skin beneath her hands. As she slipped her hands under his shirt, Nick slipped his own hands to the front of his pants, lowered his zipper and freed himself. Nick then wrapped his hands around Rachel's waist and lifted her barely an inch. He lifted her just enough so that he could find his way to her opening, lower her back down, and then plunge himself into her as deep as he could go.

But at the exact moment that Rachel grabbed onto Nick's shoulders to help lower herself around him, he stopped what he was doing. And before she could comprehend what had happened, he dropped his forehead against hers and spoke though gritted teeth.

"I don't have a fucking condom."

It took her less than a second to respond. "I do Nick. I have one right here."

Nick lifted his head and watched in disbelief as Rachel reached out for the tiny purse that was still dangling from her arm. She opened it frantically, spilling most of the contents onto the floor. Miraculously, she managed to pull out a condom, tear open the wrapper and hand it to Nick. Within a heartbeat, Nick covered himself with protection, pierced her with his eyes, and drove himself into her. In one long, smooth thrust, he had penetrated her to the hilt. And Rachel cried out with pleasure. As did Nick.

The moment Nick slipped deeply into Rachel, he had to close his eyes, because the feeling of being inside her so was intense. He found he couldn't move for a second or two, because all he wanted was to stay buried in her soft folds. But then she shifted just slightly, and that was all it took for him to practically go over the edge. Keeping her balanced against the wall, Nick thrust in and out, in and out, in and out. Then, because he couldn't stop himself, his movements became faster and harder. And finally, when he thought he couldn't hold off anger longer, Rachel screamed out his name and climaxed around him, digging her nails into his shoulders. One more deep, penetrating thrust and Nick joined her, as his own climax almost caused his knees to buckle.

It was a miracle that they both didn't crash to the floor. Nick leaned heavily into Rachel, his face buried in her hair, his breathing ragged.

Rachel was so drained that all she could do was to drop her head onto Nick's shoulder and try to draw in enough air so that she wouldn't pass out. She was absolutely, completely, shaken to the core.

It was only when Nick felt Rachel's legs begin to quiver around him that he found enough strength to step back so that she was no longer pressed up against the door. And slowly, with her clutching him around the neck, she unwrapped her legs and slid down his body. As her feet touched the ground, she was still so affected by what had passed between them that she couldn't let go. She still needed him to help steady her.

Nick responded by gently folding her naked body into his arms. And as she leaned into his embrace, he felt a stab of guilt wash over him — not for what they had just done, but for how they had done it.

"Are you all right?"

Rachel was still trying to catch her breath, so all she could manage was to nod into his shoulder.

"I'm sorry, Rachel," he whispered into her hair. "I didn't want it to happen like this."

With some difficulty, Rachel lifted her head and looked up into Nick's troubled face. Her eyes had a soft look about them, but they also seemed full of doubt. And full of something else. Something that Nick couldn't quite read.

"Are you having regrets already, Nick?"

He answered her honestly. "Not about making love to you. I don't regret that. It was way too good." He took a deep breath before he spoke again. "But I wish I hadn't been so rough and so hurried. That I do regret," he said almost to himself.

This time it was easy for Nick to read what passed through Rachel's eyes. Because it was relief — pure and simple. Which really surprised him.

"If it had been any better, Nicholas, I think my heart might have stopped."

When he just looked down at her and didn't offer a comment, she continued. "I wouldn't change a thing. Not one thing," she added softly. "I wanted you as desperately as you wanted me. And in case you couldn't tell, Nick, I felt my orgasm clear down to the tips of my toes."

Nick suddenly found it difficult to speak, because he just didn't know what to say. So instead, he reacted to her words by reaching down and lifting her into her arms, and carrying her over to the bed. With her cuddled against his chest, he leaned down and pulled the covers back with one free hand. Then he laid her gently down, placed a soft kiss against her temple, and excused himself so that he could get rid of the used condom.

Nick went into the tiny bathroom, discarded the condom, and splashed cold water over his face. He kept his eyes closed for several long seconds, before he lifted his head and stared at himself in the mirror. His eyes were full of self-incrimination, as he thought about how he'd thrown all his good intentions right out the window. He'd done exactly what he had promised himself he wouldn't do. He had taken Rachel Bennett to bed. Well, not exactly to bed, he reminded himself, as he pictured her pushed up against the door, with her long, naked legs wrapped around him. And that image alone almost made him hard all over again.

Nick knew that at this point there was no turning back. He couldn't undo what had just happened, and the truth was, he didn't really want to. He and Rachel had been dancing around the idea of having sex since the night they met. And she had made it very, very clear to him that she wanted him to make love to her. The only real problem he had with all of this was that he was still on the job. And even though he believed that she was not the least bit involved in Steven's illegal business, he was still a cop who had been lying to her since day one. And he had broken a promise to himself, which was something that did not sit right with him.

The only thing that Nick could think of to make the situation tolerable in his own mind was that he knew he was with Rachel because he wanted her. Not because he was trying to seduce her for information. He already had plenty of information to go on, and now all he had to do was get a look inside the package, which he'd noticed earlier was still on the vanity, right where it was this morning. But right at this moment, Nick couldn't care less about the package on the vanity. He was thinking about the fact, the true fact, that he had made love to Rachel tonight because he had wanted her beyond anything else, and he still did. And the fact that he wanted to have sex with her again had absolutely nothing to due with his job.

Because that thought made Nick feel somewhat better, he splashed some more water on his face and then combed his hair with his fingers. Straightening his clothes as best he could, he wanted to get back to Rachel. As he turned out the bathroom light, he looked over and noticed that she was still lying right where he had left her. The only thing she had done was to pull the sheet up to cover her. Nick walked cautiously over to her, suddenly not sure how she really felt about everything that had just happened, and even less sure about whether or not she wanted to have sex with him again. Women and their real feelings were not always easy to figure out, so he decided to play it safe and let her call the shots.

With his shirt tail hanging loose, and his hair still messed up, Rachel thought that Nick had never looked sexier as he made his way over to sit down on the edge of the bed. She smiled, but he didn't, as he watched her with a look that said he wanted to eat her alive.

"Are you sure you're all right?" he couldn't help asking her one more time.

"I'm better than all right. In fact, I feel ….. incredible."

Nick finally smiled. "Well you certainly look incredible." His voice was low and his eyes took on a hungry look.

Rachel shifted a little under the sheet, because the message in his eyes caused goose bumps to break out all over her body.

"Do you want me to go?"

"No."

"Are you sure?"

"Yes."

"Because if I stay, I'm going to make love to you again. And probably again and again and again." As he spoke, Nick let his finger wander lazily up and down her arm.

"I don't want you to go. Please stay, Nick."

"Do you have any more condoms on hand?"

"I bought a box of them at the gift shop."

Even though Rachel sounded a little embarrassed by her admission, that was all the encouragement he needed. Nick unbuttoned and discarded his shirt, stepped out of his shoes and socks, and removed the rest of his clothes without taking his eyes off of Rachel. He lifted the sheet, slipped into bed, turned on his side, and drew her to him.

As she curled up next to Nick, he threw one leg over hers, trapping her against his naked body.

"I want to take my time, Rachel," he breathed into her up-turned face. "I don't want to miss out on touching and tasting every inch of you. I want my mouth to follow my hands. By the end of this night, I want to know every one of your curves by touch, every sensitive spot on your body, and I want to take a nice, long time and do it right."

As Nick spoke, his hands had already started putting his words into action. He started by trailing the tips of his fingers down the back of her neck, which caused Rachel's heart to turn over. Next, his hand made its way slowly down her back with a light, sensual touch. When Nick reached the small of her back, he nudged her even closer with his hand, and then he allowed his fingers to slide down even further to caress her bottom. His fingers played against her skin, and he could tell that his touch was already having the desired effect as he felt Rachel starting to respond.

Nick leaned into Rachel, captured her mouth with his, and easily rolled her over onto her back. As he continued to kiss her — deep, slow, and long — his hand skimmed up her body until his fingers found and caressed her breast.

Nick set aside his own building desire, as he lifted his mouth from hers to sample a taste of her slender throat. He paused just long enough to drink in her scent. His tongue touched her neck, and he had a sudden urge to suck just hard enough so that he would leave his mark on her. But the temptation of taking her sweet, taut nipple between his lips proved too much for him, so he continued with his journey of kisses as he made his way down her neck.

Nick's hand reached under Rachel's perfectly rounded breast, and he lifted it to his waiting mouth.

As promised, Nick took his time, until Rachel cried out. And once he heard her softly moan his name, he moved on. Reminding himself to slow down, Nick's mouth left a wet trail down Rachel's body. He kissed and nipped away at her, driving her mad as his final destination became obvious.

Nick gently opened Rachel's legs with a touch of his hand, and before she could even draw in a breath, he was there. And in the very next instant, Nick lowered his head and placed his mouth right on her soft curls.

Rachel knew that she was going to experience her first orgasm against a man's mouth. She had never, ever allowed herself to let go so completely. She had never, ever had anyone make love to her like Nick Fallen was doing to her now. He had touched, kissed, teased, sucked, and caressed her beyond her wildest dreams. And now he was bringing her to the brink. Just as Rachel had that thought, Nick found her sensitive nub with his lips, and she went completely over the edge.

Nick knew the instant she began to climax against him and he let her body take over. But only for a couple of seconds. Before Rachel could recover from the force of her orgasm, Nick slid up her body, spread her legs just a little more, and forced her to look at him.

"We need protection, Rachel." Nick was so distracted by his own need for her that he almost forgot.

"In …. in the …. nightstand." Rachel could barely speak.

Nick reached over into the nightstand, had a condom in his hand, and covered himself in record time. And then he brought his eyes back to hers, and drove into Rachel with one deep, long thrust.

And it was a toss-up as to who was more affected. Rachel cried out, and Nick closed his eyes and drew in a long, hard breath.

"Don't move," he somehow managed to choke out. "You are just so tight, Rachel, and you feel so damn good." His words were so rough that she wasn't absolutely sure what he had said. But then again, she was so lost in the feel of him inside of her, she wasn't sure it mattered.

Rachel wanted desperately to run her hands down Nick's wonderful body, so she trailed her fingers over his shoulders and down his back. As her hands began to move, so did Nick. And as he began to drive himself in and out of her, he found his way to her tiny ear, whispering things that made her blush with excitement. His words were raw, raunchy, and caused a ripple of desire to crash through Rachel.

"Oh my God. I'm going to come again, Nick."

With those words, Nick knew he too was a goner. He lifted his head, slipped his fingers into Rachel's hair, and plunged even deeper. Rachel started to cry out, but Nick stopped her as his lips came down on hers. And he kissed her long and hard just as they both toppled right over the edge.

*   *   *

It was two o'clock in the morning when Nick slipped silently out of bed. He and Rachel had never left her room. They had ordered room service, drunk most of the wine she had ordered earlier, made love again, snuggled and talked, and finally drifted off to sleep. Rachel was now dead to the world, so Nick thought it was safe for him to finally get a look inside the package that was so important to so many people.

As quietly as he could, Nick made his way to the vanity. With another glance at Rachel, he reached out to turn over the envelope, and was surprised to find that it was sealed as any envelope might be. He knew that it wouldn't be difficult to open the flap and close it again without any evidence that it had been opened. And before he slipped it open, two things flashed through his mind. One, either there was nothing in it but ordinary travel documents, or two, that Steven was smart enough to know that he couldn't afford to draw too much attention to the envelope. And his second suspicion was confirmed the moment he opened the flap, and slid out the documents. The very illegal documents.

Nick turned all cop as he looked over the papers he held in his hand. There were two passports, one in the name of Miguel Ortega and the other in the name of Roberto Sanchez. Both passports contained identical information, including the passport picture. They were obviously false passports, and Nick would bet a month's wages that the picture on both was the face of Miguel Ernesto Bautista. Nick also held in his hand two social security cards and two green cards — both corresponding to the names on the passports. Even in the dim light coming in through the porthole, Nick could tell that these documents were first-rate. Anyone would be hard-pressed to identify them as false. And of course, Bautista would use them both if needed. Depending on his situation, he could pose as either man, and probably get in and out of the U.S. with ease. And that thought alone made Nick sick to his stomach.

Nick Fallen hated drug dealers. He despised what drugs did to people, especially kids. Illegal drugs easily led to murders, and he had seen way too much killing in his thirty-seven years. In his years on the police force, and especially as a detective, he'd seen prostitutes die way too young because of a stupid overdose, men kill for the drug of choice, and kids' lives completely ruined. And Nick blamed all of that on the dealers. And now more than ever, Nick was determined to help bring down not only Bautista, but Steven Jackson as well. Because Steven Jackson was just as bad as the scum pushing the drugs. He was giving them access to the U.S., and the means to distribute their shit, so he had to be stopped. And the sooner the better.

With a sigh of complete disgust, Nick slipped the documents back in the envelope and resealed it as if it has never been touched. He placed it in the exact spot on the vanity where it had been, and then made his way to Rachel. As Nick crawled back under the sheet, he thought about the woman lying next to him. And for the first time in years, he said a little prayer. Nicholas Fallen prayed that Rachel Bennett was innocent in all of this. He prayed that she was just a pawn in Steven's dirty business and that she would get out of the mess unharmed. And then, out of nowhere, he felt an almost violent need to protect her.

And before he gave it one more thought, he reached out to pull Rachel up against his body. He wrapped his arm around her waist and she moaned as she snuggled her bottom up against him. Smiling to himself, he let his hand wander up to cup her breast, right before he whispered into her ear, "Go back to sleep, sweetheart."

Rachel scooted even closer, obviously content to sleep wrapped in his arms. She let out a long sigh and went right back to sleep. Nick just tightened his hold, and prayed again that God would keep her safe. And right before he went to sleep, it crossed Nick's mind that he should have asked God not only to keep Rachel safe from Bautista and Steven, but from the cop who might very well break her heart.

CHAPTER SIX

"I really want to go with you, Professor."

"You can't."

"Sure I can."

"No …. mmmm …. You can't."

"Why not?"

"Be …. Because."

"Because why?"

"Because you …. I mean ….. I can't …. Oh God, Nick … I just can't think straight when you do that."

Nick's mouth was against her ear, his teeth pulling lightly on her earlobe. His breath was warm against her neck, and his hands hadn't been still since he woke her up.

"Do what?" he whispered.

"That," she choked out.

"What, this?" Again he took her earlobe between his teeth. "Or this?" And he let his fingers trail ever so lightly down her body. Down past her breast, stopping only long enough to run his thumb over her nipple, before lazily dragging the back of his hand down even further.

Rachel was totally lost in the sensation of his hands and mouth. She had momentarily forgotten that he had invited himself along on her delivery today, and that she was trying to explain to him why she had to go alone. Because he kept on distracting her.

"You smell like heaven this morning. You smell like woman, and you smell like sex."

Nick kissed her right below her ear before starting again on his one-sided conversation.

"Wrap your arms around me, Rachel."

His words caused a shiver to run down her spine in anticipation. Never in her wildest dreams could she have imaged the last fifteen hours. No matter how much she had wanted this and fantasized about how it would be to make love with Nick, nothing could have prepared her for this. He was so involved in bringing her pleasure and such a creative lover. Last night Nick had started out rough, urgent and demanding. And then, the second time he had made love to her, he was slow and sensual, drawing out their foreplay to the point where Rachel had been on the brink of begging him to sink into her body. And now, this morning, he was teasing and playful. But no matter his mood, each time he touched her, he was able to make her want him with such abandon that it scared her just a little. But not enough for her to put to stop to what he was doing.

So as she closed her eyes and took in a small breath, she did as he asked.

Without delay, Nick leaned over Rachel's body to reach for a condom. And right after he covered himself, he covered Rachel.

"I can't wait. I need to be inside you now."

"I can't wait either, Nick." Rachel didn't even recognize her own voice.

And for the longest time, neither one of them gave any thought to what they had been talking about. Rachel didn't think about the delivery she needed to make in less than an hour, and Nick didn't think about being a cop. They both just thought about how nice it was to wake up together, and how good it felt to be lost in the feel of each other.

"Wrap your legs around me, baby?" Rachel responded and Nick drew in his breath. "Morning sex with you is just so damn good." His words were said as he lowered his head to kiss her, and Rachel couldn't stop the orgasm that tore through her body. And the second Nick felt her convulsing around him, he followed with a blinding climax of his own.

"I'm going to be late if I don't get up now, Nick."

Nick had dragged his body off of Rachel, but he had kept one arm tightly around her and his face was buried in her neck. He was breathing deeply, trying desperately not to fall back asleep. He had gotten very little sleep last night, and the intensity of his climax had drained him beyond belief. He just wanted to bring the covers back up, wrap Rachel in his arms, and drift off for an hour or so. But her voice caused his mind to snap back to why he really couldn't do that.

"If I miss my contact, I won't make it to Mr. Bautista's to deliver his documents."

Rachel started to move away from Nick. He tried to tighten his hold and a moan escaped from his mouth.

"You may be on vacation, Mr. Fallen, but I have a job to do."

Rachel laughed as she spoke, but the words acted like a bucket of cold water had been thrown in Nick's face. So he lifted his head, turned his eyes in her direction, and tried to remind himself that he too had a job to do. And right now, he needed to pull himself together long enough to do it.

"What do you mean you can't miss your contact?"

"The way this usually works is that someone is waiting for me when I get off the ship. I don't have any problem finding them because they're either holding a sign with my name or the name of Steven's agency. Once we make contact, I'm escorted to the client's home so that they can take their time to go over the documents. When that's finished, I'm brought back to the ship. I'm usually back before lunch. Or," she added as she scooted a little further away from Nick's warm body, "I get back a little later."

Nick sat up, tucked the sheet around his waist, and looked at her with a frown on his face. "Isn't that just a little risky, Rachel?"

"What, going off with a stranger?"

"That, for one," and before she could defend herself, he started ticking other reasons off with his fingers. "Two, there is a travel advisory, warning Americans not to wander off alone, even in Mexico. Three, you are taken to who the hell knows where? And four, what if your … um … contact, doesn't bring you back before the ship sails? Just what the hell would you do then? Keeping in mind that this is a country where being on time doesn't mean a whole lot."

"Actually, to be honest, I used to be worried about all of those things."

"Used to?" he asked with a lift of his dark brow.

"Yes. Used to."

"For Christ's sake, Rachel. This is only, what, your fourth trip out of the country doing this? How in the world can you be so naïve? There are nuts everywhere. Just how well does Steven even know these people he's setting you up with?"

Rachel looked a little perturbed. "I am anything but naïve, Nicholas. I trust my brother-in-law, and so far, I've made my deliveries without a hitch. The clientele Steven services are quite harmless, believe me. No one is out to get me."

"Yeah. Well there's always a first time."

"Oh, for goodness sake. Will you stop being so dramatic? We're in Ensenada, Mexico, not down in the jungles of Bolivia."

"I don't care if you're at home in Los Angeles. You should never take off with someone you don't know. That is just damn irresponsible. And I'd think both you and Steven would know that."

Rachel slid out of bed, tossing her hair over her shoulder. "I'm going take a shower, dress, and get going. You're welcome to shower here before you go back to your own cabin. I'll find you as soon as I get back."

"Rachel…" Nick's voice was low, but had a hint of urgency in it. "If I go with you today, we both win. You can do your job, and at the same time you can humor me and let me think that I'm going along to keep you safe."

Rachel slipped into a silky robe that hit her just above her knees, before she sat back down on the edge of the bed. "It's not that I don't want you to go with me today, Nick. I'd love it. But I've promised Steven that I'd keep my deliveries completely confidential. That's one of his guarantees to our clients. Personal service, special delivery, and absolute confidentiality."

When he did nothing but continue to stare at her with a look of disapproval on his face, Rachel continued, "I can't break my promise to my brother-in-law. Not even for you, Nick. I hate liars and I don't want to become one by lying to Steven."

In that instant, Nick felt as if he had been punched in the stomach. She had just told him that she hated liars, and what had he done from the first moment he had met her? He had lied to her — over and over again. He knew that it wouldn't matter to her that the lies were necessary and part of his job. As soon as she found out the truth about him, she would see him as nothing more than a liar. God, he hated to even think about that. But luckily, he couldn't let himself think about that now, because he had to try one more time to get her to see things his way.

"I'm not asking you to lie, Rachel. Tell Steven the truth when you get back home. Tell him that you met a man aboard ship who couldn't stand to let you out of his sight for even one minute. Tell him that you met a man who is crazy about you and had only one more day to spend with you. Tell him you met a man who has fallen under your spell, and that you felt so sorry for the poor bastard that you just couldn't leave him behind."

He grinned and she almost fell for it. Nick was just way beyond charming, and Rachel came so close to giving in. But one thing that she had heard loud and clear was that Nick had said they had only one more day together. And no matter how intimate they had been and no matter how close she felt to him, it would all be over tomorrow. When they docked back in Los Angeles, he would go his way and she would go hers. And because of that, and that alone, she found the resolve to stick to her guns.

"I just can't, Nick. I don't want to violate Steven's trust in me. That's something that matters to me a great deal."

Shit was the only thing that crossed his mind. In less than one minute, Rachel had said how much she hated liars and how much she valued trust. Both of which could be directed right at Nick. He was not only a lair, but she would surely never trust him again once she found out who he really was, and why he was really here on this ship. So with that depressing thought, he decided it was time not to push her any further on the subject.

"Okay. Okay. You win. You go and do what you need to do. But you are to be very, very careful. Do you hear me? Very careful. And then you get your sweet, little tush back aboard this ship as soon as possible, because I'm not finished with you, Rachel Bennett. Not by a long shot am I finished with you."

Rachel smiled and Nick reached out to take hold of her arm, before gently pulling her down to his mouth. "And I mean as soon as possible." He brushed her lips lightly with his and then he let her go.

Rachel reluctantly pulled away. Nick just looked so sexy sitting there in her bed, with his hair soft and unruly, a morning shadow of whiskers on his face, and his green eyes still a little sleepy. God, she was falling for this man, and she was falling hard. In just three days, he had somehow managed to turn her entire world upside down. And she was enjoying every single second of it.

But right now, she had a job to do. And she had less than an hour to get ready to get off this ship.

"Stay put, Nicholas. I need to take a very quick shower and I can't afford for you to distract me. So before you even think it, the answer is no — you cannot take a shower with me."

Nick laughed out loud and ran his hand over his rough beard. "Then why don't I shave while you shower. Do you have a razor I can borrow?"

"I think so." Nick watched as Rachel rummaged around in a small cosmetic bag sitting on the vanity. "Ah, here you go. I always try to remember to carry extras." She tossed it to him and he caught the razor in one hand.

"Thanks," he murmured almost to himself.

"Any time, handsome," she responded, and then she threw him a kiss right before heading into the shower.

* * *

"*Buenos dias,* Señorita Bennett. Please come in. Señor Bautista will be right with you."

Rachel stepped into the enormous entryway and sighed in relief. The trip out to the house of Miguel Bautista had taken a lot longer than she had expected. His house, which was more like a fortress, was almost a two-hour drive from where the ship was docked. Rachel's driver spoke no English and she spoke no Spanish, so she hadn't even had an opportunity to strike up enough of a conversation during the long trip to ask how much farther they had to go. All she could do was sit back, watch the landscape become more and more remote, and think about Nick's warnings.

"There are nuts everywhere," he had told her. *"And just how well does Steven even know these people he is setting you up with?"* His words had kept ringing in her ears, and she had felt a sense of unease as they had kept on driving and driving.

But now, standing and waiting for Mr. Bautista, Rachel felt a little foolish. She had let Nick's unnecessary concern for her safety get to her, which wasn't like her at all. She knew that Steven would never put her in harm's way, and she berated herself for even listening to Nick. "God," she whispered under her breath, "I'm letting this man have way too much influence over me."

"Señorita."

Rachel was drawn back to the present at the sound of a man's voice.

"I am Miguel Bautista. Welcome to my home."

Rachel lifted her eyes and watched as he approached her, dismissing the man who had gone to fetch him with a wave of his hand. Then that large, ugly hand was extended to her, and she felt an uncontrollable urge to step back. Because Miguel Bautista was not at all what she had expected. He wasn't very tall, maybe five feet eight inches. He was somewhere in his mid-thirties, solidly built, wore his greasy looking hair in a small ponytail, and had perhaps the coldest eyes that she had ever seen. His facial features were hard and unyielding — so much so that Rachel felt momentarily unsettled. And again, Nick's words of warning echoed in her mind.

But because Rachel prided herself on always exhibiting impeccable manners, she forced herself to offer up a smile, and placed her hand tentatively in his.

"It's a pleasure to meet you, Señor Bautista."

"Please call me Miguel. And I hope that you will allow me to call you Rachel."

"Of course," she responded, as she tried to pull her hand out of his grasp. He held on just a little too long, and Rachel felt another small twinge of unease.

"Ah. I see that you have brought my package from Mr. Jackson."

"Oh yes. Forgive me. Of course you'll want to go over the papers before I'm taken back to the ship." Rachel handed him the package, thinking that the sooner she could get out of there, the better. She was a pretty good judge of people, and there was just something about Miguel Bautista that scared her a little. Actually, more than a little.

"I am in no hurry. It is almost time for lunch and I was planning for you to join me. Why don't we eat and then I can go over the documents."

Rachel felt a stab of panic. She didn't like the way he was looking down at her, and she thought he was standing closer than was necessary. She really didn't want to stay.

"I ... I appreciate your offer, but I should probably head back as soon as possible. It's a rather long drive and the ship is sailing at four."

"But I insist that you stay for lunch."

Rachel noticed that even while Miguel Bautista's words were spoken in a friendly, gentle manner, the look in his eyes was anything but friendly. "And I promise to get you back to your ship in plenty of time, Rachel. Please come along. I have planned for us to eat on the patio. It is such a lovely day."

As he placed his hand on Rachel's arm to escort her outside, another spurt of panic hit her. She suddenly felt very much alone in such a big, secluded house, with a total stranger. A stranger she didn't feel comfortable being with. So she decided that good manners were a lot less important than her need to get away.

"I'm really not hungry, Mr. Bautista."

"Miguel," he reminded her as he turned to her with his cold, dark eyes.

"Yes ... I mean Miguel. You see, I am really ..."

"In Mexico, it is really not polite to reject someone's invitation to lunch, Rachel. Especially since my staff has gone to so much trouble. And I have already promised to have you back to your ship before sailing." His arm tightened just enough on her arm to make alarm bells go off in her head. "If you're not hungry, certainly you would enjoy a nice, cold drink."

Instinctively, Rachel knew better than to turn him down a second time. "A cold drink would be very nice, Miguel." She sent up a silent prayer of thanks that her voice sounded sincere, without any hint of the sliver of fear she was feeling. "It was never my intention to appear rude."

Without further comment, Miguel Bautista led Rachel outside to a small patio table, and pulled out her chair, acting for all intents and purposes like a true gentleman. But she wasn't fooled. This man was no gentleman. He looked and acted way too dangerous.

"What would you like to drink?" he asked as he sat down across from her.

And out of nowhere a man appeared by the table, obviously ready to bring them lunch. Rachel started to ask for a glass of iced tea, but a ridiculous thought flashed through her mind: *I need to order something that can't be tampered with.*

"Do you have bottled water?"

"Of course."

Bautista nodded to the man hovering over them, and he silently withdrew back into the house.

"Your brother-in-law failed to mention to me how beautiful you are."

Rachel suddenly wanted to jump up and run for her life. The last thing she needed was for the conversation to take this sort of turn. So since she knew that the option of running was really no option at all, the best she could do was ignore the comment and chance the topic.

"Steven failed to mention to me how excellent your English is."

Miguel Bautista didn't miss a thing. She knew it and he knew it.

"Yes. That is because I did not grow up in Mexico. I was raised and educated in the United States. I live here now because I find the lifestyle more to my liking."

Rachel took a long drink of the bottled water that was placed before her. "I see," was all she could manage, because her brain was frantically trying to figure out whether or not she had insulted him. God, she hoped not.

"But is it a common assumption to make, my dear. Mexico is my homeland, and I blend in rather well here. Don't you think?"

Rachel didn't know what to think or what to say. So she played it safe and said nothing.

Lunch passed slowly, and ended up being uneventful. Rachel suspected that Miguel Bautista had lost interest in her in a big hurry, when she kept finding ways to shift the topic away from herself. She was smart enough not to give him even the least bit of encouragement. So, she kept asking about Mexico, his lovely house, the gardens, and mundane things like the food. She purposely kept her side of the conversation bland, to the point of boring. She was always careful to be polite, but stayed on her guard. There was nothing she liked about Señor Bautista. Nothing at all.

After lunch, she was taken into what appeared to be a great room, and waited impatiently while Bautista had excused himself to look over his travel documents. Minutes had ticked by, and during that time, she couldn't be sure if she was distracted by sound of the second hand on the clock, or the pounding of her own heart. Something wasn't right. Something about Miguel Bautista, his very secluded house, his obvious wealth, and his overall demeanor just wasn't right. But Rachel wasn't interested in being around long enough to find out exactly what it was.

As a matter of fact, while sitting and waiting, she had decided to have a nice, long talk with Steven when she returned to L.A. She wanted to make it very clear to him that in the future, she wanted to know a little more about his clients before agreeing to take off to parts unknown. This excursion to the outskirts of Ensenada, and this client had made her doubt the wisdom of even continuing to work for her brother-in-law for another month or two. She was shaky, and borderline queasy about the encounter with Bautista. Enough so that she was going to rethink her commitment to help Steven out.

It wasn't until she was escorted back to the waiting car that Rachel felt as though she could draw a real breath. Sitting quietly in the passenger seat of the same car that had brought her out to the house, Rachel glanced at her watch and knew that by now Nick would be going absolutely crazy. She would barely make it back before the ship sailed. His words of warning were ringing so loud in her ear, she could almost swear that he was sitting beside her. *And what if your contact doesn't bring you back before the ship sails? Just what the hell would you do then?* Rachel closed her eyes, remembering the frown on his handsome face and the rest of his cautionary words. *Keep in mind that this is a country where being on time doesn't mean a whole lot.*

It took another twenty minutes before Rachel was left off right where the ship was docked. She muttered a thank you to the driver, and flew out of the car and up the gangplank. She had a few minutes to spare, but she still wasted no time. She wanted to get back aboard the ship, safe and sound. Rachel flashed her boarding pass, and not surprisingly, she practically plowed right into Nick, who was waiting for her with an unmistakable scowl on his face.

"Where in the hell have you been?"

His legs were parted in an angry stance, he had both hands on her arms, and his eyes were a stone-cold green.

"I knew you'd be upset Nick. I ..."

"Upset doesn't even come close, Rachel," he interrupted. And she barely noticed that he was leading her away from watching eyes and big ears, and over to a small alcove with two chairs tucked away for privacy.

"I expected you hours ago. You said yourself that you're usually back before lunch. In two hours, it will be time for dinner. What the hell happened?"

Rachel didn't know quite where to start. "It took longer than I expected to make the trip out and back. The client's house is almost a two-hour drive out of town." She could tell that he wasn't the least bit satisfied with her answer.

"I've been worried sick and was about ready to ask the captain to contact the Mexican authorities." He plopped her down into one of the chairs, locked his eyes with hers, and placed both of his hands on his hips. "We sail in exactly ten minutes, Rachel. Ten minutes!"

His voice rose just a little and she wasn't sure if she wanted to laugh or cry. She could tell that Nick was trying to keep his temper, but she could also tell that he was dying to yell at her. He looked so adorable, all flustered and distraught, that against her will, a little smile played at the corner of her mouth.

"Don't you dare laugh, Rachel Bennett. I'm trying my damnedest not to reach out and throttle you. I've never been so fucking scared in my life."

Rachel, of course, didn't know that part of the reason Nick was scared shitless was because he knew who Miguel Bautista was and how dangerous the man could be. But he couldn't let on anything about that, so he concentrated on the fact that she had gone off with a complete stranger and almost didn't make it back.

"Do you have any idea how stupid and reckless your little trip was today?" *There, that should wipe the smile off her pretty face.*

"Please don't yell at me, Nick. I'm sorry if I upset you."

Nick lifted his hand and ran his fingers impatiently through his hair. He closed his eyes, drew in a ragged breath and leaned down toward Rachel sitting in the chair. Instead of throttling her, he gently reached out and pulled her to her feet. In the next instant, he drew her up against his body and wrapped his arms around her.

"I was frantic with worry, Rachel. I've felt completely help-less these past few hours because I didn't even know which direction you went in." He had softened his voice, but she could still detect a hint of anger. "And right now, I swear to God that I don't know if I want to strangle you or to kiss you."

Rachel snuggled a little closer, thankful for his arms around her, because she felt safe for the first time all day.

"You're trembling," he whispered as he reached under her chin and raised her face to his. His eyes narrowed and he searched her face. And Nick felt his heart turn over just a tad, when he saw the beginning of tears in her eyes. "I won't yell at you anymore, sweetheart." He just naturally assumed that the distress in her eyes was because of him. "Please don't cry, Rachel."

Rachel blinked back the tears that were threatening to fall. "I'm not going to cry, Nick. Really," she quickly added as she saw doubt flash through his eyes. "I'm just tired." She didn't add that she was relieved to feel safe and that she had been on pins and needles most of the day. She didn't add any of that because she didn't want to ruin the last few hours she and Nick were going to have together.

"Can't we both just forget about this wasted day and go back to my cabin?"

Nick was suddenly torn. Now that he knew Rachel was safe, he really needed to try and get whatever information he could out of her about Miguel Bautista. He knew he needed to be clever about it, and not raise any red flags, so just flat-out asking about the client was probably out of the question. He had planned to find a nice, quiet place aboard ship where the two of them could have dinner. Someplace where they could talk, and he could get her to open up about her day. The problem now was that he knew that if he went back to her cabin, they wouldn't talk at all. They would probably not even make it down to dinner again. They would end up in bed, and if he had his way, once they got there, they would stay there the rest of the night. Alex would skin him alive if Nick passed up a chance to get Rachel to tell him about Bautista. So reluctantly, he loosened the hold of his arms.

"Do you want to go and get a drink first? We can stop by one of the bars if you want."

"No," was her softly spoken reply. And when Nick looked again into her eyes, the last thing he wanted was to think about Bautista. He knew that he was the one being stupid and reckless, but he just couldn't help it. Not when she was looking at him and felt so soft and inviting.

"Me neither."

"Your place or mine?" she asked with her first real smile since she got back aboard ship.

"You have the condoms," he responded with a grin of his own.

And as they made their way to her cabin, it crossed his mind that they could always talk later.

Later turned out to be close to midnight. Once inside Rachel's cabin, they had both tumbled into bed, tearing at each other's clothes. Nick managed to get out of everything but his shirt. His shoes, socks, and pants went flying as Rachel had unbuttoned his shirt. And as she ran her hands over his bare chest, he had stripped her out of her own clothes. Rachel had then clutched so tightly onto Nick that they had literally fallen backwards onto the bed, without even bothering to throw back the covers. Nick's body had covered Rachel's, and neither seemed to notice that he was still wearing his shirt. Once they had both felt his hard body sink onto hers, he had kissed her with a sense of desperation and plunged into her a second after he had found her box of condoms.

And that had set the course for the rest of their evening. After calling down to room service and ordering the promised hamburger and fries, they had both tried to take a shower together in the teeny, tiny stall. Nick had laughed and Rachel had squealed all the way through the shower, until they finally ended up back in bed, soaking wet, and making love as if for the very first time.

Now, here it was, almost midnight. They had both dozed off for about an hour, but the bed sheets had become so tangled that it was impossible to sleep for too long. Nick had woken first, and then Rachel. Together they straightened up the bed, and crawled back in. Nick was propped up against the headboard, leaning comfortably against a pillow tucked behind his back. His one arm was around Rachel and she was snuggled up close against his side, her face buried against his shoulder.

Both Rachel and Nick were lost in their own personal thoughts. Nick was thinking about pursuing a conversation about her day, and her client, but quickly decided against it. He just couldn't bring himself to think and act like a cop right now. He knew what the plan was for tomorrow, once they docked, and he figured they would get their answers then.

It had been decided earlier, when he had checked in with Alex, that Nick would slip off the ship early. Arrangements had already been made with the captain for him to be first off, so that wasn't going to be a problem. It was also pre-arranged that Ben and Lou Jensen would be at the dock, and they would intercept Rachel as she made her way to the car she had left in the lot. They would quietly bring her in to the station and question her there. And she would either cooperate with them or she wouldn't, which he knew would tell them a lot. So, deciding that pushing her now for information really wouldn't do them much good in the long run, he was content to lie in bed with her warm body nestled against his.

Nick let his hand wander lazily up and down her exposed arm, not quite sure whether Rachel was awake or if she had fallen asleep. They hadn't said a word for a while, and he figured that if she were awake, she was probably thinking about tomorrow and how it would be the end of their brief affair. He also figured that it was not going to be as easy for her as she wanted him to think. He just knew in his soul that Rachel was not into casual affairs. And for that he was sorry. Truly sorry. But he could no more change what had happened between them than he could change the world. And all he could do was hope that tomorrow when she found out who he really was, she would find it in her heart to understand and to forgive him.

Without realizing it, that thought caused Nick to shift and draw in a deep breath.

"Are you uncomfortable?" Her voice was a little sleepy.

"I'm fine, Rachel." Subconsciously he tightened his arm around her.

"You need to get some sleep, Nick. We dock pretty early tomorrow morning."

With those words, Nick knew he had to tell her. He brought up one hand and rubbed his eyes with his fingers. "About tomorrow, Rachel." He laid his head back against the pillow and looked up at the ceiling. "I'm sorry, but I won't be able to say goodbye to you tomorrow after we get into port. I need to disembark before everyone else, because I have an early plane to catch. I'll be leaving at first light."

Nick could feel Rachel stiffen at his words. It was slight, but he noticed it all the same. And the one thing Nick was going to be glad about was that as soon as he got back to business, the lies would finally stop.

"So, are we saying goodbye now, Nick?" She tried to sound lighthearted, but failed at it miserably.

"No. I want to sleep here with you for a few more hours, Rachel."

"Will you promise to wake me to say goodbye?" This time he heard the tears in her voice.

"I promise."

Nick didn't say anything further. Besides, what the hell could he say? In just a few hours, it would all be over. So he did the only thing he could think of. He pulled the covers up, wrapped Rachel even more tightly in his arms, and leaned down to kiss her lightly against her lips. "Let's both go to sleep."

Rachel responded by snuggling even closer to Nick, and holding onto him for dear life. She felt as though her heart were breaking in two. She was a complete fool to have thought that she could actually pull off having a fling with this man, and then walk away without even a backward glance. She was even a bigger fool to think that it was impossible to fall in love with someone in just a few short days. Because here she was, hopelessly and completely in love.

As she tried desperately to stop the flow of tears, Rachel wanted to regret these past four days. She wanted to regret that she had ever met Nicholas Fallen. She wanted to regret that she had given her heart so easily to someone who had told her right from the beginning that he had nothing long-term to offer her. She wanted to blame him for the deepest despair she had ever felt in her life. But she couldn't. She couldn't and wouldn't regret these days, this man, and the pleasure she had felt in his arms. Instead, she would always remember the best four days of her life. And she would live with the memory of his lovemaking and savor the memory of each and every touch, kiss, and caress.

Rachel let her mind rest and allowed herself to replay the shared fun, the shared laughter, and the shared passion. She finally felt herself relax and could tell that Nick's own breathing had settled into the rhythm of sleep. So with her hand laid gently over his heart, she closed her eyes, kissed him softy on his cheek, and let herself drift off, thinking about how good and how perfect they felt together.

CHAPTER SEVEN

Nick waited in Alex's office, pacing around like a caged tiger. It had been hours since he'd arrived, and Ben and Lou should have been here with Rachel by now. He had left the ship at first light and headed right over to the station. Alex was waiting for him, and explained that Ben and Lou were already in place, waiting for the passengers to disembark. As Nick already knew, they would approach Rachel, flash their badges, and ask her to come with them to discuss some aspects of her sister's case. They had all agreed that she would probably not hesitate to come along if she thought they might have some good news for her. Nick knew she was anxious for some answers, and wouldn't think twice about coming down to the station. So why was it taking them so damn long and where in the hell were they?

"Sit down and have another cup of coffee, Nick."

"I've had enough coffee to sink a ship."

"So sit down. You're driving me crazy."

"Where in the hell are they, Alex?"

Alex sat back and watched one of his best detectives, and he couldn't help but wonder what was going on inside Nick's head. It had not taken a genius to notice that Nick had not been himself since he'd stepped into the station. He had been short-tempered, distracted, and borderline rude. And he kept on looking at the clock, which was driving Alex crazy.

"They're not going to get here any faster with you watching the clock every minute or two. Now either sit down or get the hell out of my office and wait somewhere else."

Nick completely ignored Alex and walked over to the window and looked out. Without realizing exactly what he was doing, he reached into his shirt pocket and took out the battered cigarette. He looked down to make sure it was still in one piece, and then fumbled around for a book of matches he knew was in another pocket somewhere. Still staring out through the window, Nick put the cigarette between his lips, struck the match, and lit up. He took in a long, deep drag. Smoke swirled around Nick and he had to squint his eyes before taking a second, deep drag.

"That bad, huh?

Nick didn't even bother to answer.

"She get to you that bad, Nick?"

That got his attention. But he still didn't say a word. He just turned slowly in Alex's direction.

"You want off the case?"

"I never wanted on this case to begin with."

"You want off now?"

Nick continued smoking, thinking about the offer on the table. He knew that if he said yes, Alex would agree to pull him off and assign him to another case. But he also knew that Alex would be disappointed in him. And even worse, he would be disappointed in himself.

"I started this, and I'll finish this."

Alex nodded and watched as Nick finished off his cigarette. Nick inhaled one last time, threw the butt into an old ashtray Alex kept on his desk for just this type of occasion, and then turned back toward the window.

"Do you want to talk about it, Nick?"

"No."

"Okay. Do you want to talk about Ms. Bennett?"

"No."

"What if she's involved?"

"She's not."

"What if she is?"

Nick looked over his shoulder and sent his boss a look that was colder than ice. And then he turned back.

"You can't just dismiss that possibility. Your job is to wade through all the known facts, gather the evidence, and then make an informed decision. All you have to go on right now are your gut feelings about this woman. We need more than that, Nick, and you know it."

Nick swung around. "You don't need to tell me how to do my job Alex. I know damn well that we need more hard evidence. A lot more. And as soon as they bring her in, we'll lay it all out on the table. She'll either agree to cooperate with us or she won't. That alone will tell you one hell of a lot about her guilt or innocence. But until Ben and Lou get here, all you've got is what my instinct is telling me. And my instinct is telling me that Rachel Bennett wasn't lying when she told me she doesn't have a clue what's in those packages she delivers."

"I hope you're right, Detective. Because it will make it a whole lot easier if you are."

Nick knew that Alex was 100 percent right. If Rachel was knowingly involved in any aspect of Steven's nasty business, they all figured that she would "lawyer up" and they would never get the chance to talk to her about their plan. A plan that she needed to agree to for it to succeed. A plan that Alex and Nick had hatched up over the phone, the last time Nick had checked in from the ship. A plan that Nick was already starting to dread.

Wishing he had another cigarette, Nick walked over and sat down in the chair in front of Alex's desk. He slumped down, crossed one ankle over the other, and stuck both of his hands in the front pockets of his jeans. "Waiting sucks." And just as the words left his mouth, the intercom on Alex's desk buzzed.

"They're here, Lieutenant."

Alex's eyes met Nick's across the desk. "Thank you. Tell Detectives Morris and Jensen to take Ms. Bennett into the interrogation room. We'll be right there."

Nick got up from his chair as Alex came around his desk. "Let's go see how much you can rely on your instinct."

Both men made their way to the interrogation room in complete silence. The door was closed, and they didn't attempt to go inside. Instead, they stood in front of what appeared from the inside to be a mirror. And it was a mirror — of sorts. A one-way mirror that allowed Alex and Nick to watch and hear everything going on inside the room, without being seen or heard themselves.

"Can I get you something to drink, Professor Bennett?"

Nick noticed that Rachel was already seated at one end of the long, scarred conference table.

"No, thank you."

"Okay, ma'am. Then let me tell you why we asked you here."

Ben's voice was smooth and gentle and he pulled out a chair and sat down. He angled his position so that he was facing Rachel. Lou Jensen didn't sit. He stood over to the side, watching them from behind Ben.

"I thought you had some good news about my sister's case." Rachel looked from one man to the other.

"We do need to talk to you about your sister's murder. But I'm afraid there's not any good news to give you right now."

"I .... I don't understand."

"Professor Bennett, we still don't know for sure who murdered your sister, but we think we have a new lead in our investigation. A lead which might help us identify your sister's killer."

"But that's wonderful news, Detective. The best news we've had in a couple of months. What did Steven say? Surely you've had a chance to talk to Steven?"

From behind the mirror, Nick and Alex both noticed that her enthusiastic response to the possibility of identifying the perp seemed genuine, which fit with what she had told him the day of their picnic.

"Well now, ma'am, that's the problem. And here's where we need your help."

"My help?" Rachel looked directly at Ben. "Again, Detective, I'm not sure I understand."

Now it was time to take off the kid gloves and lay it out. Time to watch her face closely to see if she was about to lie or tell the truth.

"Did you know that your sister contacted us less than twenty-four hours before she was killed, to report that she suspected her husband of running an illegal business out of their travel agency?"

The sudden change in subject caught Rachel completely off guard. And she wasn't sure she had heard the detective correctly.

"I …. I beg your pardon?"

"Did you know that she was scared to death when she called and talked to Detective Jensen, and that they had arranged to meet that evening? But that she never showed up, because twelve hours after her phone call to us she was found dead. Just twelve hours after she had agreed to meet with Detective Jensen?"

"Oh my God." The color drained out of Rachel's face.

"Do you know that for a while now, we have strongly suspected that your brother-in-law is supplying false U.S. documents to very undesirable individuals, allowing them to enter our country with illegal passports, visas, green cards, and more? And that we believe that your brother-in-law had his wife — your sister — killed before she could pass on any incriminating information to law enforcement?"

Rachel couldn't speak. Because she couldn't breathe. All she could do was sit there and stare from one detective to the other, trying desperately to clear her head.

Back behind the one-way mirror, Nick felt his stomach tie up in knots. He wanted to go in and take Rachel into his arms and talk her through this. He wanted to be with her, but he knew that he couldn't — because he knew that as far as he and she were concerned, the worst was yet to come.

"Do you think I could have a glass of water?"

Lou went over to the cooler and brought her a paper cup filled with water. She drank it down in one long swallow and asked politely for another. As he watched, Nick noticed that her hands were shaking.

Rachel drank the other cup of water, and she finally felt the dizziness in her head start to pass. And the realization of what Ben was saying actually sank in.

"You think that Steven killed my sister?" Her eyes were wide and her words were spoken a little louder than she had intended.

"We have reason to think that Steven arranged for your sister to be murdered."

Rachel sat in complete silence, trying to take in what was being said. She was so stunned and so distraught that the only thing she felt was a numbness that spread through her body.

"Did you hear what I said, Ms. Bennett? Do you under-stand that we think Steven may have hired someone to kill your sister?"

As the numbness began to wear off, so did the chill that ran down Rachel's spine. And finally, a bit of anger replaced some of her confusion.

"You're out of your mind, Detective. Steven would have no reason to want Cynthia dead. You can't possibly know what you're talking about."

"What do you know about the travel documents you de-liver, Professor Bennett?"

"What?"

"What do you know about the travel documents you de-liver out of the country, Ms. Bennett?"

"It's …. It's a part of our business. We provide … um. … It's a service we provide." Rachel faltered as her mind slipped back to yesterday and the awful Miguel Bautista. But she didn't have time to dwell on that, because Ben kept on throwing more questions at her.

"And exactly what type of travel documents do you deliver as part of this ….um …. this service?"

God, the questions were causing her more and more distress. And unexpectedly, as she thought again about her dreadful visit to Señor Bautista, she felt a deep-rooted fear. Because recalling how he had made her feel, and recalling his secluded and well-protected house, for the first time, she wondered herself just what was in that package.

"I ….. Can you please repeat the question?"

"Sure. Let me put it to you this way: Have you ever checked out for yourself those personal documents that you so diligently deliver for your brother-in-law?"

"No."

"Okay. That was easy," Ben responded with a smile. "So why not, Ms. Bennett? Why haven't you ever taken a look inside those packages you carry around?"

Rachel shifted a little in her chair. "Because Steven has always stressed the need for guaranteed confidentiality. And respecting one's privacy is part of the service we provide, Detective."

"So you mean to tell me that you've never been curious enough to look inside? You've never been curious enough to take a little peek?"

"Are you accusing me of something, Detective?"

"No, ma'am. I'm just asking you a question."

Although Ben's tone of voice was non-threatening, Rachel was still suspicious and uneasy.

"I believe I've already answered that question."

Ben could have accepted her response and let the matter drop, but he decided to push a little further so that he could observe Rachel a little more closely.

"I'm going to ask you this one more time, Ms. Bennett. In all the times you've taken possession of packages that you've been told hold travel documents for your brother-in-law's clients, have your ever once been tempted or curious enough to look inside? A simple yes or no will suffice."

"Do I need an attorney?" She asked this very softly.

"You tell me, Professor. Do you think you need an attorney?"

Rachel didn't like what he was insinuating. She also didn't like this entire line of questioning. She had done absolutely nothing wrong, and she had nothing to hide. She was sick and tired of being looked at as though she were some kind of criminal, and she wasn't going to let these detectives intimidate her anymore.

"Listen, Detective Morris. I don't know what you and Detective Jensen are talking about. It is completely insane to even think that my brother-in-law might be involved in Cynthia's murder. Please don't try to shift the blame for my sister's murder to Steven just because you can't solve this case. And it's equally insane to think that he would ever be involved in anything illegal. I have never bothered to look inside the packages I deliver because I've had no reason to. So unless you can prove to me that those packages I carry contain illegal United States documents, then I suggest we call it a day. Either show me some proof, or let me go. Because I know just enough about the law to know that without any proof, you cannot hold me here, Detective."

Both Ben and Lou remained silent and a stillness settled over the room. Rachel thought that she had obviously made her point so well that they would forget about their crazy theory and finally let her go. But instead, as she waited, the door to the interrogation room opened, and Rachel watched in total disbelief as Nick walked in.

Rachel was so delighted to see him that she almost jumped out of her chair. All she could process was that he was an attorney, and that somehow Nick must have heard about her dilemma and had come to her rescue. She didn't care how he knew that she needed him, all she cared about was that he was here. She was never so happy to see anyone in her entire life. She gave him one of her brightest smiles, and in a flash, her eyes took him in. But in the very next second, her smile faded and she felt as though she was going to faint.

Because standing before her was Nicholas Fallen, dressed in jeans, a white shirt with the sleeves rolled up to his elbows, a tie that he had pulled slightly loose, and *oh my God,* a shoulder holster with a gun, and a badge clipped to the front of his belt. A badge that told her in an instant that he wasn't an attorney coming to save her, but a cop. A cop, her mind screamed — a cop now standing in the same room as these detectives who were accusing her brother-in-law of killing her sister. A cop, obviously working with the other two men in the room, and apparently very involved with this case. A dirty, rotten cop who had lied to her, and then made love to her one last time, right before he had slipped out of her bed at five o'clock this very morning.

Ben got up out of the chair and everyone could hear the scraping of the legs across the wood floor. He joined Lou, and without another word, both men left the room.

Rachel's eyes never left Nick's impassive face, and her hands were clutched tightly together in her lap. She still couldn't believe that he was a cop. And with a sick feeling, she realized that probably everything he had said and done since the moment they met had been a lie. He had lied to her about who he was, what he did for a living, and probably why he was even interested in her. God, she hoped that last part wasn't true, but something deep down inside told her that it was.

With a feeling of total despair, Rachel was absolutely determined not to speak the first word. She was absolutely determined that he was going to speak first. Because, hopefully by then, she would be able to find her voice.

"If you need proof that Steven is dealing in illegal U.S. documents, Rachel, I have it." His voice was calm and quiet, and she resented him for that. She resented him for a lot of things, but right at this moment, she resented him most of all for his cool and calm tone of voice.

"As you've probably figured out by now, I was on that ship as part of an assignment to try and get information for our case against Steven. I got a good look inside that package you were delivering to Miguel Bautista, and everything in it was false. Everything in it provided a scumbag like Bautista a golden opportunity to cross our borders with little or no problems. And Bautista got everything he needed from your brother-in-law. Nice and easy. Nice and dirty. Nice and illegal. There is your proof, Rachel."

Those words did it. He had just confirmed her worst fear that he had lied to her about everything. Even about wanting to be with her. Even about wanting to make love to her. Because the only time he could have seen what was in that package was sometime during the night. It could only have been sometime during the night, after they had made love, and she had fallen into an exhausted sleep. And with that realization, something in Rachel snapped. Because now she knew without a shadow of a doubt that he had used her. Used her all along. As her temper came to a fever pitch, she jumped from her chair, giving no thought whatsoever that he was an officer of the law.

"You bastard. How can you stand there and tell me this as though you had every right to lie to me and violate my trust? Everything you ever said to me was a lie. How can you stand there and look me in the eye? Who do you think you are, Nicholas Fallen? Who the hell do you think you are?"

A slight twitch at the corner of Nick's mouth was the only indication that her words had hit their mark.

"I'm a homicide detective with the LAPD. And right at this moment, I can't afford to worry about how you feel about me violating your trust. We have a murder to solve and that should be what we're concerned about. You need to remember that the victim was your sister, and that we believe that Steven arranged to have her killed. That's what's important now, Rachel. Not us. The issues between us will need to wait until this case is solved."

Nick had strolled closer to her as he spoke. He had watched her closely as his words penetrated her brain, and for an instant, he thought that maybe he had gotten through to her. But her next words told him otherwise. Actually, her next words told him and those who were listening behind the one-way mirror otherwise.

"But you slept with me!"

Oh shit, Nick thought, because he knew that Ben and Alex were standing on the other side of the mirror.

"You actually took me to bed just so you could get information out of me. You lied to me about how much you wanted me, and I believed you. I believed every word. What a fool I was. I thought that you were special. I even thought that I had fallen in love with you. But you are nothing but a lying son of a bitch. How could you take me to bed and make love to me the way you did and have it all be just a part of your job? How could you do that to me?" Her voice ended on a sob.

"Listen, Rachel." Nick reached out to touch her arm, but she shrugged off his hand.

"Don't you dare touch me."

Nick dropped his hand, but not his eyes. His eyes never wavered from the stricken look on her face. "Taking you to bed was a mistake, Rachel. My mistake. But we both need to put that aside for now and deal with your sister's case."

Nick had no way of knowing that admitting that making love to Rachel was a mistake was just about the worst thing he could have said to her.

"You have absolutely no idea just how big of a mistake it was."

Rachel had to fight with herself to stop from screaming those words at him at the top of her lungs. The best she could do was to mentally count to ten, and hope that she could speak more calmly than she felt.

"Tell me something, Detective. Didn't it ever occur to you to simply ask me if you could see what was in that package that I was delivering? As close as we'd become, didn't it ever occur to you at any time to just tell me the truth and see if I'd cooperate with you?" Rachel could feel her enforced calmness slipping away.

"It occurred to me," was Nick's emotionless reply. "But I wasn't absolutely certain of your innocence. And even though my gut was telling me that you weren't involved, I couldn't risk this case on my gut feelings."

His brutal honesty was so hurtful that Rachel jerked at his words. And she fought back.

"That makes what you did to me even worse!" Her voice was raised and her eyes were glazed over with pure rage. "The fact that you slept with a woman that you not only didn't trust, but someone that you considered a possible suspect, is positively despicable."

Now it was Nick's turn to mentally count to ten. "One had nothing to do with the other, Rachel."

"One had everything to do with the other!" she spat back at him.

They were getting absolutely nowhere, and Nick started to say so, but Rachel spoke before he did. "I want to ask you just one question. Just one."

She lifted her chin in defiance and her eyes challenged him to try and stop her. Nick's eyes met her challenge and he said nothing while she waited long enough to be sure she had his complete attention.

"Since this little vacation of yours was really just part of your job, will you get a one-time bonus for taking me to bed, or do you get paid extra for each hour that you screwed me?

Personally, if I were you I'd go for the hourly rate, because as many times as we ended up in bed, payment by the hour will be much more profitable."

Nick's temper got the better of him and without thinking, he fired back the first words that came to his mind. "If you will recall, Rachel, you were the one who practically begged me to take you to bed. Actually, come to think of it, you did beg me, so to speak."

Her hand came up out of nowhere, and the slap could be heard like a clap of thunder. An absolute, dreadful silence settled over the room. Nick was rooted to the spot and Rachel felt a slight ringing in her ears. Neither one seemed capable of looking away from the other. Hard green eyes were locked in combat with big, soft brown eyes. Finally, after what seemed like a lifetime, Nick lifted his hand to touch his burning cheek, just as Rachel's legs failed to support her — so she sat down before she fell down.

"Feel better now?" His voice was like steel.

Rachel looked down at her hand, and found that she was shaking like a leaf. "I've never struck anyone in my life." Her voice was so soft and spoken with a quiver.

Nick refused to allow himself to let down his guard. He couldn't afford to be anything but a cop right now. He had failed at that enough over the last four days, and now with Alex, Ben, and God knows who else listening in and looking on, he needed to put aside his feelings for Rachel and treat her like he would anyone else.

Nick reached for the same chair that Ben had sat in, swung it around, and straddled it. He waited for a few more seconds to give himself time to calm down. He also wanted to give Rachel time to compose herself so that she would listen to what he was saying. When he figured that the time was right, he forced himself to speak in a quiet, yet authoritative voice.

"We know several things, Rachel. We know that Steven prepares and distributes illegal documents to the scum of the earth. We know that he used both you and Cynthia to deliver those documents. We know that your sister called and wanted to meet with one of our detectives the night she was murdered. We also know that she had evidence against her husband that she wanted to give us, and that she was scared. Really scared. And we know that at three o'clock the following morning, a homeless man found your sister's body in an alley, with a gunshot wound to the head. These are the things we know."

He waited and waited because while he spoke, Rachel had not lifted her head. She was still staring down at her hands in her lap.

"Your sister must have been worried sick about her own safety the day she called us, but she did it anyway because she knew it was the right thing to do. And before we could help her, she was murdered. Shot in cold blood. Now are you going to help us? Or are you going to bury your head in the sand and let your sister's killer go free because you're pissed off at me?"

Rachel lifted her head, and seemed surprised that he was sitting so close. He had draped his arms over the back of the chair and was leaning forward, close enough for her to reach out and touch him. But all she did was look him straight in the eye, refusing to drop her gaze from his. Finally she spoke.

"All I've wanted for the last three months is for the police to find Cynthia's killer. No one, absolutely no one deserves to die the way she did. I want to see whoever murdered my sister brought to their knees. I want to see him brought to justice. Even…" she had to take a deep breath before she could continue. "Even if that person turns out to be Steven."

"So you'll work with us?"

"So you believe I'm not involved?" she countered, not bothering to answer his question.

"Yes."

"And you're asking me to help with this investigation?" Finally, she was able to sound at least somewhat simmered down.

"Yes." Again a one-word response. Nick waited to see if she had any more questions to throw at him. When she remained silent, he asked her again, "So you'll work with us?"

It took a moment for Rachel to process his question. "I will not work with you. If I have to, I'll work with one of the other detectives, but I will not work with you."

"You don't get a choice in this, Rachel."

"Then I'll talk with your supervisor." She had to place some distance between them, so she stood up and used her own chair as something to hold onto.

"Feel free to talk with Lieutenant Kendall anytime you want. I'll even set up the meeting. But understand this: I'm on this case until the end. And like it or not, if you decide to cooperate with us, then you'll be working with me."

"But I can't trust you!" she almost screamed at him.

Nick hated more than anything to hear that from her, but he couldn't let her know it. Because now he was Detective Fallen and he had on his cop face.

"You can trust me as a cop. Have no doubt about that. And right now, that's all that matters. Because right now, all you need is to be able to trust me as a cop."

Nick stood and let a long silence drag on between them. God, he wanted to reach out for her. But he kept his distance. One reason was that there was an audience just outside the door, and the other reason was that he suspected that Rachel might actually try to slap him again if he tried to get too close. She was so mad that he could see it in her eyes, on her face, and in the way she was standing.

"I need to think, Detective Fallen, and I can't do it with you standing there. I need for you to get away from me so I can think." He didn't miss that she would only refer to him as Detective Fallen.

When he didn't immediately respond, she spoke again. But this time the anger in her eyes was replaced by pleading. "Won't you please leave me alone? I just can't deal with you any longer."

Nick felt a stab of guilt, regret, and compassion. But he couldn't act on any of those feelings, so instead he simply nodded his head and turned on his heels. "I'll be back in thirty minutes. Detective Jensen will keep you company. If you need anything while I'm gone, let him know."

He threw his words over his shoulder and walked out of the room. He recognized that it was a good idea for both of them to get away from each other for a while, so that they could put a little distance between them. And he needed some time to himself anyway. But luck wasn't on Nick's side when he walked out of that room, because he ran right into Alex, Ben, Lou, and three other detectives.

"In my office now, Detective Fallen."

Alex didn't wait for any kind of response. He gave the order and stomped off, expecting Nick to be right behind him.

Ben tried to give his partner an encouraging pat on the back, but even he knew that nothing was going to help. Alex was pissed beyond belief and Nick wasn't in a much better mood. Ben suspected that the fireworks would begin the minute they shut the office door. And they did.

"I COULD suspend you right this minute!" Everyone outside could hear Alex's words.

"You could." Nick's voice was low, calm, and lethal.

"I SHOULD suspend you right this minute!" Alex was even louder this time.

"You probably should. But you won't."

"And why the hell won't I?!"

Finally, Nick lost his temper too. And he could be heard just as clearly as his boss. "Because you fucking set me up, Lieutenant . I didn't want this assignment, but you sent me out on this suicide mission anyway. And you practically ordered me to seduce the woman. So I did. But in the process, I also managed to get us the information that we needed. The information we need to move this damn case forward. So if you want to suspend me, go right ahead."

"It would serve you right if I did, Detective Fallen!" Alex didn't even try to lower his voice.

"No one's stopping you! Least of all me!"

Nick blew out a long, hard breath and Alex did the same. Both men were so much alike that sometimes it was hard to tell them apart. They both had short tempers, they were both dedicated to their jobs, and they both respected each other. So the yelling was just a way to vent and get rid of their anger. Nothing more. And they each knew it. And so did everyone listening beyond the closed door.

"Jesus Christ, Nick, what were you thinking?" Alex had lowered his voice and sat down almost wearily into his chair. "Did you really need to take her to bed?"

Nick sat down in the same chair he had been in less than an hour ago. He ran his hand down his face, and tried to figure out how to answer that question. How could he possibly explain the sexual attraction between him and Rachel? How could he even begin to explain how he had tried, really tried, not to give in to her? How could he explain that in the end, it was just too much for him, and he couldn't fight the pull any longer? How could he explain any of this to Alex when he couldn't even explain it to himself?

"I don't know what to say, Alex. It just happened."

"You knew that she was a possible suspect. You knew that we might even have to arrest her. You're too good a cop to just let it happen. At what point did you forget you were on the job?"

Nick's eyes stayed focused on the look of disapproval on Alex's face, and he knew that even now, he could not lie to this man.

"I'm not proud that I ended up in bed with Rachel while I was on the job." Hearing himself say the words out loud made him realize how much he meant it.

"You could have compromised this entire case. It could still be compromised if Ms. Bennett decides not to go along with us. Did you even bother to think of that?"

"I think we've already established that I crossed the line, and I can't go back and change things, Alex. And if this case goes to shit because of me, you won't have to suspend me. But I'm also not going to stand here and lie and tell you that I'm sorry that it happened. Because I'm not. I'm sorry that it happened during this assignment because that's unprofessional, but that's all I'm sorry about."

"Well, Nick, you may not be sorry that it happened, but from what I heard from Ms. Bennett, my guess is that she is sorry enough for the both of you. As a matter of fact, I would bet my next paycheck that she pretty much hates your guts."

"Gee, Alex. Why don't you tell me what you really think."

Alex looked him straight in the eye. "I think we should both put your lack of good judgment behind us and get on with this case. What's done is done. And you're right, neither one of us can change it. But what we can do is concentrate on getting Ms. Bennett to work with us so that we can put that son of a bitch Steven Jackson behind bars. And," he added, "anyone else who's involved in his wife's murder."

The level of tension in the room dropped considerably.

"So I take it that you agree with me that Rachel is innocent of collaborating with her brother-in-law."

They were back on familiar ground. Both men knew there was nothing left to say on the subject of Nick and Rachel. Alex had made his point and Nick had made his. It was now time to move on.

"Yeah. No one can be that great an actress. I'm afraid the young woman has trouble hiding her true feelings. No way could she have faked her reactions to our news about Steven."

Nick rubbed one hand along his jaw, thinking about Rachel's true feelings. During her tirade, she said that she had thought that he was special and that she may have fallen in love with him. And those words had nearly brought Nick to his knees — not because he wanted Rachel to fall in love with him, but because he believed her. And he had never set out to cause her so much pain. But right now, even he had to admit that her feelings for him were far from love. Hatred, anger, mistrust, and disgust probably best described her feelings for him now.

"So how are you planning to convince her to work with you? And are you sure you want to see this thing through? I can have someone else on the team take over from here."

Alex's voice brought Nick back to the matter at hand.

"That's the second time today that you've asked me if I want off this assignment, and my answer hasn't changed. I'll finish what I started."

"Okay, Nick, I won't ask again. So with that said, you need to get your ass back in there and lay out the plan, because we need to get Ms. Bennett on board. And if she insists on meeting with me, don't worry. I'll meet with her and I'll explain to her that this case is yours."

Nick felt grateful for Alex's support, but he was having problems expressing it out loud. Actually, he always had problems expressing his gratitude out loud. So he didn't even try.

"I think that once Rachel gets over her anger and thinks about things with a clear head, she'll come through for us. And even if she stays mad at me, I think I know her well enough to bet my own paycheck that she'll still come through. She loved her sister, Alex, and she won't let her personal feelings get in the way of helping to find Cynthia's killer."

"Is thirty minutes long enough for her to get over being pissed at you?"

"Probably not."

"Then I guess you have your work cut out for you."

"Yeah. I guess I do."

Alex chuckled. "Well then, good luck, my friend."

The meeting was over. Alex had his say and Nick had his. And between the raised voices and the unspoken reproach, they both knew that Nick was going to need a lot more than just luck on his side. When he walked back into that interrogation room, he was going to need a hell of a lot more than luck.

Ben was waiting for Nick when he came out of Alex's office. He didn't say a word. He just threw his partner a look that said it all.

"Save the lecture for later, Ben. Right now, we have work to do."

"You going back in there?"

This time it was Nick's turn to throw out a look that said it all.

"Because I'd think about that if I were you, buddy. The good professor looks like she'd like nothing better than to blow you away. We didn't bother to pat her down for a concealed weapon, so she might actually have one. You know, just ready and waiting for you to waltz back through that door. God, she is royally pissed off at you."

"I said to save it, Ben."

Ben wanted to keep on teasing, but they reached the one-way mirror. Nick stopped and looked in, and just watched Rachel for a minute or two. She was sitting down again, sipping at a cup of coffee someone had obviously gotten for her. She looked a little pale, lost, sad, and tired. With a deep breath, he looked over at Ben. "Time to face the music," were his only words as they stepped into the room.

Rachel looked up and said nothing. She just took another sip from the coffee mug she had cradled in both of her hands.

Nick and Ben both walked over and sat down. Like before, Nick straddled the chair and draped his arms over the back, lacing his fingers together. He wanted to watch Rachel up close for a little while to see if he could gauge her mood, but she surprised him by setting her mug down and speaking as though she had thoroughly calmed down. Which he doubted was the case.

"So what's your plan?"

CHAPTER EIGHT

Rachel seemed way too composed. And Nick was suspicious. He found it hard to accept that she could be spitting nails when he left the room and now, in less than thirty minutes, she appeared almost docile. He didn't completely trust her outward subdued appearance, but since gaining her cooperation was their goal, he decided not to push his luck and question her sudden change of mood. But he did ask the question that needed to be asked.

"So, does this mean that you're willing to work with me?"

"You were very clear, Detective, that I don't have a say in the matter. I would meet with your superior and ask to work with someone else, but something tells me that would be a complete waste of my time."

The look she gave him was as cold as ice. All softness was gone from her eyes. And that made Nick all the more suspicious. Because beneath her cool demeanor, he could tell that she was really a volcano ready to explode.

"Why the sudden change of heart, Rachel?"

She didn't miss a beat, and her gaze never wavered from his. "Make no mistake. I don't want to work with you. In fact, if it were up to me, I'd never lay eyes on you again. But I couldn't live with myself if I didn't do whatever I can to help catch Cynthia's killer. And if that means working with you, Detective Fallen, then so be it."

He could actually feel her indignation, but decided to ignore it. Especially since he could understand why she felt the way she did about him. He had violated her trust in the worst way, and other than the fact that he was doing his job, he could see no reason for her to forgive him.

"Okay. Here's the deal." Nick decided to be equally as blunt. "This team has put in countless hours trying to solve your sister's case, and the reality is that we need you now in order for our plan to have any real chance of working. Your investment in this investigation should be one week of your time — two tops. After that, other than the possibility of seeing each other in court, you'll get your wish. I will promise you that after this case is solved, you'll never need to lay eyes on me again."

Something flickered through Rachel's eyes and Nick almost missed it. He knew his words bordered on being insensitive, but he figured those were the words she wanted to hear. But now, watching her expression change, he wasn't so sure. Actually, where she was concerned, he wasn't sure about anything. So because of that he did what he did best — he waited and he watched. He didn't have long to wait.

"Then we have a deal." The coldness was back in her eyes.

Nick nodded and looked over at Ben, who was sitting across the table. Lou left his place by the door and joined them.

"I'm not going to lie to you and tell you that this plan isn't risky, Rachel."

"That should be a new experience for you. Not lying, that is."

Nick completely ignored her comment and continued as if she hadn't spoken, even though he felt as though she'd slapped him all over again.

"You have the guarantee of everyone at this table that we'll do absolutely everything to minimize the risks. No matter how badly we want to catch the bad guys, it's more important that we keep you safe. If you can't or won't believe me about this, Professor, you can believe Detectives Morris and Jensen. They have nothing to gain by lying to you."

Suddenly, Rachel felt trapped. Nick was still sitting too close, and she was having trouble dealing with the intensity in his eyes. He was so serious and so coplike, that it was impossible for her to equate this man with the one she had joked and laughed with over the last four days. The charming, flirtatious, almost carefree lover was completely gone. And in its place was a stranger. A stranger with intense green eyes.

Needing some breathing room, Rachel got up from her chair and walked over to the water cooler. She filled a paper cup with water she didn't really want, and drank it down anyway. Then she walked back to the table where the three detectives were sitting. Hoping that she wasn't too obvious, she scooted her chair a little further away from Nick before she sat down again. As she tried to get comfortable, she glanced over at Nick and saw a flash of amusement cross his face. He hadn't missed her little attempt at putting more distance between them. In fact, he didn't even try to disguise his grin. And for a split second, Rachel felt another spurt of anger. Anger she didn't have time to deal with, because Nick was once again taking charge.

"When will you be making your next delivery for Steven?"

Rachel swallowed back her newfound hatred and answered his question. One thing she quickly figured out — the sooner she cooperated, the sooner she could get away from him.

"I'm not certain. I usually make one trip a week and I won't know about my next assignment until I see Steven on Monday."

"Do you think he'll already have something lined up?"

"More than likely," was her reply. And it didn't get past Nick that she was addressing her responses to Ben and Lou.

Both men looked a little uncomfortable, but Nick couldn't do anything about it. If Rachel wanted to play such an immature game and not speak to him directly, Nick couldn't stop her.

"Our plan is relatively simple, and it involves your next trip." She still refused to look at him. "On Monday I want you to tell Steven that you met a man aboard the cruise ship and that you think we've fallen in love."

Now *that* got her attention, and she whipped around to look at him as though he had lost his mind.

"It's important that you convince Steven that we've fallen for each other, and fallen hard."

"Now wait a minute. I don't see …"

"Please let me finish, Rachel." Nick, Ben, and Lou watched as she struggled to sit still and listen. "The reason it's important for Steven to believe we're in love is because I'm going on the next trip with you. You need to tell Steven that I'm taking an extra week off work just so I can be with you. You need to seem so taken with me, Rachel, that he'll have no reason to doubt you. Tell him whatever you think he'll believe. It's that important." As he spoke he watched conflicting emotions cross her face.

"Isn't there any other way to go about this? What you're asking me to do is so out of character for me that I'm afraid I won't be able to pull it off. I'm just not very good at lying."

Left unspoken was the fact that she thought that Nick was an extraordinarily good liar.

"You've told me yourself that Steven insists that you make these deliveries on you own, and I doubt that he'd agree to me tagging along without a good reason. A very good reason. We've also considered that he may decide to have me checked out. And if he does that, nothing should alert him that I'm anything other than your new boyfriend. I do have a law degree, my father is senior partner in a law firm in San Francisco, and you and I did meet and spend all of our time together aboard the ship."

Reminding Rachel of that sent a dagger straight to her heart.

"So unless you can come up with a better idea, we'll go with this."

Rachel knew she couldn't win this battle. Besides, everything Nick said made perfect sense. And along with everything else, she now hated him for that as well.

"I wish there was another way, but I can see the logic in your idea so I'll give it a try. After all, those lies certainly worked well enough with me. And I'll also try to do the impossible and convince Steven that I'm crazy about you. Now let me see." She paused for effect. "I guess I'll just have to tell him that from the moment I met you, I was swept away by your charm, sex appeal, and irresistible powers of persuasion."

The note of sarcasm was so unmistakable that Ben and Lou both looked anywhere but at Nick. But Nick refused to let her words draw blood. Instead, he sat and looked at her with a face that was set in stone. Only the deepening of the green in his eyes gave him away.

"Like I said. Tell him whatever you think he'll believe."

Nick tried to keep the sarcasm out of his voice, but everyone could pick up on it. He didn't want to start another fight with Rachel and he didn't want to upset her any further. She deserved better. He believed in his soul that it wasn't her fault that she felt betrayed by him, so he tried another approach.

"I'm sorry, Rachel. I know this is hard for you. You've had to take in a lot these past two hours, and if you'd like, we can call it a day. You probably need to get some rest and I'm sure you'd like some time to sort through everything we've thrown at you. If it's all right with everyone, we can arrange to meet for a while tomorrow and finish going over the rest of the plan. It's your call."

Now this was the Nick she knew. The man speaking to her was not a stranger. He was being sweet, kind, and thoughtful. And with all of the differing emotions swirling around in her mind, Rachel could feel the threat of tears she had fought so hard to keep from falling.

All three men watched in horror as she tried not to cry. Anger and sarcasm they could deal with, but God help them if she really did let the tears flow.

Swiping away at the one tear that feel onto her cheek, Rachel sat up straighter in her chair, swallowed hard, and brought her raw emotions under control. She told herself that now was not the time for her to fall apart. And even more important, she refused to let Nick think that his words bothered her enough to make her cry.

"Don't worry, I'm not going to break down," she said as she looked from Nick to Lou to Ben and back to Nick again. "And I'd really prefer not to delay this until tomorrow." There — she felt better already.

"You sure, Rachel? It's really no problem to put this off for a while if you want."

Rachel couldn't help it. Against her will, she softened just a touch because of the gentleness in Nick's voice. And she couldn't seem to stop the words that came out of her mouth.

"Please don't be nice to me, Nick. Not now. Not when I need to hold onto my anger. I've already lost my trust in you and my pride in myself, and I might just fall completely apart if I don't keep focusing on my anger. It's all I've got left right now." Her voice was very faint, and her eyes were filled with the tears that she refused to cry.

It took awhile for the men in the room to recover from her softly spoken words. Nick felt like he had just been sucker punched, and he couldn't seem to come up with anything to say. Thankfully, after a minute of silence, Ben saved the day.

"So you want to go on, Ms. Bennett?"

Rachel looked up and nodded, and Nick suddenly felt like she had a few minutes ago. He suddenly felt trapped. Without saying a word, he got up, walked away from the table, and leaned back against the wall. He crossed his arms over his chest and gave Ben a silent message to continue.

"Well, ma'am, like Detective Fallen said, it's important that he's with you on the next trip you take out of the country. Just having illegal documents in hand is not enough. We need to be able to point the FBI in the direction of the recipient of those false papers."

"You've called in the FBI?"

"We're working on that right now. Our Lieutenant, Alex Kendall, is probably on the phone with the Bureau as we speak."

Rachel didn't ask any more questions, so Ben proceeded to fill her in.

"Here's our plan, Ms. Bennett. You and Detective Fallen will deliver your package, following your regular routine. We don't want to send off any warning signals, so you two need to follow the same routine as usual. The only difference being that on this trip, you're taking your new boyfriend along. Then you make contact with the driver, you deliver your package, and after that, the two of you do nothing more than hightail it back here. And we will have you covered every step of the way. Lieutenant Kendall is going to get his hands on a nice little FBI tracking device that we will plant on Nick. We will be monitoring your every move, while at the same time get an exact location on where you've been. Once you two are back here safe and sound, the FBI will move in and pay a little visit to the bad guys. It shouldn't be a problem getting the Mexican authorities to work with the FBI, so if everything goes according to the plan, we should have Steven behind bars by the end of the week. And of course, the frosting on the cake is that we also get to put some very mean criminals behind bars as well. Criminals who we are hoping will sell out your dear brother-in-law. You see, somewhere in the pipeline, we should be able to get enough evidence to tie Steven to your sister's murder."

As Ben talked, Rachel lowered her lashes and risked looking over at Nick, still leaning up against the wall. And she felt her heart lodge in her throat. No matter how much she hated him for how he had used her, he still had the ability to take her breath away. He was just so handsome. Rachel had to admit that under any other circumstances, she would have been drawn to Nick the cop. He looked so at ease wearing his shoulder holster, and there was an added sexiness about him with his badge clipped to the front of his belt, and his cell phone resting against his right hip. Everything about him left no doubt that he was commanding, authoritative, and all man. A man she had to remind herself that she couldn't trust.

"Oh, and one other thing." Rachel forced herself to draw her eyes away from Nick and concentrate on the rest of what Ben was saying.

"I will be close behind you in case you two get into any trouble. I'll be watching your backs. Lou will be here keeping an eye on your brother-in-law, and Alex will be monitoring your movements and working with our boys at the Bureau. All and all, I think we'll have everything well-covered."

As Ben finished up, Nick made his way back to the table. He swung his chair around and sat down in front of Rachel, bringing one ankle up over his knee.

"We think we've covered all of our bases, but I want to make sure you're okay with everything that Detective Morris just laid out."

Reminding herself that she couldn't trust Nick helped her to grab onto the possibility that perhaps there was another way to go about this undercover operation. A way that didn't involve her having to work with Nicholas Fallen.

"There is something I don't quite understand, Detective Morris. If all you need is to pinpoint my final destination so that the FBI can take over, why does Nick ..... I mean, why does Detective Fallen need to go along at all? Couldn't you just put the tracking device on me? It would seem to me that would be much simpler and wouldn't require such an elaborate ploy. So how about just using me undercover?"

"No!" Nick's emphatic response left no room for argument. Or at least that's what he thought.

"I wasn't asking you, Detective Fallen. I addressed my question to Detective Morris."

"I'm afraid that doesn't change the answer, Ms. Bennett." Ben responded before Nick did.

"And why is that?" If I'm willing to be wired, or bugged, or whatever you call it, then why can't I do this alone?"

"Because you are a civilian." This time Nick beat his partner to the punch. "And we don't send untrained civilians out alone to do our jobs for us."

Even though Rachel could tell just by the look on Nick's face that it was time to drop the matter, she persisted in pushing her point.

"Well, gentlemen, the way I see it, I can refuse to go along with your plan and do a little undercover work all on my own. Granted, I will not have the advantage of your tracking system, but I'd bet I could provide the FBI with good enough directions so that they could find the bad guys again. And this way, I don't need to even bother lying to Steven. I just go about my business, pay close attention to where I've been, and work directly with the FBI when I get back."

Because no one so much as blinked an eye, she added, "And truthfully, I think my plan might actually work better than yours."

This time she got a reaction. Slowly, Nick stood, planted one hand on the table, and leaned down into Rachel's face. "Think again, Professor."

"You think you can stop me?" Even as she asked the question, she was pretty sure she knew what his answer was going to be.

"You do this our way or not at all. I go along — period. And if you even entertain the idea of going off half-cocked on your own, I will slap you into protective custody so fast it'll make your head swim. And I'll keep you locked up for as long as it takes. On this I am not lying, Rachel, so unless you want to end up behind bars, you'd better promise us right now that you won't do anything so stupid."

One look at Nick told everyone in the room that he meant every word. And Rachel wanted to fight. She wanted to challenge him and force him to back down. But looking up into his face, she knew instinctively that he wasn't going to budge. She also had a very strong feeling that he would throw her in jail if she gave him no other choice. And that she would not tolerate. So, swallowing her pride again, she met his eyes with a look that was meant to kill.

"I couldn't dislike you more if I tried, Nicholas, which, believe me, is saying quite a lot. But since you have given me no choice, I'll cooperate and go along with your plan. You and I will make my next delivery together. But," she added as she stood up to look at him face to face, "I'm going to hold you to your promise that after this is over; I'll never have to deal with you and speak with you again. That is my one condition, and it is not negotiable."

Nick secretly admired Rachel's guts, but he knew better than to say so, because he was certain that she would throw any compliment he paid her right back in his face.

"Then it appears we understand each other perfectly." Nick straightened to his full height as he spoke. "As soon as you get your next assignment from Steven, you call me on my cell phone and we'll set everything up. Don't call the station. Only call me on my cell." With that, Nick passed her a piece of paper with his cell number scribbled on it. "Alex will work with the feds, Lou will watch Steven, Ben will watch our backs, and you and I will be partners. Temporary partners," he added before she could. "So if everyone does their job, there should be no problems. Agreed?"

"Agreed."

Nick knew that her agreement cost her a great deal. And again he felt sorry for how he had hurt and disappointed her. But that would be for another time and another discussion that the two of them would need to have.

"Good." Then let's call it a day. There's nothing more we can do here. Come on, Rachel, I'll walk you to your car."

Rachel snatched up her purse and flew past Nick, heading straight for the door. "Don't bother. I'm perfectly capable of finding my own way out."

She flung open the door, but was stopped short by Nick's impatient tone of voice. "Call me. If I don't hear from you by Tuesday …" but the next thing the three detectives heard was the door as it slammed shut.

"Now, that is one hell of a woman." Lou let out a long whistle. "One hell of a woman indeed."

Ben and Lou looked at Nick, waiting for a response. Both were disappointed when he didn't say a word. Instead, Nick threw Lou a narrow look and headed through the door that Rachel had practically rattled off its hinges. Ben and Lou followed. And not surprisingly, Alex was waiting for all three of them.

"Okay, so she's agreed to cooperate. That's good." Obviously, Alex had been listening in.

"Did you get in touch with the feds?"

"Yeah, Lou, I did. And they're on board."

"And are they going to share some of their toys?"

"Yeah, well that took a little more discussion. Seems they have this thing about sharing their high-tech tracking devices with us lowly LAPD detectives. But I told them without it, it's a no go. And since they really want in on this bust, they gave in. Somewhat reluctantly, but they gave in all the same."

Nick laughed, knowing just how persuasive Alex could really be. When he set his mind to something, it was pretty much a foregone conclusion that he was going to get it. Even if it was some high-tech shit that the FBI didn't want to share.

"Well, I don't know about you guys, but color me gone. It's Saturday afternoon, and I plan to pay a visit to my girl-friend." Lou was walking away, but kept on talking. "This damn case has taken up so much of my time, I need a nice long afternoon of mind-blowing sex so that I can start again fresh on Monday. See ya."

"More information than I need to know," was Alex's response as he took off in the direction of his office — which left Nick and Ben alone. Well, not exactly alone. They were in the middle of the squad room with a few other detectives working on a Saturday afternoon, but that could be considered pretty much alone.

"I know it's early yet, but you want to grab a beer?"

"No thanks, Ben. Why don't you go on home to Betty and the girls." Nick sounded almost weary.

"Betty and the kids are at her sister's this afternoon for some baby shower. They probably won't be home for a couple more hours. It's only two, so if you don't want a beer, want to grab a sandwich?"

Nick didn't really know what the hell he wanted. But he knew that he was going to have to talk to his partner sooner or later. So he decided that he might as well get it over with. Nick looked over at his friend. "Sure. A sandwich sounds good."

"Great. Let's go on over to Cantor's Deli. I'll drive."

"The hell you will." And the few detectives in the room smiled as they heard the familiar argument of the two men who headed out the door.

Nick had decided to have a beer with lunch after all, and he could feel himself finally start to relax. He hadn't eaten all day and the food and alcohol seemed to be just what he needed. Ben was good company too. He kept the conversation light, right up until they finished with their double-decker deli sandwiches. And then, as expected, he turned serious.

"You do know that Alex could have very easily suspended your ass?"

"Yeah, I know."

"And you do know that if he had, you'd have no one to blame but yourself?"

"Yeah …. I know."

"You've also got to know, Nick, that what you did was way beyond stupid."

"Yeah, I know that too."

"So what the hell happened, partner? And why the hell couldn't you keep your pants zipped up for four days?"

Nick took a long drink from his bottle of beer. And for the second time that day, he found he didn't have an answer to that question. First Alex had asked him pretty much the same thing, and now Ben.

"I'm not sure why I let it happen. I knew better, but I let it happen anyway. And I'll tell you what I told Alex. I'm not proud that I crossed the line. Not proud at all. But I can't change it either."

The two friends drank in silence for a while, before Ben continued. "I just don't understand it, Nick. My God, having sex whenever you want is the least of your problems. Women just seem to throw themselves at you. I should know. I took down those phone messages while you were gone. So, why this woman? Why couldn't you keep your hands off of this one?"

"It isn't what you think, Ben. I didn't set out to get Rachel into bed. And whether you believe this or not, I actually tried to talk her out of it. More than once I tried to talk her out of it. But then," Nick had to take another drink of beer before he could continue. "Then one night we were getting ready to go down to dinner, and one thing kinda led to another. And before we realized it, we didn't exactly make it out of her cabin. And after that … well …. after that first time, I couldn't seem to remember why it wasn't a good idea to make love to her."

Nick drained the rest of his beer, thought about ordering another, and decided against it.

"Do you like this woman?"

"Why the hell would you even ask me that? I know you think that I'm some sort of a player, but regardless of what you think, I don't make it a habit of going to bed with women I don't like. Jesus Ben, give me some credit, will you?"

"Don't get so testy, buddy. That's not what I meant and you know it. I asked the question because you seem ..... I don't know, you seem a little different with this woman. Maybe you like her more than even you want to admit. Have you thought of that?"

Nick didn't answer; he just sent Ben a look that said something along the lines of *mind your own damn business.* But Ben never paid much attention to his partner's menacing looks.

"So you think I might be right? You think you might have a thing for Professor Bennett?"

"Give it up. I have no intention of sitting here with you and analyzing my feelings about Rachel. And what difference could it make anyway? In case you didn't notice, she's probably put me in the same category as pond scum. She doesn't exactly trust me anymore, and my guess is that she'd love nothing more than to see me suffer a long and painful death. So don't make more out of this than it is. I met a woman I liked and respected, and then I screwed up. End of story."

"Not so, my friend. Not by a long shot is this the end of the story."

"I'm finished talking about this, Ben. Finish your beer and let's go."

Ben laughed and very slowly took another sip. He was having way too much fun watching Nick squirm.

"You know, it's not the end of the world to admit that you've fallen for someone, Nick. For Christ's sake, in your case it's about friggin' time."

"What don't you understand about me telling you I'm finished talking about this?"

Now Nick was getting mad, which as far as Ben was concerned, was just another sign that Rachel meant more to him than he would concede.

"Yeah, yeah, I heard you. But you should know by now that I won't let up until I get an answer. That's what makes me such a crackerjack detective."

Nick just closed his eyes, dropped his chin, and shook his head. He wanted to laugh, but couldn't quite bring himself to find any humor in the situation. So instead he drew in what he hoped would be a deep, calming breath.

"I think Rachel Bennett is a very special lady. And if the circumstances were different, I would've liked to see where this thing between us would have gone. But the circumstances aren't different, and there's no chance in hell for us to put this behind us and start over. We'll get through this case, and we'll never see each other again. Which in the long run is probably a good thing. So, now that I answered your question, can we please get the hell out of here?"

Ben drank the last of his beer and placed his empty bottle next to Nick's. "Your treat, Nick. You fucked up, so you treat for lunch."

That was the unspoken rule throughout the squad room. Whenever a detective screwed up, no matter how minor, they brought their partner lunch. So without argument, Nick reached in his pocket and threw enough on the table to cover lunch and a pretty good tip.

"So lunch is over and the subject of Rachel is closed. I will not discuss her again except for her involvement in this case. Understood?"

"Sure, sure, whatever you say, buddy. Rachel Bennett is not open for discussion. She's a closed subject except for this case. Got it."

Ben was trying hard not to snicker and Nick was trying even harder not to strangle his best friend. Because both men knew that even after this case was behind them, Rachel Bennett was going to be anything but a closed subject.

CHAPTER NINE

"Hello."

"Your sister-in-law left the police station about an hour ago. I followed her after she left, and she headed straight home. She hasn't come out of her house since."

"I thought I told you never to call me at my home."

"I'm sorry, Mr. Jackson, but I didn't think you'd want to wait for this news until Monday."

Steven Jackson felt a thin bead of sweat form on his upper lip. He knew that having Rachel followed this past month was a good idea, and his instincts had finally paid off. But now he felt a prick of real fear, because his instincts had not only paid off, they were telling him that she had betrayed him just like his bitch of a wife had tried to do.

"Did she come in on her own?"

"She came to the station willingly, if that's what you're asking?"

No surprise there was the thought that stuck in Steven's mind. He was just waiting for something like this to happen.

"Is she cooperating with them?"

"Yes, Mr. Jackson. She's agreed to work with the cops to try to set you up."

There was a long silence, as the informant let his words sink in. He hadn't looked forward to making this call, but had decided that it couldn't wait.

"Go on." Steven Jackson felt a stranglehold on his throat.

"Well, sir, she's agreed to team up with the hotshot detective she met on the cruise ship. The one I told you about earlier, Detective Fallen. Looks like while he was screwing your sister-in-law, he also got a chance to look inside the package she was carrying, and he can prove that the papers were false and illegal as hell."

Steven broke out in a sweat all over his body. He could feel the heat form under his armpits and he started to feel his shirt cling to the wet spots on his back. He had always had a real problem with perspiration when he got nervous, and he was nervous now. Very, very nervous. He had worked too long and too hard to let his bitch of a sister-in-law ruin everything now. Reaching out for the cold glass of water he had set by the phone, he picked it up and drained it in one long gulp.

"Are you there, Mr. Jackson?"

"I'm still here." The ice-cold water had helped and he felt his body temperature returning to normal. "Go on. How are they planning to set me up?"

"It's pretty simple, really. She's planning on convincing you that Nick Fallen is her new boyfriend and that she wants to take him along on her next trip out of the country. He'll be wired, of course, and they plan to turn the location of your customer over to the FBI. They've already got Fallen's eyewitness testimony about the false papers, so now all they need is to tie you to some of your … shall we say, less-than-desirable customers. They also want to link you to your wife's murder."

"I see." Another long silence ensued.

Steven Jackson's mind was racing. Ever since Cynthia's death, he had been waiting for the other shoe to fall, and he was not surprised to find Rachel the cause of his problems. She had always been such a goody-goody. He had thought long and hard before asking for her help in his little side business, and had only gone to her because he hadn't had any other choice. He needed help getting his packages out of the country, and playing on her sympathy for him as the grieving widower, he had convinced himself that she wouldn't question him. But even though she had readily agreed to work with him for a couple of months, he had still kept close tabs on her, never trusting her completely. And a good thing, he decided, as he felt himself start to perspire again.

"What do you want me to do, Mr. Jackson? Should I still keep an eye on her?"

Again, there was a long, almost unbearable silence, while Steven thought about his next move. Getting rid of Cynthia had been fairly easy, and he figured he could handle Rachel as well. But throwing a cop into the mix complicated things. Not that it really mattered — because Steven knew it might be a good time for him to pack up and move on. He certainly had enough money, so that he could lay low for a year or two out of the country. Then, when things cooled down, he could probably slip back in and set up shop again without much trouble at all. He would need to eliminate his sister-in-law, of course, but that was more of a nuisance than anything else. After all, now that she had betrayed him, he figured that she deserved it.

"There's not much point in watching her any further. She's no good to me now. The only thing left to do is to get rid of her and the hotshot cop."

"Wait just a minute, Mr. Jackson. I had no problem taking out your wife for you, and to tell you the truth, I don't have much of a problem getting rid of your sister-in-law. But I never signed on to take out a cop."

Steven closed his fingers so tightly around the glass he was still holding that it almost shattered. "You are forgetting that I pay you very, very well. What I paid you to kill my wife is more than you make in a year. And need I remind you that you are in too deep to back out now. I own you and don't you forget it."

"But killing a cop isn't as easy as you seem to think. That's too fucking risky."

"Do you think I don't know that!" Steven was losing it big time. "We need to eliminate both of them, and we can do it so that it looks like an accident. Do you think I'm stupid enough not to realize that the cops will be all over my ass if my sister-in-law shows up murdered like her sister?"

"Okay, okay. An accident sounds good. Really good." Some of the panic had left the informant's voice. Do you want me to handle it?"

"No. We'll have it happen in Mexico." Steven already had a good idea of how to get rid of his current problem. "After a certain amount of convincing, I'll finally give in and agree to let Rachel take her new boyfriend on her next trip. I think I'll send them back to Miguel Bautista. I can explain to Rachel that he's asking for a few more documents. I'll fly them to San Diego, and then have someone pick them up at the airport for the trip to Bautista's. Once there, we'll arrange for … oh, let's say, a car accident."

"But what about the driver? How can you arrange for a car accident if Bautista sends out a driver?"

Steven was already one step ahead of his informant. "That's what will make this look all the more real. Mr. Bautista owes me a favor, a big favor, and I'm sure he'll have no problem offering up one of his men for the cause. I'm sure he has someone on his payroll that he considers dispensable. Can't you just see it now? Three people found dead at the bottom of a ravine, the result of a fast curve, faulty brakes and a leaky gas tank. How sad to find two Americans and one Mexican killed from such an unfortunate accident. Yes, three people dead is much better than two. Don't you think?"

Now that Steven had laid out his plan, he felt his entire body start to cool down. He didn't have any doubt that Miguel Bautista would help him out of this little jam he was in. In fact, Mr. Bautista would probably see it as an opportunity to wipe the slate clean. Because he really did owe Steven a favor, and now was the perfect time to cash in on what was owed.

And the best part of all, with both Rachel and the cop dead, there would be no hard evidence against him. Speculation that he might be involved, of course — but all the evidence will have all gone up in smoke, along with three very dead bodies. So now Steven could relax and plan a nice little getaway. Yes, all and all, this was going to work out very well. Except for one, little, nagging concern.

"So is this Detective Fallen going to be a problem?"

"I'm not sure what you mean, sir. He's not married and he has no kids, so other than his folks, his death won't be a big deal."

Steven had to work at not losing his temper. Cops, especially dirty cops, could be so fucking stupid.

"I don't give a shit about who's going to mourn the guy. I'm asking if he's going to be trouble when they're picked up at the airport. Getting into a car with a complete stranger will most likely go against his instinct as a cop."

"Not to worry, Mr. Jackson. Fallen won't be a problem."

Steven wasn't so easily persuaded. "You're sure?"

"Yes sir. I understand that his instructions are very clear. He's to escort Ms. Bennett on this little trip, and then get them both back here so that he can turn the tracking device over to the feds. They'll take it from there."

Cradling the phone against his ear, Steven walked into the kitchen and filled his glass with ice-cold water. He took a long, soothing drink.

"What kind of tracking device will he have on him?"

"I don't know, but I'm sure I can find out."

Steven Jackson's control snapped. "You had damn well better find out! I can't afford to have cops sniffing anywhere around that asshole Fallen and Rachel once they cross the border. We'll need to make sure that the device he's wearing is destroyed and that means we'll need to know exactly what we're looking for. I'm sure that Bautista won't want to take any chances. So you find out and you find out fast."

Steven spoke as if he were scolding a six-year-old, and he could sense that the informant on the other end of the line was getting irritated. And that pleased Steven. He liked to insult dirty cops, knowing full well that the man on the other end of the line couldn't do a thing about it. Steven Jackson was in complete control, and that thrilled him to death.

"I'll get you the information you need, Mr. Jackson. You can count on it."

"I am counting on it, and so will Mr. Bautista. You would be wise to remember that."

When there was no immediate response, Steven let his words sink in and drank down the rest of his cold water. "Oh, and one other thing, don't call me again at my home unless it's an emergency. If you need me, call me on my cell phone. Let it ring once, hang up, call again, let it ring once and hang up. I'll find a pay phone and I'll call you on your cell. I don't want anyone connecting the two of us."

That was a dismissal. Steven was finished with this conversation.

"Yes sir, I understand."

And before the informant could utter another word, the line went dead.

CHAPTER TEN

Rachel spent all of Saturday night vacillating between em-barrassment, anger, and a deep feeling of loss. Right after she had returned home from the police station, she had continued to burn up with a fierce resentment and a raging anger. As the evening progressed, and she calmed down, some of her anger toward Nick subsided, and she was left feeling embarrassed over how easily she had let him fool her and how easily she had succumbed to his charm. And then, by the time she had fallen into bed, the only feeling she could relate to was a sense of sadness. Sadness over her foolish heart, sadness over Nick, and sadness over the unexpected turn of events in Cynthia's case.

As expected, Rachel slept restlessly on and off during the night. She would drift off to sleep only to wake up after having more than one nightmare. She was just so troubled.

Sunday morning, Rachel's mind was still whirling. She was still having trouble accepting that Steven could have been part of a plot to kill Cynthia. Funny, she didn't have any problem believing that Steven was involved in trafficking illegal docu-ments. He always seemed to have a dark side to him, one that Rachel thought was just a personality flaw and none of her business. He was also way too secretive, now that she thought about it. Both in his personal life and certainly in his busi-ness. But to think that he could have arranged to have his wife killed was more than she could bear to think about. Her heart was actually breaking over that possibility. And if it ended up being true, then she wanted to bring him down. She wanted to stand back and watch him brought to justice, even if it meant working side-by-side with Nicholas Fallen.

The thought of Nick was another reason Rachel couldn't get her mind to settle down. No matter how hard she tried, she kept thinking about him. She kept seeing him leaning up against the wall, silently watching her, looking and acting like a cop. Not the man she had halfway fallen in love with, but a cop. And each time she thought of that, embarrassment would wash over her and win out over her feelings of despair.

Another reason Rachel felt rattled was because there was a small part of her that understood why Nick had needed to lie to her. She didn't like it and she didn't condone it, but perhaps she understood it. Because now that she was a part of the plan, she would do whatever it was gong to take to help catch her sister's killer. She would even lie, which was exactly what she would be doing the very next time she laid eyes on Steven.

The other truth that Rachel had to face was that while aboard the cruise ship, she had quite literally seduced Nick. She had made up her mind that she wanted to get him into bed, and that nothing was going to stop her. She had done everything in her power to get him to succumb, and it was hard to blame him completely for what had been the final outcome. Sure, he could and should have said no more force-fully, but in her heart she knew that she had given him very little choice. And for that, she was sorry. She wasn't sure she was sorry enough to forgive him; she only knew that she was sorry for the way things had turned out.

Deciding that she would go stark raving mad if she thought about these things any longer, Rachel poured herself a cup of coffee. Then she wandered into the living room, set-tled down on the couch, and reached for the remote control so that she could tune in to the first NFL game of the day.

Rachel loved professional football, and she hoped that she could lose herself for a while in the morning game between the San Francisco 49ers and the Miami Dolphins.

The knock came at four o'clock, with just six minutes left in the afternoon game between the Oakland Raiders and the Dallas Cowboys. The game was tied at ten to ten, and Rachel considered not answering her door. The Oakland Raiders were her favorite team and they had the ball. It was third and long and they were on the fifty-yard line. Ignoring the knock at the door, Rachel stood and held her breath as the Raiders' quarterback, Kerry Collins took the handoff, stepped back, scrambled out of the pocket, and then threw a nice long pass downfield to his wide receiver. The ball hung high in the air, a perfect spiral, and Rachel watched in disbelief as the receiver caught the ball by the tips of his fingers, but lost control and dropped it as he was tackled to the ground. Incomplete pass.

"Oh, that is just great." She said to the TV and the knock came again. But this time, the knock on her front door was a little louder and a little more persistent.

Normally, Rachel would never answer her door without looking through her peephole, but she was so distracted by the dropped pass that she flung open the door without thinking. And to her utter surprise, there stood Nick, with his hand raised as if he were getting ready to knock again.

It was hard to tell who was more caught off guard. Rachel did not expect to find Nick standing on her doorstep on a Sunday afternoon, and the last thing Nick had expected was for Rachel to answer her door all decked out in an Oakland Raiders jersey and tight black jeans. He could hear the game on in the background and couldn't stop the grin that spread across his face. Rachel Bennett was just so full of surprises.

The grin made Rachel's heart turn over. It also brought back some of the anger of the day before.

"What do you want?" Her tone was anything but inviting.

"I need to talk with you." Even though the smile was gone from Nick's face, there was still a hint of amusement in his eyes.

"Can't it wait?"

"It could. But I'd rather talk with you now."

"Well, I don't want to talk with you."

The flicker of amusement had finally left his eyes to be replaced by a look that Rachel couldn't read.

"It won't take long, Rachel."

"Do I have a choice, Detective? If I refuse to let you in, will you read me my rights and then drag me back down to the station?" She was being purposely stubborn and sarcastic, and she suspected that Nick knew it.

"This is not an official visit. I'm off today, so feel free to slam the door in my face if you want to. There are a couple of things I wanted to talk with you about before you see Steven tomorrow, but it's up to you. We can always do it later."

God, she hated it that he was coming off as the voice of reason, and she was coming off as the irrational one.

"Fine," she replied with obvious irritation. "Come on in. But whatever you want to say needs to wait, because there's less than five minutes left in the game." Rachel turned and all but stomped back into her living room, leaving Nick to let himself in.

Nick walked in, shut the door, and followed close behind, noticing how sweetly Rachel fit into her snug black jeans. Her silver-and-black jersey was tucked into her waistband, and he noted that she wore a thin, silver belt. Her hair was tied back in a cute ponytail, and it swung as she walked. She looked so adorable and so sexy that he had to fight down the sudden sexual pull he felt in his groin. Watching her from behind, he could remember all too well how perfect her body was, and how she had looked naked and flushed with desire. Nick had to shake his head to clear his mind of her naked image because he had to admit that this woman could quite literally take his breath away, along with whatever common sense he possessed. He was also absolutely certain that the last thing he needed was for Rachel to catch him with a hard-on, because that, if nothing else, would get him thrown out faster than he could imagine. So Nick drew his eyes away from her nice, rounded bottom, and forced himself to concentrate on the TV screen.

"Looks like a good game," was his only comment as he noted the tie score, and sat down on the couch. And again, he couldn't help but grin as Rachel scooted as far away from him as possible.

Nick settled back and watched Rachel as she watched the game. She sat almost as stiff as a statue carved in stone, her eyes focused straight ahead. He was certain that she was trying her damnedest to pretend that he wasn't there at all, and that he wasn't sitting almost close enough to reach out and touch her.

The minutes ticked by, and they both watched the game in complete silence, all the way down to the two-minute warning. And right before the game clock struck two minutes, the next play brought Rachel to her feet.

The Raiders' quarterback had responded to the defense's pass rush by taking three quick steps back and releasing the ball straight downfield. The ball was thrown right into a crowd, and was missed by the Raiders' wide receiver. Rachel was immediately on her feet, screaming "Pass interference!" as if the referee cold actually hear her.

"Pass interference!" she persisted when there was no penalty flag thrown in the field of play. "Did you see that? It was obvious pass interference." It took Nick a second to realize that she was finally talking to him.

The wide receiver on the field was pointing frantically at the defensive free safety, trying to get a ref to throw the flag. Rachel was standing on her feet, yelling at the screen. A replay was finally shown.

"My God, that was blatant pass interference. Why won't they call the penalty?"

Nick couldn't help it. He knew that he should probably keep his mouth shut, but where football was concerned, he was pretty opinionated himself.

"Actually, Rachel, I didn't see any interference. Looks like it was a good defensive play, if you ask me."

"Are you crazy, Nicholas? That safety was all over my wide receiver. My guy didn't have a chance."

"Look again, Professor."

Rachel leaned forward, staring intently at the screen as they showed the play one more time.

"I don't know what you see, but I see pass interference!"

She was not going to budge from her point of view, but then again neither was Nick.

"Sorry, Professor, but the safety was playing the ball all the way. He didn't even touch your wide-out."

"You're as blind as the ref!"

When Rachel planted her hands on her hips, Nick completely lost it. He burst out laughing. Rachel didn't see any humor in the situation. She glared down at Nick, crossed her arms under her breasts, and plopped back down on the couch.

After the two-minute warning, the Raiders punted to the Dallas Cowboys. The Cowboys got a first down, but failed to convert another first down, so the Raiders got the ball back. The only problem was that the Cowboys had taken ninety seconds off the clock, and the Raiders had only one timeout left. They were also on their own twenty-yard line. All of this Nick wisely did not comment on.

He did notice though that Rachel never sat down after her team got the ball back. As tempted as he was to keep his eyes on her, he was drawn back to the game. Kerry Collins, the Raiders' QB, converted a long, thirty-yard pass, taking eight seconds off the clock. Oakland used their final timeout.

It was now first and ten. Collins was in the shotgun position, and Dallas was preparing for an all-out blitz. Because of the blitz, Kerry Collins was forced to scramble, wasting precious seconds. He stumbled, avoided a tackle, and somehow managed to complete another thirty-yard pass. Oakland was now on the Cowboys' twenty-yard line, with ten seconds left in the game.

Rachel was going crazy, yelling out her own plays. She was completely beside herself, and Nick was enjoying her immensely. He was getting a real kick out of watching her.

Back on the field, Kerry Collins obviously didn't like the look of the defense, so he called an audible at the line. The center snapped the ball, Collins stepped back, faked a pump pass, and with only seconds left on the clock, he threw a screen pass to his running back, who fought and scratched his way across the goal line. Time ran out and the Oakland Raiders beat the Dallas Cowboys, sixteen to ten.

Rachel's arms were up, indicating a touchdown, and she had a smug and victorious smile on her face. "So much for cheating us out of a pass interference call," she threw over her shoulder and Nick could only sit there and watch as she disappeared into the kitchen. His low, masculine laughter followed.

Nick could hear Rachel rattling around in the kitchen and his patience gave out, so he clicked off the TV and joined her, uninvited. He walked into the neat little kitchen just as she placed two cups on a tray, which also held a freshly brewed pot of coffee. Without asking permission, he took the tray.

"Where do you want this?"

"I'd planned to have coffee in the living room." Now that the football game was over, her mood was impossible to gauge, so Nick didn't even try. He just walked back into the living room, set the tray down on the coffee table, and settled back in his spot on the couch. Rachel followed.

"You said that you had a couple of things you wanted to talk with me about."

She poured them each a cup of coffee. Nick noted right off that all friendliness was gone from her voice and she was determined to remain cool and aloof. But because he liked the woman of a few minutes ago a whole lot better than the one sitting before him now, he decided to see if her could break through her suit of armor.

"Yeah, well now I have three things to talk with you about. The first being how in the world did you ever become such a fan of the Oakland Raiders? The Raiders may be a good team, but they're also considered the bad boys in the NFL. I'd have thought you'd go for ... shall we say, a more conventional team."

"I know you didn't come over here on your day off to discuss football, Detective. You said that you wanted to talk with me before I see Steven tomorrow. So let's talk about that, shall we? Because I really don't have anything else to say to you."

So much for breaking her down. If possible, she was sitting even more rigidly than before. Nick was tempted to reach over and shake her, but instead he drilled her with a look of exasperation.

"Okay. You don't want to talk about football, then let's talk about Miguel Bautista." Not surprisingly, Rachel flinched when he referred to Bautista. "We didn't get a chance to ask you about him yesterday." Rachel took a sip of coffee. "You should know that Bautista is on the DEA and FBI watch list, and I'd like to ask you a few questions about him."

It didn't get past Rachel that Nick had instantly turned into the man of yesterday. He had on what she was starting to think of as his cop face, and for a brief second she was sorry she'd refused to talk about football.

"Is that really necessary? I can't stand to even think about that man, much less talk about him."

"It's important, Rachel. Any information we can pass on will only help the authorities grab the bastard. Bautista is a known drug dealer and he's wanted for questioning in an attempted murder of a federal deputy DA."

Rachel had to shake off the fear she felt ripple through her. "What exactly do you want to know?" Her tone was a little less defensive, which he figured was a step in the right direction.

"How about your overall impression of the guy? Let's start with that." Nick took a small notepad and a pen out of his shirt pocket. He was all business.

"That's easy, because I remember my first impression very clearly. Mr. Bautista made me so uncomfortable that I felt my skin crawl when I was around him. He was quite menacing to look at and he had the coldest eyes I've ever seen. He's not a big man, maybe five-foot-eight or five-foot-nine. He speaks perfect English, and he told me that he was actually born in the U.S. but prefers to live in Mexico. I know this may sound rather dramatic, but he had a sense of evil about him. And he wouldn't take no for an answer."

Nick had been jotting down notes, but looked up sharply at her last comment. "What do you mean he wouldn't take no for an answer?"

"Well ..." Rachel had to pause because suddenly she felt a little nervous. She just knew that Nick wasn't going to like what she had to say, but she said it anyway. "Do you remember that I told you that I barely made it back aboard ship that day because the client lived further out of town than what I expected?"

Nick merely nodded.

"Umm ... well, that was only part of the reason why I was so late in returning. You see, when I arrived at Bautista's house, it was almost 12:30, so he invited me to stay for lunch. I turned down his invitation and asked to be brought right back to the ship. Only .... only he wouldn't take no for an answer and he insisted that I stay for lunch. He made it very clear to me that refusing his invitation was considered rude."

Nick's eyes turned a dangerous shade of green.

"Anyway, to tell you the truth, I was more than a little scared. His eyes and his touch told me clearly that I was not going anywhere until he was good and ready to let me go. I can still recall how awful it felt when he touched me."

"His touch? Bautista touched you? That son of a bitch laid his hands on you?" Nick's voice was as dangerous as the look in his eyes.

"Calm down, Nicholas. Bautista just put his hand on my arm to lead me outside to the patio. But even that slight touch held somewhat of a warning and I couldn't stand the feel of his hand against my skin. I can't really explain it because all he did was take my arm, but I felt threatened all the same."

Nick wondered briefly if she realized that for the second time she had called him by his first name, and he doubted that she realized she did.

"Why in the hell didn't you tell me this at the time?"

"You're kidding. Right?"

Nick got up from the couch and started pacing. The thought of that bastard laying a hand on Rachel made him half-crazy.

"I wish you had told me. I hate the thought of you being so scared and all alone with someone like Miguel Bautista. God, Rachel, you must still have been shaken up when you got back aboard ship. We could have talked about it. Damn it, I knew that I shouldn't have let you go there without me."

Rachel watched and let him pace, trying to determine whether or not she should respond to him honestly. Deciding that she really had nothing to lose, she told him the truth — which she was pretty sure he didn't really want to hear.

"I didn't tell you any of this at the time because I knew you'd go nuts, and I didn't want to ruin our last night together. The hours we had left were too precious to waste, Nick. I wanted to be your sole focus on our last night together. I wanted you thinking only about me."

Nick stopped dead in his tracks and looked over at Rachel. He immediately noticed two things. One, that everything about her seemed to have softened, and two, she had spoken the truth. A truth that made him a little sick to his stomach, but the absolute truth all the same. Nick's eyes took on a gentle look as he digested what she had just said. And he knew that he wasn't ready to go there yet, so he kept the conversation focused on Bautista. And he kept pacing.

"What else can you tell me, Rachel? Can you describe his house?"

She felt a pang of disappointment that he passed on making any sort of comment about their last night together. For some crazy reason, she really wanted to hear him say that he had felt the same way about their last night together. But he didn't and she realized that she should've known better. *But then again,* she thought to herself, *what had I really expected?*

"I remember thinking that his place was more like a fortress than a home. It was large, secluded, and probably well-protected."

Nick finally stopped pacing. "Why do you say it was probably well-protected?"

Rachel shifted on the couch, tucking one leg up under the other. "It was just a feeling I had. I didn't actually see guards or anything like that. But there was just something about the place that made you feel as if someone with a gun could step out of the shadows at any moment."

"How much of the house did you see?"

"Not much. I was escorted from the … will you please stop pacing? You're making me dizzy."

Nick stopped and turned toward Rachel. He waited and she waited. And he realized that she was not going to say another word until he sat down. Which he finally did — almost unwillingly.

"Sorry. It's a bad habit of mine. I seem to think better when I'm moving around."

"Well, I can hardly think at all with you traipsing back and forth."

"Yeah," Nick responded with a hint of a smile. "It drives my partner crazy too. He's always hammering at me to sit down."

"Which detective is your partner?" she asked without thinking. "It wasn't clear to me yesterday."

Nick put his pen and notepad on the table and poured himself another cup of coffee.

"Ben Morris and I've been partners since I came to the LAPD two years ago. Detective Jensen, the other cop who was in the room, is part of the team assigned to your sister's case."

Rachel's mind flashed back and she could easily pick out Ben as Nick's partner. Thinking back, there seemed to be a silent communication between the two men, a communication that was obvious to her now. She started to ask Nick more about his relationship with his partner and then stopped herself. Rachel didn't want to know anything more about Nicholas Fallen on a personal level. She knew that he was a cop, and she knew that he was a very good liar, which was all she needed to know. Of course, she also knew that he had a great sense of humor and that he was an incredible lover, but both those things she pushed right out of her mind.

"As I was saying, I didn't get to see any rooms in the house except one. We ate lunch out on the back patio, which was located right off the large entryway. After lunch, I waited in a room that could be considered a den. And then I went straight out the front door into the car waiting to take me back to the ship."

"You said you didn't see any guards. But how about other people? Who else did you see while you were there?"

"I'm afraid I can't be much help there either, because besides Bautista, I saw only three other people. The driver, the man who let me into the house, and a man who served us lunch. I had no idea Bautista was a criminal, so I wasn't paying a whole lot of attention. All I knew was that I didn't like being around him, and that I wanted to get back to you."

Nick stopped writing and lifted his brow when she made that statement. So she quickly added, "I mean that I wanted to get back aboard the ship where I could feel safe."

Nick started to say something, but changed his mind.

"So are we finished here? There's really not anything more I can add."

Nick sensed that she was almost ready to flee. And he wasn't ready for that yet. "I just have two more questions. How about the driver? What did you two talk about? And do you think you could give us any idea at all where Bautista's place is located?"

Rachel shook her head in response to both questions, and Nick noticed how a few strands of hair escaped from her ponytail.

"The driver didn't speak English and I don't speak a lick of Spanish. So there was no conversation between us. And the house was located so far out of town that I completely lost my sense of direction. I'm sorry, but I haven't a clue where his house is located. The only thing I remember that may be of any help is that as we got closer to his place, we took a narrow, steep, curvy road. But that road only lasted for about five miles. Other than that, the landscape all looked the same. I'm sorry, I wish I had paid more attention."

"Don't be sorry. You had no reason to try to remember where you'd been. I'll give the FBI this information anyway, because you never know what will help."

"Then we're finished?" As she asked the question, she got to her feet.

Nick knew that she wanted to get rid of him and he really couldn't blame her. But he had come over today because he wanted to talk to her about two things — only one of which was Miguel Bautista. He still had one more subject to broach with her. The one subject that was the real reason why he was here.

"Can you give me five more minutes? There's something else I need to talk with you about."

He could tell she wanted to say no. He could also tell that she was trying to figure out what it might be that he wanted to talk about. So as she stood, looking a little uncertain, Nick took the opportunity to take advantage of her hesitancy.

"Just five more minutes and then I'll go."

Rachel's eyes met the determined look in Nick's and she knew it would do her no good to try to put off whatever it was he wanted to say. So with a faked look of indifference, she sat back down.

"Okay. You've got five minutes. Starting now."

Nick laughed, which caused her to immediately regret not throwing him out on his sexy ass. "Boy, you won't give an inch, will you?"

"You're wasting your five minutes, Detective Fallen."

In a blink, Rachel watched all laughter disappear from Nick's expressive eyes. He shifted his position on the couch so that he was looking directly at her, and then he let his eyes search her face for a few seconds.

"Will you promise to hear me out?"

Her stomach took a nose dive because this couldn't possibly be anything good, but she agreed with a slight nod of her head. And again Nick's eyes roamed over her lovely face.

"Listen, Rachel." Surprisingly, Nick had to clear his throat. "I want … no, I need to talk to you about what happened between us."

This was going to be even worse than what she'd expected. But Rachel had promised that she would hear him out, so she sat without drawing in a breath.

"I'm not going to sit here and give you a bunch of excuses about my past behavior. I stepped over the line with you and nothing I can say will justify that. I don't even expect you to forgive me. But I do need for you to be able to trust in me again, if that's at all possible."

Rachel started to speak, but Nick held up his hand to stop her. "I wish you'd let me finish." He waited for a heartbeat and when she said nothing, he continued. "I knew going into this investigation that I'd be lying to you right off the bat. We all did. And even though none of us liked that idea, we all felt it was necessary." Nick let his words sink in and he watched her for any sort of reaction to his words. When there was none he went on. "We thought we had a pretty good handle on what Steven was up to, but we hadn't a clue if you were knowingly involved in his side business, or if he was using you as a pawn, like we believe he used your sister. None of us on this case felt comfortable with the fact that you are a college professor who took a leave of absence to take on the job as errand girl for your brother-in-law. So we …. I mean, so I was assigned to get to know you and to see if I could flush things out. So I lied to you, Rachel. I lied to you about everything. Everything that is, except for one very important matter."

"Please, Nick. I don't …"

"I know that it won't make any difference to you now, but I still need to say this. I need you to understand and to believe me when I tell you that I never lied about wanting to be with you. Making love to you was never a part of this job. I was with you because I wanted you, and I thought I could separate being a cop from all the other feelings I was having about you. It was wrong, Rachel, and all I can say is that I'm sorry. I'm sorry that I let lust and desire rule out over what should have been good judgment. I'm sorry that you feel cheated and betrayed by me. And most of all, I'm sorry if I hurt you."

Nick ended on a deep breath. And for several long minutes, Rachel couldn't think of anything to say. But as the silence between them stretched on and on, she cleared her throat and tried not to look away from Nick's steady gaze.

"You didn't hurt me, Nick. You disappointed me, but you didn't hurt me." She lied because she couldn't bear for him to know the truth — that he had quite thoroughly broken her heart. "I was so caught off guard yesterday by what Detective Morris was saying about Steven, that I couldn't even think straight when you walked through that door and I realized that you were a cop. Everything was just too much for me to grasp. Steven's illegal operation, his possible involvement in Cynthia's death, and you not being who I thought you were. It was all just too much."

Nick waited, suspecting that she wasn't finished.

"I will not apologize to you for my behavior yester-day. I will not even apologize to you for slapping you, even though I've had some time to think things through a little more clearly. I can't ever remember being as upset with anyone as I was with you. But having said that, I'm also not as irrational as I might have seemed yesterday. I'm smart enough to sort through everything you and the other detectives told me, and to realize that you lied to me so that you could catch a killer. My sister's killer. And that I do understand. But as for the rest of what happened between us, that I'm not sure I'll ever understand."

"I'm not very good at having this sort of conversation, so I'm not sure what else to say, Rachel. Except that I meant it when I said I never set out to hurt or to disappoint you."

Rachel closed her eyes for a brief second and willed herself to be as honest with him as she could. "I believe that you never intended to hurt me, Nick. I really do. But what I may never be able to understand is how you could make love to me the way you did, when you knew that I was a case you were work-ing on. How you could make love to me so convincingly one minute, and then lie to me the next. I truly understand why you had to lie, but I'm not sure I'll ever understand how you could do both."

Nick thought for a second that he actually preferred the irrational Rachel. He was pretty good on fending off her anger, but this calm, logical Rachel was harder to deal with. Espe-cially since what she was saying was right on the mark.

"No one knows better than me that I was wrong to try to mix business with pleasure. At the time I didn't stop to think about any of the consequences. If it's any consolation, my lieu-tenant almost suspended me over my lack of judgment, and truth be told, I probably deserved the suspension."

"Your lieutenant knows that we slept together?" He could tell she was appalled by that possibility.

"It's hard to keep secrets when we're working as closely as we do on a case." He wasn't about to tell her about the one-way mirror. "You were pretty pissed at me yesterday, and it didn't take long for everyone to put two and two together."

Rachel could feel herself starting to blush. "I'm not sure how I'm ever going to be able face your partner Ben and Detective Jensen again. I can only imagine what they must think of me. And I don't ever want to meet your lieutenant."

She looked so stricken that Nick had the urge to reach out and take her in his arms. He knew he couldn't do that, but he had the urge all the same. So the best he could do was to reach out and lay his hand on her arm. And he was surprised when she didn't try to pull away.

"You don't need to be embarrassed over this at all, Rachel. I can promise you that no one thinks anything other than that I crossed the line. As a matter of fact," he added when she didn't look convinced, "Lou thinks you're one hell of a woman. And that is a direct quote."

Rachel felt as though she wanted a hole to open up in the floor so that she could disappear. Regardless of what he said, she was just so embarrassed.

"I think I was better off when I was so angry at you that I couldn't see straight. Anger has a way of overshadowing all my other emotions, and even though you don't think I need to be embarrassed, I am."

"Why?" he asked gently, and was immediately sorry that he did, because the answer was obvious.

"We had sex after knowing each other for just a few days. That may be an everyday experience for you, Nick, but not for me. I've never had a fling before, and you were it. But even though I know that's totally out of character for me, your work colleagues don't know that about me. They must all think I'm just an easy …. well, you know, they must just think I'm easy."

"What happened between us is personal, Rachel, and is no one's business but ours. No one on this case will judge you, I can promise you that. I can also promise that it won't affect what we have to do now to get your sister's killer. I know that, the other detectives know that, and my boss knows that. Now the only thing left is for you to believe it."

She wanted to believe it — she really did. So she made herself dismiss the fact that Nick didn't deny that causal sex was routine for him, which was really bothering her, and forced herself not to care what everyone else might think.

"You're right. What happened between you and me didn't involve anyone else. We were two single, consenting adults who were sexually attracted to one another. So we acted on that attraction. We had lots of fun and great sex. No big deal. Right?"

Nick knew that she was trying to convince herself as much as she was trying to convince him. And he felt a stab of guilt. He couldn't deny that he had always taken sex less seriously than he should. Sure, he loved women and he loved the act of sex, but the emotional strings were never very tight. Because he made sure of that. He loved women and he loved sex, but he never let himself fall in love with anyone. He had been there once, and it had ended in a bad divorce. Love was not for him, and he knew that it never would be. And since he didn't want to lie to Rachel any longer, and he didn't want to lead her on any more than he already did, he told her what he knew to be the truth.

"We were terrific together, Rachel, but I think we both know that we can't go back in time and start again on a romantic level. I think I've known all along that you would never be completely comfortable with a casual affair, and I can't give any woman more than that. I don't want all the things that come with a committed relationship. I'm no good at that. But if anything good can come out of this, other than solving your sister's murder, maybe we can go forward as friends."

Rachel felt her heart crack, just a little. But she was absolutely determined not to give herself away.

"Do you think that's possible?" she asked very quietly.

Nick wasn't exactly sure what she was asking. Was she asking if it was possible for them to really not step into another romantic relationship, or was she asking if it was possible for them to become friends? He decided to respond to the latter possibility.

"I would like to be your friend, Rachel. And yes, I think it's possible. But for us to even get to that point, you have to be able to trust me again."

Rachel felt saddened by his words and tried to convince herself that all she really wanted from him was friendship. She believed that if she told herself that often enough, she might actually start to believe it.

"I'm not sure what it will take for us to be friends. There's still a part of me that is pretty mad at you, and I'm not willing to let go of that yet. But for the next week or so, while we are forced to work together, I'm willing to give it a try."

Nick felt relief wash over him. "That's all I can ask. Well, except for one other thing."

Rachel suddenly felt completely drained. Her sleepless night, and the emotional tug-of-war with Nick seemed to be catching up with here. She just couldn't deal with him any longer.

"Can this one other thing wait? My mind is starting to shut down. I don't think I slept more than three hours last night, and the night before that, you hardly let me sleep at all. I'm exhausted Nick, so can we please call it a day?"

Nick's mind immediately flashed back to the night before last. Rachel was right when she said he had not let her get much sleep, but at the time, neither of them seemed to mind. They were both too busy finding new ways to please each other, and sleep had just not been much of a priority. But now, he noticed that Rachel did look as tired as she said. He knew he should just get up and go, but he wasn't quite ready to leave. There was one other matter that had to be settled between them.

"I'll leave in a second so you can get some rest. But I need to be absolutely certain that we have an understanding about working together."

She threw him a drowsy look, and tried to stifle a yawn. All she wanted to do was go and lie down, but instead she sat and waited for him to finish his thought.

"Hopefully, during this next week, you and I will be taking off to deliver your next package of dirty papers. Between Alex, Ben, Lou, the FBI, and myself, everything should be covered. But no matter how well we plan, Rachel, there is always the possibility that something could go wrong. And that's where I need to ask you to trust me. On this assignment, you need to do exactly as I say, when I say it, without questions or any argument. Do you think you can do that?"

"I'm not very good at taking direction without asking questions. You've probably figured that out about me. But I can try."

Her response was exactly why Nick had felt that he needed to bring the subject up at all.

"That's what I was afraid of. Trying is not good enough. I can only keep you safe if you do precisely what you're told. If things go to hell, I won't have the time or the luxury of explaining anything to you. I need to be able to rely on you to do as I say without any, and I mean without any, hesitation. This will involve trusting me, Rachel, and I need to know that you can do that. At least during this assignment."

There, he had laid things on the line. If she couldn't give him 100 percent assurance that she would act without question, he would call this whole thing off.

"It's that important?"

"Yes. It's that important." He could have added that *she* was that important, but didn't.

"Okay, Nicholas, I'll do whatever you say, whenever you say it. And I won't give you any sort of trouble. But," she added for good measure, "don't think for a second that I'm going to like it. I'll do it, but I refuse to like it."

"Is that a promise?"

"Yes," she replied with a sigh. "It's a promise."

"Good." He sent a real smile Rachel's way and for a second, she felt the urge to slap him like she had yesterday. His smile was just too much for her heart to take in, and the look in his eyes was just too knowing. And because she had little or no defense against him, she wanted to slap the smile right off his face. Instead, she got up from the couch and headed for the front door.

"You need to leave and I need to get some rest." Her tone of voice gave him no choice in the matter.

Nick got up and followed her. She opened the door, and stepped aside to let him out. But he didn't move.

"Make me one other promise, will you?"

"One promise a day is enough." Even as worn out as she was, she refused to give in to him. But Nick ignored that warning.

"Promise me that you'll eat something tonight and go to bed early. You look pretty wiped out."

She looked up at him with tired eyes, and he felt his fingers flex at his side with the need to reach out and touch her.

"I'm a big girl, Detective Fallen. I can take care of myself without you having to worry about me. Believe it or not, I've managed just fine for years now."

"Well, like it or not, I do worry about you, Rachel."

Now where in the hell had that come from? he asked himself as he saw a look of surprise flash across her face. But the surprise passed so quickly, to be replaced by a look of caution.

"If it will get you to leave, I'll promise you anything." She replaced her surprise with words that she hoped would get him out the door.

Nick knew it was time to go. He had said all he came to say today, and much more. He had probably outstayed his welcome and he felt thankful that she hadn't thrown him out earlier. So before she pushed him out onto the front steps and slammed the door in his face, he needed to go. But as he looked down at Rachel, he felt a real reluctance to leave. He wanted to close the door, pick her up, carry her over to the couch, and lie down with her. He wanted to wrap her in his arms, and feel her soft body up against his. And as he thought of snuggling up together on the couch, with her bottom tucked up against the fly of his jeans, he felt a knot of desire crash into him. A pure, unadulterated sexual desire that he didn't want to feel, accept, or deal with. So, without saying another word, Nick reached out and lightly touched her cheek. But just for a second — a split second.

"Call me as soon as you know something. You have my cell number."

"I'll call," was all she could manage, as he dropped his hand. And Rachel stood at the door, watching as Nick walked down her driveway to his sweet, little sports car parked at her curb. And without even glancing in her direction, he got behind the wheel, started the engine, and put in a Janis Joplin CD. With the top down on his car, and with the sun just beginning to set, Nick let the wind blow through his hair, and he felt the sorrow of the music deep in his soul.

CHAPTER ELEVEN

"I'm sorry if I seem a little shocked, Rachel, but it's not like you to fall head over heals for anyone in ... what was it ... five days?"

Rachel squirmed in her chair, more uncomfortable than she thought possible.

"I know it's not like me, Steven, but if you'd meet Nick, I think you'd probably understand. He's everything I've ever looked for in a man, and he feels the same way about me. He needs to be back in San Francisco next week, so I don't want to go anywhere this week without him."

"What does he do in San Francisco?" Steven had to make this look good, so he asked the question.

"He's an attorney in his father's firm. They practice corporate law, and his father is the senior partner." It was easy for Rachel to tell this particular lie, because just a couple of days ago, this is what she believed Nick did for a living.

"I see."

When Steven didn't offer anything further, Rachel filled in some more of the blanks.

"Nick was actually expected back in the office today, but he called and extended his vacation for another week. He did this just for me, Steven, and now I want to do something for him. I don't think I'm asking too terribly much."

"But you know, Rachel, that a large part of what makes our service so valuable is that we guarantee personal delivery and confidentiality. Most of our clients are quite wealthy, and privacy is vitally important to them. And it's only one day. You could go and make the delivery for me and come back the same day."

This conversation was going pretty much as Rachel had expected, so she was prepared. She had rehearsed her response on and off all last night, until she had finally drifted off into another night of restless sleep.

"I don't want to put your business relationship in jeopardy, Steven, but please try to see things my way. Nick and I only have this week to be together before he heads back home. With both our schedules being so busy, it's hard to tell when I'll get to see him again. I'm sure if you explained the situation to your client, he will be reasonable and allow me to bring Nick along."

Even to her own ears she sounded fairly convincing. Which was pretty astonishing, given the fact that she was such a lousy liar.

Steven sat back in his chair and grinned at Rachel. A grin that belied what he was really thinking.

"Okay, my dear. Far be it from me to ruin your love life. And after all, you have been good enough to take a leave and help me out this summer. So I'll speak with Mr. Bautista and since he's already met you, I'm sure there'll be no problem if you bring your boyfriend along."

Rachel forced herself not to fidget in her chair. "Mr. Bautista? I'm going back to Miguel Bautista's?"

A look that could have been described as sinister flashed through Steven's eyes. But the look was so brief that Rachel thought she might have imagined it.

"Looks like you need to pay another quick visit to Mr. Bautista, my dear. He contacted me first thing this morning. He needs to make an unexpected trip out of the country and he'll need to file for a visa right away. I'm working on his visa application right now."

Rachel paled at the thought of having to lay eyes on Miguel Bautista again. She could vividly picture his cold, bottomless eyes and she shivered at the thought of how his hand had felt against her skin. And even though she hated to admit it, she was thankful that Nick would be going along on this trip. Because there was absolutely no way she would agree to go off alone to Miguel Bautista's secluded home. Especially now since she knew that he was wanted for questioning by both the DEA and the FBI.

"So when do you want me to go?" She surprised herself at how calmly she asked the question.

"Mr. Bautista's expecting you on Thursday. I'll make arrangements for you to fly to San Diego, and he'll have a driver meet you at the airport. If you want, you can fly home that same day. Or," he added, "you and your boyfriend might want to spend the night in Mexico together."

Rachel ran her hands up and down the front of her pants, more nervous than she wanted to let on.

"Why don't I take care of making our flight reservations this time? I'm not sure what Nick will want to do. I'll let you know once we decide, and then you can notify Mr. Bautista of our flight plans." She felt nauseated at the thought of seeing Bautista again.

"That should work."

Steven got up, anxious to end this little farce of a meeting. He wanted to get rid of Rachel so that he could get in touch with Bautista. Now that she had shown him her true colors, he was actually anticipating her demise. And it pleased him immensely that she would die at the bottom of a ravine with her cop lover. To Steven's way of thinking, Rachel and Nick were getting no less than what they both deserved.

"Let me know what your plans are as soon as you can, Rachel, so I can firm things up on this end."

Rachel stood up, noticing that the palms of her hands were still damp. But she didn't want to give herself away, so she resisted the urge to wipe them again against her pant legs.

"I think I'll take a late lunch, Steven, if you don't mind?" She was eager to get away so that she could call Nick.

"Sure. Go ahead. It's been quiet all day. Take as long as you like."

Rachel didn't wait. She walked out of Steven's office as quickly as she could, making sure that she didn't draw undue attention to herself. With a smile to the woman she still didn't know was an undercover cop working for Alex Kendall, she picked up her purse and headed out the door.

Once outside, Rachel drew in a long, deep breath. *How could Nick have lied to me with so much ease?* She asked herself. And she felt a wave of depression wash over her. Because what she had just done with Steven went against everything she believed in. She had looked him right in the eye and she had lied. And she had done it without any remorse — guilt for lying yes, but remorse, none at all.

Rachel got behind the wheel of her reliable Honda Accord, started the engine, and pulled out into L.A. traffic. As she began driving, she had no idea where she was headed. Even though it made no sense at all, she felt that she needed to get far way from the office before she dialed Nick's cell phone. Plus she needed to drive for a while in order to calm her nerves. So she kept on driving, trying not to think about how her life seemed to be made up of nothing but lies. Steven had obviously lied to her forever, Nick had knowingly lied to her, and now every aspect of her life seemed caught up in a web of lies.

Rachel drove for close to fifteen minutes, and before she even realized it, she pulled into the parking lot of the USC campus. She always loved the campus, and no matter how busy or how crazy her days were, she always felt at peace here. So she allowed herself the luxury of sitting for a few minutes, looking out over the campus that would soon be her home again. She missed teaching very much, and suddenly she regretted her decision to give up teaching summer school to help out Steven.

Thinking of Steven brought Rachel right back to the present, and reminded her that she had to get in touch with Nick and fill him in. So she grabbed her purse, reached in for her cell phone, and dialed the number he had given her. It rang three times before he picked up.

"Detective Fallen."

Her heart skipped a beat at the mere sound of his voice. God help her, that she could be so affected just by his voice on the other end of the line.

"Nick, it's Rachel." She got out of the car because she needed a gulp of fresh air.

"Did you talk with Steven?" He was all business. There wasn't so much as a *How are you?*

"It sounds like I caught you at a bad time."

There was a brief pause before Nick responded. "Yeah, actually you did. I'm at another crime scene right now."

Being at another crime scene could only mean one thing in Nick's world — that another murder had just taken place.

"Oh my God, Nick. I'm so sorry."

Rachel couldn't even begin to imagine a job like Nick's. How he could deal with murder day in and day out, and keep his sanity, was something she couldn't quite comprehend. Respect yes, but comprehend, no way.

"Listen. We don't need to get into this now. So why don't I call you later? Or do you want to call me back when you have a chance? I can fill you in on my conversation with Steven anytime."

Rachel could hear lots of commotion in the background.

"I should finish up here in a couple of hours, Rachel. I'll need to go back to the station for a while, but how about I call you at … hold on a second, will you?" Rachel didn't have a choice. "Will someone please check on how the witness is doing? And don't let the M.E. get away, I want to talk to him myself. And I need someone to move all these spectators back behind the yellow tape. And I need it done now!"

Rachel could hear him yell out his orders, even though she could tell he had placed his hand over the phone.

"Sorry. Things are a little hectic at the moment. Tell you what, I'll come by your place as soon as I can manage to get away. I should be able to get there by seven. We can talk then."

Rachel could tell that he was in a hurry to hang up. "Okay, Nick. That'll be fine."

"Oh, and Rachel, don't eat dinner. I'll pick something up for us on my way over.

With that, the line went dead — before Rachel even had a chance to tell him not to bother.

Rachel opened her door at seven thirty to find Nick standing on her doorstep with Chinese takeout in one hand, and a duffel bag slung over his shoulder. He looked more than a little tired, and her heart went out to him. His hair was so attractively messed up, it looked as if he had run his fingers though it a hundred times during the day — which she suspected might actually be the case. He wore a sport coat over a pale blue shirt, and she noticed that he had already pulled out the knot in his tie, because it now hung loosely around his neck. His eyes were guarded and weary.

Because Rachel suddenly found it hard to take in the man standing before her, she just stepped aside and said nothing as he walked in. Nick nodded his thanks as she closed the door behind him. He let his duffel slip from his shoulder, dumping it on the floor of her small entry.

"Do you like Chinese?" he asked before she had a chance to question him about the duffel bag.

"I love Chinese."

Nick held up the bag of food and Rachel took it from him, accidentally brushing her fingers against his. Even that slight touch was like a shockwave crashing through her, causing her pulse to kick up a notch. Embarrassed that Nick could still affect her in such a way, Rachel avoided looking into his eyes and instead headed straight for the kitchen.

"Take off your jacket and get comfortable, Nick. We'll eat in the kitchen."

Rachel fled and Nick shrugged out of his jacket, draping it over the back of the couch, along with his tie. He followed closely behind her, wondering what was making her so nervous. She seemed a little jumpy to him, and he hoped that it wasn't over her conversation with her slimeball brother-in-law. Although he guessed that was probably the case, since he figured she more than likely spent all morning dreading her encounter with Steven.

Rachel could feel Nick standing behind her in the kitchen, and against her will, she drew in his wonderful, masculine scent. She knew it was silly, but for a moment she closed her eyes, imaging how nice it would be to be able to give in to temptation and lean back against him. It would be so easy for her to take one small step back, and she had to resist the urge to do so. So instead of giving in, Rachel set the bag of food on the counter and reached up to get two plates out of the cupboard.

"Oh no you don't." Nick's hand on her arm stopped her in the act. "That's not the way to eat Chinese takeout."

Nick reached over, grabbed the bag, and took it over to the kitchen table. He removed four little, white containers and two sets of wooden chopsticks.

"Now here's how you eat Chinese takeout." He picked up one set of the chopsticks and extended them toward Rachel.

And before she could stop herself, she smiled. Because even though Nick looked tired, he also looked adorable standing there in her tiny kitchen with chopsticks in one hand and a devilish grin in his eyes. He winked, and she laughed softy, thinking that he really had a way of making her completely forget how mad she was at him just two days ago.

"Do you want a glass of wine or would you prefer a beer?"

"Well, you see Rachel, that's another thing about Chinese takeout. You gotta have a beer with it. Beer just goes down a whole lot better than wine when you're eating out of a carton."

It took all of Rachel's willpower not to fall under Nick's spell. She felt so off-balance that she had to mentally remind herself that the only thing Nick Fallen could give her was a shattered heart. He had made it eminently clear where he stood on committed, long-term relationships. He wasn't in the market for one — pure and simple. And no matter how badly she might want to change his mind, she just knew that she wouldn't be able to. He would be out of her life forever once this case was over, and no amount of wishing otherwise would change that. So with that reminder firmly planted in her mind, Rachel turned away from Nick and took two bottles of beer out of the fridge.

"I suppose drinking out of a glass would also spoil the whole Chinese takeout thing?" she asked, trying to match his mood.

"You bet it would."

Nick reached over, took both cold bottles out of her hands, and twisted off the caps. He set both bottles on the table and pulled out a chair for Rachel, waiting for her to come and sit down. Even after such a long day, and as worn out as he probably was, she noted that he didn't forget his good manners. Which, of course, just added to his disarming charm.

Rachel took the chair he offered, picked up one of the cold beers, and took a long swallow. She needed something cool and wet to soothe her parched throat.

"That's my girl," was Nick's only comment as he tilted his own bottle and took a nice, long drink.

Nick and Rachel ate in silence, passing the white containers of food back and forth between them. It was a surprisingly relaxed and rather intimate time. It didn't matter that they were sitting in a brightly lit kitchen, because there was just something incredibly personal about sharing food out of a carton. Personal, sweet, and a lot of fun.

Nick had purposely not pursued any conversation while they ate, wanting to wait for Rachel to unwind before he broached the subject of Steven. When he first arrived, he had sensed that she seemed a little anxious, and he wanted her to take her time and not feel pressured. They were just beginning to get back on the right footing, and he needed to be careful not to blow things. So he sat quietly, sipped at his beer, and watched her from across the table.

"You're staring."

That was the absolute last thing he had expected her to say.

"Yeah, well it's kinda hard not to, Rachel. No matter how you feel about me now, I still think you're one of the most beautiful women I've ever seen."

That was the absolute last thing she had expected him to say. And because those words made her nervous, and because she didn't want to go there with him, she blurted out the first thing that came to her mind.

"I wish you didn't have to wear your shoulder holster. It makes me uncomfortable. Can't you take it off?"

The abrupt change of subject should have surprised him, but it didn't. Knowing Rachel, she was just going to sit there and ignore his comment that he still thought she was beautiful. Which was fine with him, because he probably shouldn't have said it in the first place.

"I'm still on duty. I officially go off the clock at nine. I'm already breaking the rules by having this beer, so I'd better keep the holster in place."

"You're good at that, aren't you?"

He was pretty sure he knew what she meant, but he asked her anyway.

"Good at what?"

"Breaking the rules."

Nick didn't respond. Instead he scraped back his chair and gathered up the nearly empty containers. He cleared the table in record time, and then he came back and sat down. But this time he didn't sit down across the table from Rachel. This time he pulled up a chair and sat down right in front of her.

"The rules are actually pretty simple. I'm here and I'm going to do everything I can to keep you safe. Lou is in place keeping his eye on Steven, but until your brother-in-law is behind bars, I can't afford to let my guard down. And that means my gun stays right by my side. I'm sorry if that makes you uncomfortable, but that's the way it is."

Everything about him told her that he would not budge on this issue.

"You didn't answer my question."

"And I don't intend to."

Rachel didn't like his response one little bit, so she decided she couldn't quite let the subject drop.

"It's a fairly simple question, Nick. And like Detective Morris said to me the other day, a yes or no answer will suffice. So let's try it again, shall we? Do you ever follow the rules, or do you always make up your own as you go along?"

For Christ's sake, he thought to himself, *she is every bit as stubborn as I am.*

"I'll tell you this much, Rachel, but I'm only going to say it one time. I have as much respect for the rules as the next guy. But you need to know that I won't think twice about breaking every damn rule in the book if it means keeping you out of harm's way. This case has been handed over to me and I'm in charge. That means we do things my way, with or without the benefit of any rules."

She immediately felt as though she had just been put in her place and she wasn't sure how to react. Pressing him any further on this ridiculous subject would get them nowhere, and she would be doing it just to push his buttons. And what would she accomplish anyway? Nothing. Absolutely nothing. So with as much grace as she could muster, she grabbed her bottle of beer, sent him a quelling look, got up and headed into the living room.

Nick followed her, trying not to laugh. He didn't think she'd appreciate it. She was trying to give him the impression that she was fed up with the conversation and put out by his response, but he knew better. He was getting to know her better and better the more time he spent with her, and he figured that if she really was put out, she would make absolutely certain he was aware of it. So swallowing back his laughter, he went into the living room and sat down on the chair across from Rachel, who was sitting on the couch.

"Okay, Professor. You don't want to talk anymore about my ability to follow the rules, so how about you tell me what you and Steven talked about today?"

That did it. She was trapped. She had walked out on one conversation she didn't like, only to find herself having to face an even more unpleasant topic.

"Do we have to?"

Nick didn't even bother to answer her. He just threw her a look that said *What do you think?*

Rachel snuggled into the corner of the couch, and tucked both legs under her, trying to get comfortable. She picked up a small accent pillow, fluffed it, and put it back in place. Under Nick's very watchful eye, she then clasped her hands together and laid them in her lap. Still not comfortable, she wiggled around a little more.

"Okay, enough." Nick's deep voice stopped her in mid-wiggle. "Stop stalling, Rachel. We need to talk about Steven, and if you're finished trying to find the perfect spot for your sexy little bottom, can we please get started?"

Rachel had the immature but overwhelming urge to stick her tongue out at him. Instead, she sat completely still and sent him look that was meant to kill.

Nick ran his hand down his face, more tired than he wanted to admit. But they still needed to get this over with, so he lifted his head and took a deep, sobering breath.

"Why don't you start from the beginning?"

"Do you want me to tell you everything about my day from the time I got up, or just my conversation with Steven?"

"Just your conversation with Steven."

"What do you want to know exactly?"

"I want to know everything. Don't leave anything out."

Rachel didn't want to rehash the entire episode with Steven, so she thought she might move things along by asking Nick to be a little more specific.

"Well, do you think we could approach this a little differently? How about you ask me questions, and I'll answer them. You're a detective, so you must do that all the time when you interrogate people. So go ahead, Nick, interrogate me."

Now the breath that Nick took was full of frustration. She was being purposely obtuse, and he could throttle her. But he needed answers, so he decided to play it her way — at least for a while.

"Okay, Rachel, I'll ask, you answer. First, does Steven have an assignment for you this week?"

"Yes."

He waited for her to elaborate, and when she didn't, he went on. "Second, did you tell him about me?"

"Yes."

Again Nick waited and again she said nothing more. "Third, did he buy off on our sudden … umm … our sudden love affair?"

"Yes."

"Fourth, did you convince him that you needed to take me along with you?"

"Yes."

"Fifth, did you … dammit Rachel, talk to me. I need more than one-word answers from you and you know it."

Nick was getting angrier by the second. She was playing with him and he didn't like it. The games were now over as far as he was concerned, and he decided to tell her so.

"Question and answer time is over, sweetheart, so start talking. And start from the beginning. I need to know exactly what you said to your brother-in-law and what he said to you. And if you think you can, I want you to try to describe his body language to me. Anything you can think of that was different about him will help."

For the second time in minutes, Rachel was trapped. And she decided that it was time to give in. This wasn't a game, this was serious business and she needed to start treating it that way. So with a little smile of apology, she shifted around on the couch one final time, and then she started to talk.

Rachel talked and Nick listened. Like the day before, he took a little notepad out of his shirt pocket and started taking notes. Every now and then, he would look up from his notepad and watch Rachel with his penetrating eyes, but other than that, he just let her talk. She explained to him how she had convinced Steven to let him go along, and how she needed to make their flight reservations for a trip to San Diego on Thursday. Once Rachel got started, she told Nick every word of their conversation. She left nothing out. And after twenty minutes, he finally put his notepad down.

"Good job, Rachel. I know this wasn't easy for you, but you did everything we needed you to do."

Rachel didn't respond to Nick's compliment. Instead she got up, turned on the lamp by the table next to Nick, then sat back down. It was a little past nine o'clock and she thought that they needed more light in the room, because the one lamp by the couch had cast too much of a romantic glow around them.

"So I guess we're going to San Diego," he added when she remained silent. "Do you know who the client is?"

With or without the extra light, Nick wouldn't have missed the look of distress that flashed through her eyes. And he was suddenly more alert than tired.

"You won't believe this, Nick, but Steven is sending me …. I mean us, back to Miguel Bautista's. Mr. Bautista called this morning and told Steven that he's got to go out of the country unexpectedly, and he needs a visa right away. So we're to take his visa application to him on Thursday."

Nick didn't like this at all. Turning around and going back to Miguel Bautista's sounded like a setup to him. He didn't know why exactly, but something just didn't ring true.

"Is this normal, Rachel? Have you made return trips before on such short notice?" He tried to hide the concern in his voice.

"I don't really know. I've only been doing this for a month, and I haven't a clue what Cynthia's schedule used to be like. She was always coming and going. It's likely that she made more than one trip to the same client. Why do you ask?"

"No reason, really. I just want to check all the facts." He didn't want to alarm Rachel, especially since he was most likely alarmed about nothing at all. His suspicious mind might just be working overtime. Which was a definite hazard of his job.

"Well here's one fact for you, Nick. I hate the idea of seeing Miguel Bautista again, and I wish we were going anywhere but there. My skin crawls just thinking about that man."

Nick wanted to try to make Rachel feel a little better, so he got up from his chair and went over to sit down next to her on the couch. Without thinking about what he was doing, he reached out and took one of her hands in his.

"Here's another fact for you to think about, Rachel. If we can get a shot at nailing Bautista, then it's worth the trip back there. We weren't kidding when we told you the other day that Bautista is a very dangerous man who needs to be brought in. I'm sure the feds will be thrilled about our delivery on Thursday. I'll bring Alex up to date tomorrow and he can pass the good news on. This is a chance to really put that bastard away for good."

As Nick spoke, his thumb was rubbing back and forth across Rachel's hand. She kept her eyes downcast, but he could tell that she was aware of him and his closeness, because he could feel the rapid beat of the tiny pulse in her wrist. He was so tempted to reach out and pull her into his arms, but a voice in the far recess of his mind told him that holding her close wasn't a good idea. So instead, he let go of her hand, reached down to unsnap his cell phone from his belt, and flipped it open.

"I need to call Ben. I can fill Alex in tomorrow morning, but right now I should let Ben know that we're on for Thursday."

Rachel had been almost drugged by the pleasure she had felt from the touch of Nick's thumb rubbing lightly against her skin, and it took her a full minute to realize that he was now talking on the phone.

"Could you have him call me when he gets in if it's not too late, Betty? Have him call on my cell."

Betty must have said something funny because Nick started to laugh. And again Rachel felt drugged by his deep, masculine laughter.

"Yeah, well it's past nine now, and Home Depot doesn't close till ten. So if he gets home before ten, have him call, otherwise I'll see him in the morning."

With that, Nick hung up. He tossed his cell onto the coffee table and stood up.

"How about some coffee? I'll make it, if that's okay with you? Just tell me where you keep the coffee."

Rachel suddenly wanted Nick gone. She was starting to feel way too comfortable around him. There was little or no anger left over from two days ago, and he was looking way, way too good for her peace of mind. It was definitely time to get him going.

"It's almost nine thirty, Nick, and I think I'll make it an early night." Rachel stood as she added, "So at the risk of being rude, I'll see you out."

"I'm not going anywhere. I'm spending the night."

That stopped her cold. And all the anger that she thought was gone came back to her in a flash. She couldn't believe that he could take her so easily for granted. Well if that's what he thought, he had another thing coming, and she wasted no time in telling him just that.

"The hell you are, Nicholas Fallen. We may have struck some sort of truce, but that does not mean that we're going to pick up right where we left off. How dare you even suggest such a thing? I told you before that I'll work with you, but I have absolutely no intention of ..."

"Hold on, Rachel. I'm sorry, but I think you've misunderstood." Nick lifted his hands out in front of him, palms up, trying to declare his innocence. "I didn't mean that I'm spending the night with you in your bed. If there's not a place to sleep in your extra bedroom, the couch will do just fine."

Now instead of anger, Rachel felt puzzled. She didn't have a clue what he was talking about. She started to ask him to explain, but before the words left her mouth, she remembered the duffel bag sitting on her entry floor.

"You planned to spend the night here all along, didn't you?"

"I plan to stay not only tonight Rachel, but I'm here until we close this case."

In an instant, everything became crystal clear, and Rachel was embarrassed because she really had misunderstood. But no way was she going to offer up an apology for lashing out at him. Hell would freeze over first.

"For goodness sake Nick, I don't need you to watch over me all night. There's no way I'm not safe here in my own house. Trust me, Steven doesn't suspect a thing. Now can we please call it a night and will you please go home?"

Nick didn't budge. He just looked at her and she couldn't even fathom what was going on in that head of his.

"I still don't think you understand."

"I understand that I want you to leave," she replied with both hands on her hips. "But I'm having trouble understanding just how to get you out of here." *That should do it*, she thought. But as usual, she was mistaken.

"Sit down and listen to me." When she didn't move, he walked over, placed his hands on her shoulders, and gently pushed her back down onto the couch. Before she could jump back up, he sat down and grabbed her knee, keeping her in place.

"I believe you when you say that Steven doesn't suspect anything, but I'm not going to take any chances. If he has second thoughts about your story and decides to have you watched, how would it look if your new boyfriend, who has taken a week off just to spend it with you, is not actually here with you? Especially at night. Don't forget that I'm supposed to live in San Francisco, so where would I be if not here?"

Now Rachel was even more embarrassed, because everything he said made perfect sense.

"You were able to convince Steven that we are so much in love that you just about refused to go out of the country without me. Well, people that much in love become lovers, Rachel, and they spend their nights together. So, until this thing is over, I'm here to stay. And don't look so appalled," he added when he saw a look of unhappiness on her face. "I promise to behave myself, and you have my word that this time around I won't try to mix business with pleasure. I won't forget that I'm on the job."

First embarrassment and now sorrow. Rachel was feeling both of those things and much more. And both of those emotions centered around the fact that no matter how hard she fought it, she still wanted to be with Nicholas Fallen. He was able to draw her like a moth to the flame. She could try to stay mad at him, but even anger paled in comparison to how she really felt about him. She wanted him, but she couldn't have him, because he'd made it clear that he didn't want her back. And she knew that she had to accept that. Just like she had to accept that he was going to be in her life until this case was over. And that meant he would be spending his nights in her house, but not in her bed.

"My second bedroom doesn't have a bed in it because I use it as an office, but the couch is pretty comfortable."

"The couch will do just fine. I can sleep just about anywhere."

For a moment, Rachel wasn't able to look at Nick. All she could remember was what it was like sleeping next to him, and her heart turned over a little at the memory.

"I'll make you some coffee, Nick, and then I think I'll go on to bed."

Nick stopped her before she could get up. "I'll make the coffee. Just tell me where it is."

She was just too worn out to argue with him. "Coffee's in the fridge."

Nick didn't say anything, not even goodnight. He just squeezed her knee and then got up and went into the kitchen. Almost in a daze, Rachel decided that the least she could do was make up the couch while he was in making coffee. He was giving up his own bed in order to help catch her sister's killer, so it won't hurt her to try to make him as comfortable as possible.

Rachel was just finishing making up the couch into a nice comfy bed, when Nick's cell phone started to ring. She glanced around and found it still sitting on the coffee table, where he had tossed it after talking with Ben's wife.

"Get that, will you, Rachel?" Nick yelled out from the kitchen. "It's probably Ben."

Rachel picked up the phone and flipped it open.

"Hello."

"Oh dear, I'm sorry. I must have the wrong number."

Uh oh, this was not Ben. This was the voice of a very sexy woman.

"No, no. I'm sorry," Rachel quickly responded, "this is Detective Fallen's phone."

There was a breathy pause on the other end of the line.

"Then may I speak to Nicky please? This is Darla."

Rachel thought she might actually throw up. If the woman on the phone looked anything like she sounded, then Rachel was in big trouble. This woman sounded absolutely gorgeous. And a little impatient.

"I'll ….. I'll get him for you. Can you please hold one minute?"

Before Rachel could call out to Nick, she looked up to find him making his way back to her with a mug of coffee in his hand.

"It's for you," she said as she all but threw the phone at him. "It's someone named Darla."

Nick caught the phone and had to steady the mug in his other hand to keep the coffee from spilling out all over him.

"It's who?" he asked with an element of surprise.

"Darla," Rachel muttered as she flopped down onto the chair.

Nick still looked a little uncertain. He gazed over at Rachel, and then frowned down at the phone as if it was something from another planet, before finally bringing it to his ear. "Fallen," he almost snapped into the phone, which wasn't at all what Rachel had expected him to do.

The sexy voice must have told him who was calling, because Nick's next words were again not what Rachel had expected.

"How'd you get this number?"

Nick took a sip of coffee as he listened to Darla explain how she had called the station so many times looking for him, and that a nice detective named Ben had finally given her this number.

"I see."

Now Nick looked a little embarrassed. He glanced over at Rachel, obviously wanting her to leave the room to give him some privacy, but she refused. She just sat and listened, because she loved the fact that he was the one feeling off-balance for a change. So she ignored the look he was giving her, and stayed her ground. Waiting and listening.

"Listen, Darla. I haven't had a chance to call you back because I've been really busy. As a matter of fact, I'm here working on a case right now and I really need to keep this line open."

Rachel couldn't hear what the woman on the other end was saying, but she could only imagine.

"No …. no really, Darla, I'll call when I have a chance. But it's probably going to be awhile 'cause I have a lot going right now."

Rachel's felt a little sorry for the woman because she could tell that Nick probably had no intention of calling her back anytime in this decade. His tone of voice was anything but encouraging. And she wondered if the woman knew him well enough to realize that.

"Yeah, well, and one other thing. This cell is for official business only, so I'd appreciate it if you wouldn't call me on it again. Ben shouldn't have given it to you. He's not supposed to give it out to anyone." He tried to be kind when he said it but there was just no kind way to ask someone not to call you.

"Sure, sure, I understand." Nick looked really uncomfortable now, but even so, his voice softened and turned into a nice, slow drawl. "Of course I had a good time. Of course I meant to call you. But right now I've got several cases I'm working on and there's no way I can tell when I'm going to be free. So why don't you go ahead and invite someone else along, darlin'. That way you won't have to wait on me."

Nick was finally turning on some of the charm that Rachel had come to recognize as his way of getting out of awkward situations. She figured he could get away with just about anything, even not returning phone calls to beautiful women, when he used his sweet, sexy tone of voice. And suddenly she wished that she'd gone to bed and given him some privacy.

"Don't give it another thought, Darla. You go and have a good time."

Rachel noticed that this time he didn't promise to give her a call.

Nick finished the call, flipped the phone shut, and glared over at Rachel. "Having fun?" he asked.

She sat up straight and refused to let him intimidate her. "It's my house. If you'd wanted some privacy, you could have taken the phone into the kitchen."

"And deprive you of an evening's entertainment?" Nick was trying to act miffed, but his eyes gave him away. There was just a hint of laughter he couldn't quite disguise.

"So who's Darla?" She hoped her question would wipe that laughter right out of his eyes. And it did.

"Just a woman I went out with a couple of times." Nick sat down on the couch, messing up the neat, little bed she had made for him.

"Did you sleep with her?" *My God, why in the world did I ask him that?*

"Do you really want to know?"

Now it was Rachel's turn to feel uncomfortable. And scared — scared of what his answer was going to be. "No. I really don't."

"Well, I'm going to answer you anyway, little miss nosy." And before she could stop him, he continued. "I went out with Darla twice and I did not sleep with her. I didn't even try, in case you were going to ask. I don't go to bed with every woman I take out. I wasn't all that interested in her then, and I'm not interested in her now. So there, are you satisfied?"

Rachel sank down in her chair, completely mortified. She had had no business listening in on his private phone call, and even less business asking him such a personal question. She had gone way too far, and now she needed to see if she could redeem herself.

"I'm sorry, Nick. I have no right to …… well, let's just say I have no rights, and that I'm really sorry."

Nick didn't know what to think at that moment. He wanted to get pissed and stay pissed at Rachel, because that might stop him from wanting her. Anger was better than the ache he felt each time he looked at her. Anger he could deal with, longing to have sex with her again he couldn't deal with.

So it was best for both them if he could stay good and mad. But then, out of the blue, she had to go and apologize. Christ, but this woman was the most unpredictable woman he had ever met. And God help him, but that was just one of the things that he liked about her — along with her beauty, her brains, her spunk, and her sweet, sweet nature.

"Let's not talk about Darla anymore. It's getting late. You're tired, and I'm beat, so why don't we both go to bed?"

Rachel figured that was as much of an acceptance of her apology as she was going to get from him.

"All right." She stood and started in to move in the direction of her bedroom. "Anything you need, you can find in the linen closet. The bathroom's down the hall to your right."

"Goodnight, Rachel," was all he said.

"Goodnight, Nick," was her softly spoken reply.

*   *   *

It was one o'clock in the morning, and Nick had still not closed his eyes. He was wide awake. He had spent the last three hours trying to get comfortable on the couch, and trying even harder not to imagine Rachel sleeping in her bed, just a few feet away. He could easily see her all tangled up in the sheets, as she was prone to do, quite possibly with one long, slender leg hanging over the edge of the bed. He had found her that way himself on more than one occasion, and the sight of her like that had always led to something more. Both mornings that he had woken up with her aboard ship, he had not been able to leave her bed without making love to her. Never mind the fact that they had had sex more times than he could count during the night, every morning when he would see her all tangled and soft and sleepy, he would need to be inside of her. Nothing else seemed to matter to him. Just slipping into her as deep as he could go, and losing himself in her hot, sweet body.

Thinking about sex with Rachel was the absolute last thing Nick needed to do. He could not allow himself to go there again. He had broken all the rules, put her trust in him at risk, and taken advantage of a woman that he really, really liked. And to make matters even worse, the more he got to know her, the more certain he was that Rachel Bennett was a woman who wanted to be with someone in a committed relationship. She would never admit it to him, but he knew that's what she wanted and what she deserved. He knew that just as strongly as he knew that he wasn't the right man for Rachel. She needed someone who would come home at the same time each night. She needed someone who could plan a vacation and not have to change plans at the last minute because there was a break in a case that couldn't wait. She needed someone who could sleep through the night without the phone ringing, sending him off at three in the morning because there was another body found in another alley. Rachel Bennett needed someone, anyone, except Nick — and he knew it. So with that in mind, he tried again to get some sleep, burying his face into the pillow, trying not to even think anymore about the woman that seemed to consume his every thought.

But as luck would have it, as Nick turned over onto his back, still wide awake, he caught the sight of Rachel trying to sneak quietly by him on the couch. She had slipped on a short, white, flimsy robe, which made her look like an angle gliding by. Because Nick had not so much as dozed off, his eyes were adjusted to the darkness and he could see her perfectly. So he lay back and enjoyed the loveliness of her as she walked silently by.

He watched as she disappeared into the kitchen, trying to decide what was the gentlemanly thing to do. Stay put and try to go to sleep was one option — get up and join her in the kitchen was another option. In less than a second, Nick threw his legs off the couch and reached for his jeans.

He slipped them on, grabbed his discarded shirt, and put it on, but didn't bother to button it up. In the next second, he was on his way to the kitchen.

Nick swung open the kitchen door and spotted Rachel filling a tea kettle with water from the tap. Not wanting to startle her, he cleared his throat before stepping in and letting the door swing shut behind him.

Rachel whirled around, almost dropping the kettle in the process. "My God, Nicholas. You scared me half to death."

She was clutching the kettle against her chest, her eyes turning from fright to awareness. Awareness that there was nothing to be afraid of.

"Sorry if I startled you. I tried not to," he muttered as he walked over, reached around Rachel, and turned off the tap.

Both Nick and Rachel felt the instant heat that rose up between them. And it was hard to tell who was more affected. Nick had just meant to turn off the running water, but standing this close to Rachel, his mind latched onto other things. Like how good she looked in her tiny, white robe, how incredibly good she smelled, and how much he wanted to run his hands through her soft, inviting hair.

It would have surprised Nick had he known that Rachel was thinking almost the exact same thing about him. Her eyes had taken in his wonderful chest, exposed because he hadn't taken the time to button up his shirt. His hair was just long enough so that it started to curl slightly at his collar, and she wanted desperately to run her fingers through its thickness. Everything about him screamed out at her to reach out and touch him. Everything that is, except the look of warning that suddenly appeared in his eyes.

Nick could pinpoint the moment he figured out what was going on in Rachel's head. She was just no good at hiding her emotions. And he had to remind himself that he was not here to take her to bed. He wanted to. He wanted to more than he wanted to breathe. But he wouldn't let himself, because he would never forgive himself if he did. So before he could allow Rachel to do something they would both regret, like reach out and touch him, he took a step back, just out of her reach. And he tried to do so without being too obvious.

"What are you doing up?"

It took her a moment to regain her composure. She could hardly stand to look at him all rumpled and sexy, but she figured if he could resist her, then she could resist him. At least she would work really, really hard at it.

"I couldn't sleep, so I thought I'd make some tea." It suddenly dawned on her that she was still clutching onto the tea kettle. So she calmly walked over to the stove and sat it down on the burner. "Sorry if I woke you. I tried to be very quiet."

"I was awake." He started to add that he couldn't sleep either, but thought better of it. He didn't want to give her any reason to ask him why.

"Would you like some tea? It's herbal and doesn't have any caffeine. It's actually supposed to help you sleep."

Nick didn't want tea, he wanted a drink. A nice, stiff drink. But since tea was all she was offering, he accepted.

"Sure. Sounds good." He wondered if she might have some brandy to put in it.

"Well, sit down and make yourself comfortable. It should be ready in a minute."

Nick pulled out a chair and sat down at the table. He ran his fingers through his hair, and then down over his chin, thinking that he probably looked pretty bad at the moment.

Rachel, of course, thought just the opposite. She thought that Nick had never looked sexier to her. He needed to shave, which made him look dark and handsome, and his green eyes had a slumberous look, which made Rachel's mouth water. He was just too good-looking for his own good, and she had to fight the desire that wound its way through every inch of her body.

As the minutes ticked by, a silence settled over the kitchen. Rachel took a peek at Nick and thought about going right over and plopping herself down on his lap. She could see herself wrapping her arms around his neck, sliding her fingers through his hair, and leaning in to kiss him. And just as she imagined what his response would be, the kettle started whistling, bringing her back to the real world, and forcing her out of that particular fantasy. She jumped, he grinned, and she prayed that he hadn't figured out what was going on in her mind.

Rachel made two cups of the herbal tea, handed Nick a mug, and sat down with him at the table. She took a sip to try to calm her nerves. Sitting with him in the wee hours of the morning in her quiet kitchen was even more intimate than when they had shared dinner together just hours earlier. Way more intimate.

"Thanks," he said and then he took a sip of tea. After the first taste, he grimaced because he hated tea.

Rachel laughed, and he raised his eyes to her face. Her laughter was something that he'd missed over the last couple of days, and he as drawn to it now.

"Would you like something added to your tea?"

Obviously she hadn't missed the frown on his face.

"What are you offering?"

"How about some cognac? I have a nice bottle stashed away."

He wasn't about to turn down her offer, but he also wasn't about to waste good cognac on a cup of tea.

"I'll take the cognac, but how about in a glass. I'll pass on mixing it in the tea."

Rachel had the bottle down from the cupboard and was already reaching for a glass. She poured him a generous serving and brought it over to the table.

"You're not having any?" he asked as she sat back down.

"I think I'll stick with the tea."

"Okay, if you're sure," he said softly, right before he took a sip. The nice, rich drink went down smooth as silk. Cognac was good stuff. Really good stuff.

"Can I ask you a personal question, Nick?"

Rachel's voice broke the silence, and Nick was a little leery. He was never really comfortable with personal questions. Asking them was one thing, but answering them was quite another. He also didn't want to get into any questions about his past sex life, and he couldn't imagine what other personal questions she could be referring to. But because he couldn't think of a tactful way to say no, he responded in the affirmative.

"Sure. What do you want to know?" He decided that he could always plead the Fifth if he didn't like what she was asking.

"You mentioned once that you had been married, and that it was a long time ago. What happened?"

Nick really didn't want to talk about this ex-wife, but thought that it was safer than talking about his past indiscretions.

"It's kinda a long story." He took a stab at trying to get out of talking about it, but she wouldn't let it go.

"That's not fair. You and your detectives have investigated me and know an awful lot about my life, both past and present. And I'm still not sure who the real Nicholas Fallen is. I'd like to know a little more about who you are. Who you really are," she added, knowing that he would get the message.

And he did. Nick didn't miss the meaning behind her words. He had told her so many lies that she was trying to figure out the truth about what made him tick. And he supposed he owed her that much. Actually, he probably owed her much more, but he decided that he would start with answering her question.

"I met Nancy my last year of law school. She was working as a legal assistant in my dad's firm. She was pretty, full of life, and seemed to be ready to settle into a permanent relationship." Nick hated this, but went on just the same. "We dated until I got my law degree, and then we got married. She quit work right after I passed the Bar because I started working for my dad one week later. And all was well. At least for the first two years of our marriage, and right up until the time I quit being a lawyer and became a cop. Then everything changed."

Nick stopped talking only long enough to take another sip of cognac. "Anyway," he continued, "the first year I became a cop, my marriage went straight to hell. Seems that Nancy loved being the wife of a lawyer a whole lot more than she loved being a wife to me. She kept begging me to give up law enforcement and go back to work for my father. But I just couldn't do it. Not for my father and not for Nancy."

He paused, waiting to see if Rachel had anything to say, and when she didn't, he went on with his story. "The first year I was a cop, all we did was fight. The second year, we stopped fighting, but we also stopped talking. And the last six months of our marriage, we had completely stopped making love. You see, Nancy figured that if she withheld sex, I'd give in and do whatever she wanted. Which only confirmed what I had long suspected — that we cared very little about what really mattered to each other. So at the end of four years, my marriage came to an end. Nancy asked me to move out of our nice, little condo in the heart of the city, and I did. She filed for divorce, and we split what little we had fifty-fifty. And we both got on with our lives. So there you have it, Rachel. The condensed and rather boring story of my divorce."

"So where is Nancy now? Do you even know?"

Nick finished his cognac in one long swallow and then got up to pour himself another taste. Talking about his failed life with Nancy was harder than he thought.

"Yeah, I know where she is. She's still in San Francisco, married to a very successful attorney in a firm that specializes in filing medical malpractice cases. The firm's quite well known and Nancy is in her element. Her husband makes tons of money and they rub elbows with all the other snobs in San

Francisco. She's probably happier than a pig in shit." There
— he had told his story and he was finished. Finished answering her questions, that is, because he now had a few questions
of his own.

"Okay, Professor, it's your turn. How about you? Why is it
you've never been married?"

Rachel should have expected this, because knowing Nick,
he would simply consider turnabout as fair play. And for a
second, she almost refused to answer him. But in the end, she
decided that it really didn't matter, so she told her own story
just like he had told his — straight and to the point.

"I almost got married last year to a math professor. He
teaches at USC and we dated for almost two years before he
proposed. His name is Kevin, and he's a really nice guy. We
discovered that we had a lot in common, enjoyed each other's
company, and we both seemed to be at a point in our lives
where it made sense to get married and start a family."

Rachel looked down into her cup of tea, debating with
herself as to how much more to tell Nick. Should she just tell
him it didn't work out and leave it at that, or should she tell
him the reasons why she hadn't gotten married? She was still
struggling with how to proceed when he asked the question
that helped her make up her mind.

"Well, obviously things didn't work out between the two
of you. How come?"

Rachel knew he had been truthful with her about his
breakup with Nancy, so she'd be just as truthful with him.

"Like I said, Kevin is a really nice guy." She looked up
from her cup of tea and caught Nick's eyes focused directly at
her. "The truth is that a couple of months before the wedding,
I realized that I just couldn't go through with it. I liked Kevin,
I liked him a lot. But I didn't love him. Not the way you're
supposed to love someone your about to marry."

Nick's eyes never wavered from her face, and she felt compelled to tell him all of it. So without looking away from him,

as she was tempted to do, she went on. "And there was one other thing. There was one other part of our relationship that I just couldn't overlook."

She figured that he'd already guessed what was coming, but she said the words out loud anyway. "There just wasn't enough spark in our sexual relationship. I never felt a burning need to be with Kevin that way. Sex was nice, but it wasn't what … well, it wasn't … it wasn't like what you and I had together. It was never hot, or reckless, or demanding, and it was never all-consuming. And that's what I wanted it to be like. That's what I wanted from the man I was going to marry."

Rachel wouldn't allow herself to think about what she was telling Nick, and she wouldn't allow herself to stop. He wanted her story, so he was going to get her story. All of it. She kept talking.

"So I called off the wedding. And the truth of the matter is that Kevin was pretty relieved. He knew that something was missing between us, but he didn't have the nerve to call off the wedding himself. Plus, he was willing to sacrifice having a great sex life for the chance to have children. But I wasn't willing to make that compromise in my life. Because what I really want is to have it all. I want to marry a man that I love, I want to have great sex, and someday I'd like to have children."

Boy, if that confession didn't make Nick run for the hills, then nothing would. But he wasn't running, Rachel noticed, at least not yet.

"So you want to have kids someday?" His green eyes were as compelling as his question to Rachel.

"Yes," she answered without hesitation. "I love children and someday when the time is right, I'd love to have a family. I sometimes daydream about having both a boy and a girl. I know it's silly to daydream about such things at my age, but I can't help it."

"That's not silly at all," was his only comment, so Rachel asked him another question.

"How about you, Nick? Do you ever think about getting married again and having children?"

She had successfully turned the tables and was again asking him a personal question. But Nick didn't really mind.

"It's not that easy for me. Being a homicide detective doesn't lend itself to having a wife and kids. Our hours stink, our days are long, and we're always on call. Most marriages to cops end in divorce. It's tough on the families and I can understand why the divorce rate is so high."

"That's all fine and well, Nick, but once again you didn't really answer my question. Taking all of that into account, do you ever see yourself getting married again and having a family? Or is that something that's not even in your realm of thinking?"

Nick wondered for a brief second where Rachel was going with all of this, and then he decided that it was nothing more than two people having a conversation. A late-night, very personal conversation. But somehow it seemed appropriate for two o'clock in the morning, so he just shrugged his shoulders and then answered her.

"Sure, I think about both of those things. I sometimes wish there was someone waiting for me at home, especially when I come in at some ungodly hour. I miss sleeping next to a woman every night, and I miss waking up with someone in the morning. And even though I don't think I've ever said this to another human being, I think I'd love to be a father some day. I like kids, and I'd love to have a couple of my own."

Rachel was momentarily at a loss for words. She hadn't expected this from Nick, so she wasn't sure what to say. And fortunately for her, she didn't have to say a thing because Nick went right on talking.

"But I'm realistic enough to accept that having a wife and kids is probably not in the cards for me. At least not in my near future. I told you once or twice that I'm no good at long-term relationships, and it's true. I just don't have it in me right now. That may change someday, but then again it might not. I could very well spend the rest of my life alone."

Rachel couldn't stop the next words that popped out of her mouth. Somehow whenever she was around Nick, her brain didn't seem to know when to remind her to keep her mouth shut.

"You may never get married again, Nicholas, but something tells me you'll never be alone either. You, women, and sex just seem to go hand-in-hand. You may not have a wife in your life, but I figure you'll always have plenty of girlfriends."

Even though Nick thought her words were outrageous, he laughed. He hadn't meant to, but he couldn't stop himself.

"You think so, do you?"

"Yeah, I do," she replied with a grin of her own. "I think there will always be a Darla somewhere, calling Nicky, and inviting him to go heaven-knows-where,"

Nick laughed again, and this time his low laughter caused a ripple of desire to spread through Rachel. He had a very masculine and a very sexy laugh.

"Well God help us all if that turns out to be the case. Darla and her type are fine for now, but I hope I'll make better choices in women in the next five to ten years."

Nick was teasing, but Rachel realized that many times, the truth was said in jest. And the sad truth here was that at this time in his life, Nicholas Fallen preferred women like Darla. Not women like Rachel. So with that cruel reminder, Rachel pushed her empty cup aside and stood up. It was time to call it a night.

"I think I'll be able to sleep now." As she spoke, her eyes took in the man who had somehow managed to turn her world upside down. Even just sitting innocently in her kitchen, he was almost too much for her to handle. "So I'm going to head off to bed." She didn't mean to sound alluring, but her voice had taken on a slightly husky tone. A tone that didn't get past Nick.

Nick finished off the last of his drink and stood up, standing toe-to-toe with Rachel. For one minute, his mind closed down and he forgot he was a cop. All he could see before him was a beautiful woman who touched him in a way that no other woman had before. Not even Nancy. And without thinking, he reached out for her and drew her slowly, very slowly, into his arms.

"I wish we could meet again in five years, Rachel."

Her hands had taken hold of Nick's shirt, and at his words, she clutched onto it as if it were a lifejacket.

"And for what it's worth," he said in a soft, deep voice, "even though I can't give you what you want in a man, you are worth more than all the Darlas I've ever met in my life. I really do care for you, Rachel. I really do."

His last words were whispered into her ear, right before he laid his mouth against her neck. But all Nick did was close his eyes, tighten his hold on her, and breathe in her scent. And when Rachel didn't pull out of his arms, he allowed himself one small taste. Just a touch of his lips and a sweep of his tongue.

Rachel knew that this was a mistake, but she couldn't seem to find the will to step out of his embrace. His arms felt so good around her and his mouth was doing glorious things to her senses. She felt drugged and exhilarated, both at the same time. And as she clung to the front of Nick's unbuttoned shirt, she let a small moan of pleasure escape from her parted lips.

What Rachel would never know was that her small, soft moan was what finally broke through Nick's muddled brain. Somehow he realized where this was leading, and he remembered who he was and why he was here. So, reluctantly he lifted his head, loosed his arms from around her waist, and took a step back.

"I promised that I'd behave myself, but if I keep on holding you, I'll never be able to keep that promise."

The look in Nick's eyes completely betrayed his words. He was trying to take full responsibility for a fragile and potentially dangerous situation. And because Rachel was still shaken up by his mouth against her neck, she was grateful that he was giving her a chance to walk way from him before it was too late. Not having a clue what she was doing, Rachel lifted her fingers and touched the spot on her neck where Nick's mouth had been. It still felt warm and wet.

All Nick seemed to be able to do was stand and watch her while he tried to get his raging hormones under control. His eyes followed her hand as her trembling fingers rested against her neck. Every part of him began throbbing with a need to bury himself as deep inside of her as he possibly could. And he fought down the urge to reach out for her again.

"I guess I'll see you in the morning," she managed to choke out, realizing too late that it was already morning. Two o'clock in the morning, to be exact.

When Nick said nothing, not even goodnight, Rachel was suddenly rooted to the spot. Her feet just wouldn't move. The only thing she seemed capable of doing was watching Nick watch her. Which wasn't good for either one of them, because the sexual tension in the air was enough to set the house on fire.

"Go to bed." Nick finally found his voice. "Please go to bed."

She didn't wait another second. Because if she didn't move now, she had a pretty good idea of where they might end up. And knowing Nick, it would very likely be right there on her kitchen floor. And even as enticing as that was to her, she just couldn't risk her heart any further. So before he had a chance to try to change her mind, she fled, leaving behind her a very frustrated, albeit a somewhat honorable homicide detective.

CHAPTER TWELVE

"Did anyone try to follow you?"

"No. I was careful. I drove around a little after I left Rachel's, but no one was tailing me, so I came on in."

"Do you think that's odd, Nick?"

"Not really. Rachel's satisfied that Steven bought her story about us, and if that's the case, then there's no reason to have me followed."

"Yeah. I suppose you're right."

Nick could tell that Alex wasn't convinced and he wondered why. But before he had a chance to ask, Ben joined them.

"Sorry I'm late. Betty had an early dentist appointment this morning and it was a little hectic with just me and the girls."

"No problem, Ben. We're still waiting for Lou. As soon as he gets here, we'll get started."

Alex's words must have conjured Lou up, because in the next second, he came through the door.

"Hey, lover boy," he said as he slapped Nick on the back. "How's it going?"

Nick knew that he would never live down having slept with Rachel while on assignment. That little piece of news had spread through the station faster than a speeding bullet.

Yesterday, most everyone had avoided looking him in the eye, but today he figured he was going to be fair game. And Lou was taking the first shot.

"Don't start with me, Lou."

"What's the matter, Fallen? You go undercover and you get laid. Sounds like a pretty good assignment if you ask me."

Lou chuckled at his own remarks, and Nick felt an uncontrollable urge to punch the guy's lights out. Which was ridiculous since he had expected this — this and probably a whole lot more before the day was out.

"Why doesn't everyone sit down." Alex was always the voice of reason.

Ben had already grabbed a chair, Lou found a chair next to the window, and Nick chose to lean up against the wall. He felt too restless to sit.

"Okay, Nick, you're on. Bring us all up to date."

"There's not much to tell," he started, but then he stopped for a second when Ben lit up a cigarette. He wanted one so badly that he could actually taste it. But he had broken down and had one the other day right here in Alex's office, and he wasn't going to give in to temptation again. So he ignored the craving and continued.

"Everything's going pretty much according to plan. Rachel got Steven's blessing for me to go along with her this Thursday for her next delivery. We're taking a hop over to San Diego, where we'll be met at the airport. We'll make the delivery, get back here, and turn what we have over to the feds."

"If you're flying to San Diego, does that mean you're heading back over the border?" Ben asked between puffs of his cigarette.

"Yeah, and that's the good news and the bad news. The good news is that we're finally going to get our chance to bring down Miguel Bautista. Steven's sending Rachel back to his place with some more papers. Story is, the guy needs a last-minute visa, so we're delivering the application."

Ben stopped smoking, Alex's eyes snapped up in surprise, and Lou was the only one who said what everyone was thinking.

"Christ, Fallen, that's fucking great news. We've wanted to get our hands on that bastard for two years. What in the hell could be the bad news in this?"

"The bad news is that Ms. Bennett is scared to death of the man. She's only doing this to help us catch her sister's killer, otherwise she wouldn't go within a hundred miles of the guy."

"She won't back out, will she?" Ben asked as he leaned over and put out his cigarette.

"No, she won't back out."

Nick wondered briefly if anyone in the room felt the same twinge of guilt that he felt. They were all using Rachel, and it didn't seem to matter that he'd just told them that she was scared to go back to Miguel Bautista's. But then he reminded himself that they had used her from the very beginning, and she was still the key to solving this case.

"How's Ms. Bennett holding up, Nick?"

Nick met Alex's eyes and he knew then that Alex did feel a little of the same guilt that Nick felt. It was easy for him to recognize it, because he figured it was just a reflection of his own troubled eyes.

"I don't think she's sleeping too well. Last night, she was up in the middle of the night. I don't think she got more than four hours' sleep, and that worries me."

"I can't believe it." Lou's words came out louder than intended. "You're still sleeping with her?" Lou sounded astonished by that possibility.

"I'm sleeping at her place." Nick sounded totally fed up.

"Well I'll be damned." Nick didn't say a word to Lou; he just drilled him with a look that said it all.

"I'll say this much, Fallen. After watching her with you the other day, I can't believe that she'd let you through the front door. How in the hell did you talk your way back into her bed?"

Nick leaned away from the wall and slammed his eyes onto Lou's laughing face. One more word, just one more, and he would not be held responsible for beating the shit out of his fellow detective.

Luckily, Ben knew the look on Nick's face better than anyone, and he came to Lou's rescue, even though Lou didn't realize he needed rescuing.

"Cut it out, Lou. You heard what Nick said. He said he was sleeping *at* her place. He's there to make sure the story holds up, in case Jackson has someone watching Ms. Bennett. How would it look if her new boyfriend wasn't around? Especially at night."

Lou wasn't stupid, and even he could feel some of the tension in the room. "Sorry, man, I didn't mean anything. I was just givin' you a hard time."

Nick drew in a deep breath before he walked over and sat in a chair next to his partner. He looked over at Lou and realized that he had overreacted. Any other time, he would've been able to dismiss Lou and his dirty mind with no problem. But because Lou's dirty mind had included Rachel, Nick was having trouble keeping his cool. Which he now needed to get under control.

"Forget it, Lou. I'm just tired myself. I probably got less sleep than Rachel did last night."

Alex had sat back in his chair and watched the exchange, trying hard not to let his own amusement show. It was obvious to him that Detective Nicholas Fallen had finally met his match. And that match came in the form of a beautiful brunette, with soft eyes and a temper that could take him on when necessary. Nick was doing everything in his power not to let his feelings for this woman show, and Alex thought that he failed at it miserably. He just looked so tired, so lost, and so confused, and it delighted Alex to no end.

"Anything else we need to know, partner?" Ben's question brought everyone back to the matter at hand.

"Nothing right now. Rachel may have some more information tonight, and if she does, I'll give you a call. By the way," he added as he stretched out his long legs, trying to relax, "have the feds coughed up a tracking device yet?"

"It'll be here sometime tomorrow. God forbid they give it to us any sooner. They don't trust us with their toys, so they won't send it to us until the last possible minute." Alex sounded put out.

"What's it going to be?"

"I asked for something simple. We don't want to draw attention with anything out of the ordinary. My guess is that they'll plant something into a wristwatch. That's what I suggested anyway. But we'll just have to wait and see."

"Okay, well, if there's nothing else, I have some work to do on that poor slob we found stabbed to death yesterday." Lou was already heading out the door.

"Hold on a minute, Lou. What's the story here?"

He turned back to all three men in the room. "Looks like the guy was the victim of a gang killing. From what we found out yesterday, he's a member of one of the gangs that hang out in Chinatown. There's a gang war going on right now, and he might've been a commissioned hit. We've got one witness who we believe belongs to a rival gang, and I guess you two are going to interview him. Are you also planning to go back into Chinatown?"

"Yeah, Nick and I are heading out there later today."

"And you're going where?" Alex asked Lou, because it was his hard and fast rule that his detectives keep him informed of their whereabouts at all times.

"I'm heading over to the coroner's. I thought I'd look in on the autopsy."

"Okay. But keep me posted. If this is gang-related, we might need to come up with some answers before the press makes the connection."

"Will do, boss." With that Lou was gone.

"So you two heading out?"

"Yeah, we've got the witness to interview again and then we're heading into Chinatown to see who we can round up."

"Well the same goes for both of you. Keep me posted, will you? If this is a gang kill, then it's the third one in three months. That's a coincidence we can't ignore and one I'm sure the press will pick up on. We need to stay ahead of the game, so call in and let me know what you find out."

Ben and Nick both got up and turned toward the door. They were already running behind schedule, so their day was going to be even longer than usual.

"Ben, can you give me a second with Nick?" Alex hated to ask, but he really wanted to talk with Nick alone for a few minutes.

Ben didn't give away his surprise. He just threw his partner a look that said *better you than me.* "I'll wait for you outside, buddy."

"I only need a minute," Alex responded even though Ben had been talking to Nick.

"Shut the door, will you, Nick?"

Nick walked over, closed the door, and turned to face his boss. "What's up, Alex? You know anything you have to say to me you can say in front of Ben."

"Sit down and don't get so defensive. I just want to ask you a question."

"I'd rather stand."

"Well, I'd rather you sit."

Nick wasn't about to start his day off with a fight with Alex. He'd already had enough trouble with Lou. So he walked over, sat down, and resumed the position he had been in earlier. He stretched out his long legs, crossing them at the ankles, and rested his elbows on the arm of the chair. He lifted his hands, steepled his fingers, and watched Alex without so much as blinking an eye.

"You look like shit, Detective."

Nick couldn't help the grin that spread across his face. God, but he really liked Alex Kendall, and the way he got right to the heart of things.

"Yeah, well, it comes with not getting enough sleep."

"And that's what I wanted to ask you about."

"What? You concerned about how much sleep I'm getting, Alex? How touching." Nick wasn't trying to sound like a smart ass, but somehow his words came out that way.

"Don't push me, Nick. Not today. I've got a lot going on, and so do you. Frankly I don't give a damn how much sleep you're getting. I know you've functioned before on little or no sleep, and I figure you'll do just fine either way. But I am concerned about Ms. Bennett."

Now *that* got Nick's full and undivided attention, just as Alex had suspected it would. "You said that Ms. Bennett didn't sleep much last night and that you were worried about her. Well, tired people make mistakes, and that makes me worried about her too."

"You don't need to worry about Rachel. I've already thought about giving her one of those over-the-counter sleeping pills if it looks like she's going to have another restless night. She'll fight me on it, but I have to believe that in the end she'll want a good night's sleep badly enough to take the stupid pill."

"I know I don't need to tell you this, but we need her to be on her toes. We're too close for her to slip up."

"She'll be fine, Alex. She just needs to get some rest, and I'll make sure she does."

"So how's the couch?" Alex changed the subject so fast that Nick responded before he even realized it.

"Uncomfortable."

"How much sleep did you actually get last night?"

"Not much."

"You figure you'll sleep any better tonight?"

"I thought you didn't give a damn about how much sleep I'm getting."

Alex grinned, Nick didn't. He knew that this conversation was heading somewhere, but for the life of him, he couldn't figure out where. So he resolved to let Alex do the talking and lead the way.

"Listen, Nick. When this case is over, I want you to take some time off and have yourself a little vacation."

Now Nick was suspicious. "Why?"

"Because you haven't had any time off to speak of in the two years since you've been here. You've earned it. Take a week, or two, and find yourself a nice little island to visit somewhere in the Caribbean. I'm sure you can find someone to take along with you. Someone who can help take your mind off work for a while."

Nick's suspicion was turning to awareness. He looked over at Alex and could swear that he could see the wheels turning in the man's head. So he decided to push things along, just a little.

"And you wouldn't by any chance be thinking that I might want to take an English lit professor along to this nice little island with me, would you?"

"Well, now that you mention it, I personally think that Ms. Bennett would be a great …"

Alex stopped when Nick stood up and looked down at him with eyes that flashed a clear warning. "Don't sit there and treat me like a fucking teenager, Alex. I don't need you or anyone else looking out for my sex life. I do just fine on my own, thank you."

Alex just sat back in his chair, trying to keep his grin from turning into an all-out smile. "It's not your sex life I'm concerned with, Nick. I figure you probably get more offers for sex than anyone I know. It's actually your love life that I'm trying to look out for. And I think even you're smart enough to know that there's a difference."

Nick was so appalled by the turn of this conversation that he found it hard to speak. But only for a second.

"I don't believe this. I just don't believe this. I am not going to stand here and discuss my love life with you. With all due respect, Alex, it's none of your damn business."

"Well, I just thought …"

"And furthermore, get Rachel Bennett out of your head. I am not in love with her and she's not in love with me. For Christ's sake Alex, how could you even think such a crazy thing?"

"Well, I just thought …"

"No, don't answer that. I have no intention of discussing this with you. I don't want …"

"Hey, are you guys finished in here yet?" Nick stopped in mid-sentence when Ben poked his head in through the door. "Excuse me, boss, but we really need to get going. They're holding the witness for us."

Nick wasted no time in getting the hell out of Alex's office. "Yeah, we're finished." And when Alex said nothing, Nick asked, "Right, Lieutenant?"

"Right, Detective."

And without another word, Nick stormed out of the office, with Ben following close behind.

"Hey, wait up."

Nick kept on walking, right out the door, straight for his car. He was so mad, he couldn't see straight. He wanted to go back and yell at Alex some more, and to tell him to mind his own damn business and to stay the hell out of his life. Ben caught up with him just as he flung open the car door.

"What's got into you, partner? And what happened in there?"

"Nothing happened." Nick was still fuming.

"Well if nothing happened, then how come you look like you're about ready to explode?"

"I'll be fine," Nick said through clenched teeth. "Just give me a second."

"Well you don't look fine, and you look way too mad to drive. So I guess we'll just have to take my car."

Knowing that he would probably regret this later, Nick tossed his car keys over to Ben, who was standing on the other side of the car. "Here, you drive."

Ben caught the keys in one hand, looking over as if his partner of two years had lost his mind. "You're actually gonna let me drive your car? Boy, whatever didn't happen in there between you and Alex must have been good."

"You want to drive or not, Ben?" Nick started walking over to the passenger side of the car. "You've been bellyaching and begging to drive my car for two years. Well, here's your chance. Take it or leave it."

Nick flung open the passenger side door, plopped himself down into the seat, and scowled at his best friend.

"You can drive my car but only if you don't ask me one thing about Rachel Bennett. I do not want to talk about Rachel today, is that clear?"

Ben laughed all the way around to the driver's side of the car. He now had a pretty good idea of what Nick and Alex had been talking about. And he loved it. And better yet, he loved the fact that he was going to get to sit back and watch his best friend fall at the feet of one very beautiful and very deserving woman. And he was going to enjoy even more that Nick would fight it all the way. Of course, in the end, Nick would lose, but right now Ben and perhaps Alex were the only two who had figured that out. But what fun it was going to be to watch it all. Because it couldn't be happening to a nicer guy.

Ben slipped behind the wheel of Nick's baby, flicked on the ignition, and flew away from the curb. He knew he'd probably never get another chance to drive this sweet car, so he gave it his all.

"You crash my car and I swear I'll shoot you."

Ben pretended that he hadn't heard a thing and kept on driving. But even though they were in a hurry to get to the county jail, where they were holding the only witness to the murder yesterday, Ben slowed down so he could savor the experience.

"Man oh man. Driving is way better than being a passenger. How about we trade off driving this baby? You drive one week and I'll drive the next. I'll even chip in for gas."

"I knew I shouldn't have given you my keys. And no way will I make that mistake again. You're a terrible driver."

Nick made the comment just as Ben swung the car into a parking space. He threw Nick an envious look, revved the engine, and then turned if off with a sigh.

Nick felt some of the tension leave his body, and he couldn't help but be thankful for his crazy partner. He was still pissed off at Alex, but he needed to put that aside and get on with what he and Ben needed to do. They had a busy day ahead of them, and being mad wasn't going to help. So instead he reached his hand out, palm up, and looked over at Ben.

"Car keys."

Ben looked like a little boy about to give away his favorite toy. "How about I keep them for a while?"

"How about you give them back to me?"

"I'll give them back if you promise that I get to drive again."

"No way. You drive like crap, and you could have gotten us killed. Now give me the car keys."

Nick and Ben argued about the keys all the way into the jail. It was only when they reached the interrogation room to interview the witness that Ben dumped the keys into Nick's hand. And for an instant, just an instant, Nick thought that all was well with the world.

But that feeling didn't last long at all, because this day had turned out to be one hell of a bad day. Their one and only witness had suddenly developed amnesia, taking back everything he said he'd seen the day before. Nick and Ben sat with him for hours, trying to get him to cooperate. And it wasn't until he'd started screaming police brutality that they finally gave up. They had just lost their witness to a brutal stabbing, and unless they could get some gang members to come forward, they were back to square one. And square one meant that they didn't have shit.

It wasn't until Nick and Ben had scoured every inch of Chinatown, trying to pin down members of the victim's gang, that Nick realized he needed to check in with Rachel. It was already five o'clock and he hadn't called her all day. Since both Nick and Ben needed a break, they decided to duck into a Chinese restaurant and see if they could scrounge up a cup of coffee.

Getting coffee instead of tea was no easy task, but finally a pot of hot, black coffee was brought to their table. Ben poured and Nick flipped open his phone to call Rachel.

"Hello?"

"Can you talk?"

"Well hello to you too, Detective Fallen." Luckily for him, Rachel was in a pretty good mood, so there was a hint of laughter in Rachel's voice.

"I guess that's a yes. You must be out of the office."

"It's after five and I left the office over an hour ago. I'm at the grocery store now, so it's safe for me to talk."

"The grocery store? What are you doing there?" Nick knew that was a stupid question, and he looked over just in time to see Ben roll his eyes. Obviously Ben thought it was a stupid question too.

"Would you believe that I'm buying groceries so that I can make dinner for us tonight?"

Boy that sounded really nice to Nick, but he didn't want Rachel to go to any trouble.

"You don't need to cook, Rachel. I can pick something up again on my way over. Just tell me what you'd like."

"Do you like lasagna?"

"I love lasagna. And I know a pretty good place to pick some up. What do you want to go with it?"

He could hear noise over the phone, and guessed that Rachel was already in the checkout stand.

"Don't you dare pick up lasagna and bring it to my house. My specialty is lasagna and I will not eat anyone else's. Just tell me when you think I should have it ready."

Nick looked over at Ben, not really wanting his partner to hear this conversation. But it was clear that Ben was not going anywhere, so unless Nick got up and walked away from the table, he had no choice.

"You really going to cook dinner for me? How sweet."

Rachel's laughter rang out into Nick's ear and he felt a warmth spread throughout his body. "Don't lay on the charm for me, Nicholas. I'm already planning to cook dinner for both of us. I'm sick and tired of restaurant food and I want a home-cooked meal. You just happen to be spending the night, so I guess that means you're invited."

Nick didn't take offense because he could tell she was teasing. And he was tempted to tease her right back, but thought better of it because there were two big fat ears that were hanging on to his every word.

"Ben says hi." That was his way of letting her know that he wasn't alone.

"Tell him I said hello," she responded, a little tentatively because she was still embarrassed that he knew about her fling with Nick. "So what time should I have dinner ready?"

"We still have one more stop to make here and then we need to head over to see the M.E. about the case last night. It'll probably be close to eight by the time I get to your place, so if you don't want to hold dinner, that's okay."

"Don't worry about that. Lasagna is better the longer it cooks. Eight will be just fine. And don't worry if it's later. Dinner will keep."

"Okay, thanks, Rachel. I'll see you as soon as I can."

"You and Ben be careful," were her parting words, and Nick nearly dropped his phone. It had been years since anyone had told him that. Nancy had stopped telling him to be careful after his first year on the force. And his parents never bothered to tell him that at all. God, but it sounded nice coming from Rachel.

"She cooking you dinner?" Ben had a big fat smile on his face to match his big fat ears.

"No. She's cooking dinner for herself and she said I could join her. That's different from her cooking dinner for me. I'm just sort of tagging along."

"Oh yeah," Ben said, "I can see that there's a really big difference. And who are you trying to convince anyway, buddy, me or yourself?"

"You know what, Ben? You're a real pain in the ass and I swear I don't know how Betty has put up with you all these years. That poor woman should be nominated for sainthood."

Ben pushed his coffee cup aside, enjoying the joking between friends. "Betty stays married to me, my friend, because she still can't get enough of me. If you know what I mean?"

Nick started to say something, but Ben was too fast. "I know that you're considered some great catch, and that most women throw themselves at you, partner. I guess you're good-looking enough, and you do have the advantage of driving that hot little sports car. But here's something you probably don't know about me. I'm considered somewhat of a stud myself, and my pretty Betty stays married to me because I'm so good in bed."

"I do not want to talk about this, Benjamin. Don't even go there. That's way more than I want to know about you. Betty is still a saint in my mind, and don't you go ruining that for me."

"Jealous, Fallen?"

Nick's mind flashed back to his conversation with Rachel about having a wife and kids, and he realized that maybe he was a little jealous of Ben. But he would never admit it out loud.

"You have Betty and the girls, and I have my hot little sports car. What else could I possibly need?"

It didn't go unnoticed that Nick had asked *what* else did he need? As opposed to asking *who* else did he need?

But since Ben was having too much fun, he decided not to point that out.

"Pay for the coffee, will you? I let you drive my car, so you can pay."

Ben didn't even try to argue over who was going to pay. He just threw some money down for the coffee and then they both headed back out on the street.

"Well, should we try to hit a couple of more shops to see if we can flush out some gang members, or should we head on over and meet Lou and the M.E.?"

Nick hated to concede that their visit to Chinatown had been a waste of their time, but now he was more anxious to see what the autopsy had revealed.

"Let's go see what the body can tell us. We're not going to find anything here."

"Yeah, that's what I thought."

They headed to small parking structure where they had parked Nick's car and had paid some kid to make sure it wasn't touched.

"Say, buddy, it's my turn to drive. You drove over here from the jail."

"Give it up, Ben." Nick tossed the kid a twenty-dollar bill, and opened the door to the driver's side.

"Oh come on, let me drive. I'll drive real careful, I promise."

Nick laughed at how pathetic Ben sounded, but he stood his ground. He slipped in behind the steering wheel, fastened his seat belt, and waited patiently for his partner to get in the car. Like a ten-year-old, pouting because he didn't get his way, Ben got in and slammed the door, shooting Nick a look that said *so there.*

"Now that is real mature behavior, Ben. Real mature."

"Yeah, well I learned it from Becky. She does that to me all the time. You'd be surprised how fast a six-year-old can master the fine art of pouting."

With the top down on the car, Nick laughed into the wind, picturing Ben's precious little six-year-old having a bit of a tantrum. Laughing felt good, and he started to relax just enough so that he could begin to look forward to the end of the day. He was anxious to see Rachel and see how her day had gone with Steven, but he was even more anxious to sit down to a meal she was cooking for the two of them. He had tried to make light of the whole thing with Ben, but he was secretly touched and pleased that she was cooking tonight. He hadn't guessed that she had a domestic side to her, and it was a side that he knew he was going to like. Because now he had discovered another piece of the puzzle named Rachel — a puzzle that he was having a lot of fun putting together.

*   *   *

Rachel pulled the lasagna out of the oven at exactly eight o'clock, figuring that Nick would be walking through the door any minute. She had given him a key this morning, telling him that it would be better for him to come and go at will. It felt funny giving a man a key to her house, but now she was glad she did, because she could stay in the kitchen and finish up the salad without having to answer her own door. Everything was pretty much ready, and all she had to do was make the salad dressing and open the wine so it could breathe.

She had decided to set the dining room table this time, and not eat in the kitchen. It had been a long time since she'd served dinner in her dining room, and she was looking forward to it. She had pulled out a white lace tablecloth, used her fine china, and had two candles ready to light.

Over the last two hours, Rachel had told herself over and over that she wasn't setting up a romantic dinner. She was simply setting a nice table, more for herself than for Nick. She liked having company for dinner and she rationalized that she would set a nice table for anyone she was cooking for. It just so happened that the "anyone" tonight was a man who could still cause her heart to turn over, just by walking into a room.

Rachel finished up her homemade salad dressing and glanced over at the clock. It was almost eight thirty and still no sign of Nick. She thought about putting the lasagna back in the oven to keep it warm, just as her phone rang.

"Hello?"

"Hi, Rachel. It's Nick."

She thought to herself that he didn't need to identify himself, because she would know his low, sexy voice anywhere.

"You must be running late."

"Yeah, we were just getting ready to head out, when we got a call from the county jail. Seems our murder witness, who conveniently lost his memory this morning, has his memory back and now he wants to talk. Ben and I are driving over to see him now."

"Well, that's good news, isn't it?"

"It is if the guy tells us what we need to know."

Rachel wasn't sure what to say. She knew so little about his line of work, and she hated to think that he was on his way to interview a witness after already putting in a twelve-hour day.

"It's hard to tell how long we'll be, but it's unlikely that I'll make it back to your place before ten. I'm really sorry about dinner."

Even though Rachel was deeply disappointed that he wasn't going to make it to dinner, she decided that the guy really needed a break.

"Please don't worry about dinner. I'll leave a plate for you in the oven so you can have something to eat if you're hungry when you get in."

"I hope you didn't go to too much trouble."

She looked over at her lovely table, her perfectly prepared lasagna, her homemade salad dressing, the open bottle of red wine, and she lied through her teeth. "It was no trouble at all. I just baked a pan of lasagna and threw a salad together."

"Well promise me that you'll eat something and promise not to wait up. You need to get some sleep tonight, Rachel, so if I'm too late, I'll let myself in as quietly as possible."

Nick had no idea how that sounded. But Ben did. Nick sounded like he was talking to a loving wife, rather than to a woman who was nothing more to him than a job.

But Ben also knew better to say a word about his observation, so this was a little secret he would keep all to himself.

Rachel hung up the phone and felt a sadness sweep over her. She had wanted to have this dinner with Nick more than she realized. It was silly and not practical, but she wanted it all the same. So now, with her appetite completely gone, and the evening stretched out before her, she did the only thing that made sense — she went over and poured herself a nice, big glass of wine.

Sipping the red wine, she did as she'd promised and cut into the lasagna, putting a generous portion on a plate. She covered the plate with foil and placed it in the oven to stay warm. Then she put everything away in the fridge. She didn't have enough motivation to clear the dishes from the table, so she left them there, figuring that she could do it later.

Rachel glanced again at the clock and hated the fact that it wasn't even nine o'clock. She knew that when Nick had said he'd be back by ten, he probably meant eleven or even later. And the real problem was that she had the rest of the evening ahead of her, and she wasn't the least bit sleepy. "Well maybe another glass of wine will help me sleep," she muttered to herself. So, grabbing the bottle of wine, she went into the living room, put on a new opera CD she still hadn't found the time to listen to, and settled down to see how many glasses of wine it would take to put her to sleep.

Nick slipped his key in the door at ten thirty, bone tired and fed up with the entire day. He and Ben hadn't gotten much out of their reluctant witness, but they had made some headway. They would start in on the guy again tomorrow, and hopefully his fluctuating memory would improve overnight.

Trying to be as quiet as possible, Nick could hear his own stomach growl and he wondered if Rachel had left him some of her lasagna, as promised. He made his way into the living room, and started straight for the kitchen, when he stopped short. Nick was surprised to find that the lights were still on, music was playing, the dining room table was still set, but there was no Rachel. And he wondered if she had already gone to bed. It was late, and he hoped so, but looking around the house, he somehow doubted it.

And then he heard her. One minute, all he could hear was the sound of Pavarotti's voice, and the next minute, he heard Rachel singing along, as if she could actually sing. Which even to his unschooled ears, she could not. Nick flinched, and continued making his way to the kitchen, where the awful sound was coming from. He opened the kitchen door, stepped in, and stopped short again for the second time in less than two minutes.

Rachel was dressed in her sweet, white robe, which didn't cover nearly enough skin. Her hair was haphazardly piled on top of her head, with loose, wet strands hanging down her back. She had a carton of ice cream out on the counter, and held a spoon in one hand and a glass of wine in the other. Her back was to Nick, and in between bites of ice cream and sips of wine, she was singing along with the opera. She was swaying her bottom in time to the music, and she was obviously drunker than a skunk.

"Rachel?"

At the sound of Nick's voice, she turned around, a little unsteady on her feet. She still held both the spoon and the wine, and Nick noticed that the wine glass was nearly empty, which he wasn't sure was a good thing or a bad thing.

"You're home." She smiled over at him.

"Yeah," he said as he watched her drain her glass. "And you're drunk."

Rachel looked around the kitchen as if he'd been talking to someone else. And then she swung her eyes back to him.

"Who me? I'm not drunk." Her words were slightly slurred.

Nick chuckled and then walked over and took the empty wine glass out of her hand.

"Just how much of this stuff have you had?"

"Not that much," she responded, trying to keep her eyes focused on him. Which was proving a little more difficult than one would expect.

"Yeah, well, let's see." After Nick placed the glass in the sink, he reached over and lifted the wine bottle that was sitting on the counter next to the ice cream. It was almost empty.

"You drank this whole thing?" he asked, turning just in time to catch her around the waist as she stumbled.

"Of course I didn't drink it all. I saved some for you."

Attempting to prove her point, Rachel slipped out of Nick's hold, retrieved a clean wine glass, and went over to the nearly empty bottle. She tipped it down, poured the liquid into the glass, and frowned as less than half the glass was filled. The look on her face was priceless and Nick had to swallow so that he wouldn't burst out laughing.

"Oh my goodness. Where did all the wine go? I know I didn't drink that much." She turned toward Nick with a confused look in her eyes. "Do you think it could have evaporated?"

This time Nick couldn't stop the laughter. *Of course such a question could only come from someone truly drunk,* he thought as he stepped closer and looked down into her worried eyes. She was so serious and so cute, and he felt a tug on his heart.

"Don't worry about it, sweetheart. I don't need any wine."

She looked troubled for about one second, and then she completely changed gears. "Then how about some ice cream?"

Before he could stop her, Rachel dug the spoon into the carton. With a delightful smile on her face, she put one hand on Nick's shoulder, leaned in a little closer, and lifted the spoon up to his mouth. At her gentle urging, he opened his mouth and she fed him the smooth, creamy dessert. As he swallowed, his eyes never left her face, and somehow his hands found themselves clasping onto her waist.

Nick knew that he needed to pull away, but he seemed unable to move. Especially since Rachel seemed so intent on feeding him some more. As he stood rooted to the spot, she dug again into the ice cream, first taking a tiny bite herself before bring the spoon up to Nick's lips. Because her aim was just a little off, she left a small dab of ice cream at the corner of Nick's mouth. And before he knew what she was doing, she leaned up, poked out her tiny, pink tongue and licked away the spot of cream. At the touch of her tongue, every part of Nick's body stiffened, and his fingers actually clenched at her waist. This entire situation as just way too dangerous.

"Want some more?" she whispered, and Nick knew that it was time to get her out of this kitchen and into bed. She needed to get some sleep and he needed to get away from her. Because if he didn't, he figured that in about one more second, he'd find other more inventive things to do with that ice cream.

"Come on, Rachel, let's put the ice cream away. It's really late and I think it's time for bed." That didn't come out exactly the way he'd meant it, but Rachel didn't seem to notice.

"But I'm not sleepy." Again her words came out in a soft slur.

"You will be as soon as your head hits the pillow. Trust me, I should know."

Nick forced himself to release his hold on her waist, step back, and grab onto the back of a kitchen chair with both hands. He just had to keep his hands off of her.

"Okay, Nick. I guess I am a little tired," she finally admitted, as she turned back to him after putting the ice cream away.

"I'm tired too. It's been a long day and …"

"Nicholas, could you please stand still? You're making me feel a little seasick."

Uh oh, thought Nick, *this is not a good sign.* Especially since he hadn't moved so much as an inch. So wanting to avoid what he feared was coming, Nick acted very quickly.

"Come on, sweetheart," he said as he went over the wrapped his arm around her waist, "let me help you."

Thankfully, Rachel didn't try to pull away or argue with him, so he led her gingerly from the kitchen, through the living room, down the hall and into her bedroom, turning out lights along the way. Once in Rachel's bedroom, he took her right over to the bed. Keeping his arm around her, he reached down and flung back the covers, and then stacked one pillow on top of the other, wanting to make the bed as comfortable as possible.

"Now, let's get you out of this robe and into bed."

Without conscious thought, Rachel responded to Nick's soft and soothing voice by slipping out of her robe. But instead of climbing into bed, she turned toward him and leaned into his body. And without conscious thought on his part, Nick wrapped both of his arms around her, not stopping her as she snuggled up against him.

"Will you stay with me until I fall asleep?"

As Rachel breathed out the question, Nick could feel her lips skim against his neck, and he knew that he had to tell her no. There was just no way he could stay with her in her bedroom and keep his hands off of her.

"Of course I'll stay."

Nick couldn't believe those were his words and he wondered if he'd lost his mind. And then, as Rachel snuggled even more closely against him, he thought that maybe he was at risk of losing more than just his mind. Because that thought scared the holy shit out of him, he dismissed it as quickly as it came. And before he could do any more damage, Nick lifted Rachel up into his arms and laid her gently into bed. He tucked the blankets around her, and then he sat down on the edge of the bed and took one of her small hands in his.

"Close your eyes and try to sleep."

But she didn't do as he suggested.

"Can I tell you something, Nick?" As she asked, she lifted her free hand and slowly traced his lower lip with the tip of her finger.

Nick felt an immediate, familiar, and unwanted stab of desire. He knew that it would be really easy to give in and touch Rachel, but he also knew that it would be a big mistake. A very big mistake. So he made himself fight down the desire, and he reached up to capture her wandering hand. Now he held both of her hands in his.

"What do you want to tell me?" He had to force himself to remember that Rachel was too tipsy to realize what she was doing.

Rachel closed her eyes, and because she was quiet for such a long time, Nick thought that perhaps she had fallen asleep. He studied her lovely face for a few minutes and was jut about to lean over and place a small goodnight kiss against her temple when her eyes fluttered open.

"I've been thinking."

So she hadn't fallen asleep, was his thought as he reached over and brushed a damp strand of hair away from her cheek.

"What have you been thinking?" His fingers trailed down her cheek to rest against her neck.

"Well," she responded on a sigh, "I was wondering if …"

Nick had to hide his grin. "What were you wondering?"

He could see a struggle going on in her eyes, so he sat and patiently waited for her to continue.

"Nick, do you think that in five years, if both of us are still not married, that we could find each other again and think about having a baby together?"

Her words were so completely unexpected and caught Nick so off guard, that suddenly he felt like he'd just been stabbed in the heart.

"I know that I'm a little drunk, Nick, but I also know that I could never find a more wonderful man to have a baby with. And in five years, if you're ready to let a woman like me into your life, I would love to give you a child."

Nick sat as still as a rock, unable to breathe and unable to think of a thing to say. Never in his life had someone told him something so sweet or offered him something so precious.

"You wouldn't even have to marry me," she added. "Although you could if you wanted to."

Her words were spoken barely above a whisper and Nick could tell that she was fading fast. She was also struggling to keep her eyes open.

"It's all right if you don't love me, Nick, because I …." She yawned and finally shut her eyes. "I know that you would love …. our …. child …. enough."

She finally drifted away into sleep and Nick actually felt as if he were going to pass out. He was so affected by Rachel and her softly spoken words. He would never have predicted in a million years that she would tell him such a thing. And he was having trouble dismissing away what she had said. And worse yet, in a small place in his heart, he didn't want to dismiss away her words. Because for a brief second, Nick could actually see him and Rachel having a child together. He could easily picture a beautiful little girl, who would have Rachel's luscious black hair and his deep green eyes. A beautiful little girl who would climb up into his lap at night, wrap her tiny arms around his neck, and call him Daddy.

Nick closed his eyes, but before he completely lost himself in such an unlikely fantasy, he reminded himself that he was no good at falling in love. And no matter what Rachel had just said, he knew without a doubt that she deserved to be loved — especially by the man who would be the father of her child. So as his brain took over his heart, he accepted that he would never be that man, because the last thing he wanted in life was to fall in love. And even though this woman could touch him like no other woman he had ever met, he knew that their time together would soon come to an end.

Still holding one of her hands in his, Nick let his eyes draw her into his soul. He took in every one of her features, until he finally rested his gaze on her softly parted lips.

"If I could fall in love with anyone, it would be you, sweetheart," he confessed as he lowered his mouth to hers. "But I can't love you. I just don't have it in me," he whispered. And then he kissed her softly — a light, sweet, but very meaningful goodnight kiss.

CHAPTER THIRTEEN

Nick was sitting at the kitchen table reading the paper and savoring his second cup of coffee, when Rachel stepped tentatively into the room. Nick lifted his eyes, and his coffee cup halted halfway to his mouth at the sight before him.

Less than an hour earlier, he had heard the shower going. It had crossed his mind then that Rachel might wake up with a hangover, and one look at her now only confirmed that possibility. Because she looked like she felt terrible.

Standing in the doorway, Rachel seemed almost afraid to enter her own kitchen. She had quickly donned a pair of jeans and a pink halter top. She had made a half-hearted attempt at putting on some makeup, she was barefoot, and her hair was loose and hanging down her back. He thought that she looked frail, a little sick, and completely hung over. And she also looked like she didn't know whether she should come in or flee. And the last thing Nick wanted was for her to flee.

"Good morning." Nick finished his sip of coffee.

"Good morning, Nick."

Rachel finally shut the kitchen door behind her, took baby steps over to the coffeepot, and Nick noticed that she hadn't looked him straight in the face. Her eyes had been downcast when she'd entered the kitchen, and now she was focusing way too much on pouring herself a cup of coffee. A much-needed cup of coffee, he surmised.

Rachel stood with her back to him and took a long sip of the dark brew. With a hand that wasn't very steady, she filled her cup back up to the rim. And knowing that she could put it off no longer, she turned toward Nick.

Nick sat quietly and continued reading the paper, seeming perfectly content to ignore her presence - which irritated her just a little. But is also gave her time to gather her scattered thoughts, and to study him sitting at the table. Today he had on a pair of dark brown khakis, a light brown shirt, and a striped tie. He wore the dreaded shoulder holster, his badge of course, and his ever-present cell phone. And she noticed that a tan sport coat was hanging over the back of his chair. He looked so good, and she felt so worn out, that a spark of resentment bubbled up inside her. And before she could do something completely irrational, like throw her cup of coffee in his handsome face to get his attention, she pulled herself together and went over to sit down.

Nick still didn't look up from his paper, so Rachel sat and drank her coffee in silence. She would die before she would be the first one to speak. If he wanted to ignore her this morning, she would ignore him as well. And anyway, after what she remembered of last night, she wasn't sure what to say. So saying nothing seemed like the safest bet.

"So how are you feeling this morning?"

She should have known that he just couldn't leave well enough alone. And since she didn't want to answer his question, she stalled by asking one of her own.

"How are *you* feeling this morning?"

With his own question thrown back at him, he finally lifted his eyes from the paper.

"I feel great. I got a solid seven hours' sleep, showered, shaved, and had my first cup of coffee before eight." His eyes were now crinkled with laughter. "And it looks like it's going to be a beautiful Southern California day. The sun is shining, and there's not a cloud in the sky. Good day to be out and around, wouldn't you agree?" Now he was making fun of her and she felt irritated at him all over again.

"Life would be much better if you would please stop shouting. There is no reason to speak so loudly. I can hear you just fine without you raising your voice."

Nick didn't know whether to laugh or to get up and wrap his arms around her. She looked so forlorn and he knew exactly how she was feeling on the morning after — because he had been there, way too many times. But he refused to give in to her fragile mood, because he was having way too much fun teasing her.

"How about I not speak at all, Rachel, and make you some breakfast instead? How does that sound?"

The idea of food made her stomach turn over. But she would never admit such a thing to Nick. There was no way she wanted him to know what a lightweight she was when it came to drinking a little wine. So after taking another sip of coffee, she plastered a fake smile on her face.

"I didn't know you could cook." Maybe if she avoided the subject of eating breakfast long enough, he would have to leave for work.

"I don't cook much, but I can whip up a pretty good omelet."

God, the thought of an omelet was going to make her throw up. And the only good thing about that possibility was that she would make sure that she would throw up all over the man responsible for her churning stomach.

Nick must have read her mind. "Something tells me an omelet isn't what you want this morning. How about some soft scrambled eggs and a piece of dry toast?"

That sounded a little better, but not much. But because Nick was trying to be nice, and because he had finally gotten his nose out of the paper and wasn't ignoring her any longer, Rachel finally gave in to defeat. She just couldn't keep up the pretense any longer.

"God, Nick, I think if I try to eat anything at all, I might just die."

Nick's soft laughter seemed to envelop both of them in the cozy kitchen. "Trust me, sweetheart. You may wish you could die right now, but you aren't going to be that lucky. You'll just have to tough it out."

She moaned and lifted her hand to rub at her temple. "And how long before I feel like I'm back among the living?"

Without thinking, Nick reached over and took her hand. Then he brought her fingers to his lips and kissed them softly. "You'll feel better in a few hours, Rachel. I promise."

"How long is a few hours?"

She sounded almost desperate, so he got up from his chair and stood behind her, placing both of his hands on her shoulders. As he gently rubbed away the tension, she sighed and leaned back into his hands. "Oh God, Nick, that feels so good. Please don't stop, because if you do, I swear I'll shoot you with you own gun."

He laughed softly and leaned down to speak into her ear. "I'm going to fix you something to eat. I know it sounds awful right now, but you need to put something in your stomach. You'll start to feel better once you do."

Since he seemed to know what he was talking about, Rachel nodded, and then almost broke into tears when he took his hands away from her shoulders.

Nick poured Rachel another cup of coffee and then he went to work on her breakfast. In no time at all, he was placing a plate of eggs and toast before her. She grimaced, he noticed, but he didn't remove the plate.

"Eat whatever you can, sweetheart. I promise it'll do you a world of good."

When had he started calling me sweetheart? she wondered, as she picked up the fork. "How about you? Aren't you eating?"

Again she was stalling and he knew it. "I fixed something earlier." He sat back down and pushed the plate closer to her. "And I'm not leaving here until you eat. So quit stalling."

The best she could do under the circumstances was to glare at him as she forked up the eggs. And with her stomach rolling, she took a tiny little bite.

Nick watched her over the rim of his coffee cup, doing everything in his power not to laugh. He had to hide his smile, which was harder than hell to do. But he had a sneaking suspicion that if he laughed at her now, she just might find the strength to pick up her plate and throw her eggs right in his lap.

"So how come you know so much about hangovers?" she asked around a small second bite.

"I've had enough of them to last me a lifetime. At least I did when I was younger. And believe me, no matter how many years it's been, you never quite forget how bad it feels the next day."

"So when was the last time you had too much to drink?"

He noticed that Rachel was actually nibbling at her toast, which was a good sign.

"That would be about two years ago. It was my last night on the SFPD and my fellow cops gave me a going-away party that got a little out of hand. And before that, the last time I got rip roaring-drunk was on November 17th, nine years ago."

She placed the rest of her uneaten toast next to her eggs, and looked at him with a definite question in her eyes.

"You're tying to figure out how I can pin it down so precisely, aren't you?"

"I figure there must be a good reason that you can recall that particular date."

Nick encouraged her to take one more bite of eggs, and then he answered her unasked question. "November 17th, nine years ago, was when my divorce became final."

"I see," she managed as she put down her fork and pushed the plate away.

"No, I don't think you do." Nick could have stopped there, but something pushed him to tell her the rest. "I didn't get totally shit-faced because I was no longer married to Nancy. I got shit-faced because I was only twenty-eight years old, and I already had a failed marriage behind me. That depressed the hell out of me, so the night my divorce was final, I drank myself into oblivion. Of course, I felt like I wanted to die the next day, so I swore off drinking altogether. Needless to say, the promise never to drink again didn't last long, but I can honestly say that I didn't get drunk again until the night before I came to L.A. And that just kinda happened by accident."

Rachel smiled over at him because she liked hearing him tell about his past. Even if it was about his failed marriage. Somehow, she felt more and more connected to Nick each time she learned a little more about him.

"But how about you, Professor? Is this the first time you've actually been drunk enough to feel like the walking dead the next day?"

Again Rachel smiled. "Would you believe that I've never been, as you put it, shit-faced before?"

"Never?" he asked, grinning at her use of his foul language.

"Never."

"Well, good for you. Getting drunk is never a good idea." Nick got up and took her unfinished breakfast over to the sink. "Although I have to admit that you were pretty cute last night."

Rachel dropped her head into her hands, closed her eyes, and prayed that he would let the subject drop. She wasn't sure she would ever be able to talk about last night.

"Aren't you late for work?" she muttered into her hands as he came back to the table and sat down.

"I've got a little more time before I need to leave." She could hear the seriousness in his voice. "So why don't you look at me and we can talk about it?"

She lifted her eyes to his, but shook her head. "I don't want to talk about last night."

"I think we should."

"Well I think we should just forget last night ever happened."

"How much do you remember, Rachel?"

"Enough."

He couldn't let her get away with dismissing last night, and the things she had said to him. He thought that they needed to talk it through, because he was afraid that if they didn't, last night might end up being one more barrier between them.

"Do you remember wanting to feed me ice cream for dinner?" He figured he'd start with something easy.

"I remember …. I mean, I seem to remember …" She stopped in mid-sentence and looked down at her clasped hands. "Why are you doing this, Nick?"

"I think we should talk about last night, Rachel, because I don't want you shying away from me as your memory comes back in bits and pieces."

He had no idea that her memory was already back in full force. And much to her embarrassment, she remembered everything. "Can't we just forget about how much of a fool I made out of myself last night?"

Nick thought for a second about letting things go, but he didn't want any more walls between them. "You were anything but a fool. And I'd rather we talk things through. Last night, when I put you to bed…."

She jumped up from her chair, forgetting about her pounding headache. "Okay, okay, I remember everything, absolutely everything. Are you happy now?"

"Sit back down and let's …"

"I remember feeding you ice cream, I remember both of us with our arms around each other, I remember you tucking me into bed, and I remember asking you if you and I could have …"

At the shrill sound of his cell phone, Rachel stopped. Nick glanced down, saw that it was Alex's number, and snatched the phone from his belt. "Fallen," he said more sharply than he had intended.

"Nick, it's Alex. When are you coming in?"

"I'm getting ready to leave now." He spoke to his boss but never took his eyes off of Rachel.

"Good, we have another lead on the gang killing and I've got the tracking device from the feds."

"Is Ben in yet?"

"Yeah, he just walked in."

"Okay, I'll be right there." Without waiting for a reply, Nick snapped his cell shut. He stood up, took his sport coat from the back of the chair, and put it on, never once taking his eyes off of Rachel. "We'll finish this tonight," he said, wanting her to be very clear that this conversation wasn't over.

Rachel was so relieved to get rid of him that she didn't even bother to argue the point, although she had no intention of continuing this discussion. He now knew for certain that she remembered asking him to be the father of her child, and she couldn't bear to discuss it further. There was no point, and no matter what he said, or how many times he said it, she had made a humongous fool out of herself. And she was not about to go there again. Not tonight, not tomorrow night, and not ever.

"Call me on my cell when you get a chance. I'll be in and out, but call me when you can get away from Steven." He was all business now, his mind switching very easily back to being a cop.

"I need to make our plane reservations to San Diego," she told him as she followed him to the front door. "Do you care what time we leave tomorrow?"

"About that." Nick turned toward her with his hand on the doorknob. "Make the flight out tomorrow anytime you want, but don't make our return flight until the next day. We want Steven to think that we've decided to stay over in Ensenada."

"Why, are we spending the night there?"

"No, but Alex and the FBI will be waiting for us in Ensenada. Once we deliver the package to Bautista, we'll have the driver take us back into town and drop us off at one of the hotels, where we'll hook up with Alex. The feds will take over from there."

Rachel was relieved to be talking about anything but last night. "All right, I'll call you when I've made our flight reservations and as soon as I can get away from the office. It'll probably be around lunchtime." The mention of food still made her stomach queasy.

Because he couldn't help himself, Nick leaned over and placed a small kiss on Rachel's cheek. "Drink some ginger ale, it'll help settle your stomach."

Rachel was trying to figure out if he was some kind of a mind reader, when he opened the door and started down the front steps. But before he got very far, he turned and came back toward her. And she noticed right away that he had a troubled look on his face.

"Listen, Rachel, there's something I should tell you." She felt a little uneasy, but just stood holding onto the door. "You're probably going to get good and pissed that I haven't told you this before, but it was for your own good."

She couldn't even imagine what he was about to say. The only thing she knew for sure was that when most people said something was for you own good, what they had to say was usually going to be pretty bad.

"The new receptionist in your office, Ms. Lacy — well, she's not exactly a receptionist. She works for Alex and she went uncover last month as part of this operation." When Rachel's mouth dropped open, he continued. "We didn't tell you because we didn't want you acting any differently around her. But now I want you to be aware of who she is, and if anything, anything at all goes wrong during the day, she's there to protect you."

Rachel finally found her voice. "But what could go wrong?"

"Nothing that I can think of off hand, but I don't know Steven and I don't want to take any chances. So if you think he may suspect what's going on, or if you feel the least bit threatened, you let our officer know. Do you understand?"

"Yes, I understand." But she really didn't. Because she truly believed that Steven had no idea what she was up to. And she wouldn't allow herself to think for even a second that she was in any real danger. But before she could relay any of that to Nick, he was already halfway down the steps.

The rest of Rachel's day was pretty uneventful. She made her way into the office around ten, scheduled their flight reservations, and had as little to do with Steven as possible. She was very aware now of who the woman at the front desk was, and she wished that Nick hadn't told her. Because it was hard for her to be completely natural around someone she now knew was a cop.

"Rachel, dear, can you come into my office for a moment?"

Rachel froze at the sound of Steven's voice, but turned and smiled at him like she would've done before she knew him to be a suspected killer. He might not have pulled the trigger, but if he had hired someone to kill Cynthia, in her mind, he was a killer all the same.

"Sit down for a minute. We've hardly seen each other since you returned from your cruise. You've left early every day this week. This new boyfriend of yours must be taking up every minute of your spare time."

Rachel sat and tried to act natural, but it was hard. She just wanted to get as far away from Steven as possible.

"Well, Nick has some friends here in town who he visits during the day while I'm at work, but I like to get home to him as soon as possible. He can only spend so much time catching up with old friends." That was the story that she and Nick had hatched up yesterday morning over coffee, in case the house was being watched and Steven got curious about how Nick was spending his days. Seeing him leave her house each morning in his car might cause someone to get suspicious. She they had come up with something that seemed fairly plausible. "Also, Nick returns to San Francisco this weekend. He needs to be back to work on Monday, so he's driving home on Sunday. "

"I was hoping I'd get a chance to meet him, Rachel. Is it possible we can get together for dinner tonight?"

Oh my God, Rachel thought as she tried not to turn pale at his suggestion. This was something they hadn't expected. "I believe we already have plans for tonight," she lied through her teeth. "Nick said something this morning about wanting me to meet some of his friends over dinner."

"Well, that's too bad, dear. I thought that since you seem so serious about the guy, it would be a good idea for me to meet him. We're the only family each other has, Rachel, and I've come to think of you as my own sister."

Now Rachel really wanted to vomit. "Maybe it will be possible after we get back from Ensenada," she suggested, realizing that she was becoming a pretty good liar.

"Ah, and talking about your trip." Steven reached into the desk drawer and brought out the all-too-familiar package. "Here's the visa application for Mr. Bautista. I called and gave him your flight information, and there will be a driver waiting for you and Mr. Fallen at the airport."

Rachel took the package and stood up, wanting to get out of his office before she gave herself away. She was finding it harder and harder to look Steven in the eye, and like yesterday, she felt a sudden urge to wipe her damp hands down the skirt she was wearing. She was just no good at these undercover games and she wondered how Nick managed to live this life day in and day out.

"Nick and I have decided to spend the night in Ensenada and return here on Friday. I hope that's okay with you, Steven?"

"No problem at all, my dear. You enjoy your free time and I'll see you back at work on Monday."

Rachel detected a little sarcasm in his voice, but decided to ignore it. After all, it was probably nothing. Probably just her mind working overtime.

As Rachel left Steven's office, clutching onto the illegal package, she decided that now was as good a time as any to make her getaway. It was after one o'clock and she needed to check in with Nick. "I think I'll call it a day, Ms. Lacy. There's not much for me to do around here anyway. Could you let Steven know that he can call me on my cell if he needs me? Otherwise, I'll see him on Monday."

The undercover cop turned receptionist never batted an eyelash. She nodded at Rachel and kept on typing, as if she'd been working in an office all her life. And again, Rachel was amazed how all the people who worked for Nick's boss could so easily deceive everyone around them. And it saddened her to think how easily Nick could deceive her as well. And even though she didn't want to dwell upon that possibility, it was all she could think about as she drove home.

Rachel wanted to believe that Nick cared about her. He had told her so himself the night before last, and she really wanted to hold onto that. Because if she couldn't believe that he had some real feelings for her, she just might fall completely apart. She didn't think for a moment that they had a future together, but even drunk, she had meant what she had said to him last night. If they could meet again in five years, she would love to have a child with him.

Recalling her words to him in the late hours of the night, she felt a blush spread over her entire body. She knew that he wasn't going to let the matter drop. He had made that clear this morning. But even though she had meant every word last night, now in the light of day, she could think more clearly — and she could see that she would never be able to follow through with her own proposal. Because she would never be able to have a child with Nick without having his love. And that was something she knew was beyond her reach. Nicholas Fallen might care for her, but he would never love her. And she had to accept that and make plans to get on with her life. Plans that would not include the man she had fallen completely and hopelessly in love with.

Twenty minutes after Rachel had gotten into her car, she walked into her house and called Nick.

"Detective Fallen."

"Are you busy?"

"It's about time you called. I was getting worried. You said you'd call at lunch and it's already 1:30."

Maybe he really did care, she thought, *maybe just a little.* "I just got home with the package for Bautista."

"Are you finished for the day?"

"Yes. I told Ms. Lacy, who by the way is so good at her job you'd never know she was a cop, that I was leaving for the day and I'd see them on Monday."

"Good. I'm glad you're outta there."

"Where are you?" she asked because it seemed unusually quiet. Normally when she talked with him on his cell, there was lots of noise in the background.

"I'm in Alex's office with Ben. We're going over the plans for tonight."

"Tonight?" she asked as she searched the fridge for a ginger ale.

"Yeah, we all need to get together this evening someplace away from here. Ben suggested his house."

Rachel felt her stomach tie up in knots and it had nothing to do with the last twinges of her hangover. "You mean I have to face Ben again and meet Lieutenant Kendall in person?"

"Come on, Rachel, I thought we talked about this." Nick had gotten up from his chair and walked over toward the window so he could have a little privacy. "I told you that you've got nothing to be embarrassed about, and you've just got to believe me." He was almost whispering into the phone.

"I'm trying to, Nick, I really am. It's just that for some crazy reason, I seem to act totally out of character whenever I'm around you. And then I can't help but be embarrassed, because I do things I never thought I'd do. "

"Like what?" he asked, forgetting that he had an audience, but too curious to let the subject drop.

"Like sleeping with you two days after we met," she responded. "Like getting angry and losing my temper enough to slap you. Like getting totally drunk in my own house, and then asking you if we could have a..." She stopped and took a deep breath when she realized what she had almost said. "Well, you know what I mean. All of those things are just not like me. And Ben and your boss know that I slept with you and they probably know that I slapped the hell out of you."

Nick chuckled softly into the phone. "They know, and the only one they blame for what happened between us is me. Our sleeping together involved us, Rachel, no one else. And I deserved that slap, even if I didn't think so at the time."

When she said nothing further, Nick continued, "Okay, so we're agreed that you have no reason to feel embarrassed around Ben, Alex, or anyone else." When she didn't immediately respond, he added, "Right?"

"Right." And when she said it, she felt like she was starting to believe it.

"Then here's the plan: Alex and Lou will meet us at Ben's sometime after eight. I'll pick you up at the house at six, and we'll head over to Ben's for dinner first. Betty is cooking a pot roast and we're invited."

Ben's house, dinner, pot roast — her mind was swirling. "What can I bring?" She knew there was no use trying to get out of going to Ben's for dinner, so why even try?

"Nothing. I'll pick up a bottle of wine."

When she groaned into the phone, he felt a little sorry for her, because he had forgotten about her hangover. "Not that you have to drink any, sweetheart." And then he asked, "How are you feeling, by the way?"

"I was feeling okay until you brought up the subject of wine." She was joking, of course — at least he hoped she was.

"Well, not to worry, the adults can drink wine and you can have milk along with the kids."

"Very funny, Detective Fallen. Very funny indeed."

This time, Nick's chuckle turned into all-out laughter. "Go take a nap and I'll see you around six. And if you need me before then, call, okay?"

"Okay," she said softly. And like yesterday she added, "Be careful." And then she hung up.

Nick hooked his phone back on his belt and stood staring out the window. He thought about how involved he'd become with Rachel in less than two weeks, and he wondered if he was going to miss her when this case was over. Tomorrow they would deliver their package to Bautista and everything would come to an end. She would go back to teaching and her nice predictable life, and he would continue with his work and dating a variety of women. Christ, for the first time in years, that sounded hollow and empty. Because no matter how many women he dated, and no matter how many women he took to bed, he knew that he would never really get Rachel Bennett out of his system. She had become just too important to him.

"Everything okay?"

Nick was so lost in his thoughts that he had completely forgotten where he was, and that Alex and Ben were sitting in the room.

"Everything's fine." Nick turned away from the window, but made no effort to go back and sit down.

"So tell me something, buddy. You make a habit of calling all of your women sweetheart, or just this one?"

Nick walked over, snatched the cigarette out of Ben's hands, took a long, deep drag, and handed it back.

"That's what I thought."

"Don't make more out of this than what it is, Ben. And that goes for you too," he added with a glance over at Alex, who was sitting behind his desk with a knowing grin on his face. "For Christ's sake, don't the two of you have anything better to do than sit around and speculate about what's going on in my life?"

"Not really," replied Ben before Alex could add his two cents. "Your personal life right now is a hell of a lot more exciting than either of ours. You're completely screwed up over this woman and you don't even realize it. Hell, Fallen, you're more fun to watch than the wrestlers on TV."

Nick decided to completely ignore both of them and their obsession over his relationship with Rachel. So he glared at each man, piercing them with eyes that turned so deep a green that they were almost black. Ben laughed and a second later, Alex joined in.

"Glad my life is so fucking entertaining."

"You have no idea," Ben said between hoots of laughter, "no idea at all."

Nick was close to losing it. He was thirty-seven years old, had been married and divorced, and they were treating him like he was some kind of a kid with a schoolboy crush. He could take teasing around the squad room as easily as the next guy, but this whole thing about Rachel was getting out of hand. And he wasn't sure what to do about it. So he just jammed both hands into the front pockets of his pants, sent his partner a threatening look, and tried to turn the conversation back to business.

"Where's Lou?"

Alex and Ben knew that the teasing was over. They were getting a real kick out of seeing Nick squirm, but the fun and games were over. At least for the time being.

"He left a little while ago to keep an eye on the brother-in-law. I told him to stay on the guy and check in by phone. He'll meet us at Ben's house around eight."

"Okay, so what about the rest of the afternoon? You want to head back into Chinatown?" Nick directed his question to Ben.

"Yeah, I guess we should. Didn't you want to check out one other place we think our victim may have frequented?"

Before Nick could answer, Alex jumped in. "First I want the two of you to finish your report on the Roberts case. That case is over two weeks old, and I'm still waiting on your final report. Do that and then head over to Chinatown."

Both men groaned, hating the thought of spending a couple of hours behind a computer. "Your turn to type, buddy. I did it the last time."

"Yeah, yeah, I know." Nick pulled a couple of dollars out of his pocket and threw them over at this partner. "Go get us a couple of Cokes and I'll get started."

Both detectives left Alex's office, muttering about the evils of report writing. No one on the force liked spending their time behind a computer, when they could be out doing what they were really paid to do — solving a murder.

Nick sat at his desk, typing away, when Ben returned with the drinks. He sat down in the chair at the side of Nick's battered desk, waiting for the right moment to interrupt his partner's train of thought. He didn't wait long.

"Hey, man, sorry about teasing you in there."

Nick just kept on typing, preferring not to respond. But Ben was persistent.

"I mean, I like giving you a bad time and all, but I can tell this lady means more to you than you're willing to let on."

Nick kept typing.

"It's nothing to be ashamed of, my friend. Even when the best of us fall in love, we usually make damn fools of ourselves. That's just the way that God meant for it to be. So why fight it? Why not sit back and enjoy it?"

Nick's fingers finally stopped hammering away at the keyboard. He sat for one second, looking blankly at the computer screen, and then he slowly turned toward his partner and best friend.

"I know we've had this discussion before, Ben, but I guess you weren't listening the first time. No one is in love here. Got it? And I have no intention of falling in love. I happen to like my life just the way it is. So why don't you do both of us a favor and let it be?"

Nick spoke calmly and quietly, trying to send his message as clearly as possible. He didn't want any more misunderstanding.

"Okay, but let me ask you just one thing, Nick. And I'm asking this with all kidding aside. You say you like your life just the way it is. But don't you ever think about how nice it would be to have someone in your life to share it with? And I don't mean the Betsys and the Darlas and all the other women who flock around you all the time. I mean a woman like Betty, who would be your best friend, your lover, and the mother of your children. Can you honestly say that you wouldn't like to have a life like that?"

Nick sat and stared at Ben. He knew that his friend meant well, but it was a subject that he didn't want to think about or talk about. He didn't want to examine his life that closely, because he was afraid of what the answers might be. So instead of saying another word on the subject of love, Rachel, family, and children, Nick turned back to the keyboard.

"What day did we bring in the perp on the Roberts case? Was it the seventeenth or the eighteenth?"

Ben knew that the conversation leading up to Rachel was over. And since he respected his partner's feelings, he didn't push the matter any further.

"It was Tuesday, the seventeenth."

"Yeah, that's what I thought."

So for the next two hours, Nick typed and Ben watched, helping to fill in the blanks whenever Nick had a question.

CHAPTER FOURTEEN

"Hello."

"You called?"

"Yes. Alex Kendall has the tracking device. The feds delivered it to him this morning."

"Have you gotten a look at it?"

"No sir. No one has."

"Well, as interesting as this bit of information is, it doesn't help me or Mr. Bautista if we don't know what we're looking for."

"Yes sir. I know that and I'm working on it."

The silence on the other end of the line was intentional and meant to intimidate.

"I'll get you the information, Mr. Jackson."

Again another long pause.

"I thought I made myself clear the last time we talked. I need to know exactly what they'll be using to track Fallen and my sister-in-law. Without this information, you're of no further use to me."

The threat in Steven Jackson's voice was unmistakable.

"I'll have what you need before morning. You can count on it."

"Then this call is a waste of my time. Contact me again only when you have the information. And if you can't get me what I need, don't bother to call. Our association will be over."

The informant felt a spurt of hatred, but he couldn't afford to let it show. Not right now. Because he wanted something else from Steven Jackson — and that something else was the real reason for this call.

"I have another matter to discuss with you, Mr. Jackson."

He could tell that Steven was debating whether or not to hear him out or to hang up the phone. And his hatred turned to rage.

"Make it quick. I haven't got all day."

The informant had to swallow back the bile in his throat. "I want to be there when this thing goes down. I want to see for myself that Nick Fallen and the bitch he's been fucking are dead."

"I'm not sure that's a good idea. You're no good to me if your cover's blown."

"My cover won't be blown. Trust me on that. I can slip across the border, have the satisfaction of seeing them at the bottom of the ravine, and slip back without anyone realizing I've been gone."

Steven's curiosity got the better of him. "I thought you didn't want any part of killing a cop. You said it was too risky. Why the sudden change of heart?"

"That's easy. I've changed my mind because I hate that son of a bitch Fallen enough to take the risk. That bastard waltzed into the LAPD two years ago, and became the golden boy practically overnight. Kendall and the guy are too much alike. Fallen's way too smug and I want to be there when the bastard dies."

Steven's mind was working a mile a minute. He knew that sooner or later, he would have to eliminate his informant, and now he was being given a golden opportunity. One more body thrown into the mix was no big deal. As a matter of fact, the informant's death right now might just work to his advantage. If the feds didn't buy the staged car accident, they probably wouldn't look much further if a fellow cop was also found dead at the scene. Especially a fellow cop who had no business being in Mexico. Steven believed that the feds were just stupid enough to figure that the informant was a dirty cop, out to eliminate Fallen, and had gotten himself killed in the process.

"Just be sure you're not missed. I'll let Bautista know to expect you."

The informant's rage left him the instant he was given the go-ahead. His excitement at watching Nick die overtook everything else.

"I'll expect a call from you with the information on the tracking device before morning. No excuses."

And like always, when Steven Jackson was finished talking, the line went dead.

CHAPTER FIFTEEN

Nick pulled up to Ben's house at exactly 6:15. He and Ben had finished up their report on the Roberts case and headed back into Chinatown for the rest of the afternoon. He left the station close to 5:30 and stopped to pick up a nice bottle of Chardonnay before swinging by to get Rachel. She was ready right at six and they wasted no time in heading over to Ben's.

On the drive over, Nick could tell that Rachel was a little nervous, even though she was doing her best to hide it. More than once, he had glanced over to find her nibbling away at her bottom lip, a sure sign that she was on edge. But he decided not to say anything about it. If she wanted to talk about being nervous, she would. If she didn't, well, he could respect that too.

"You look beautiful tonight, Rachel," he commented as he helped her from the car. He loved the long, gauzy skirt she wore, and the white, sleeveless blouse tucked into the tiny waistband.

"Thank you," she said softly, and then started in again on her bottom lip.

"You feeling any better?" he asked as they walked up the front steps.

"I feel fine. The hangover has finally worn off."

"That's good."

And with that, Nick knocked on the front door. Within a matter of seconds, the door opened and a lovely woman smiled over at both of them.

"Nicholas Fallen, I swear that you just get better and better looking," she said as she ushered them into the house, throwing her arms around his neck. And Rachel watched as Nick kissed her squarely on the mouth.

"And you must be Rachel?" she said as she released her hold on Nick. "I'm Ben's wife, Betty."

"It's nice to meet you." Rachel extended her hand and Betty took it without hesitation. "And thank you for inviting me to dinner."

"Well, you're certainly welcome, my dear. It's been too long since this handsome guy came by for dinner. Every now and then, I insist he come over and eat so that I can make sure he gets something nutritious into him. And anyway, the girls miss him."

This was all said as Betty linked her arm through Rachel's and led them in the direction of a nice, cozy family room. "The roast needs a few more minutes and then we can eat. But come on in and Ben will get you whatever you'd like to drink."

Betty took the wine from Nick and then Ben took over as host. "What can I get for you, Ms. Bennett?"

"Please call me Rachel. And I'd love a soft drink of any kind, if you have it."

"No problem there. One beer and one Coke coming right up."

Ben disappeared into the kitchen with Betty, Nick took a seat on the sofa, and Rachel wandered over to the fireplace. On the mantel were family pictures of every size and shape, and she was intrigued by them. There must have been fifteen picture frames crammed on top of the mantel. And she wanted to see them all. So she took her time, carefully picking up each picture before setting it back down in its place.

"Here you go, Rachel."

She turned at the sound of Ben's voice, accepted the soft drink, and smiled her thanks. "These are wonderful pictures. I hope you don't mind my taking a look."

"Be my guest," Ben responded as he handed Nick his beer and sat down.

Both men watched as Rachel continued to lift one picture frame after another, looking at the pictures with such honest interest. She loved the pictures of the family, especially the little girls, and it showed on her face.

"Your daughters are lovely, Ben."

Nick wondered if he was the only one who heard the wishfulness in her voice.

"Thank you. Betty and I are really proud of both girls. They can be a handful at times, and we threaten to give them to the gypsies every other day, but they are the apples of our eyes. And speaking of a handful," he added, as they heard the pounding of little feet, "here comes one now."

"Uncle Nick! Uncle Nick!"

Rachel turned just as the cutest little girl she had ever seen came running into the room, heading straight for Nick. And in less than a heartbeat, she flung herself into the air and was caught around her tiny waist, landing smack dab on Nick's lap.

"Hey, princess," he laughed as she flung her arms around his neck, "what took you so long? I've been waiting for my hug for five minutes."

Little Becky giggled into Nick's neck as she hugged him for all she was worth, and Rachel's heart turned over at the sight. Here was the man she had fallen in love with, holding in his lap a precious little girl. He was laughing, hugging, and showing a side of him that she had no idea existed. And she couldn't pull her eyes away.

"Guess what, Uncle Nick?"

"What, princess?"

"I went to a baby shower with Mommy last weekend. And I was the littlest girl there. Except for the baby in the other mommy's stomach. That baby's younger than me because it isn't born yet."

"Did you have a good time?"

"We had lots of fun. I helped open presents and I got to eat two pieces of cake."

"Well, good for you."

"Rebecca, get off of Nick's lap and let him enjoy his drink." Betty had come in from the kitchen and sat down, urging her young daughter to behave.

"Oh she's no bother, Betty."

Rachel watched in total disbelief as Nick wrapped his arms around the little girl, keeping her on his lap.

"Where's Amanda?" he asked, as Becky squirmed to get more comfortable.

"She's where she always is. On the phone. I swear to God, I can't even begin to imagine what a thirteen-year-old can talk about all day. It's never-ending."

Rachel went over and sat down on the sofa with Nick, as everyone started talking about teenagers and whether or not they should have their own cell phone. Betty said yes, Ben said no, and Nick stayed out of it. The conversation was all in good fun, and while they debated the pros and cons, Rachel sneaked another peek at Nick and Becky. The little girl seemed totally content to sit on Nick's lap and listen to the grownup conversation, which didn't surprise Rachel all that much. What did surprise Rachel was how content Nick seemed to be. He seemed so at ease and she could tell that he really didn't mind that his lap had been taken over by a six-year-old. In fact he seemed to completely enjoy it.

"Well, here's our oldest angel now."

Betty's words caused everyone to glance in the direction of a very lovely young girl. And Rachel noted as she entered the room that she was dressed like all teenagers these days. She had on hip-hugger blue jeans, a shirt with the name of some rock group emblazoned across the front, and her feet were bare. And she had a huge smile that she directed right at Nick.

"Hi, Nick. Boy am I glad you're finally here." Rachel watched as she sat down on the arm of the chair that her father was sitting in. "I need you to help me convince Mom and Dad that I'm old enough to go out on a date with a nice boy that I've known since grade school. He's invited me to the movies this Saturday night and I think I'm old enough to go. Don't you?"

Rachel glanced over at Nick, and the look on his face was one of pure, unadulterated astonishment.

"Are you kidding me?" No one was sure for a moment who Nick was talking to, but he cleared that up with his next words. "You're not seriously thinking about letting Mandy go out on a date, are you, Ben? My God, she's only thirteen."

Becky, finally getting a little restless, wiggled off of Nick's lap and headed over to climb up next to her mother.

"Nick!" Amanda jumped up, looking at him like she'd lost her one and only friend. "I thought I could count on you to be on my side."

"Don't put Nick on the spot, young lady."

"But Mom!"

"But Mom nothing. And mind you manners." Betty's voice left no room for argument. "Amanda, say hello to Nick's friend, Ms. Bennett. And Rachel, this is our oldest daughter, Amanda."

Amanda said hello and Rachel asked the young girl to call her by her first name. With introductions out of the way, Amanda turned right back to her own situation.

"But can I ask Nick just one more question?" All eyes turned toward Amanda, who was perched again on the arm of her father's chair. "How old do you think I need to be to go out on a date? A real date."

Nick looked over at Ben, silently seeking some help, but his partner just sat there with a grin on his face. Obviously, Ben and his daughter had already been through this.

"Well …." And when no one came to his rescue, Nick continued. "If it were up to me, Mandy, I'd say you should be able to date at, say … oh, age eighteen."

"Eighteen?"

Again she sprang up from the arm of Ben's chair and then suddenly total chaos ensued. Ben burst out laughing, Amanda tried to convince everyone in the room that Nick didn't really mean eighteen, Becky squealed with laughter along with her father, and Nick tried to get a word in edgewise.

"Welcome to my world," Betty said as she got up and motioned for Rachel to follow her into the kitchen. "Will you help me put dinner on the table while they fight this out?"

Rachel almost hated to retreat into the kitchen, because she was having so much fun. But she got up laughing herself as the argument about dating continued.

Dinner progressed along the same lines, with everyone talking at once. The conversation was lively, the food wonderful, and Rachel was having a thoroughly good time. And so was Nick. It was apparent that Nick felt like he was a part of this very special family, and Rachel felt a twinge of envy. Envy because once Steven was behind bars, she would have no family at all to turn to. Not that she would miss Steven — quite the opposite. But the fact still remained that once he was locked up, she would be all alone, because even Nick would be out of her life.

Shaking off the sudden feeling of loneliness, Rachel's attention was drawn to Nick, who was sitting beside her at the table.

"Do you want a sip of wine?"

He was tilting his wine glass in her direction. His eyes were watching her over the rim of his glass, and she felt drawn into his stare. Without giving it any thought, she wrapped her hand around Nick's fingers on the stem of the glass, brought the wine to her lips, and took a sip.

"Mmm, that's nice," she whispered as her tongue swept over her bottom lip, and Nick felt an immediate tightening sensation in his groin. And he almost moaned in frustration. But luckily he was saved from that embarrassing possibility when Amanda asked Rachel a question.

"Mom told me earlier that you're a teacher. What do you teach?"

"I teach English literature at USC." Rachel found it hard to draw her eyes away from Nick and to concentrate on Amanda.

"Boy, that's pretty cool. I think it would be fun to be on a college campus all day. Do you like it?"

"Yes," Rachel responded with a warm smile. "I love teaching and it is pretty cool, if I do say so myself."

"Can I come and visit you sometime?" The enthusiasm in Amanda's eyes was unmistakable.

"I'd love that. If it's all right with your parents, you can come by anytime. Just give me a call and I'll give you the grand tour."

"Cool."

In that instant, Rachel realized that she really liked Ben and his family, and she wondered briefly why she had been the least bit nervous earlier. But just as that thought popped into her head, Amanda's next question made her more than nervous — it made her incapable of speech.

"Nick has never brought any of his girlfriends over here for dinner before. He must really like you. So how long have you two been dating?"

Rachel sat stone still, and was having trouble coming up with any kind of an answer. But not Nick. He answered Amanda as if her question was no big deal.

"Rachel and I met on a cruise ship almost two weeks ago, Mandy."

"You went on a cruise? I didn't know that. How completely cool."

Just like that, the topic of conversation shifted away from Nick and Rachel, as Amanda fired one question after another about what it was like to go on a cruise. She asked about the food, the activities, and all the ports of call. She had endless questions, and Nick sat very patiently sipping his wine, answering each and every one, until Betty finally announced that it was time for dessert.

Dessert was homemade apple pie and it was served in the family room. Amanda excused herself and took hers up to her room so that she could talk on the phone, and Becky ate hers curled up next to Nick on the couch. When everyone finished with dessert, Rachel asked if she could help with the dishes, but Betty refused to let her.

"Alex and Lou will be here shortly, Rachel, and I'll clean up then. Please just relax."

Betty smiled at her husband and nodded toward Becky, who was now snuggled up against Nick, fighting to stay awake.

"And as for you, little one, say goodnight to your dad, Uncle Nick, and Rachel. It's almost past your bedtime." Like all six-year-olds, Becky insisted that she wasn't the least bit sleepy. "Well it's time for bed anyway, Rebecca, so give your dad a goodnight kiss."

"Can Uncle Nick tuck me in?" she asked as she climbed back up on Nick's lap.

"Go on with your mom, Princess, and get ready for bed. I'll be up to tuck you in in a minute."

Becky climbed off Nick's lap, gave her dad a goodnight kiss and headed off with her mom. Then without warning, she turned, ran over to Rachel, and gave her a big hug and a kiss goodnight. Rachel's arms went around the little girl, and for a second, she held onto her for dear life. When Becky pulled away, Rachel felt tears well up in her eyes, and she had to fight to keep them from falling.

Nick watched Rachel's reaction to Becky and he wanted desperately to go over and put his arms around her. But he was way too aware of Ben watching him watch Rachel, so he stayed right where he was. He had made his point earlier that he wasn't falling for Rachel, and now was his chance to prove it. Whether he was proving the point to himself or to Ben, he wasn't entirely sure.

"So are you two ready for tomorrow?" Ben's question broke into both Nick and Rachel's thoughts.

"Yeah. Rachel booked our flight out and we arrive in San Diego at …?" He looked over at her when he realized that he didn't know what she had arranged.

"We leave Burbank Airport at three tomorrow and arrive in San Diego in about thirty minutes. I couldn't get a flight out any earlier, so we're stuck with the late afternoon."

"That means we should get to Bautista's sometime around eight at night," Nick added. "Rachel said the drive out to his place took close to two hours from downtown Ensenada. So if there are no delays, I figure we should get there in about four hours."

"Okay, buddy. I'll be waiting for both of you at the San Diego airport. You won't see me, but I'll stay as close as possible. Alex is bringing the …" Ben stopped at the knock at the front door. "Speak of the devil." He excused himself and went to answer the door, which left Nick and Rachel alone for a second.

"You okay?" he asked, and all she could do was send him a shaky smile.

Before Nick could remind her not to feel awkward over meeting Alex, Ben came into the room with Alex and Lou, and Betty came down the stairs. Because the dinner party had now turned to business, Betty quickly said her hellos and excused herself to go and clean up the kitchen.

"Lou, you remember Ms. Bennett?" Ben stated the obvious. "Ms. Bennett, this is Lieutenant Kendall, and Lieutenant, this is Rachel Bennett."

Rachel saw only friendliness in the eyes of the man these men called their boss, so she stepped forward and extended her hand. "It's a pleasure to meet you."

When Alex took her slender hand in his, he was reminded of Rachel's stunning beauty. He could see in an instant how easy it had been for Nick to fall for her. And glancing over Rachel's shoulder at Nick, who was standing behind her, he felt a little sorry for the guy. Because Alex knew, as he drew his eyes back to Rachel, that Detective Nicholas Fallen simply didn't have a chance.

"It's nice to meet you too, Ms. Bennett."

"Please call me Rachel."

"Thank you, I will." Alex let go of her hand and got right down to business. "All right, we're all here, so let's talk about tomorrow."

"Listen, Alex, give me a second, will you? I've got to go up and say goodnight to Becky." Nick didn't wait for permission; he just turned and bounded up the stairs.

"Sorry, Alex, but Nick promised he'd tuck Becky in, and she's probably upstairs in bed refusing to close her eyes until he gets there. You see, my daughter insists on calling him Uncle Nick and she thinks he hung the moon and the stars. The kid is crazy about him."

"Well, it looks to me like the feeling is mutual, Ben." Rachel hadn't intended to voice an opinion, but the words tumbled out anyway.

"Yeah. Nick's kinda partial to Becky. He spoils her rotten and no matter what Betty or I say, we can't seem to stop him."

Everyone, especially Rachel, noticed the pride in Ben's voice. It was obvious that he was delighted that his youngest daughter worshipped the ground his best friend and partner walked on — and vice versa. And for the second time that night, Rachel felt a pang of envy.

Five minutes after Nick disappeared, he came back down the stairs and they went to work.

"Before we go over the schedule, let me give you the watch with the chip that will allow us to follow you guys. This chip has a state-of-the-art tracking device, and a microphone so that we can hear what's going on."

Alex passed the watch to Nick and gave Ben what looked like some sort of small, hand-held navigation device.

"What's the range?" Nick asked as he slipped the watch-band over his left wrist.

"Pretty damn far. Ben and a couple of FBI boys can stay up to two miles behind you and still track your every move."

"Good. So Ben and two FBI tag-alongs will be on our tail, and Lou I take it you're still staying behind to keep on eye on Steven?"

"Hell yes." Lou said the words with a frown on his face because it was no secret that he wanted to go along on this operation and not stay behind and baby-sit.

"And I'll be with the rest of the feds in Ensenada. Ben will keep in touch by cell phone and we'll wait in the hotel for you and Rachel. I want you two to make the delivery and head back to town pronto. We want you both accounted for before the feds take over."

"When I made the last delivery, Mr. Bautista refused to have his driver take me back to the ship until he was ready to do so, Lieutenant. He insisted I stay for lunch, even though I tried to beg off. It may be difficult to get him to agree to let us return to town right away."

Nick walked over and sat down on the couch next to Rachel. And without thinking about what he was doing, he reached over and took hold of her hand.

"Don't worry about that, Rachel, because that's where I come in. When I'm finished fawning all over you, Bautista will see how anxious I am to get you back to Ensenada so that we can be alone. I'll make a big fuss about having to head back to

San Francisco in a couple of days and about how romantic I think Ensenada is. I plan to be all over you, Rachel. So much so that Bautista won't be able to wait to send us packing."

Rachel felt a deep blush rise to her cheeks and she just prayed that no one noticed. But she should have known better. Because the second she glanced over at Nick, his smile told her that he hadn't missed a thing. And even if the smile on his face hadn't told her so, his fingers tightening his hold on her hand gave her a clear message.

"Just be sure that you're convincing, Nick." Alex's voice interrupted Rachel's thoughts. "I don't want you and Rachel hanging around Bautista any longer than what's absolutely necessary. You won't be carrying a weapon, so I want you in and out. If we sense there's a problem and Bautista won't let you out of there, we're heading in. Remember, Ben will be able to hear everything that's going on."

"No problem, Alex. I'll get Rachel out of there. Leave it to me."

"I don't see why the hell I can't go along with Ben instead of a couple of federal agents." Lou finally added his two cents and he was looking directly at Alex. "Once this goes down, who gives a shit what Steven is up to? Anyone on the force can be assigned to follow him."

A stillness came over the room as everyone waited for Alex to respond.

"We've been over this, Lou. Outside of the FBI and Ms. Bennett, there are only four of us who know about this plan, and I want to keep it that way. So you'll stay here and keep watch over Mr. Jackson. If the man even looks like he's up to something, you call me. I don't care if you call me a dozen times. Anything out of the ordinary and you let me know. You're a cop and you need to rely on your training and your instinct. And you stay close to the bastard while we're gone. He gets a funny look on his face, he leaves the office earlier than usual, he does anything at all that you don't like, you pick up the cell phone and you call."

Alex left absolutely no room for a debate. He knew it, Lou knew it, and so did Nick and Ben. Even Rachel, who'd never seen Alex in action before, knew that the subject was closed. Lou would stay behind and watch Steven and that was the end of it.

"I'll do it, Lieutenant, but I refuse to like it."

"Now you're starting to sound like Nick."

Lou looked put out at Alex's comment, Ben looked like he was trying hard not to laugh, and Nick looked like he didn't like the comparison Alex had just made. But no one said a word, letting Alex take the lead.

"So what's the schedule for tomorrow?"

Nick was the one to speak up. "Rachel and I land in San Diego around three thirty. It'll take us a little over two hours to get to Ensenada, and from there, it's about another two hours to Bautista's place. We should get there before eight."

Alex got up from the chair he was sitting in and started to pace. And Rachel was struck by how similar Alex and Nick were. When Nick was trying to figure something out, or if he was troubled about something, he had a tendency to pace. Just like Alex was doing now.

"All right, Nick, everyone will be in place by the time you two arrive in San Diego. Except for you and Rachel, the rest of us will stay in touch by cell phone. Ben, I'll expect you to check in every thirty minutes, once Nick and Rachel leave the airport. Lou, I'll expect you to check in every three to four hours, unless our friend gives you any reason to check in earlier."

Everyone said okay at the same time, and Rachel figured that the meeting was over. But Alex surprised her when he stopped pacing and turned to look straight at her.

"Ms. Bennett …." Alex stopped and started again. "I mean Rachel. I haven't taken the time to tell you how much we all appreciate the fact that you're helping us. We couldn't pull this off without you. But having said that, I feel it's important to say that we're all well trained for this type of assignment, and I want to assure you that our number one goal is to keep you safe. Nick knows what he's doing, and he won't let anything happen to you. But in order for him to do his job, you must do exactly as he says, starting the moment you get off the plane in San Diego."

"We've already been through this, Alex." Nick assured him. "Rachel and I've had this exact conversation. There's no need to repeat it."

Alex didn't look completely convinced, so Rachel chimed in.

"Nick made it very clear that I'm to do what he says, when he says it, with no questions asked. I'm inquisitive by nature and I don't always go along without some sort of an explanation. But for this plan of yours to be successful, I really do understand that I need to do things Nick's way. So I give you my word that I will do exactly as I'm told. I'll do it Nick's way, Lieutenant Kendall, even if I refuse to like it."

She knew the instant she had won Lieutenant Alex Kendall over. As soon as she'd said that she would agree to go along and do things Nick's way, but that *she refused to like it,* she knew she had him. And for the first time since he and Lou entered the house, Alex smiled.

"What is it with everyone who works for me anyway?"

Rachel knew that she was included in his definition of *everyone,* and she was so pleased that she smiled back.

"You all have your assignments, so let's call it a night. Tomorrow's going to be a very busy day for all of us."

Now that the meeting was finally over, like magic, Betty came out of the kitchen. She walked over to where Ben was sitting, and like her daughter did earlier, she sat on the arm of the chair.

"Before you send everyone out into the night, Alex, can I offer up some coffee?"

"None for me, thanks, Betty."

Lou echoed Alex's response and so did Nick. And suddenly, before Rachel could take another breath, everyone was heading toward the door. *Boy,* she thought as Nick stood and pulled her to her feet, *when a meeting is over with these guys, it's over.*

When everyone was gathered on the front porch saying their goodnights, Betty took Rachel aside.

"I hope you'll come back with Nick again, Rachel. We would love to have you anytime."

Nick was busy talking with Alex, so Rachel felt it was safe to speak freely. For some reason, she couldn't find it in her to mislead this kind woman.

"After tomorrow, unless something comes up about the case, I don't think I'll see Nick again…" Saying those words out loud was harder than she could have imagined.

"Well, even though it's none of my business, I have to say that I think you're wrong about that."

"I wish it were true Betty. But …"

"I don't think you see what I see, my dear," Betty interrupted. "Even though we've only known Nick for two years, he's like a member of this family. And I feel very close to him. Close enough that I can tell you that I've never seen Nick look at anyone the way he looks at you. It's hard for him to let his guard down, but I can tell that there's something there. And I believe you feel the same way about him. Am I right?"

Again Rachel couldn't bring herself to lie. There was just something about Betty that made her want to confide in her.

"I've never felt this way about anyone, Betty. Not until I met Nick. But even though he may care about me, he doesn't …" She stopped the second she felt Nick's hand at her waist.

"Thanks for dinner, Betty. It was great, as usual."

Ben came over to stand by his wife, and Rachel and Betty exchanged a look of silent understanding right before Nick led her down the porch steps and into his car.

Rachel turned to wave goodbye as Nick slipped in behind the wheel, snapped his seat belt into place, and pulled away from the curb.

"See, now that wasn't so bad, was it?"

"I had a wonderful time, Nick. I'm really glad I came."

He glanced over and even though it was fairly dark inside the car, she could see the smile he threw her way.

"Betty and the girls are terrific. And it's not hard to see the bond that's developed between you and Ben."

Nick kept his eyes focused on the road. "Ben's the best partner I've ever had. There's no one I'd rather have watching our backs tomorrow."

Thinking about tomorrow caused a tightness in Rachel's throat, and she couldn't respond. Just the thought of seeing Miguel Bautista again sent shivers up and down her arms. But more than that, with the thought of tomorrow came the reality that she would probably never see Nick again. And that she could hardly bear to think about.

If Nick noticed her sudden quietness, he didn't let on. And for that, she was grateful. So grateful that she swallowed back her unexpected tears and peeked over at the man she knew she would never forget.

Rachel's eyes were drawn like magnets to one of Nick's hands on the steering wheel and the other draped lightly over the stick shift. He had beautiful, sexy hands, and Rachel felt a pool of desire as she recalled how his fingers had felt against her skin. There hadn't been an inch on her body that he hadn't touched, and she ached for him. She wanted desperately to be with him again. She wanted to feel his mouth on hers, to feel his hands roam over her body at his leisure, and to feel him slide deep into her. She wanted him so badly that her mind couldn't focus on anything else. And she was surprised when Nick pulled his car into her driveway and shut off the engine.

Nick stepped out of the car and walked over to give Rachel a hand. He opened the passenger door, reached out to take her hand in his, and helped her from the car.

"It's later than I thought," he mentioned as he shut and locked the car door. "I'll need to go into work for a few hours in the morning before we leave for San Diego. We might have a break in the gang stabbing and I want to follow up on a few things."

He kept her hand in his as they walked up to the house. As they reached the front door, Rachel reached into her purse for her key, only to have Nick take it from her. Wrapping his arm around her waist, he inserted the key, pushed open the door, and escorted her inside.

"I know it's not even ten yet, Rachel, but I need to make it an early night. I want to leave here no later than six tomorrow morning."

"Why so early?"

Nick took off his shoulder holster and dropped it onto the coffee table. Rachel knew that he wanted his gun close at hand.

"Ben and I want to ride around town and make sure this tracking device works as well as the feds claim. We also need to do some legwork on our recent stabbing before Ben can take off for San Diego. He's driving and wants to be in place at the airport before we land."

She felt almost guilty for asking. He and Ben put in such long hours.

"Do you need to set an alarm?"

"No. I'll have no problem getting up. And I promise I won't disturb you. I'll be as quiet as a mouse."

Nick took off his badge and his cell phone, and laid them next to his holster on the coffee table.

"Okay, Nick. Just give me a second to get the bedding to make up the couch for you."

Rachel took two steps toward the linen closet and then stopped. She whirled around, took one look at Nick, who was watching her, and made an instant decision.

"You don't have to sleep on the couch tonight." Her voice actually cracked.

Nick was still standing by the couch, and he felt his stomach tighten at her implied invitation. Every part of his being wanted to be with Rachel again, even if for only one more night. But no matter how much he wanted her, or how badly he wanted to sleep beside her, his brain told him he had to keep his distance.

"I think I'd better stay on the couch."

"Why?"

He was surprised that she even asked, but since she did he decided to be honest. "Because I can't give you what you want."

"You're wrong about that, Nick. I think you can give me exactly what I want."

"For one night maybe. But even if we both get what we want, in the end I can't give you any more. And I think you need so much more."

"Again, I think you're wrong about that. What I want and what I need happen to be one and the same. I've learned enough over the last ten days to realize that all we can do in life is to take one day at a time. There are no guarantees that we'll always be happy, Nick. And no one knows what their future will hold. So right now, what I want and what I need are very simple. I want and need to live for today."

She was making it nearly impossible for him to say no to her, but he knew that he had to find the willpower to stick to his guns.

"I'm still on the job, Rachel. And even if I wanted to, I can't just dismiss that away. I'm here to work with you and to protect you, not to take advantage of you. I did that once already and I don't want to do that to you again."

Rachel threw what little pride she had left right out the window as she took a couple of steps closer to Nick.

"I'm not naïve or foolish enough to believe that we have any kind of a future together. You've been honest about that from the very start. I know that after this case is closed, we'll never see each other again. But I also know that I don't want to regret not being with you one more time. So I was hoping that we could forget about this case for a few hours and share one last night together."

She looked so beautiful and so vulnerable that Nick almost reached out for her. But he knew he'd be totally lost if he touched her, so he fisted his hands at his side, telling himself over and over that he couldn't give in to the desire he felt in every bone of his body.

"No matter how much I want you, Rachel, I need to stay here on the couch tonight."

Her soft eyes looked up and she studied him as if the answers to all her questions were locked away in his deep, green eyes.

"Do you still want me?" She whispered the question, her eyes never leaving his.

"I'm not going to answer that, sweetheart."

And with his softly spoken words, Rachel knew the battle had come to an end. Nick may still want her, but not enough to be with her. And she had to accept that. No matter how badly it hurt, she just couldn't push him any more. So trying not to look as heartbroken as she felt, she stood up on her tiptoes, leaned in, and kissed him gently on the lips.

"Goodnight, Nick."

Her warm breath against his mouth was almost his undoing, and already Nick was regretting his decision. But now, as she stepped away from him, he knew that it was too late to change his mind. The damage was done. He had turned Rachel's offer down and she would never forget. And with that realization, Nick felt his heart crack just a little as Rachel turned without another word and headed for her room.

*   *   *

Nick looked at his watch one more time, irritated that it was midnight and he was still wide awake. No matter how hard he tried, he couldn't get Rachel out of his mind. The more he tried not to think about her, the more his mind betrayed him. And once his mind latched onto thoughts of her, his body was close behind.

He tossed and turned on the couch, flinging off the covers, cursing at his lack of control. He was actually throbbing with the need to lose himself inside of Rachel. Finally, in pure desperation, he sat up, ran his fingers through his hair, and then dropped his head into his hands.

"What the hell is the matter with me?" he muttered to himself. But the answer was obvious. Nick was driving himself nuts because the woman he wanted to make love to was sleeping in another room just a few feet away.

Not able to sit still another second, he got up and started to pace. Back and forth he went, until he couldn't stand it any longer. And with a curse beneath his breath, Nick stood and stared at the hallway, willing Rachel to come out of her room. And as the minutes ticked by, he found himself losing the battle between his brain and his body. Slowly at first, and then with absolute determination, Nick walked straight to Rachel's bedroom, opened the door, and went right in. Because he was so good at barely making a sound, he was able to make his way over to her bed without waking her.

Nick crouched down beside the bed, lifted his hand, and brushed a lock of hair away from Rachel's cheek. And just as his fingers skimmed over her skin, her eyes fluttered open. She didn't appear the least bit alarmed that he was crouched beside her bed, nor did she appear the least bit surprised.

"I thought you were a dream." Rachel's soft voice broke the silence. "But when I felt the touch of your hand against my face, I knew you were really here."

"I'm really here," was Nick's only comment as he reached out to touch her again. But this time, he let his fingers move slowly down the side of her neck, and over her bared shoulders, before reaching over and throwing back the covers.

Rachel didn't say another word as Nick got up from his crouched position, and sat down on the edge of the bed. He placed one of his hands gently on her shoulder and turned her so that she was lying flat on her back. Then, in complete silence, Nick pushed aside all of his doubts and removed the flimsy nightgown she was wearing. He brought it slowly up her body, slipped it over her head, and let it drop to the floor.

Nick's green eyes swept up and down Rachel's exposed body, needing to touch her but wanting to take his time. He let his eyes linger on her a moment longer, appreciating the swell of her breasts before he allowed himself to reach for the inviting peak. He began his exploration of her body by dragging the back of his fingers across her nipples. Rachel closed her eyes and sighed his name.

As he began to tease her with his lips and tongue, he felt Rachel's hand reach out for him.

"Oh no you don't, sweetheart."

Nick lifted his head and captured both of her hands in his. Piercing her with the intensity in his eyes, he lifted her hands above her head and placed them on the brass headboard, wrapping her fingers around one of the rails.

"If you move your hands before I'm finished, I'll get my handcuffs and cuff you to the headboard."

He spoke into her mouth and waited for a second for his words to penetrate her brain. Her sudden intake of breath told him that she understood his threat, and feeling confident that she would not remove her hands from the headboard, he continue with his slow exploration.

Nick let his tongue lick at the corner of Rachel's mouth before he dipped his head and buried his lips against the side of her neck. With a deep groan of pleasure, he kissed his way down her throat with a hot, wet, and open mouth. As he kissed his way down across her breasts, he stopped just long enough to suckle her extended nipple.

Rachel couldn't stop herself from thrusting her body upward to give Nick even more of an advantage. His teasing mouth was driving her crazy, and she almost let go of the headboard to reach out and drag him down on top of her. But even as exciting as the possibility was of being handcuffed to the bed, his words of warning kept her fingers wound tightly around the brass rails.

Only after Nick had gotten his fill of her sweet, rounded breasts, did he move on lazily down her body. First his hand trailed hotly down Rachel's stomach. Then he let his fingers play lightly with the soft curls between her legs. And then, finally, he moved down to the end of the bed, and bent his head so that he could taste her with his scorching mouth. And like a flash of lighting, Rachel exploded into an all - consuming, never - ending climax.

Rachel was still trying to come back to earth when Nick finally lifted his head. He got up from the bed, stripped out of his briefs, and noticed that her hands were still clutching onto the headboard. As he watched Rachel's eyes begin to focus, he leaned over and placed both of his hands over hers. He released her fingers from around the brass rail and turned her over onto her stomach. He then fumbled in her nightstand for a condom, stretched his naked body on top of hers, and lifted her hands back up to the headboard. And without being told what to do, Rachel tightly gripped the brass rail.

"All I can think about is being inside of you. I've never wanted anything more."

Nick dropped his head and whispered into her ear, his voice low and husky. And Rachel moaned.

She was so lost in the feel of Nick's erection pressed against her bottom, that a little sob escaped from her as he lifted himself up.

Nick brought himself up on both knees, placed his hands around Rachel's waist and brought her up so that she was kneeling on her knees with her back pressed against him. With her hands still holding onto the headboard, Nick wrapped one arm around her, cupped one of her breasts with his free hand, and without waiting another second, he thrust deeply into her from behind.

Rachel called out his name, and tightened her hold on the headboard as he began to move in and out of her. He started out nice and easy, keeping up a slow, even rhythm. But as he heard the catch in Rachel's voice, and as her breathing started to get deeper and faster, so did his thrusts. Holding onto her for dear life, Nick closed his eyes and buried his face into her hair.

"Come with me, sweetheart. Come with me now."

His words were all it took. With one final, deep plunge, Rachel screamed out her climax just as Nick threw back his head, took a deep breath, and followed her with a blinding climax of his own.

Both of them tumbled back down into the mattress as their knees suddenly gave way. Rachel's hands finally dropped from the headboard, her fingers throbbing with pain from clutching the rail so tightly.

Nick's limp body followed Rachel's down, and he shifted just enough so that he was draped over half her back, with one of his legs still between hers. His breathing was labored and he had to struggle to turn his head so that he was facing her.

Rachel was lying on her stomach, with her eyes closed, and her breathing was every bit as erratic as Nick's. It was only when she sensed that he was watching her did she find the energy to open her eyes.

"I tried to stay away from you, Rachel. But I just couldn't. No matter how hard I tried, I just couldn't stay away."

"I'm glad you couldn't, Nick." Rachel had trouble getting the words out because her throat was so dry.

At first, Nick didn't say anything. Instead of talking, he was content to just lie beside Rachel and watch her. And then, because he couldn't help it, he reached over to lightly stroke his thumb over her cheek.

"Your skin is as soft as satin, and I get hard just thinking about touching you."

Rachel sighed into the pillow.

"Even now, just lying here looking at you, and feeling your skin beneath my fingers is enough to make me want you again."

Nick's hand swept down her neck, and then he trailed his fingers every so slowly all the way down her back.

Rachel stirred beneath his touch. And as one minute turned into two, she started to lift her head so that she could get a better look at him.

"Don't move," he finally whispered to her. "I'll be right back. I need to get rid of this condom."

With a great deal of effort, Nick forced himself to get up. He headed into the bathroom, quickly cleaned up, and was back in bed before she even had a chance to turn over. Smiling at the sensual picture she presented, he climbed in beside her.

"My God, Rachel," he breathed out the words. "I really do want you again."

Nick worked at gently turning Rachel onto her side. Then he scooped her up against his body, wrapped her tightly in his arms, and bent his head to kiss her. The kiss was long, wet, and very thorough. And before she had fully recovered from his lovemaking, she was leaning into his kiss, letting him know that she was ready for him again.

"But this time it's my turn," she barely managed to get out as she pulled her mouth away from him. "This time it's my turn to touch you, to tease you, and to taste you."

She could tell that what she'd just said hadn't really registered with Nick, so she put action to her words. First she pushed him onto his back. Second, she took hold of his hands, brought them up to the headboard and wrapped his fingers around the brass rail.

"If you move your hands before I'm finished," she whispered against his lips, "I'll get your handcuffs and cuff your hands to the headboard." She had remembered his exact words to her.

Nick swallowed back a deep moan, but the desire in his eyes was all the encouragement she needed to put her sexual plan to work. So slowly, very slowly, Rachel began her own exploration of his glorious body. As she continued her torturous assault, she could feel Nick's body responding. She could tell he was right on the edge, and she was determined to push him over. She wanted to give him as much pleasure as he had given her, and she knew exactly how she wanted to do it. So with one quick glance to make sure that his strong hands were still holding onto the headboard, Rachel's hands, mouth, and tongue continued to touch, to tease, and to taste.

In the stillness of the night, Nick thought that maybe he'd died and gone to heaven. As Rachel worked her way down his body, he couldn't tell what was driving him crazier — the feel of her mouth against his skin, or the feel of her silky hair as it trailed over the same path her lips had taken. Whatever it was, mouth or hair, Nick was on the brink of losing control. And the fact that he couldn't touch her was making it even worse.

But because he was already so close to the edge, all Nick could do was to close his eyes, clutch his fingers even more tightly onto the headboard, and let Rachel take him to the ends of the earth.

CHAPTER SIXTEEN

"Buenas noches."

"Fallen will be wearing the tracking device in his wristwatch."

"Very good, Señor Jackson. I will tell my men."

"Is everything in place?"

"Everything is ready. The only problem is there will be a slight delay in getting rid of the cop and your sweet sister-in-law."

Steven felt perspiration begin to form on his upper lip. Delays could only mean trouble.

"I don't understand. I thought you'd arranged for a car accident."

"Everything's arranged. But in order to make this accident look real, I have to dispose of one or two of my own men. The two men I plan to sacrifice are finishing up another little job for me, and they should get to my villa tomorrow night around ten."

Perspiration was now forming under his arms. This wasn't going according to plan. But Bautista was a master at getting rid of problems, so Steven tried his best to calm down.

"Okay, so how's it going to happen? Remember, I can't have anything traced back to me."

Miguel Bautista wasn't accustomed to explaining himself

to anyone, but since he owed Steven Jackson a favor, he decided to make an exception this time. But after this business transaction was completed, he would never contact the man again. He had all the false papers he needed and besides, Jackson was starting to feel like a liability.

"Three of my men will pick Fallen and Ms. Bennett up at the airport and bring them here. En route, they will dispose of the FBI tracking device. Once they arrive at my villa, the cop and Ms. Bennett will be my guests for about two hours. As soon as Sanchez and Moronez arrive, I will turn Fallen and Ms. Bennett over to them. They will be instructed to take our guests out into the desert to get rid of them. Only problem is, no one will make it very far. The accident is arranged and all four will be dead within an hour of leaving the villa. It will look like Detective Fallen and your sister-in-law were being taken back into town when the tragic accident occurred."

Steven's spirits were starting to lift. With both Nick and Rachel dead, there would be no witnesses against him and no hard evidence. Bautista's plan was solid and should work like a charm. That is, as long as Fallen was kept under control.

"Nicholas Fallen will fight you as soon as he realizes you're on to him. The minute you try to get the watch off him, he'll know he's as good as dead."

"Detective Fallen will have very little say in the matter. He will have a hard time fighting us with a gun pressed to his and Ms. Bennett's temple."

"So that's why you're sending three men to pick them up?"

Bautista didn't bother to reply. The answer was obvious.

"Are you going to tell them that they're going to die?"

"Of course," was Bautista's calm and eerie response. "I shall deliver that message to them myself. I didn't like the way your sister-in-law treated me when she was a guest in my house, and I shall delight in watching her face as I tell them both they have only two hours left to live."

Steven was a cold-blooded man, but even he wasn't sure he would go that far. He preferred to remove himself from the unpleasant side of his business. And thinking about what was unpleasant, reminded him of his informant.

"I have a small favor to ask." Bautista waited, so Steven went on. "My informant wants to be there. He hates Fallen's guts and he wants to see for himself that the cop and my sister-in-law are dead."

"I don't want him here, Mr. Jackson."

Steven's calm state slipped away. He refused to beg, but he needed to deal with the problem of his informant. And Bautista was the only man he knew who could do it.

"I wish you'd reconsider, Mr. Bautista. You see, I was hoping that he'd show up and have a little accident of his own, and that perhaps his body could be found with the others. I'd like to create confusion about the accident, and I figure with another cop thrown into the mix, the feds will be so perplexed that some of the pressure will be off me. They'll be scrambling around trying to figure out if they're dealing with a dirty cop. And they won't be sure who's dirty — Fallen or my informant. With all that going on, it will give me time to disappear for a while."

Miguel Bautista thought that Steven Jackson was a complete fool. No way would the body of one more cop take the focus off of him. Sure, it might confuse things for a while, but since the cops already knew about Steven's little side business, with or without their star witness, they'd still go after him. But if the fool thought he was safer getting rid of his informant, then so be it. One more dead cop, even a dirty cop, was no skin off his nose.

"I'll expect your informant before Detective Fallen and Ms. Bennett arrive. I want to speak with him myself. And he is not to bring a weapon. Understood?"

"Understood."

Steven hated being the one having to take orders. He was much better at giving them. But he needed Miguel Bautista right now, and even though the man owed him big-time, there was no mistaking who was in charge.

"When this is over, Mr. Jackson, you and I are even. I will owe you no more favors, so don't ask for one. Don't ask me for a favor ever again. I hope that too is clearly understood."

It wasn't a question, really, but Steven knew the man expected a response.

"Of course, Mr. Bautista. That too is understood."

"Then I will wish you a good night."

And like Steven did to so many others, Miguel Bautista hung up the phone, without waiting for a reply.

CHAPTER SEVENTEEN

The plane ride from Burbank to San Diego left on time, and Nick and Rachel arrived to find a man holding a sign with her name on it. The day was turning out lousy, by Nick's way of thinking, and all he wanted was to get this assignment over with. He hated being undercover without a weapon. He hated that Rachel might be in danger and he had jack shit to protect her. He hated that he was worried, on edge and not much in the mood for talking.

He had gotten up early and left the house without waking Rachel. They had made love on and off all night, but the funny thing was, other than being a little tired, he felt sharp as a tack. He had met Ben at headquarters at six, and they took advantage of the light traffic and rode around testing the tracking device. It worked perfectly. Then they followed up on what they thought was a lead to their gang stabbing. Unfortunately, the lead went absolutely nowhere.

The morning passed pretty much as expected, but what made the day start to turn was the argument Nick had with Alex. All morning, Nick had a nagging feeling about this trip to Mexico. A bad feeling he couldn't quite shake. He knew that everything was lined up and everyone was in place. He knew that Ben would watch their backs and that Alex and the feds were close at hand. But still, he had a gut feeling that something was going to go wrong. And he didn't want Rachel any-where around if things went to shit. So Nick had approached Alex with a change in plans, which Alex promptly shot down. Which promptly pissed Nick off, and he still felt pissed.

Nick had mentioned to Alex that this assignment was too risky for a civilian. He purposely hadn't mentioned Rachel by name, because he didn't want Alex accusing him of being too involved to be objective. So, downing a cup of coffee in his of-fice, Nick laid out his new plan to both Alex and Ben.

He casually suggested that they leave Rachel behind, and send him on alone to deliver the package to Bautista. Nick said that once he got to San Diego, he could explain in his lim-ited Spanish that Rachel had come down with the flu, and that he was making the delivery for her. They would accomplish the same thing, as far as Nick was concerned. They would get to Bautista's, pin down his whereabouts, turn the matter over to the feds and the Mexican authorities, and call it a job well done. And Rachel would be safe.

The only problem was that Alex had dismissed his plan, not giving it any consideration. Alex claimed that they weren't about to jeopardize this operation by making changes at the last minute. Bautista was expecting Rachel, and Alex was con-cerned that the driver would leave Nick's ass behind if Rachel wasn't with him.

So the argument had started. Nick ended up raising his voice, Alex ended up slamming around his office, and Ben sat still, deciding that now was not the time to interfere. He knew these two needed to fight this thing out between them.

In the end, it was no surprise that Alex got his way. The plan would go forward with Rachel. No more discussion. And from that minute on, Nick felt madder than hell. He was mad at Alex, but even madder at himself for ever agreeing to let Rachel get involved in this. He should have figured out a bet-ter way to get what they needed. But like everyone else, he was so focused on the opportunity to finally get his hands on

Bautista that nothing else seemed to matter. And all he hoped now was that he wouldn't regret it. Because of all this, Nick was still in a bad mood when he picked Rachel up and drove them to the airport.

Rachel had noticed the minute she slipped into Nick's car that his mood had altered. She could see how rigidly he was sitting, and how tightly his fingers were wrapped around the steering wheel. She couldn't see his eyes because they were hidden behind sunglasses, but she could sense that he was in no mood to talk. So, wisely, she left him alone. She knew without a shadow of a doubt that his sullen mood had to do with work and not with her. Last night, they had been as close as two people could be. They had made love, laughed, made love some more, and slept tangled together under the sheets. The night couldn't have been better. And this morning, she had found a sweet note scribbled by him next to the coffeepot. It had simply read, *Hey, sleepyhead, I'll pick you up at two. Call me before that if you need me.* It was signed Nick, and the P.S. brought tears to Rachel's eyes. *P.S. Last night was incredible. I'm glad I didn't listen to myself.*

Since nothing had happened between them from the time Nick left the note to the time he'd picked her up, she knew that he was drawn into himself for the job ahead. So she didn't take his mood personally. The best she could do was to let him work through things in silence and hope that his mood would improve. But the plane ride wasn't much better. They got aboard, got settled, and because he still hadn't felt like talking, he had reached over and placed her hand in his.

As she rested her hand in his, and just as the plane took off for San Diego, Rachel had simply leaned over and kissed him lightly on the cheek.

Please God, don't let anything happen to her, he prayed, and then he closed his eyes for the rest of the quick trip.

Right before landing, Nick opened his eyes, and suddenly he was all cop. He had reminded her to do exactly as he said, and she had simply nodded her agreement. So here they were, making their way through the airport to the man holding the sign bearing her name.

Rachel shouldn't have been surprised, but Nick switched his mood again so quickly, she had to blink twice in order to get into character. The second he spotted the man with the sign, he became the fawning lover. He was carrying their small overnight duffel in one hand, and slung his other arm around Rachel's shoulder, bringing her in close to his body. He suddenly seemed totally relaxed. He had a smile on his face, his step was light, and he looked to all the world like he was getting ready to go on a little vacation.

As soon as they reached Bautista's man, Nick dropped the duffel at his feet and extended his hand. The man with the sign shook Nick's hand, and smiled over at Rachel.

"Please come with me. The car is waiting."

Rachel was surprised that this man spoke English. The driver Bautista had sent before knew nothing but Spanish, and Rachel had expected that to be the case this time as well. She knew Nick hadn't expected anyone to speak English, but he didn't miss a beat. Without taking his arm from around Rachel, he reached down to grab the duffel, and followed the man with the sign.

What did surprise Nick, though, was that when they reached the black SUV, he could see two other men inside. There was one man sitting in the front seat, and one in the back seat on the driver's side. His stomach tightened, and all his senses went on alert. And for about the hundredth time, he cursed under his breath that he didn't have a weapon.

"We had some business to attend to before we could pick you up at the airport," explained the man who tossed the sign into the back. "But the car has lots of room, so the trip should be most comfortable." His English was excellent, and Rachel wondered if he, like Bautista, was born and raised in the U.S.

"No problem," Nick said as he helped Rachel up into the SUV. But in reality, he knew that this could be a big problem. His only saving grace was that he knew that Ben and a couple of feds were close behind.

The drive across the border was uneventful. Hasty introductions were made and after that, everyone seemed content to sit in silence. Nick played the boyfriend to the hilt. Rachel was sitting between Nick and the man called Roberto, and he scooted her as close to him as possible. He kept her hand firmly clasped in his, and pretended to watch the scenery go by. But behind his sunglasses, Nick was more interested in studying the driver and the man sitting directly in front of him. He wanted to be able to give the FBI as accurate a description as possible.

Every now and then, just to make things look real, Nick would lean over and kiss Rachel lightly on the temple. He kept her snuggled so close to him, there could be no misinterpreting his intentions. He was the boyfriend, crazy in love, and that was why he was along.

Rachel knew that Nick was only playing a role, but she felt so much safer tucked up against his body. They were pressed as closely together as they could get, and Nick had a firm and protective hold on her hand. He kept sweeping his thumb over the back of her hand, and she felt his caress deep in her heart.

There was a part of Rachel that couldn't wait for all of this to be over with, but there was another part of her that couldn't bear the thought of saying goodbye to Nick. She was so torn, especially after last night. She loved Nicholas Fallen and she had almost said the words to him as they'd made love. But she had forced the words back, knowing that those were words he didn't want to hear. He had been with her last night because she had offered him a night of sex without any commitment. And he had taken her up on that. Nothing more. And even though her heart was breaking at the prospect of never seeing him again, she wouldn't have changed last night for the world.

The SUV made its way through Ensenada, and was heading out of town. Rachel had no idea if they were heading in the same direction as before, but she was very watchful as they made their way deeper into the desert. Nick was watching everything around him, wondering how far behind Ben and the feds were. He'd glanced at this watch earlier just to check the time, and realized that they'd been on the road for a little over two hours. There were about two hours to go.

As the SUV turned off onto a dirt road that seemed to lead to nowhere, Nick glanced down at Rachel to see if she could shed some light on the route they were taking. She looked up at him and barely shook her head, giving him the message that she wasn't sure. He was just about to ask casually how far to their final destination, when Rachel spoke up, surprising him.

"I wonder if this is the same way we went the last time." Purposely, she was speaking to no one in particular. She just wanted to see if she could get a response.

"We are taking a little shortcut, Ms. Bennett," said the man sitting beside her. "We will be back on the main road once we get closer to Mr. Bautista's villa." Again, such perfect English, noted Rachel, and not for the first time, she wondered where Bautista found these men.

Nick shifted beside Rachel, suddenly more alert than he wanted anyone to know. He couldn't ignore the alarm bells in his head, and he thanked God that the tracking device included a microphone that transmitted to Ben everything being said. But just as he thanked God that Ben was not far behind, the car came to a screeching halt, and suddenly without any warning, there were two guns pointed right at Rachel and Nick. The man sitting beside Rachel had a pistol pointed directly at her temple, and the man in the passenger seat turned and pointed his own pistol right at Nick's forehead.

"Make one move and you'll live to regret it, Detective Fallen. Because if you so much as move a muscle without being told to, Ms. Bennett will be the first to die."

Nick did as he was told. He didn't move, because he believed these guys. If he did anything rash, Rachel might die, and Nick couldn't live with that possibility. Besides, he didn't have a damn thing to use to protect them, so he didn't have any choice but to sit absolutely still.

The driver got out of the car, went around to the passenger side of the back seat, and opened the door. With a gun still pointed at his forehead, Nick didn't so much as blink an eye as the driver reached over, pulled at his left arm, and yanked off his watch.

"I'll just take this, Detective." And with that, Nick and Rachel watched as the watch with the tracking device was thrown onto the ground and smashed into the dirt with the heel of his boot.

"I know your friends probably aren't too far behind, but right about now, they've discovered that they've just lost any trace of you."

Rachel let out a little whimper that Nick hoped only he could hear. They were still holding hands, and her nails were digging deeply into his flesh. Nick knew that she was scared to death, but there wasn't a thing he could do about it right now. His only hope was that Ben would figure out a way to catch up with them. But even he knew that the possibility of that was one in a million.

The driver reached into the back of the SUV and extracted two pieces of rope. In no time at all, he had Rachel and Nick's hands tied behind their backs. And only once they were securely tied up did the other two men put their guns away.

"Just sit back and enjoy the ride. We'll be at Mr. Bautista's in no time. He's expecting us before eight."

They turned around on the dirt road and started heading back toward the main highway. And in less than ten minutes, they were back on their way, flying down the road. Nick looked over to see if Rachel was all right, and she was as white as a ghost. His heart sank into the pit of his stomach. The bad feeling he'd had all morning had finally caught up with him. He wanted to be able to reach out to her, but all he could do was lean down and lay his cheek close to her temple.

"You okay?" he whispered, and when she turned her eyes to his, his heart lodged in his throat. She was obviously scared out of her wits, but she was trying to be very brave. He could tell.

"I'm okay," she whispered back, and behind him, he maneuvered his tied hands as close to hers as he could. She moved her hands tied behind her back toward his, and their fingers touched. It was just a light touch, but Nick hoped like hell it was comforting all the same.

The rest of the drive was made in complete silence. It took almost two more hours to reach their destination, and when they finally did, it was pitch black. There was no moon out and there were no lights on around the villa. The entire place had a deserted look to it. Which, of course, wasn't the case at all.

Nick and Rachel were helped out of the back seat of the car, dragged out by their arms. They were pushed up the front steps, Rachel nearly stumbling into Nick. Right before they reached the door, it swung open, and there in all his glory stood their host — Señor Miguel Bautista.

Bautista was standing in the glow of the lights that were on within the house, and Rachel thought he looked as menacing as ever. And she felt her skin crawl.

"Well, well, well. We meet again, Ms. Bennett. And I see you've brought along another guest. Please, do come in, Detective Fallen."

Nick was shoved from behind into the entryway, with Rachel right behind him.

Bautista nodded his head in the direction of the room Rachel had been in during her last visit, and both of them were literally pushed forward. As they were both practically thrown into the room, Miguel Bautista followed behind, closing the door behind him. It was understood that the three men from the car were now standing guard. As Rachel and Nick stood side by side, Bautista walked over and poured himself a drink, talking a long sip. He then walked over to a chair, sat down, and crossed one ankle over his knee. He looked like he had all the time in the world.

"Figure it out yet, Detective?"

Bautista was sneering at him and Nick wanted to kill the man with his bare hands. And he decided that if he could get free, that would be exactly what he would do. But for now, Nick couldn't afford to lose his focus. He had to stay calm and try to figure out a way to escape.

"The watch was obviously no surprise to you. You knew exactly what you were looking for, so we must have a leak in the ranks. Any fool could figure that out."

"And you are anything but a fool. Right, Detective?"

Bautista was baiting him. But for what reason Nick didn't know.

"That's where you're wrong. I'm a fool, all right. I was a fool to come out here without a gun to blow your fucking brains out." That probably wasn't the smartest thing Nick could have said, but he couldn't help himself.

Bautista took another swallow of his drink, and Nick had the suspicion that he wanted to throw the rest of it in his face. But their host pretended to ignore his comment, and played it cool. "So, Detective Fallen. Any guess as to who the dirty cop is in your shop?"

Now Nick was certain that Bautista was taunting him, but he wasn't in the mood to play along, so he remained silent.

"No matter," Bautista continued. "You'll find out soon enough."

While Bautista sat quietly, sipping his drink, Nick worked at the rope tied around his hands. If he could just get his hands free, he would have the element of surprise on his side, which should give him the chance to overtake the bastard.

Rachel was standing next to Nick, completely silent and not moving so much as one inch. Nick guessed that fear kept her quiet and immobilized. He didn't know what Bautista's little waiting game was, but he didn't have to wait long for the answer.

"It would seem, my dear, that you and your association with the cops have made your brother-in-law a very nervous man. And because of that, I've found myself in a position of having to do Mr. Jackson one little favor." He took another sip. "It's a pity, though, that you got yourself involved in something that is obviously way over your pretty little head." His evil eyes swept slowly up and down Rachel's body. "A pity indeed."

If Nick could get free and get hold of a gun, he knew he would put a bullet hole right through Bautista's skull.

"And you, Detective Fallen. Did you and your friends really think I would allow you to just waltz in here and lead the FBI right to my front door? You may be a fool, but I am rather surprised that you and the LAPD are that stupid."

"If there hadn't been a leak within our department, you would already be in custody. We are not stupid, Bautista, just unlucky. And it sickens me that we were not able to bring you down because one of our own has turned out to be a no good son of a bitch.

"You give yourself too much credit, Detective Fallen. Better men than you have tried to … take me down, as you so eloquently stated, and they too have failed."

"We may have failed tonight, but mark my words. Your time will come. You can count on it."

As Nick talked he worked at the rope around his wrists. If he could keep Bautista distracted long enough, he might just be able to work his hands free.

"You are dead wrong, Detective. I didn't need a leak to help me stop you. No one gets into my villa uninvited. Absolutely no one."

Nick started to respond, but was stopped cold when he heard the door open and close. Nick and Rachel turned around at the same time. Rachel gasped out loud, and Nick said nothing. The look in his eyes said all there was to say.

"Oh my God." Rachel felt her knees start to buckle and Nick stepped closer to her, silently urging her to lean on him.

"Oh come on, Fallen. Don't tell me you're not surprised that I'm the leak?"

Nick never knew that he could feel such hatred for another human being. Hating Bautista was just a natural reaction because of his job and the fact that Bautista was a lowlife criminal. But the hatred he felt when he looked at one of his own who had betrayed everything he stood for was a deep-rooted hatred. And it was a feeling he would never forget.

"You're disappointing me, Nick old friend. The hotshot detective I know would be trying to talk his way out of this right about now. What's up? Cat got you tongue?"

Nick forced all emotion off his face, and his eyes turned a deadly green. "I hope you burn in hell, Lou." Nick sent him there with the look in his eyes.

With all the swagger he could muster, Lou Jensen stepped forward and backhanded Nick so hard across his face that Nick lost his balance and fell to his knees. Rachel let out a small cry as blood started dripping from the corner of Nick's mouth, and she fell to her knees beside him. Lou bent down and grabbed a handful of her hair, pulling her painfully back to her feet.

"Keep your dirty hands off of her," Nick managed right before Lou kicked him in the ribs with such force that he crashed to the floor on his side. Lou lifted his boot to kick a second time, and Rachel started begging Lou not to hurt him anymore. Lou tightened his hold on Rachel's hair and planted another blow to Nick's body.

"Enough!"

The sound of Bautista's voice stopped Lou, and Nick struggled back to his knees. He had to blink several times in order to clear his head.

"Bring both of them over here to me."

Lou let go of Rachel's hair to roughly pull Nick to his feet. Then he shoved both Nick and Rachel toward Bautista, who hadn't moved from the chair.

"I have no intention of looking up at the two of you any longer. Down on your knees."

Rachel dropped without any further urging, but Nick wasn't as cooperative. So Lou landed a swift kick to the back of Nick's legs, bringing him down to his knees beside Rachel.

"Making me angry will do you no good, Detective Fallen. I am in charge here. Make no mistake about it."

Lou moved to stand behind Bautista's chair so that he could watch the rest of the show about to unfold. This was what he came for and he didn't want to miss a thing.

"I'm sure you and Ms. Bennett realize by now that you will not live to see the morning. You're death is not in question. Neither I nor Mr. Jackson can afford to let you live. And you should be thankful that I've decided not to kill you here on the spot. In less than two hours, you two will be going on a little ride. The desert is very beautiful this time of night, and it seems a fitting place for both of you to die."

Nick looked over and watched as Rachel swallowed back a lump of fear. She had a knowing and terrified look in her eyes, and Nick would have given anything in the world if he could get her safely out of here.

"Detective Jensen will escort you to a room upstairs, where you will be locked in and untied for the next two hours. Don't even waste your time tying to escape. Windows will not open and no one will come if you call out."

Miguel Bautista looked from Rachel to Nick. He was pleased to see fear in Rachel's eyes, and irritated that Nick's face showed no expression at all. So he took one more stab at riling him. Bautista got to his feet and stared down at the couple on their knees.

"There are few people in this world that I despise more than cops, Detective Fallen. So know this. If I had my way, I would turn Ms. Bennett over to my men and force you to watch each man take his time and pleasure with her. Then, I would kill her right before your eyes. And finally, I would find a most painful way for you to die. But this is not my show, and I have agreed to have you both meet with a most unfortunate accident. So for now, you will have two hours to say goodbye to each other. I suggest you make good use of that time."

Bautista's sarcasm was not lost on Nick or Rachel. Nick also knew that Bautista's goal was to get a rise out of him, so he refused to let any hint of emotion show. And Rachel was just too stunned and too scared to speak.

"Get them out of here before I change my mind and kill them both this instant." Bautista barked this order at Lou Jensen, who moved around and jerked both Rachel and Nick to their feet. He dragged them out of the room, and instantly the three men who were standing guard came to attention.

"You, come with me. And bring your gun. If either one of them makes one move, shoot the woman." Lou was back in charge for a few minutes, and loving every minute of it.

Nick and Rachel were pushed up the stairs and into a small, furnished bedroom. With the gun pointed directly at Rachel, Lou untied Rachel's hands first and then Nick's.

Rachel stood rubbing away the pain around her wrists caused by the rope, but Nick was too angry to feel any pain, so he stood with his hands tightened into fists at his side.

"What, Fallen? Still nothing to say? Or are you scared too shitless to speak?"

Lou headed for the door, when Nick asked a simple, one-word question.

"Why?" That was all he said, but that was enough to get Lou's attention.

"You really are one stupid son of a bitch. Why in the hell do you think I did it? I did it for the money. Lots and lots of money."

"So just how much is lots and lots of money, Lou? How much did Jackson pay you to kill Rachel's sister?"

"More than I will ever see on this stinkin' job. Being a cop is fine if you don't want anything more in life than to fucking serve and protect. But I want a lot more, and Steven Jackson was able to help me get it. And having the pleasure of knowing that you are going to die is frosting on the cake."

"So you sold your soul to the devil?"

"Not quite, Nick. To my way of thinking, I already am the devil." And with that, Lou laughed his way out the door, slamming and locking it behind him.

Nick instantly turned toward Rachel, and she almost fell into his outstretched arms.

"Nick, are you all right?" Rachel reached up and touched a finger to the caked blood on his lip. "Are you hurt?"

"I'm fine." He responded to the concern in her voice by tightening his hold. "Really, I'm fine."

He held onto her, trying to soothe away some of her fears. He wanted to keep on holding her, but time was running out, and there was something he had to tell her. But he had to check out the room first. So very carefully, Nick led Rachel over to the bed, urged her to sit, and placed a finger up against his lips, telling her without words to stay perfectly quiet.

Rachel sat in stunned silence and watched as Nick took his time looking at every nook and cranny in the room. He searched through the empty closet; he searched every light, under the bed, along the doorframe, as well as in, out, and around both nightstands. Finally, satisfied that everything was in order, he came and sat down next to Rachel.

"I can't find any evidence that the room is wired, but let's speak softly just the same."

"Does it even matter?" Her question was filled with despair.

"Yeah, sweetheart," he replied as he wrapped her again in his arms. "It does."

Rachel tightened her arms around Nick and shuddered into his shoulder. She was scared beyond belief, but she wanted him to think that she was brave enough to look death in the eye without making a scene.

"I need you to listen to me for a minute, Rachel." He loosened his arms from around her, but kept her close by reaching out and taking hold of one of her hands. "I need to tell you something important."

Nick was speaking very quietly, and Rachel wondered what he could possibly say that had to be kept a secret. There was no way they were going to get out of this alive. She knew it, and she knew that Nick knew it. But because she felt some urgency in him, and because she too had something important to say, she reached up and placed a couple of her fingers against his lips.

"I'll listen, Nick," she said quietly. "But first, I need to say something to you."

Nick kissed the tip of her fingers and then captured her hand with his. Now he was holding both of her hands. "Me first, sweetheart. You need to hear what I have to say."

No way was Rachel going to let him go first. "Please, Nick. I've done absolutely everything you've asked of me and I haven't asked much of you in return. But I'm asking you now. Please listen to what I have to say. It's important to me."

"But, Rachel, what I need to tell you may change ..."

"Please." Her words and her eyes were begging him, and at that moment he could deny her nothing. So he just sat and quietly looked at her, waiting for her to continue.

Rachel looked down into her lap for a long minute, and Nick wondered if she had changed her mind. But he guessed that what she was really doing was gathering her thoughts, so he calmly waited.

"This is very hard for me, Nick, so please don't interrupt me. I know that will be almost impossible for you," she added with a touch of a smile, "but please let me get it all out."

When she looked up into his eyes, he leaned over and kissed her ever so lightly against her parted lips. "Okay. I won't interrupt."

Rachel knew it was now or never. And since their time together was running out, she plunged right in.

"I need you to know that no matter what I said to you last week, I know in my heart that you never meant to mislead me or to take advantage of me. I fell hard for you on that cruise ship, and I did everything in my power to get you to take me to bed. And when I needed to blame someone, I blamed you. I was embarrassed, hurt, and angry, and I took it all out on you. It was so much easier than accepting how I really felt about you." Rachel took a breath, looked again into Nick's eyes and went on before she lost her nerve. "But I've gotten to know you, Nicholas Fallen, and I want you to know that I admire everything about you. I think you're the most honorable man I've ever met. You are a good person, and you're someone I am so proud of. I …"

"Rachel," Nick interrupted even though he said he wouldn't because he was getting a little embarrassed.

"Please. You promised to let me finish."

"Okay," was all he said when he caught the catch in her voice.

"All of that's important, Nick, but what's really important is for me to tell you that when we made love last night, that's exactly what it was for me. I know you don't want to hear this, but I need to tell you that I've fallen in love with you. I love everything about you. It's not just the fact that you're the most incredible lover, or that you've shown me a sexual side of myself that I never knew existed. I love you because you can make me laugh, you make me want to try new things, in and out of bed," she added with a shaky smile. "You have a mind that's as sharp as a tack and you have a wonderful sense of humor. I believe in you, Nick, and my biggest regret in dying is that I'll never know if there was any chance that you would have fallen in love with me." Rachel wanted to be brave, but she couldn't stop the tears that were now falling from her eyes. "I don't need or want you to tell me you love me back. It was just so important before we die that I tell you that I love you."

Rachel dropped her eyes and wiped away at her tears. She had poured out her heart and suddenly she couldn't quite look Nick in the face. And that was too bad, because if she'd looked up at him at that moment, she would have seen something in his eyes that she would never have expected to see. She would have seen love. A love as strong and as open as the one she'd just confessed having for him.

Nick sat and absorbed Rachel's words, knowing in that moment that everything he had felt about her and about falling in love had just changed. Looking down at her, he felt a love so overwhelming that he couldn't find any way to put his feelings into words. Bautista had asked him earlier if he was a fool, and he could say with certainly that where Rachel was concerned, he was nothing but a fool. He had tried to deny his feelings for her all along, never wanting to give her a chance to be a permanent part of his life. He had spent so much time shutting Rachel out that he hadn't been able to see what was right before his eyes. He hadn't been able to see that day by day, he was falling more and more in love. Nick could hear Ben asking him if he thought he might ever want a wife and kids, and for the first time in too many years to count, he did. He wanted this woman to be his wife, his best friend, and his lover. And now he knew that if he could change things, he would do so in a minute. But before he could tell her any of this, he first had to tell her something else, something that might actually change the way she feels about him.

Nick reached over, placed a finger under her chin, and lifted her face to his. He lifted his other hand and brushed away her tears with the tip of his thumb. Then he leaned over and kissed her. Just a brief kiss — but a kiss full of love and promise.

"First I'm going to tell you something, and then we're going to talk about us, Rachel."

Because Rachel was still trying to get her own emotions under control, all she could do was nod. Which Nick took as his cue to start talking.

"What I'm going to tell you is going to make you so mad at me that you'll probably take back everything that you've just said. But even if you try to take your words back, I won't let you," he added when she looked thoroughly confused. "Because I just so happen to love you too, Rachel Bennett, but we'll talk more about that in a minute, because I need to ask you a question first, okay?"

The look on Rachel's face was priceless. She looked at Nick with such a surprised look on her face that even in this desperate situation they were in, he almost started to laugh.

"Don't look so startled, sweetheart." He was a little startled himself that the words *I love you* had come out of his mouth so easily.

"You don't have to say something you don't mean, Nick." She felt compelled to give him a way out, just in case he was only telling her he loved her to try to make her feel better for the few hours they had left.

"And when have you ever known me to say something I don't mean?"

Rachel held her breath, and looked deeply into Nick's eyes. "You mean you really do love me?" She couldn't help but ask.

"I really do love you," he responded, never taking his eyes away from hers. And there was no doubt in his words at all. "And as much as I want to convince you of that, right now, I really do need to tell you something, so I want you to listen to me."

Rachel shook herself out of her daze and came crashing back down to reality. They only had hours left to live and she had promised to hear Nick out. Although anything he had to say now would only pale in comparison to the fact that he had just told her that he loved her. But he looked so serious that Rachel agreed to hear him out.

"I'm listening."

Now it was Nick's turn, and he could only hope and pray that she would see the logic in what he was about to confess.

"Do you trust me, Rachel?"

"Yes," she answered without thought, because she trusted him completely.

"Okay, that's good. Because I need you to trust in me right now more than ever."

Rachel was already dying to ask tons of questions — like *what are you talking about?* — but she kept quiet.

"If all goes according to plan, we'll be safely out of here in less than two hours."

Rachel's mouth dropped open and Nick pretended not to notice.

"Right now, Alex, Ben, the FBI, and the Mexican authorities are within a stone's throw of here. They've been on our tails all along. We've had this whole thing set up to catch Lou right from the beginning. The wristwatch was only a decoy. I have a tracking device built into my belt buckle, and Ben and the guys have been able to trace us every inch of the way and they've been able to hear every word. They've been ready to come through these doors as soon as I give them the word. But we don't want to take any chances of gunfire inside the house. It's too dangerous. We need to get outside where we have a better chance of protecting you."

The haze was starting to lift and Rachel couldn't keep her mouth shut any longer. Everything Nick had just told her was just too much for her to take in.

"I don't understand. You mean our guys are surrounding the house?" Rachel spoke very low, now understanding why Nick wanted to be sure the room wasn't bugged.

"That's exactly what I'm saying. As soon as we set foot outside, all hell will break loose. The last thing we are going to do is get into any car, so there will be shooting, Rachel, and I want you to do what I say, when I say it. That hasn't changed."

"But … Nick, I still don't understand. You said you set this up to catch Lou? How and when did you know about Lou?"

Nick ran his fingers through his hair, obviously hating to have this part of the conversation.

"Alex became suspicious of Lou right after your sister's murder. It's all true what he said about taking a call from Cynthia and arranging to meet her at a coffee shop outside of town. But Alex later found out that what he said about your sister never showing up for the meeting wasn't the truth. You see, Alex wanted to follow up on an interview with the gal who worked the cash register the night of your sister's murder. Lou was tied up, so Marc, one of the other detectives on this case, went over to the coffee shop. It wasn't any big deal, so Marc went without even mentioning it to Lou. And what he found out changed everything. The lady at the coffee shop said that your sister did show up. She also said that Cynthia and Lou left the coffee shop together around the time that the M.E. sets as the time of death."

"Oh my God," was about all Rachel could manage.

"Anyway," Nick continued, "Alex immediately started checking around, because there was no way he'd nail a cop just on the say-so of one witness. And what Alex found over the next couple of months confirmed that Lou was up to something. There were large sums of money deposited in Lou's bank account one week before and one week after Cynthia's death. Traces on Lou's phone showed calls to Steven Jackson. But we needed more than that. We needed more evidence to tie him to your sister's murder. And that's when Alex brought me and Ben in on the case. Then the opportunity came to get aboard that cruise ship and see where you fit in, and we took it. And then you gave us Miguel Bautista on a silver platter. And, well, you can figure out the rest."

Nick sounded exhausted and Rachel's head was swimming with so much information. So much surprise information.

"And why are you just now telling me this, Nick? Trust works both ways, you know. Couldn't you, Alex, and Ben trust me?"

Finally, Nick thought. *She was getting around to the anger.* The anger he had expected.

"I don't blame you for being pissed as all get-out that I let you think our situation here was hopeless and that we had just a couple of hours to live. But we had a good reason to keep you in the dark."

Nick looked over to see if he could gauge her mood, but she was sitting stone still with little expression on her face. He hoped that was a good sign.

"I needed you to feel, act, and look scared. Bautista's too clever to fool, and we couldn't risk the fact that Lou might've been able to tell if you were faking it. And I still need you to act and look scared Rachel, even though you know the truth of our situation. Everything hinges on them getting us outside to take our little joyride. Once outside, Alex and the boys will take over."

Rachel wasn't really mad. She could see the logic in their plan, and in some ways, she was glad she hadn't known the real situation. Her fear earlier was so real that she could taste it, and what Nick didn't realize was that she was still scared out of her mind. So there would be no play-acting on her part.

"Believe it or not, Nick, I'm not mad at you. And I have complete faith in you, Alex, and Ben. But until we get as far away from Miguel Bautista as possible, I'm still scared . So don't worry about me giving anything away. Just looking at the man puts the fear of God into me."

"Fear is healthy in this case. It'll keep you on your toes. And that's a good thing, because I refuse to let anything happen to you. We have too much to talk about when we get home. There's a future for us somewhere in all this, and we need to get out of this mess to figure out what that future is."

She noticed that he didn't say that their future was marriage and a family, but Rachel had too many other things to worry about right now. She would cross that bridge with Nick when the time came. And now was not the time. So she asked a simple question, instead of dwelling on the one she really wanted to ask.

"So what happens now?"

"We wait."

Rachel thought waiting was a really good idea. She needed time to wait so that she could sort through everything Nick had just thrown at her. Starting with the fact that in his belt buckle was a tracking device, with a built-in …

"Nick, please don't tell me that everything we've just said to each other has been overhead by Alex, Ben, and the entire FBI."

He wondered when it would dawn on her that there were ears listening in on their every word.

"Okay," he said with a grin, "I won't tell you that everything we've just said to each other has been overheard by Alex, Ben, and the entire FBI. Because the only people actually listening in are Alex, Ben, and maybe three or four feds, not the entire FBI."

Rachel groaned as she recalled that she had just announced that she and Nick had slept together again last night.

"Are you going to be in trouble again with Alex?" she whispered even more softly, hoping that her words couldn't be picked up.

"Probably."

"Well, can you tell him it was my idea? Maybe if you explain that I was the one who suggested you not sleep on the couch last night, he wouldn't be quite so mad." She was talking so low, Nick could barely hear her himself.

"I think you just did that yourself, sweetheart."

"Surely they can't hear what I just said?"

"This puppy can pick up the slightest sound, Rachel, even the softest whisper. That's why it's so effective."

Rachel looked horrified and Nick swallowed back a laugh.

"But don't fret. I'm sure that Alex will go easy on me. After all, if he suspends me, or worse yet, fires me, I'd be so pissed at him that I wouldn't invite him to our wedding. And God knows he won't want to miss out on that."

Rachel thought she was hearing things. "What did you say?" She wanted to hear him say it again — and again and again.

"I said that if Alex …"

The door suddenly swung open and Lou stood there with two men that Nick and Rachel hadn't seen before. And one of the men was holding a gun that was aimed smack dab at Rachel.

"Just get up and don't give us any trouble, Fallen. One move I don't like and Rachel will die right here and now. We're all heading downstairs and into the waiting car. These two gentlemen arrived earlier than expected and they're here to take you two for a little ride. One you'll remember for the rest of your lives."

Lou threw the man who was not holding a gun two pieces of rope. "Tie their hands as soon as you get outside."

True to her word, Rachel didn't have to pretend or try to act scared — because she was. Even though her mind told her Alex, Ben, and FBI reinforcements were outside somewhere, she wasn't sure they could get them out of this. These guys meant business and Rachel still had doubts that she and Nick would make it out alive.

Nick put his hands on Rachel's waist, urging her down the stairs in front of him. He leaned over and whispered into her ear. "When I tell you to drop, you fall to the ground." That's all he had time to tell her, because the man behind him shoved a gun into Nick's back.

"Shut up and just keep walking."

Nick did exactly as he was told. He needed to get outside, where he knew things would start happening.

Bautista was standing in the entryway, watching their descent down the stairs with eyes as cold as ice.

"You know what to do with the bodies," Bautista said without any emotion. "Just make sure nothing can be tracked."

"Yes sir," the two men responded in unison, never imagining that they were being set up themselves and would soon be lying at the bottom of a ravine along with Nick and Rachel.

Rachel refused to look at Bautista as she passed by him on her way out the door. She was not going to give him the satisfaction of seeing the fear in her eyes. And she was also trying desperately to focus on being outside and waiting for Nick's instructions. It was so dark that she couldn't see a thing, other than the outline of a sedan sitting at the end of the long dirt drive.

Nick was so attuned to getting himself and Rachel outside that he too walked right past Bautista without so much as a glance. He needed to be ready the second he saw or heard Alex and Ben, so all his attention was focused into the night.

Once they reached the porch, Bautista stepped out of the house and Lou stopped and stood next to him. Rachel, Nick, and the two henchmen continued on down the steps and walked toward the waiting car. They were just a few feet from the car when one of the men growled at Rachel and Nick, "Stop and put your hands behind your back. Both of you."

Nick knew that he only had seconds now. He couldn't let them tie his hands or he would be useless. *Where in the hell were Alex and Ben?* he thought, and in the very next second, a blast went off to the right of the villa, sending flames and smoke swirling into the darkness.

And then everything happened at once. Nick sensed, more than saw, a group of men in black come out of nowhere. He swung around and slammed his fist into the man trying to tie his hands, sending him to the ground and knocking him out with the first blow. He yelled at Rachel to fall and that is when the bullets started flying.

Nick lunged at the other man holding the gun, and they tumbled to the ground, wrestling for possession of the gun. As Nick struggled for control, he could see Bautista's men coming from all directions, weapons drawn and firing. As he continued to wrestle on the ground, he could hear the gunfire from his men, with shouts of "FBI, drop your weapons." Which was to no avail, because there were shots ringing out in all directions.

Nick was finally able to position his body up and over Bautista's man, cutting off his breath in a hold that was meant to kill. But he knew that killing this man wasn't necessary, so with a hard left uppercut to the chin, he knocked the guy out cold.

The very next instant, Nick felt a hand wrapped around his arm, pulling him up to his feet so forcefully that he thought his shoulder might be dislocated. But he ignored the pain and swung around with an intent to do some serious damage. That's when he felt a gun slapped into his hand, and at the same time he looked up into his partner's face.

"Lou and Bautista high-tailed it into the house. Want to go after them?"

Bullets were still flying and Nick took one quick look at Rachel and saw that she had done exactly as ordered. She was lying face-down on the ground, close to the car so that she was somewhat protected. "Don't move!" he yelled at her and then he grabbed onto one of the feds dressed in black. "Stay with her and make sure she doesn't move an inch." When the FBI agent knelt down beside Rachel with his gun drawn and ready, Nick took off with Ben.

"Cover us!" Ben yelled out to Alex and a few others, and both Nick and Ben made their way onto the porch. Nick plastered his back up against the wall on one side of the front door, and Ben plastered his back up against the wall on the other side. Some of the shooting outside had died down, with Alex, the feds, and the Mexican authorities rounding up most of Bautista's men. There were still some shots fired from one or two holdouts, but it was only a matter of time before the FBI took them down.

"On the count of three," Nick mouthed and Ben nodded. Nick put up one finger, then two fingers, and when his third finger went up, Ben jumped in front of the door, fired directly at the lock, and slammed the door open with his raised foot. Ben crouched low and Nick went high, gun ready to fire. Both men stayed outside the door for the count of two, and then they made their way inside. With guns drawn, they went into the entryway, and to no surprise, it was empty.

Neither one knew the layout of the house, so it was a guess as to which way to go. The shooting outside had completely stopped, so Nick guessed that the feds had everyone under control and had more than likely surrounded the house by now. So if Bautista and Lou tried to get out by way of the side doors, or if they tried to go out through the back way, they would be easily apprehended.

"You guys need any help?" Alex had joined Nick and Ben in the entryway, with weapon drawn.

"Sure makes it easier," Nick replied. "If they want out of the house, it makes no sense for them to head upstairs. So I'll go toward the back. Ben, you check out the rooms and on right, and Alex, how about checking out the rooms on the left."

Nothing was said. Nothing needed to be said. Each man had a job to do and each man knew how to do it. Ben moved cautiously toward his right, Alex moved cautiously toward his left, and Nick moved cautiously toward the back of the house. None of them had taken more than ten steps, when they heard two shots that sounded as if they'd been fired high into the air.

"FBI. Throw down your weapons and put up your hands. Miguel Bautista and Lou Jensen, you are under arrest."

Nick stopped, Ben stopped, and Alex stopped, just as several more shots were fired. And then more came in rapid succession. All three men turned and tore out of the house, and ran in the direction of the shots being fired. At the side of the house stood at least a dozen FBI, all with weapons raised and ready to fire.

"Where are they?" Alex asked the question as they reached the FBI.

"They both headed back into the house. I think one's been hit. Maybe both."

Without another word, Alex, Nick, and Ben headed for the back of the house. The door was standing wide open, and there was no sign of either Bautista or Lou. The three men entered slowly, with their guns aimed and ready. Blood was splattered on the floor, confirming that either Bautista or Lou had taken a bullet. Nick, Alex, and Ben cautiously followed the trail of blood.

As Nick rounded a corner into a long and deserted hallway, Alex and Ben covered his back. The trail of blood was even thicker. And it didn't take long to find the reason why. Lying with his back up against a wall at the end of the hall was Miguel Bautista. His eyes were wide open, completely still, totally blank, and there was no question that he was dead. But because Nick wanted to be absolutely sure, he took a second to kneel down and check the pulse at his neck.

"The bastard's dead. Now we need to find Lou."

Ben had already noticed that there was more blood on the floor leading away from Bautista's body. The trail of blood wasn't nearly as thick, but it was there all the same. Which meant that Lou had probably taken a hit as well. Ben quietly began making his way around Nick, heading for a closed door at the end of the hall. Alex and Nick were right behind. Very carefully, Ben tested the doorknob and found that the door was unlocked. He looked over his shoulder at Alex and Nick, signaling with his eyes that he was ready to go in. On a silent count of three, Ben threw open the door and like before, he crouched low, while Alex and Nick went in high.

The second the door crashed open, all three men caught a movement in the corner of the room. A side door leading outside was slid open and Lou was making his way out. He had just cleared the door and was ready to flee into the darkness.

"Take one more step and I'll blow you to hell and back."

Nick meant every word he said. If Lou so much as moved a muscle, he would blow his head off. And Lou must have known it, because he stopped and turned around slowly, looking down the barrels of three guns pointed directly at him.

"Drop your gun, Lou." The order came from Alex.

But Lou wasn't about to give up so easily. He stood outside on the other side of the door and faced each man, almost daring them to fire their weapons. He had one hand pressed against a wound in his side, and in his other hand he held his gun. Blood was dripping into the dirt.

"I want to cut a deal."

"You have nothing to deal with, Lou. Now drop your gun."

"I have plenty to deal with, Alex. How would you like Steven Jackson on a silver platter? I can give him to you. But I want to deal first."

Nick and Ben stayed quiet. This was Alex's call.

"Not interested."

"But I can tie Jackson to the hit on his wife. And I can give you details about his entire operation."

Because Lou had still not dropped his weapon, all three men stood with their feet slightly apart, pointing their own weapons at Lou. No one so much as moved an inch.

"I won't deal with a dirty cop. You should know that about me by now. So let me tell you one more time, drop your weapon."

Lou tried again. But he changed his tactic.

"You know I can take one of you out before you get me. And it might be you, Alex. So think again. You agree to cut me a deal and I'll drop my gun. You refuse and I swear I'll blow one of you away."

"No deal."

Alex, Nick and Ben were ready — and Alex was counting on it.

With blood still dripping down his side, Lou made the slightest of moves. But it was just enough. His trigger finger barely twitched. And before he got a clean shot at Alex, Ben threw himself at Alex, knocking him to the ground in the exact same second that Nick fired the first shot. Lou crumbled to the ground, still clutching onto his gun. He had gotten off a shot of his own, but the bullet had not found its target.

Nick, on the other hand, had hit his target right in the chest. Alex was the first one to make his way over to Lou. Ben and Nick followed. None of the three had put away their guns. And even though Lou was lying face down in the dirt, he was still breathing. His eyes were closed and he looked like he might not make it.

"Don't you dare die on me, you fucking bastard." Alex's words rang out into the night. "I want your sorry ass back in the United States where you will stand trial for the murder of Cynthia Jackson."

The rest of whatever Alex said was drowned out, as two choppers came hovering over the villa. They were choppers called in by the FBI, and were a welcome sight. Everyone looked up and watched as the pilots set the things down, and when Ben turned to say something to Nick, he noticed his partner was gone.

Nick ran over to where he had left Rachel, tucking his gun into the back of his jeans. He saw that she was no longer where he'd left her, and guessed that she'd gotten up when all the shooting had finally stopped. But he had guessed wrong. Because from the corner of his eye, he saw someone lift Rachel's limp body onto a stretcher.

Nick just turned and stared at the sight before him, unable to move. Terror swept through every bone in his body, and he seriously thought that he might die himself right there on the spot. It was only when he felt Ben's hand on his shoulder that he was able to move. And with Ben by his side, he walked over to the stretcher like he was in some kind of a trance.

Rachel was lying on the stretcher with her eyes closed, and a gunshot wound to her chest. She had been hastily patched up by one of the federal guys who had some paramedic training, but she still looked like she was barely holding on. Blood was all over the place and she was so deathly pale. Nick took hold of her hand, and just looked up at one of the men holding onto the stretcher.

"We're taking her by chopper to the naval hospital in San Diego. It's close and we should be there in less than thirty minutes."

They were lifting the stretcher up into the chopper, and without a word, Nick climbed in with them. He was still holding onto Rachel's hand, refusing to let go. And his heart was in his throat. The pilot jumped in behind the controls and Nick finally looked down at Ben, standing on the ground, looking up at his partner and best friend.

"I'll clear things with Alex," Ben yelled into the chopper, because just up and leaving the scene of a crime was something Alex would not like. Especially by the man heading up this investigation. "And I'll find you at the hospital."

"Thanks, Ben," was all Nick could manage, as the blades started whirling and drowning out everything else. And in seconds, the chopper was up and off the ground.

Nick looked down at Rachel and suddenly he felt so helpless that all he could do was close his eyes and try to draw in a deep, calming breath.

"Just hang on, sweetheart." Nick whispered down to Rachel. "Please just hang on." And this time, the words that he whispered were said more for himself.

CHAPTER EIGHTEEN

Nick sat in the waiting room, alone. He had sat in the same chair for more than five hours, not moving and barely breathing. It was three o'clock in the morning and Rachel had been rushed into surgery more than five hours ago. No one had come out to see him or given him any news. He was as numb as he could ever remember being in his life, and equally as scared.

Quite simply, Nick's heart was breaking in two. He had finally found someone that he could love, and now she might very well be taken away from him. And there was nothing that he could do. This was one situation that he had absolutely no control over, and that made it even harder for him. He was always so much in control, and more times than not, calling the shots. But now, Nick wasn't calling any shots. The doctors were in charge and none of them had given him the time of day. No one had even bothered to give him an update. They were all so busy taking care of Rachel. And because that was the case, he sat quietly, sending up one silent prayer after another.

When another half hour went by and there was still no word, Nick was terrified that the worst had happened and that everyone was afraid to give him the bad news. He knew that he must look like hell. He still had Rachel's blood all over his clothes, he still had a gun tucked into his jeans, he desperately needed to shave and comb his hair, and his eyes had a tired and frantic look to them. He was getting desperate and more and more frightened by the second. So, dropping his head down into the palms of his hands, Nick decided that maybe a prayer said a little louder would be easier for God to hear.

"Dear God," he choked into his hands, struggling to hold back the tears, "I know it's been a long time since you've heard from me, but I need to ask you a favor. I need to ask if you will please save Rachel." Nick swallowed and let the tears fall. "I'm not asking this for me, God, but for Rachel. She has so much living to do, and she can touch so many people just by being alive. Please give her that chance, God. Please let her live. Please."

Nick slowly lifted his head and found Ben and Alex standing before him. And he wasn't the least bit embarrassed that they caught him crying out a prayer. Because all he could think about was Rachel.

Ben took a chair on one side of Nick and Alex took the other. All three men looked like hell.

"How's she doing?" Alex risked asking.

"She's been in surgery since we got here. And no one's told me a damn thing. The only thing the doctor said before they took her into the operating room was that the bullet appears to be lodged very deep in her chest and that her condition is very serious. He said she has a fifty-fifty chance of surviving the surgery."

"Rachel's a strong and healthy woman, Nick. She'll pull through."

Nick knew that Ben was trying to be encouraging, but he couldn't stand to even discuss the possibility that Rachel wouldn't recover, so he changed the subject.

"How's Lou?"

"He's alive. We left him in a Mexican hospital, surrounded by the FBI. He'll live to stand trial." There was definite satisfaction in Alex's voice.

"That's good. Because I want to look the bastard right in the eye when I testify against him."

"You might have to stand in line for that, Nick. We all want a chance at him. Especially me."

At Alex's words, Nick's lips twitched and he nearly smiled for the first time in hours.

"We also gathered up almost twenty of Bautista's men and turned them over to the authorities. Bautista had a sizable army of men around him, but they were pretty inept. The takedown was easier than we thought."

Nick flashed back to Rachel lying on a stretcher with a hole in her chest, and there was no way he could ever be convinced that the takedown had been easy.

"The feds have taken control of Bautista's villa. They're hoping to find leads to other names on their watch list. Scum like Bautista usually hang with other scum, so the feds are hopeful that they'll make some connections. They're rifling through every scrap of paper in the place."

Nick wasn't fooled for one second. All of this could be passed on to him later, but Alex was trying to take his mind off of Rachel.

"Other than Bautista, the body count tonight was six. All Bautista's men. Three federal agents were injured, but nothing too serious."

Nick had hardly heard a word Alex just said, because his eyes were focused on the doctor who was heading straight for him.

The doctor heading their way had obviously just come out of surgery. He wore surgical scrubs, paper booties covering his feet, and a paper cap. His surgical mask was hanging loosely around his neck. But even though Nick took all of this in at a glance, what he really noticed was the look of caution that rested in the surgeon's eyes.

Nick stood as the doctor approached.

"Are you Detective Fallen?"

"Yes."

"I'm Doctor Keating, Detective, and I understand that you came in with Ms. Bennett on the chopper?"

"How is she?" Nick couldn't waste time on formalities.

"Are you related to her?"

Nick knew the drill. If he wasn't related, they wouldn't tell him shit. So he looked right at the doctor and lied.

"I'm her fiancé."

Dr. Keating either knew Nick was lying or thought that he looked like anything but a fiancé.

"Does Ms. Bennett have any other relatives we should contact?"

Alex stood and decided that now would be a good time to jump in and save the doctor, because Nick looked like he was about ready to kill.

"Look, Doctor Keating. I'm Lieutenant Kendall with the LAPD. And the only living relative Ms. Bennett has is being escorted to jail as we speak. He's being charged, among other things, with providing known drug lords and possibly terrorists with false U.S. documents. He arranged to have Ms. Bennett's sister killed, so we also have him on murder one. Now Detective Fallen is here, he's engaged to Ms. Bennett, he's been waiting for more than five hours, and he also has a gun tucked into the waistband of his jeans."

Alex added that last with a smile, trying to lighten up the mood. Even though he strongly suspected that Nick might actually use the damn gun if the doctor wouldn't answer his question.

"You had me the second you talked about the terrorists, Lieutenant. Remember, you're in a naval hospital. I'm not only a doctor, but I'm also a commander in the United States Navy. And fiancé or not, if you helped bring down someone associated with terrorists, then I'll tell you anything you want to know."

Before Nick could ask, the doctor filled him in.

"The surgery was touch and go for a while. As we suspected, the bullet was lodged pretty deep. But we got it out, and Ms. Bennett is in recovery now. She'll be in recovery for a couple of hours and then we'll move her into the ICU. She's still in very serious condition, and the next twelve hours or so are critical. But she's young and strong, so I see no reason for her not to pull through with a complete recovery.

"Can I see her?"

"Not now, Detective Fallen." There was a hint of sympathy in the doctor's voice. "After we move her into the intensive care unit, you can see her for about five minutes. But she won't know you're there, because we've got her heavily sedated. So let me suggest that you find yourself a motel and try to get some sleep. You can see Ms. Bennett when you return."

"Thanks, Doctor, but I think I'll stay right here, if you don't mind."

Doctor Keating knew when to argue and when to give in. And just seeing the determined look on Nick's face told him that no amount of persuasion would get him to leave.

"I'll have a nurse come and get you when you can see Ms. Bennett."

"Thanks," was all Nick muttered as he reached out to shake the doctor's hand.

"You want us to stay?" Ben's voice broke into Nick's thoughts.

"No. I know you need to get back to L.A. and see what's going on with Jackson. I'll be fine here."

"Are you sure, Nick?" This time it was Alex.

Nick looked over at the two men who had become his best friends. Ben was his partner and almost like a brother to him. And even though Alex was technically his boss, Nick considered him to be a good and trusted friend.

"It might be hours before she wakes up, and there's no need for you to stay around and baby-sit me. I'll be okay."

"You realize that you look like shit, don't you?" Ben had such a way with words.

"Yeah. I think the doctor actually thought I was one of the bad guys." Nick looked over at his boss. "Thanks, Alex."

Alex slapped Nick on the shoulder. "A navy pilot has of-fered to take us back to L.A. in one of their planes. Call us as soon as you know anything."

Ben started to shake his partner's hand, then at the last minute, he threw both his strong arms around Nick. "Call me if you need me, buddy, and I'll come right back."

Nick nodded at both Ben and Alex. And without any more words, Alex and Ben left. Nick watched them walk into the elevator before he collapsed back into the same chair he had been sitting in for hours. He stretched out his long legs, crossed his arms across his chest, and closed his eyes. *I need just a couple hours' sleep,* he thought. But before he could allow himself to sleep, he knew that there was one more thing he had to do.

And with his eyes still closed, Nick mouthed the words that were lodged in his heart. "Thank you, God, for saving Ra-chel. Thank you for giving her a chance to pull through. Please give her the strength to beat this, God. Please give us a chance for a life together …… Please," was the last word he muttered as he was finally overtaken with a deep and peaceful sleep.

*   *   *

"Detective Fallen." Nick felt a soft tug on his shoulder. "Detective Fallen, if you will open your eyes, you can see Ms. Bennett now."

Nick was immediately awake, all sleep gone from his fog-gy mind. He'd actually slept for a couple of hours so his eyes were alert, but guarded.

"How's she doing? Is she awake?"

The nice young nurse smiled up at him. "She's doing as expected, Detective. We just moved her into the ICU and Doctor Keating said you could see her for a few minutes."

Nick followed the nurse down a long corridor and through two double doors, marked as the ICU. He went into the room and noticed immediately that there were three other patients in the unit. There was a nursing station located in the center of the room, obviously situated that way so that the nurses could see all the patients who might need attention. There was equipment everywhere and he could hear machines beeping. The nurse, who smiled at him over her shoulder, brought Nick over to a bed stationed at the end of the row.

"She's still sedated, Detective, so she won't know you're here. And I'm sorry, but you can only stay a few minutes."

Nick thanked the nurse and walked over to Rachel's bedside. And his heart nearly stopped. She looked like she was on the verge of death. There were tubes and needles sticking out everywhere. She was hooked up to at least three IVs and just looking down at her, Nick was scared beyond words. He couldn't believe that this was the same woman that he had made love to less than twenty-four hours ago. That woman was so full of life, and this woman was so close to death. And Nick would have changed places with her in a heartbeat if he could.

Ignoring the nurse's words that he could only stay with Rachel for a few minutes, Nick reached over and quietly pulled a chair closer to her bedside. He reached out and took one of her hands in his, and settled in for the night. There was no way he was going to leave Rachel now. She would need him when she opened her eyes, and he was going to be there for her. Come hell or high water, he was going to be there when she woke up, even if he had to fight with every nurse and every doctor in the hospital.

What Nick didn't know was that the moment the two night nurses looked over and saw him holding onto Rachel's hand, they were ready to break all the rules. They both thought that the handsome detective needed to be right where he was, not alone in some deserted hospital waiting room. Both the nurses were romantics at heart, and what they saw before them was the most romantic thing in the world. So together they decided to ignore the rules and let him stay.

Nick watched Rachel for about an hour, and then he closed his eyes. He was still holding onto her hand, but he laid his head back against the chair and took a deep, ragged breath. It was now six in the morning and everything was still very quiet around him. He knew he couldn't sleep anymore, but he kept his eyes closed, thinking about how dramatically his life had changed over the last two weeks.

"Nick?" The voice was whisper-soft, and a little raspy.

Nick opened his eyes and sat straight up in his chair. His heart was beating a mile a minute.

"Nick …. is that you?"

"You're awake." Nick leaned over Rachel, cupping the side of her face with one hand. "Thank God, Rachel, you're awake."

Rachel's eyes fluttered closed and Nick guessed that she'd drifted back to sleep. But a second later, she opened her eyes again.

"Where am I?" Her words were spoken so softly that Nick had to lean closer to hear her.

"You're at a naval hospital in San Diego, sweetheart. You've just come through surgery, but you're going to be just fine." And for the first time in hours, Nick allowed himself to believe it.

"Is … is everyone else all right? Are … you… are you all right?"

"I am now, Rachel."

One of the nurses stepped up to the other side of Rachel's bed, and she smiled over at Nick and then down at Rachel.

"I need to get the doctor, Detective Fallen. He'll want to know that Ms. Bennett is awake."

She left and Nick hardly noticed because he was looking down so intently at Rachel.

"My God …..Nicholas ….. you ….. look terrible." She swallowed and ran her tongue over parched lips. "Are …. are you sure …. you're all right?"

In answer to her question, Nick simply leaned down and kissed the tip of Rachel's nose. And just then, the nurse came back with Doctor Keating.

"I need to ask you to leave, Detective, so that I can look my patient over." This time, Doctor Keating would not take no for an answer.

"I'll wait outside." Nick squeezed Rachel's hand before he turned her over to the hospital staff.

Once outside the doors of the ICU, Nick called Ben on his cell. Ben picked up on the first ring.

"Hello?"

"Ben, it's me. Sorry to wake you, but I thought you'd want to know that Rachel just woke up."

"God, Nick, that's great news."

"Yeah, well I haven't had a chance to talk with the doctor yet because he threw me out of the ICU. I'll find out more after he's examined her."

"You need anything, buddy?"

"Just some time off. I want to stay with Rachel until I can bring her home to L.A. Will you clear it with Alex?"

"No problem. We both figured you'd stay. Alex will tell you to take all the time you need, you know that."

Nick recalled Alex's suggestion that after his case was over that Nick take a nice little vacation.

"Tell him I'll check in."

"Will do, buddy. Just call if you need anything. You know where to reach me."

Nick hung up the phone and suddenly felt like he could find a bed and sleep for a hundred years. He knew he must look a sight. Even Rachel had noticed and she was still loaded up on whatever drugs they were pumping into her.

"She's sleeping again."

Nick turned around. He hadn't even heard Doctor Keating walk up behind him, which just proved how tired he was.

"Just tell me she's going to be okay, Doctor."

Doctor Keating took Nick by the arm and led him over to a couple of chairs. Both men sat down.

"She's going to be just fine." Doctor Keating knew that was all Nick needed to hear, but he added more encouraging words. "It's rather remarkable how well she has come through this surgery. While she was awake, she was pretty alert. Her vital signs are better than expected, and my guess is that with a good eight to ten hours of sleep, she'll be out of the woods. We should be able to transfer her to a private room in a day or two."

"When will I be able to take her home?"

"I'd think she could be discharged in five or six days, depending on how her recovery progresses. But keep in mind that she will be far from well, Detective. She'll need to be watched carefully. Full recovery will take eight to ten weeks, maybe longer."

As long as Rachel was alive, Nick didn't care if her recovery took eight to ten years — because he planned to be with her every step of the way.

"Does she have someone who can look after her? At least for the first couple of weeks?"

"I plan to take her to my place. She can stay with my partner's wife during the day, and I'll keep an eye on her at night." Nick knew that he would be able to count on Betty.

"Well, you'll do no one any good if you don't get some rest yourself, Detective Fallen. There's a nice little motel right down the road. I'll arrange to have a petty officer drive you over."

"I guess staying here until Rachel wakes up again is out of the question?"

Doctor Keating got to his feet and laughed. "We gave Ms. Bennett a sedative that will put her out for at least eight hours, probably ten. So go and get some sleep and don't you dare show your face back here before …." Doctor Keating glanced at his watch. "Before five o'clock this evening."

Nick knew that he wouldn't wait until five to return, but no use telling the doctor that.

"And since it looks like we are about the same size, I'll have someone drop off a change of clothes for you at the motel. You might want to burn the ones you're wearing."

Nick's mouth turned up into a genuine smile. He liked Doctor Keating. He liked him a lot.

"Thank you, Commander Keating." For some reason, Nick wanted to acknowledge the man's rank.

"You're welcome."

As both men shook hands, Doctor Keating read a message of gratitude in the depths of Nick's green eyes.

"Tell me just one thing, Detective Fallen: Are you and Ms. Bennett really engaged?"

"We will be," was Nick's honest reply. "I'm afraid the bullets started flying before I had a chance to officially ask her."

Doctor Keating laughed all the way down the hall. And knowing that it would do him no good to try and sneak back into the ICU, Nick headed off to look for his ride to the motel.

As it turned out, Nick actually slept almost eight hours himself. He woke a little after three, showered, and changed into the clothes that had been delivered to his room. He grabbed a quick bite to eat and was back at the hospital, sitting by Rachel's bedside by five. There were two different nurses on this time of the day, but neither one paid Nick the least bit of attention. So he settled back and waited for Rachel to wake up.

It wasn't long before Rachel opened her eyes, and the first person she saw was Nick. He was sitting in a chair next to her bed, looking so wonderfully handsome that her heart actually turned over. He hadn't shaved, but the dark whiskers didn't detract at all from his good looks; instead, it gave him a reckless, sexy look. He was in desperate need of a haircut, but that too just added to the overall effect. And in the back of Rachel's mind, she could only think of the words *drop-dead gorgeous*.

Nick noticed immediately that Rachel was awake, but he wanted to give her a few minutes to get her bearings. So he smiled down at her, and then leaned in and gave her a light kiss at the corner of her mouth.

"I love you," were the first words out of his mouth. He wanted to clear that up right away.

"I love you too," she whispered back. And then she went right back to sleep.

Over the next forty-eight hours, Rachel faded in and out, always staying awake a little longer each time. By the end of the second day, she had been moved out of the ICU and into a private room. Nick had become very familiar with the hospital and all the nurses, so they pretty much let him come and go as he pleased.

On the third day following surgery, Nick sat with Rachel well past visiting hours, but no one seemed to notice. Or at least they pretended not to notice.

"The doctor told me earlier that you're going to be just fine, sweetheart, but it's going to take some time."

"How much time?" Rachel was sitting up in bed with a couple of pillows tucked behind her head.

"I should be able to take you home in a few days. And you're coming to my place, Rachel, where I can keep my eye on you."

"Will I be able to go back to work in September?"

Nick hadn't even thought of that. But because September was only six weeks away, he doubted it.

"Probably not. The doctor said you'll need to take it easy for at least eight weeks, maybe longer."

Rachel looked saddened by that piece of news, but she refused to let it get her down. She was too happy just having Nick by her side.

"Well, I guess I could make arrangements to start teaching again in mid-January, after winter break. That should give me plenty of time to get back on my feet."

That sounded perfect to Nick, and that fit right in with his plans — plans that he thought he'd better let Rachel in on.

"Sounds to me like you'll have more than enough time to rest, get well, and make plans for our wedding. How about we get married on Christmas Eve?"

Rachel was feeling a little woozy again, so she wasn't sure she heard Nick correctly. "I refuse to fall back to sleep until I hear you say that again, Nick. Did you just ask me to marry you?"

Nick took Rachel's hand in his, and he felt overwhelmed by his love for her. "I know this isn't the most romantic place to propose, Rachel, but I can't wait. You see, I already told the doctor that I was your fiancé so that I could get in to see you. But I'm tired of all the lies I've told since I met you, Rachel, so in order to make an honest cop out of me, I guess you'll just have to say yes and marry me."

Rachel was struggling to stay alert, but she wasn't going to miss this for the world. So she fought to keep her eyes wide open.

"Do you want to have children, Nick?"

"I want to have children with you, Rachel. I want to have a life with you. I want us to get married, have babies, and live happily ever after. I want you to be my wife, my lover, my confidant, and my best friend. I know that being married to a cop isn't going to be easy. Our hours stink and we're are always on call. There will be days when I'll be so involved in a case that I won't be able to come home at night. But I promise that I'll do everything in my power to make you happy. I love you, Rachel, and I want to marry you. So what do you say?"

Rachel's heart was so full of love that she wasn't sure she could even speak. And she was so sleepy that she could hardly keep her eyes open. But as she closed her fingers around Nick's hand, she kept her eyes turned to his.

"I've always wanted to be a Christmas bride." She was fading and Nick smiled down at her.

"So is that a yes?"

"That's a definite yes," she whispered. And Nick watched as her eyes closed, and she drifted off to sleep to dream about the life she was going to have with the man standing beside her bed, holding tightly onto her hand.

EPILOGUE

CHRISTMAS EVE

"Come on, let me drive. I'll be real careful."

"No way. I told you before that you drive like crap. And I have no intention of getting killed on my wedding day."

"But I'm supposed to drive you to the church. That's what the best man does. He drives the groom to the church."

Nick and Ben were making their way out of Nick's apartment, toward his car parked at the curb.

"I don't understand why you had Betty drop you off over here anyway. I can get myself to the church."

"I came because I'm supposed to drive you. And I figured we could take your car. That way you'll have it handy after the reception."

Rachel was over at her house getting dressed and Nick wondered if she had already left for the church. He had gotten dressed at his apartment, because of some crazy rule that the groom was not allowed to see the bride before the ceremony, which he thought was nuts. But because he didn't have to vacate his apartment for one more week, he had decided to get dressed there. He wouldn't be coming back after the ceremony, but for today, it had come in handy. He had informed the manager earlier in the week that they could rent the apartment right away, since he and Rachel had decided to live in her little two-bedroom house. At least for a while. They both knew they would need to get a bigger place as soon as they started having kids, which Nick hoped wouldn't be too long in the future.

Already, Nick's life had changed and he was happier than he'd ever been. And Rachel had made the difference. She had worked hard at her recovery over the last few months, and he had watched her with a great deal of admiration and pride.

Rachel had also learned over the months what it was going to be like married to a homicide detective. As Nick had said, his hours were unpredictable, and sometimes she would go days without seeing him. But no matter where he was or what he was doing, he always managed to find the time to call. And she always felt like she was a part of his life — a very important part.

Nick was thinking about Rachel, kids, houses, and their life together, and he didn't even notice that Ben had made his way over to the driver's side of the car.

"Toss me the keys, buddy, and I'll drive."

Nick laughed as he dug the car keys out of the front pocket of his tux and tossed them over to his partner.

"I will probably live to regret this," he said as he climbed into the passenger seat. "And what I said still stands. You crash my car and I swear I'll shoot you."

Ben looked over and smiled. Then, without further delay, he slipped the key in the ignition, turned on the engine, and sped away from the curb. They made it to the church in record time.

Nick was standing at the head of the altar, with Ben and Alex standing next to him. Betty was the matron of honor and Amanda was in her first wedding as a bridesmaid. The small church they had chosen to get married in was full, and everyone was silent as they waited for the bride to come down the aisle. As organ music started to fill the church, every eye turned to see Rachel, dressed in an exquisite gown of satin and lace. She had chosen a simple gown with a beaded, scooped neck, long sleeves, and more than a dozen tiny pearl buttons down the back. She wore her hair down, because she knew that was the way Nick liked it best. She was a vision to behold, and at the sight of her coming down the aisle, everyone seemed to be holding their breath.

Nick couldn't quite believe his eyes. Rachel came toward him looking more beautiful than he could have imagined. Her eyes were locked onto his, and they never looked away from each other as she made her way to his side. Just as she reached the first couple of steps leading up to the altar, Nick stepped forward and took her hand.

He smiled down into her upturned face, and ignoring what the minister had told him to do at the wedding rehearsal, he leaned down instead and kissed her. Nick bent his head and his lips touched hers and lingered, until she kissed him back. And everyone in the church sighed.

Nick slowly and almost reluctantly lifted his head, tucked Rachel's hand into the crook of his arm, and led her over to the minister, who was watching them with a smile on his face. Ben and Alex closed in next to Nick, while both Betty and Amanda had trouble keeping the tears from falling. But all Nick was aware of was the woman who would soon become his wife. So after placing one more light kiss at the corner of Rachel's mouth, Nick finally looked straight at the minister, urging him to begin.

"Dearly beloved. We are gathered here today ……."

THE END

About the Author

Patricia Graves lives in Los Angeles with her husband of twenty-two years. She has a Master's Degree in Health Administration and works full-time in the health care field. When she is not working, and not writing, she and her husband spend their time travelling to countries throughout the world.